cs

'The book is a [...] riguing plot and well-drawn
characters, set in a splendidly realized world.
High magic, treachery and revenge keep the
reader turning the pages."
– Katherine Kerr, author of *License to Ensorcell*

"Juliet McKenna writes classic epic fantasy at its best: with
swords, sorcery, fights, and intrigue a-plenty, wrapped
around compelling characters struggling to stay alive in an
exceptionally well-drawn world whose order has been
disrupted by violence, betrayal, and greed. McKenna's got
all the things in her books that I read epic fantasy for."
– Kate Elliott, author of *Cold Magic*

"Juliet E. McKenna invariably delivers an epic fantasy
world of real people, sympathetic motivations and
delicious consequences. I never know what's
going to happen next and I always want to find out!"
– C.E. Murphy, author of *The Walker Papers* series

"Inventive magic, devious intrigue and appealing
characters make for an exciting tale, well-told."
– Gail Z. Martin, author of *The Sworn*

"Juliet McKenna's latest mixes magic and politics in a
fully realized fantasy world. A rewarding new fantasy from
a master of the craft."

Also by Juliet E. McKenna

BOOK 2 *of* THE HADRUMAL CRISIS

DARKENING SKIES

Juliet E. McKenna

SOLARIS

First published 2011 by Solaris
an imprint of Rebellion Publishing Ltd,
Riverside House, Osney Mead,
Oxford, OX2 0ES, UK

www.solarisbooks.com

UK ISBN: 978 1 907992 76 6
US ISBN: 978 1 907992 77 3

10 9 8 7 6 5 4 3 2 1

A CIP catalogue record for this book is available from the
British Library.

Designed & typeset by Rebellion Publishing

Printed in the US

In memoriam
Anne McCaffrey
with admiration and affection

Pathfinder and trailblazer in her career and in her fiction for
so many women writers, with her work read, enjoyed and
celebrated by men and women alike.

She was the first writer I met in person, who in the course
of an evening revealed so much of both the craft and the
practicalities of being an author.

My own books would never have been written without
that first encounter. Our handful of subsequent meetings
similarly inspired and delighted me.

MANDARKIN

KRA KEREG
PENAR

SOLURA

SOLITH

MARE'S
TAIL

CASTAMARN

NADRUAD

WREDE

VANAM

SELERIMA

ENSAIMIN

OAKMONT

HANCHET

ISSBESK

THE
GREAT
FOREST

DREDE
AMBAFOST

EYHORNE

VERLAYNE

KADRAS

FRIERN

WHITE RIVER

BAY
OF
TESHAL

COL

PEORLE

DURYEA

GULF
OF
PEORI

DUSGATE

TRESIA

TRESIA

VEEL

CALADHRIA

KEVIL

FERL

SOLITH
SOLURA
PASTAMAR
NADRUAL

THE
GREAT
FOREST

MEDESHALE

GRYNTH

SELERIMA

VANAM

WREDE

GIDESTA

SHOLVIN COVE

INGLIS

ENSAIMIN

EYHORNE

AMBAFOST   FRIERN

KADRAS

HANCHET

DALASOR

BAY
OF
TESHAL

COL

GULF OF
PEORLE

PEORLE

DURYEA

DRAXIMAL   ASHERRY

BLACKLITH

CHANAUL

DUSGATE

TRESIA   TREBIN

TRESIA

ABRAY

CARLUSE

COTEBRIDGE

TRIOLLE

LESCAR

TANNAT

SAVORGAN

KEVIL

CALADHRIA

FERL

MARLIER

ADRULLE

LICANIN

CARIF

PARNILESSE

SOLLAND

ZAFER

ANGOVE

BREMILAYNE

PINERIN

CLAITHE

HALFERAN

RELSHAZ

MARKYATE

TOREMAL

NYME

KALAVEN

FEVERAD

| BELIEVED POSITION OF |
| HADRUMAL |
| (THE WIZARDS' ISLE) |

ATTAR

VEYET

LEQUESINE

MORETAYNE

KHUSRO
DOMAIN

JAGAI
DOMAIN

THE
GULF OF
LESCAR

DERRICE

SITALCA

NAHIK
DOMAIN

MIRIS
DOMAIN

REGIN

LYOUTESSELA

ALDABRESHIN

CAPE OF WINDS

— CHAPTER ONE —

Ferl, Caladhria

1st of For-Autumn

In the 9th Year of Tadriol the Provident of Tormalin

HE STOOD ALONE in the centre of the high hammer-
beamed hall. Those barons already assembled sat on
tiered benches of polished oak rising up on either side.

Afternoon sunlight poured through the wide arched
windows piercing the thick stone walls. Their sills were
level with the heads of those later arrivals forced to take
the highest, rearmost seats. Some lords leaned forward,
intent on studying Corrain's expression. Others sat back
as they conferred with their neighbours. Some went so
far as to shield their mouths with cautious hands.

Corrain turned around and walked back to the great
double doors. 'Fitrel, I want you making the rounds of
the taverns and stable yards.'

He handed a discreet purse to the older man; a grizzled
veteran already pensioned off before direst necessity
had recalled him to his livery.

'Buy a little ale to moisten some tongues. I want to
know who's turned up and their principal alliances and
feuds.'

When Corrain had been a Halferan barony guard
captain, he would have been out and about all night to
learn such vital information before the first sitting of
a quarterly parliament. He'd had no such opportunity

since they'd arrived the previous evening. Besides, such behaviour was hardly fitting for a man now claiming the barony's title for himself.

Fitrel nodded comfortably. 'I should still have some acquaintance among their noble lordships' households.'

Corrain thought it all too likely that Fitrel's one-time comrades would be fishing on some distant river bank. If they hadn't already died and been reborn, oblivious, into the Otherworld. But Corrain had precious few strings to his bow and Fitrel could surely make new friends.

There would doubtless be a good many folk hereabouts eager to learn the true story of the corsair raid that had seen the former Baron Halferan murdered, the best of his household guard slaughtered and the remnant enslaved. Until Corrain had escaped and returned to renew the fight against the corsairs this summer.

'What do I do?' Reven demanded.

'You keep your voice down,' Fitrel rebuked the youth.

Corrain held the lad's gaze. 'You uphold the honour of Halferan.'

He had no doubts about the boy's loyalty but, Saedrin save them all, Reven was as unpredictable as a colt freshly broken to harness and none too skilfully broken at that.

This was no time to lament fat old Arigo's death though. Those most eminent lords who'd sent lackeys to hold them a place on the foremost benches were arriving.

'Yes, captain,' the boy said hurriedly.

'Baron Halferan,' Fitrel barked.

Corrain heard a muffled chuckle from somewhere on the upper benches. It wasn't an amiable sound. 'Be off with you both.'

'You keep your head and you'll do right by our lady,' Fitrel assured Corrain, 'and for our lord's girls.'

Corrain saw the puzzlement on a late-come baron's face as he overheard those words. Realisation turned the man's bemusement to contempt.

'I will.' Corrain clapped the old swordsman on the shoulder by way of farewell.

Guards in the Ferl barony's blue jerkins waved Fitrel and Reven back so that the last lords could enter before ushering them out. The door wards' polished bronze belt buckles reflected the chevrons on Baron Ferl's standard flying high above the hall.

This town of Ferl hosted the parliament sufficiently often for the local barons to have built this hall to house it. Corrain had visited often enough in his dead lord's service to take full advantage of festival licence at solstice or equinox.

What muddy footprints had he left here? Corrain was uneasily aware that he'd been too easily tempted into heedless follies, ever since those days when Fitrel had first ruled the barrack hall as sergeant-at-arms. He wondered what tales these assembled lords had heard. Their own faithful retainers were doubtless out gleaning gossip in the back alleys and taprooms.

He turned to face the barons. Who would prove determined to curb the unseemly ambition of an erstwhile guard captain? Who among them would believe that his first and last desire was now to serve Lady Zurenne, the Widow Halferan, and her noble daughters Ilysh and Esnina?

Since Corrain had so grievously failed his murdered lord, this was all the restitution he could make. Since his quest for revenge on the corsairs had gone so perilously awry. Not that anyone here knew that, any more than they knew the whole truth of Lord Halferan's death. Corrain must keep all those secrets, for his own sake as much as for Zurenne's and her daughters.

His face impassive, he took a stride towards the steps up to the rear benches.

'A moment—' Baron Ferl's outrage foundered the instant he stood up. Everyone could see he didn't know what to call this interloper.

Corrain halted and bowed to the baron.

An expectant murmur swirled around the hall.

Corrain didn't say a word.

Settling his stance comfortably, he gazed at the great window at the far end of the long hall. Soaring stone tracery framed a multitude of diamond leaded panes. Bright heraldic hues coloured the outermost edges, casting jewelled patterns on the pale stone floor. Not that any individual lord's blazon was honoured. Every noble had an equal voice in this parliament.

Then let one of them speak first. Corrain had been in enough sword fights to know the wisdom of letting his opponent make the first move. He had also stood sentry outside baronial halls long and often enough for him to wager good gold that he would outlast the noble lords in this particular trial. He began counting the different coloured panes of glass.

Baron Ferl took refuge in pomposity. 'You are welcome, my lords, to our proud parliament. Thus we honour our forefathers who bequeathed us this sacred duty; to safeguard the interests of Caladhrians from the highest rank to the humblest.'

Recovering his composure, he laced his fingers across his paunch.

'We are not subject to the whims of monarchs. We do not forget how the ancient Tormalin dominion was brought low in generations past by arrogance and fallibility on their Emperor's throne. Nor are we ruled by greed and selfishness. Not when we see the merchants' guilds, accountable only to their own purses, oppress the city states and fiefdoms of Ensaimin.'

No, Corrain thought bitterly as the baron droned on. Caladhria has this parliament that's so seldom able to agree that every household would still be lit by candles if the parliament had ever been asked to debate the merits of oil lamps.

The bare minimum number of barons required to ratify a parliamentary decree could argue every facet of the simplest question for the full five days of a festival without ever coming within bowshot of a conclusion.

The Tormalin Emperor would have sent his legions if the corsairs had raided his shores. The Ensaimin guilds would have hired mercenaries to wreak their bloody vengeance. Caladhria's barons sat on their fat arses and bickered over who should bear the cost of defending their coasts while better men like Lord Halferan died in the attempt.

But he must not betray any such anger, Corrain reminded himself. The fight with the corsairs was behind him, or so he fervently hoped. He must look to the future. To secure Lady Zurenne and her daughters' future.

'Though this parliament has been called out of season—' Baron Ferl glanced at Corrain as he concluded '— let us conduct our debates with courtesy and reason.'

Corrain looked down at the slave shackle fastened around his off-hand wrist, a short length of broken chain dangling from it. That prompted another frisson along the baronial benches. Backs straightened, light summer cloaks rustled and booted feet shuffled on the oak planks.

He'd already heard three different versions of the oath that he had supposedly sworn and two other rumours as to why he still wore the manacle and had refused to cut his hair, even if he now wore it tamed in a tight braid hanging down his back.

Let them ask, if they dared. Corrain wouldn't tell them. That was between him and his dead lord and no one else, not even a god.

Still no one spoke. Quelling an impulse to a humourless smile, Corrain contemplated the distant window. That didn't stop him tallying up the headcount with discreet sideways glances.

Three hundred, give or take a handful. Definitely more than half of the five hundred or so barons required to safeguard the interests of the obedient artisans, yeomen and labourers in return for their unquestioning fealty. So any decree passed here would be binding in law.

How many might decide in his favour? Corrain knew that his noble opponents would have summoned as many inclined to oppose him as they possibly could, despatching the courier doves able to carry a message so much more quickly than a mounted man. That would have given such hostile lords more time to travel to Ferl than those summoned in the usual fashion.

On the other side of those scales, his foes had betrayed themselves with their haste to summon this parliament out of season. The decree demanding his attendance had been a disgrace; ink smudged on the parchment and half the requisite twenty-five wax seals crooked or blurred.

The decree which had arrived so late, giving him so little time to get here. Well, these noble lords might baulk at night travel under anything less than both moons at their full but no guardsman could be so timid. Corrain and his men had often ridden, as now, under the full of the Greater Moon alone.

A balding baron rose to his feet, on one of the higher benches. 'I propose the first question for debate is whether we need to be here at all.'

An exasperated nobleman promptly stood up on the other side of the hall. 'I support the proposal. It's not forty days since we assembled in Kevil at summer solstice. Why are we called away from our harvests and herds at this busiest of seasons?'

That provoked a sharp riposte from a lord on the bench below. 'Congratulations, my lord of Cathalet, on having harvests and herds to concern you. Those of us closer to the southern coasts have seen our fields go unplanted and our beasts sold or slaughtered to deny the raiders their plunder.'

Corrain was relieved to see a good number nodding their agreement with Baron Aveis.

He had hoped as much. Ferl was one of Caladhria's more southerly towns. Those nobles living hereabouts would all have seen the suffering of commoners fleeing from those coastal baronies attacked by the corsairs from the southern islands.

He had seen the knots of men and women in the doorways of taverns and merchants' warehouses, some avid with curiosity, some apprehensive. This was no routine parliament, conducting its business while the townsfolk went about their own concerns.

The locals couldn't console themselves with their

distance from the sea any longer. Everyone had heard how, this very For-Spring, those dread black ships had sailed up the river Dyal in Lescar. Their own Ferl River was navigable all the way to this town that shared its name.

'The raiders have gone,' a noble with a florid complexion said scornfully. He gestured briefly at Corrain. 'I gather we have this man to thank. His claim to the title of Baron Halferan may hardly be seemly but he has married the rightful heiress so confirmation seems a simple enough gesture of gratitude. Let us be done with the business and go home!'

Corrain tensed. Could it be so simple? Would he be back on the road to Halferan the very next day, confirmed as legal guardian to Lady Zurenne and her daughters?

Would he truly have escaped these noble lords' questions as to exactly why the corsairs had vanished so suddenly? And worse, secured the coastal barons' gratitude, for succeeding where his own dead lord had failed. For persuading the Archmage of Hadrumal to help them, by telling them where the raiders would land so that the Caladhrians could lie in wait to burn their ships.

He had told that lie to protect Halferan. Now he must stand by it. At least until he was confirmed as baron in his dead lord's place. Then Lady Zurenne and her daughters would be protected under Caladhrian law, even if Archmage Planir brought the wrath of Hadrumal down on his head, undeniably guilty of telling and perpetuating that untruth and more besides.

Lord Licanin rose to his feet from the bench on Corrain's sword hand. Steely-haired and wrinkled though far from his dotage, he regarded Baron Karpis opposite with measured dislike.

Karpis was perhaps ten years younger, his prime softening into fat disguised by his chestnut doublet's expensive tailoring. Corrain wondered if an apothecary's dye bottle was responsible for the matching colour of the baron's carefully pomaded locks.

'My noble lords,' Lord Licanin began.

Before he could say another word, something crashed into the hall's great wooden doors. A steely clash of blades outside cut through the booming reverberation.

Noble voices rose in disbelief and indignation.

'What is going on?'

'Where are the Ferl troopers?'

'Is it corsairs?'

Corrain stared at the shivering door. Could it possibly be corsairs? Of all the men gathered here, he alone knew what resources the raiders might now have to call on. Had he truly brought that disaster upon Caladhria?

Or was he about to face the Archmage's wrath? Because the wizards of Hadrumal knew that Corrain was responsible for summoning the vile sorcerer who had really destroyed the raiders. Before the treacherous bastard had decided to claim the corsairs' island lair for his own.

The Mandarkin wizard Anskal might have promised to spare Caladhria any future raids but Corrain had no faith in wizards. His own dead lord had trusted a renegade mage and that had been the death of him.

The wicket door flew open and a man fell headlong through it. He scrambled to his feet, one of the Ferl gate wards.

The man had a bloodied nose and a swelling eye. His

sword was still in its scabbard though and that clash of blades outside hadn't been repeated. It was only a common brawl, Corrain realised.

Then he heard young Reven shouting incomprehensible abuse. A moment later the lad choked on a yell of pain.

Corrain was out through the door inside a handful of long strides. He saw a man in a dun jerkin standing over Reven, ready to plant a boot in his ribs.

Grabbing the man by his shoulders Corrain flung him away. Taken wholly unawares, the man reeled backwards down the steps of the hall's grand portico.

Reven had given a decent account of himself before the blow that had felled him, Corrain noted. The man had a split lip and a bloodied nose.

Regardless, he hauled the bleary-eyed lad to his feet by the front of his already torn shirt. He shook him with all the frustration he couldn't turn on those cursed nobles cowering in their parliament.

'What fool's game are you playing? Where is Sergeant Fitrel?'

Reven pointed with a wavering hand. Appalled, Corrain saw the old man in the midst of the fracas. It seemed that all the Halferan guards were intent on beating some Karpis retainers in crimson jerkins senseless.

'Stand down!' Corrain thanked all the gods whom he didn't believe in that he could still call up a guard captain's razor-edged tones. 'Halferan, form up!'

Anger gave his words such steely authority that three of the Karpis men stood to attention before they realised what they were doing.

The Halferans in their pewter livery withdrew to the other side of the hall's broad entrance. Corrain swiftly assessed their injuries. At least he saw nothing worse than bruises, bloody scrapes and torn clothing. Better yet, the Halferans had inflicted far more hurts than they'd suffered on the Karpis men.

He caught Fitrel's eye. The grizzled swordsman could only see out of one. The other was already swelling shut.

'Report, sergeant,' Corrain growled.

'Captain!' Reven spoke up from the pillar he was leaning on. 'You didn't hear what they've been saying.' The boy could barely restrain himself. 'Mocking every one of us, aye and saying such vileness about Halferan's ladies—' He broke off, colouring furiously.

Corrain could imagine what stable yard filth had been flung. Hard-riding troopers wouldn't bother with tactful enquiries about his frankly scandalous marriage. Lascivious speculation about young Lady Ilysh's performance on her wedding night would have been the least of it.

'How can some erstwhile guardsman manage the myriad tenants and complex affairs of a barony?'

Corrain wheeled around to see the great hall's doors now standing open, revealing the barons crowding the entrance. Some were wide-eyed with curiosity. More betrayed distaste as they contemplated his dishevelment. Corrain's exertions had left his doublet wrenched askew and the shirt beneath had come untucked.

'He will never command the respect of men he rode with as a common trooper. Look at them, scuffling in the streets. Drunk, like as not.'

Now he saw who was talking. Baron Karpis had raised his voice to carry far beyond his immediate companion.

Scorning Halferan when Karpis men had started this fight. Deliberately too, Corrain didn't doubt that, not after Reven's account.

Could he convince the parliament that this scuffle had been provoked? Would it do any good for Halferan's cause, even if he did?

Would he be back on the road tomorrow, returning to tell Lady Zurenne how utterly he had failed her?

— CHAPTER TWO —

Taw Ricks Hunting Lodge, Caladhria
1st of For-Autumn

'DO WE KNOW when the—' Doratine's pencil hovered over her slate '—when he'll be home?'

At which time, presumably, they would all know what to call Corrain. Zurenne shook her head.

'There's no way of knowing how long this parliament will last. But he'll send a messenger ahead when they're on their way. If he doesn't?' She shrugged. 'He and the guardsmen will have to make do with whatever meat and bread may be found.'

'Should I prepare for other guests?' Doratine's shaking pencil betrayed her with a shrill squeak on the slate. 'Lord Licanin?'

'You have your menus. You may go.' Zurenne spoke more curtly than she'd intended.

How dare Doratine even hint that the parliament would insist on her sister's husband remaining as Halferan's guardian?

However grateful they might be for Lord Licanin's undoubted aid and indeed, his own guardsmen's sacrifice, when the corsairs had attacked, Lady Ilysh was her father's rightful heir. Zurenne had married her to Corrain with every legality observed in the Halferan manor's own shrine. The parliament could not ignore their own laws, even if Lysha was barely old enough to be blooded by Drianon.

And Corrain had sworn to Zurenne on that same altar, before the goddess of home and motherhood, that the marriage would be in name only, to ensure that she and her daughters would never again be subject to some unwanted guardian's unchallengeable authority.

But it never did to be on bad terms with the servants. Zurenne managed a conciliatory smile. 'You have my authority to tell Master Rauffe to buy whatever you wish at the Genlis market.'

'Thank you, my lady.' Doratine curtseyed and hurried from the room.

Though of course that made it all the more likely that Master Rauffe would knock on her door with some veiled complaint that Doratine had stepped on his toes. They were forever encroaching on each other's jealously guarded responsibilities.

Zurenne allowed herself an exasperated sigh. Halferan Manor had been big enough to accommodate them all separately. Doratine's spacious chamber had been the most favoured of the servants' rooms above the storehouses beyond the kitchen and its range of buildings. Master Rauffe and his wife had enjoyed the steward's comfortable dwelling beside the barrack hall and opposite the baronial tower.

All that lay in ruins. Now the entire household was crammed into this modest lodge, only ever intended for seasonal visits by the baron, his chosen guests and their handpicked servants.

Zurenne reminded herself to be thankful that some long-dead Baron Halferan had substantially extended the original timber and plastered-brick building. That had only offered a single wide hall with this sitting room and its adjoining bedchamber to the rear and a garret above for servants.

She looked at her needlework laid ready on a polished marquetry table. She had been delighted to find the delicate piece in that furnishing warehouse, when she had fled to Claithe in search of some comforts after her first few miserable days here.

Besides, she had told herself, the barony's reputation would benefit from the merchants seeing her composed and prosperous. Everyone would see that whatever their sufferings, Halferan had survived the corsairs' attacks. Now all their travails lay in the past.

So she had scattered the Archmage's blood money like a ploughboy sowing seed. She had bought Relshazri joinery, pottery from Peorle, fine wools and linens carried south by merchant ships from Col, Trebin lace and buttons from Duryea. Pewter and brass wares for the kitchen and servants' hall all the way from Wrede in northern Ensaimin.

Now her purchases looked as out of place here as she was. This lodge had been decorated throughout with a practical eye to the hazards of mud and worse consequences of a day's hunting with horses, hawks and hounds.

The frivolous chairs that framed the round table looked positively foolish beside the scarred wooden settles intended for guests taking their ease in breeches and boots after a long day at the chase. The costly new carpet in front of the cavernous, soot-darkened fire place was almost as ridiculous.

Besides, no amount of frills and fancies could distract Zurenne from the constant reminders of her beloved husband's presence here, reminding her wherever she looked that he was never to return.

The scars on the stone door jamb showed where he'd been accustomed to sharpen his knife while waiting for a groom to bring him his horse. He had inked the map in the entrance hall showing the different chases through the local forests with his annual tallies of deer and boar.

Zurenne picked up a book of Tormalin poetry. She had bought it in hopes of distraction after her daughters had been sent to bed and before they woke in the mornings. Now it reminded her too readily of that small stock of thoughtful books which she'd found on a shelf in the bedchamber, debating the natural philosophy of birds and beasts.

It was so easy to imagine her beloved sitting and reading in quiet candlelight, pleasantly weary after a day on horseback, well fed on venison or game birds. Zurenne had never begrudged him his visits here, his escape from the burdens of his barony.

Tears, so often a threat, even so long after his death, welled in her eyes.

A peremptory knock on the door startled her into dropping the book of poems.

'My lady?'

'Mistress Rauffe.' Zurenne braced herself as the door opened.

The steward's wife was as thickset and uncompromising as her husband was lean and jovial.

'My lady.' She curtseyed. 'I was wondering if you have given any further thought to my proposal?'

'I have,' Zurenne said firmly, 'and it is out of the question.'

'My lady.' Mistress Rauffe curtseyed again. 'It is hardly

seemly for the household lackeys and the maidservants to be living in adjoining rooms. If my husband and I were to take—'

'I would have thought you would be grateful to have a room to yourselves, even one so small.' So they would be, Zurenne was sure, if the former storeroom between the scullery and the kitchen wasn't right next to the other one which had been cleared out for Doratine's use.

'Everyone else is forced together like beans in a pod. You cannot see the floors for sleeping pallets.' She swept a hand towards the current great hall, built on the lodge's eastern face with all the florid ugly stonework of generations long past. Her other hand carried the gesture across towards the guest suites on the other side of the original hall, now the lodge's entrance. The servants' rooms that Mistress Rauffe coveted sat across the corridor from those suites.

'The kitchen wing is the newest building here.' Zurenne had to blink away more tears. Her own husband had commissioned a devotee of Tormalin Rational architecture to design the clean-cut wing, after she had pointed out the deficiencies of the earlier additions on her first visit here after their marriage. 'You will be warmer than anyone else, as the season turns to Aft-Autumn.'

Zurenne really didn't want to imagine what the rest of the demesne servants would endure once For-Winter arrived, crammed into the extended garrets beneath the lodge's mismatched rooflines.

'Very well, my lady.' Mistress Rauffe curtseyed a third time but Zurenne knew better than to take that as a sign of acquiescence.

Sure enough, the woman insisted on the last word as she went out into the entrance hall. 'Perhaps we can discuss it further when the baron arrives.'

Zurenne longed to call her back, to demand which baron she meant. Corrain, confirmed as Baron Halferan? Or did the steward and his wife truly believe that the parliament would refuse his claim in favour of Lord Licanin?

But she let the woman leave. This haphazard household wouldn't run half as smoothly without Mistress Rauffe's brisk attention to a myriad practical details and her talent for getting the very best work from the most dilatory maid.

Zurenne told herself firmly that was only the couple's former loyalties talking. After all, they had come to Halferan from Licanin, after their lord had so belatedly learned of the abuses which Zurenne, her daughters and the barony had suffered at the hands of that scoundrel Master Minelas with his forged claim to their guardianship.

After the villain had murdered her husband and no one had come to her aid for a year and more. After the neighbouring barons of Karpis and Tallat had given that supposed grant only the most spurious examination, doubtless bought off with coin stolen from Halferan's own coffers.

All at once, Zurenne was paralysed by terrifying memories. Of Minelas intercepting her letters. Of him dictating the lies she must write to her sisters. Of him wringing the necks of Halferan's courier doves in front of her. Of the threats the usurper had made, as he plundered her daughters' inheritance; to wed and bed Ilysh himself with all the violence he clearly relished.

Of the ruffians he had hired to replace her husband's honest guardsmen. Of the way those evil men had kept Zurenne a prisoner in her own home, even after Minelas himself had departed on whatever business had proved to be the death of him. But even that hadn't brought her salvation.

She came to her senses and looked afresh around the cluttered, inhospitable room. Once again, tears threatened, now with a headache pressing close behind.

Zurenne longed to leave but there were no gardens to walk in here, only kennel yards and stables and a deer park beyond. Besides, as soon as she stepped outside the dour sanctuary of this sitting room, she would be besieged by the expectant gazes of those who'd survived Halferan Manor's destruction. When would their true lady, their beloved lord's daughter lead them home to rebuild?

Doratine wasn't the only one who would struggle to address Corrain as the new Baron Halferan when the parliament was obliged to grant him that honour. Everyone knew that the marriage was a convenient fiction to keep the barony out of another outsider's hands. They persisted in their old allegiance and looked to Ilysh as her father's true heir.

Which was exactly as it should be. Zurenne drew a resolute breath and surveyed the plastered walls above the walnut panelling. She wouldn't remove any reminders of her husband's presence here, not even those ugly trophies wrought from the antlers of prized deer. No matter how lacerating she found daily recollection of their companionship, of the consolations of their marriage bed, of their shared joy in their beloved daughters.

Nor would she yield to the nightmares that persisted after she woke alone, night after night in the silent darkness. The fear that the parliament's barons would somehow rule against Corrain and hand her and her children to some other guardian. She could not stand the thought of even one as benign as Lord Licanin.

Zurenne's hand strayed to the triangular silver pendant on its ribbon around her neck. Adorned with her private sigil made from the upright runes shown on the bones rolled at her birth, the Archmage's gift was enchanted so she might summon his help if the corsairs ever reappeared.

She would use it to speak to him, if the parliament denied Corrain's claim. Let the Archmage use his influence to change their mind, or the coin that he seemed to be able to summon out of thin air. Whatever it took, Zurenne didn't care.

Otherwise she would tell the world that Master Minelas, that charming man who had so convincingly sworn that the lamented Baron Halferan had appointed him to care for his widow and orphaned daughters—

Zurenne would tell the world that the scoundrel had been a renegade mage. That the wizard isle of Hadrumal's so-called Council had never so much as suspected his vicious nature, much less acted to curb it.

Once they had learned of his villainy, they had only sought to conceal it. If Corrain hadn't returned, ready and willing to bear witness to the wizard isle's disgrace, Planir need never have admitted to Minelas's crimes. He had made no effort to find those Halferan men enslaved in the Archipelago, even after he had learned the renegade had sold them to the corsairs.

In the dark silence of the night, Zurenne wondered if

the magewoman Jilseth hadn't been trapped alongside them when the corsairs had besieged Halferan, would the Archmage have let Zurenne die with her children; the last witnesses able to denounce Minelas for the villain he was?

Though of course the Archmage had told her no one would believe her, when Zurenne had threatened to tell before. But if he didn't want her to keep his secret, why had he handed over so much gold and silver, supposedly making good on Minelas's thefts? Zurenne knew that coin was the price of her silence without any wizard having to say so.

She sighed. Demanding the Archmage's help, if Corrain's claim was dismissed, assumed that Planir could find some way to defend Halferan from the parliament's decree. Zurenne suspected that saving them all from slaughter by corsairs had been simple by comparison.

She realised her restless feet had brought her to the sitting room's heavy oak table, long enough to seat five men on each side. It had been pushed back against the wall opposite the hearth, sturdy benches tucked beneath it.

Now it held stacks of leather-bound ledgers and bundles of the rent rolls that had preceded them; record of the barony's dues collected at solstice and equinox. Singed and scattered remnants of folded parchments were heaped haphazard beside them. All that Master Rauffe had salvaged from the muniment room as they fled the corsairs. Along with the shrine ledgers, this was all that remained of the archive relating the barony's pact with generations of tenantry.

Zurenne had no notion what to do with them. Her

husband always dealt with such matters. Besides, there was no point her starting such an undertaking. Once Corrain was confirmed as Baron Halferan that would be one of his many challenges.

Though of course, she could address her own correspondence. Zurenne contemplated her prized writing box holding pens, ink and paper, the two halves cunningly hinged to open into a leather-faced slope. She should already have written the greetings customary at the turn of each season, sharing the latest news of her children and the household with her sisters and the neighbouring baronies ladies.

Several of their letters had arrived in the past day or so. They lay on the top of the writing box, their wax seals uncracked. Zurenne didn't want to read her sisters' protestations of affections or their excuses as they sought to explain why it had taken them so long, even after all her letters had stopped, to persuade their husbands that something was amiss in Halferan.

She didn't want to read Lady Diress of Karpis's warm and friendly advice that Zurenne should yield to the inevitable and surrender voluntarily to Baron Karpis's protection. Since the parliament would undoubtedly agree it would be wholly irresponsible to abandon the lamented Baron Halferan's tenantry, his helpless widow and her innocent daughters to some trooper more used to taking orders than to giving them.

No. Zurenne would write once she knew which way the parliament's scales had tilted. Or perhaps she should say; which way those runes had rolled.

Her hand strayed to her pendant again. As well as using the three-sided bones for gambling as the household troopers did, some of the old women used them for telling fortunes. Roll them and one rune would be hidden on the bottommost face. On the two facets that showed, one rune would be upright and the other one reversed.

Were all her hopes to be overthrown by the parliament's barons, as easily as some bone cast from a gambler's hand landing wrong sides up?

The door from the entrance hall opened, unheralded by any tap. Ilysh stormed into the room.

'Lysha.' Zurenne immediately sat down on the end of a bench and reached for those unwanted letters. 'Kindly do me the courtesy of knocking.'

'Mama, the dress-lengths have arrived from Claithe.' The set of Ilysh's jaw ominously strengthened her resemblance to her dead father. 'Evrel says that the silks are for you and the broadcloths are for me and Neeny.'

'That's correct.' Zurenne snapped a wax roundel with the Fandail seal. Would news from her remote sister Celle offer some distraction?

'I want a silk gown.' Ilysh took a step to demand her mother's attention. 'I am Lady Halferan. You cannot dress me like a child!'

'I will dress you as I see fit.' Zurenne tossed the still-folded letter aside with sudden concern. 'Where is Neeny?'

Why wasn't her younger daughter's outrage echoing around the building if Lysha had given her the slip?

'In the kitchen.' Ilysh brushed her long brown hair back with something perilously close to a shrug.

Zurenne slammed her hand on the table. 'You are supposed to be looking after her!'

'I am not a nursemaid,' Lysha retorted hotly.

'No,' Zurenne snapped. 'Your nursemaid Jora has

leave to visit her brothers and sisters as they mourn their murdered parents. Had you forgotten that? If you wish to be honoured as Lady of Halferan—' she was on her feet before she realised it '—then take some measure of responsibility!'

Ilysh stared at her, fury kindling in her hazel eyes. Then she flushed scarlet and burst into tears.

Before Zurenne could take back her words, the girl fled for the master bedchamber opening off the sitting room, which the three of them were sharing amid a similar mismatch of old and new furnishings and truckle beds.

Despite the weight of the heavy oak door, Lysha managed to give it a creditable slam.

Zurenne sank back onto the bench. It wasn't as if she wanted silk dresses. Silk came from the Aldabreshin Archipelago where the corsairs lurked, when they weren't raiding the Caladhrian coast, robbing, burning and murdering innocents. But she had to keep up appearances and such opulence spoke of a safe and secure barony, to her own people as well as to those neighbours watching for any sign of weakness.

Her head ached, this time with anger. The parliament's barons knew that the Archipelago sheltered those accursed corsairs. Yet they eagerly purchased Aldabreshin glassware, silks and spices, brought from Relshaz's merchants. The trading city on the muddy delta of the River Rel had grown rich on its inhabitants' willingness to buy and sell anything from anyone, up to and including trading slaves with the Aldabreshi warlords.

Thanks to the corsairs, some of those slaves were Caladhrian. Corrain could swear to that. Of all those

Halferan men captured when Zurenne's husband was killed, he had managed to escape after a year or more in chains. What would the inland barons say to that? How could they deny they had any duty to act? That the corsairs' raids were the coastal lords' problem and none of theirs?

How long would they have to wait for news? Jilseth looked at the four-sided timepiece on the lofty mantel shelf. It had been turned promptly to its autumn face that very morning, now showing the day and night divided by ten equally spaced chimes instead of summer's longer hours or the far shorter divisions of winter daylight.

It was going to be a painfully long time before that arrow sliding down the long timescale prompted the next silvery chime or the one after that.

A knock sounded and the door to the hall opened to reveal Raselle. 'My lady—'

'Where is Esnina?' Zurenne strove not to vent her anger on her faithful personal maid.

'In the kitchen.' Raselle sank into a deep curtsey, her round face anxious. 'Helping Doratine make curd tarts. She was crying so—'

'Very well.' Zurenne could hear Lysha sobbing in the bed chamber. She couldn't face the thought of dealing with one of Neeny's exhausting tantrums as well.

Far better that the child found some amusement in the kitchen under Doratine's watchful, loving care. Far better than shrieking incomprehensible defiance at her mother until she fell asleep, only to wake and stare hollow-eyed at some recollection of the horrors she'd seen. Men hacking each other to pieces. Greybeards, women and children cut down amid bloody frenzy.

Would either of her daughters be happier when at

least some of their current uncertainty was relieved? Zurenne so desperately hoped so.

She drew a deep breath. 'I must attend to my correspondence. Please bring me a tisane tray.'

'My lady.' Raselle retreated obediently from the room.

Zurenne meant to reach for a letter but once again she found her hand closing around the silver sigil on its ribbon.

If she could use the ensorcelled trinket to call on the Archmage, could she ask him to use his wizardry to at least find out what the parliament's barons were saying?

To ask, she thought with sudden guilt, how the lady wizard Jilseth fared? Because none of them would still be alive if the magewoman hadn't saved them and at such cost to herself.

That was something for Zurenne to remember, if she was ever tempted to give in to her miseries.

— CHAPTER THREE —

Trydek's Hall, Hadrumal
2nd of For-Autumn

THE ARCHMAGE SWEPT a hand over the silver scrying bowl. The magelight suffusing the water shifted from turquoise to emerald green. The droning voices rising from the rippling water were silenced.

Jilseth had always been awe-struck by the Archmage's talents. A stone mage by birth, his instinctive affinity was with the soil and rock. Yet he had such effortless control over all the magics of fire, water and even of the air, the element most opposed to his own. There couldn't be more than a handful of other wizards in this whole city so dedicated to the study and perfecting of magic who could work a scrying spell combined with a clairaudience.

Now seeing Planir work such complex wizardry only deepened her fear. Would her own magic ever return?

Hearth Master Kalion scowled at the bowl set on the octagonal rosewood table between the upholstered chairs that framed the comfortable room's hearth.

'The barons insist on debating all the summer's events before they deign to consider Captain Corrain's claim?'

Planir nodded, sunlight lancing through the tall windows burnishing the silver in his dark beard. 'I fear it'll be another long and tedious day.'

Kalion glanced at Jilseth, still standing on the

threshold though Planir had invited her in as his magic opened the door to her knock.

'I supposed you have an interest in the Halferan Barony's fate,' the stout mage acknowledged. 'Have you recovered from your exertions in their cause?'

That was one way to put it, she supposed. Opening pits in the earth for the corsairs to fall into. Drawing up turf ramparts to block their way. Her wizardry shaking the raiders' ladders off Halferan's walls while the topmost bricks reshaped themselves into defiant spikes.

Her magic honing the guardsmen's blades so they could hack a bloody path from the manor's gatehouse to the high road. The slightest scratch, however strongly an enemy might be armoured, opening into a gaping wound. Those gashes continuing to widen and deepen even after the blade withdrew. Within a few breaths, raiders lying dead on the ground, limbs severed and spines cut clean through.

Pouring her last breath into such devastating magecraft. Waking to find her mageborn affinity utterly exhausted, all her wizard senses numb. Waking every morning since to find that nothing had changed. Not in thirty days.

'I am recovering,' she said calmly.

Jilseth hadn't expected to find the Hearth Master in the Archmage's private study. Worse, his faithful shadow, Ely was perched on the edge of a ladder-backed chair drawn up beside the rosewood table. Jilseth wasn't about to give the slender, sly-faced magewoman any more gossip to spread in Halferan's wine shops.

'Join us, please.' Planir rose and fetched a second upright chair from the table on the other side of the room.

Jilseth desperately hoped that he wouldn't ask what had brought her here. She couldn't think of a plausible lie any more than she could contemplate admitting in front of Ely that she had come seeking reassurance. Planir had assured her that her affinity with the earth would stir anew. Once again Jilseth had woken before dawn to contemplate the appalling possibility that it wouldn't.

She tugged at a crease in the skirt of her plain grey gown as she sat down. 'Do you think that Corrain's supposed alliance with Hadrumal will sway the barons' votes?'

'I would say so. They'll decide the wisest course is to tolerate him as Baron Halferan.' Kalion smoothed the red velvet of his gown complacently. Old fashioned as the Hearth Master's garb was, it flattered his portly figure far more than a doublet and breeches in the mainland style.

'Rather than risk alienating Hadrumal and all its wizards,' Ely quickly agreed.

'They still don't believe us.' Planir shook his head wryly. 'However often we insist that we had nothing to do with the corsairs' disappearance.'

'Are you surprised?' Kalion asked. 'When scores of people saw Jilseth's magic prevail against the raiders? That tale must have been told in every tavern and market place from Cape Attar to Peorle.'

'Indeed.' The Archmage rose from his chair and walked to the sideboard where glasses framed a trio of decanters. 'Cordial? Plum, pear or almond?'

Light from the modest fire glinted on the faceted crystal. With the heat of high summer now passed, the island was exposed to the chilling winds sweeping in from the west. Though Planir was in his shirtsleeves, his favourite faded doublet hung on the back of the door.

'Pear, thank you,' Kalion inclined his head agreeably.

'I'll take a little of the same.' Ely rose in a flutter of green silk to fetch both glasses.

'I have told them time and again,' Jilseth protested. 'Baron Karpis, Lord Licanin, Lady Zurenne. When I used magic to save Halferan Manor I was acting first and foremost to save my own neck.'

'You have nothing to apologise for.' Planir's gesture quelled a surge of sparks in the fireplace. 'Any wizard is entitled to use lethal spells in direst need.'

'Few wizards ever find themselves so beleaguered,' Kalion remarked, 'or acquit themselves so well.'

'Hearth Master,' Jilseth said tightly.

She didn't seek his approval, however briefly satisfying it was to see Ely's swift distaste. The lissom magewoman couldn't shake her apprehension that Jilseth might rival her own beloved Galen as one of Hadrumal's most noted stone mages.

'It does no harm for the mainland populace to be reminded of what magecraft can do.' The Hearth Master sipped his cordial, content.

'No?' Planir queried. 'When some barons will be all the more inclined to oppose Corrain precisely because they fear what he might achieve with a noble's rank in one hand and an alliance with Hadrumal in the other?'

'Archmage?' Ely looked perplexed. 'Ah, of course, that business at the last parliament in Kevil.'

Jilseth wished she had asked for some cordial. Taking a sip might hide her embarrassment at the memory of her confrontation with Lord Tallat.

She had publicly called the younger nobleman to task

for daring to hint that Halferan and the coastal baronies could now call on magical aid. He had made the mistake of disbelieving her and she'd made the mistake of using her magecraft to get his full attention, in full view of all Caladhria's barons attending the Summer Solstice Parliament. Which had of course only served to convince Tallat and doubtless many others that Corrain truly had the Archmage's ear.

Pouring himself a small glass of amber liquor, Planir savoured the scent of almonds. 'That Kevil encounter would have been a ten day tale if magic hadn't driven all the corsairs out of Caladhrian waters. Now they naturally assume that we drove the raiders off at his bidding and it's well known that we returned strongboxes of stolen coin to Halferan. Other baronies that suffered such raids have seen no recompense.'

'How long is Hadrumal to pay for Minelas's crimes?' Kalion demanded testily. 'Will we be filling Halferan's strongboxes until the widow and the new baron are both laid on their funeral pyres?'

'It hardly seems justice,' Ely nodded. 'Especially since the traitor himself is long dead and beyond any punishment.'

'You don't think we should make amends for all that Lady Zurenne and her children suffered?' Jilseth was provoked into a sharp retort. 'And Halferan Manor has been utterly laid waste. Barely one brick still stands on another.'

Planir raised a quelling hand. 'We cannot know that Minelas has escaped punishment. The priests may be correct when they say Poldrion sends his demons to claw those whom Saedrin turns back from the door to the Otherworld.'

Returning to his seat, the Archmage grinned as the other wizards all looked at him, astonished.

'Since priestly claims can neither be verified nor disproved, we will abandon the question of Minelas's fate. The important thing for Hadrumal is that he is dead and there is no doubt of that.'

He inclined his head towards Jilseth. She smiled dutifully, trying not to recall the sight of the renegade mage gutted by a vengeful dagger; well-deserved payment for him trying to sell his skills to the highest bidder in Lescar's recent civil war.

'Our concern now is with this world and those living in it, notably the innocent and honourable mageborn on the mainland,' the Archmage continued, serious. 'They will be the first victims of the mundane populace's fear and suspicion if word spreads of a corrupt and vicious wizard such as Minelas so successfully defying Hadrumal.'

'Captain Corrain and Lady Zurenne cannot tell that tale without dishonouring their own dead lord's memory.' Once again, Kalion's tone was somewhere between rebuke and challenge 'It was the former Baron Halferan who first sought the aid of illicit magic.'

'Only after I had so grievously disappointed him, when I told him that the Edict of Trydek expressly forbids any magical engagement in warfare.' Planir held up his hand and the diamond on the great ring of his office blazed in the sunlight falling through the window. The gems set around the great stone glowed; sapphire, amber, ruby and emerald.

'You can hardly feel guilty on that score,' Kalion said tartly. 'You upheld the Edict just as every Archmage to wear that ring has done since Trydek first established this sanctuary.'

Though Jilseth waited for the Hearth Master to remark that of course, the lamented Baron Halferan might yet have lived, if Planir had accepted Kalion's oft-repeated contention that driving Archipelagan raiders away from Caladhria's shores was in no sense the same as taking sides in some battle between the mainland's realms or princes.

She knew what else he would go on to say. That taking an interest in mainland realms' affairs was not in any sense forbidden. Indeed, with Hadrumal's guidance, strife that might lead to warfare could be soothed away. So Hadrumal's Council had a duty to keep abreast of developments and to cultivate a measure of influence with the ruling powers. Barely a fifth of the wizards were born in Hadrumal after all.

True, but Jilseth, of Hadrumal blood since her twice-great-grandsire had set foot on these shores, found that precious few of the mainland-born spared much thought for the family or friends who had so hastily shipped them off to this safely distant isle when hitherto unsuspected magebirth manifested on the cusp of adulthood.

But Kalion's thoughts were elsewhere. He shook his head, jowls wobbling. 'Besides, their precious dead baron will be shown for a fool as well as a knave. He was no great judge of men if he couldn't see that Minelas would betray him as readily as the swine betrayed his oaths to Hadrumal.'

'Perhaps.' Planir set his cordial glass down, his grey eyes flinty. 'Well, what's done is done. Let's look to the future.

'If Corrain is indeed confirmed as Baron Halferan,' he said more briskly, 'the captain will have to bear all the burdens of that rank. Halferan's tenantry and yeomen will all be looking to him for guidance as the barony rebuilds. They cannot delay if those who lost their homes and livelihoods to the corsairs are to have food and shelter for the winter. At best, he has the two halves of autumn before the harsh weather arrives. All the while, his enemies will be wishing him ill. Baron Karpis and Lord Licanin in particular will be ready to pounce on the first sign of any failing.'

The Archmage swept a lean-fingered hand over the scrying bowl and the emerald magelight in the water brightened. 'With every eye turned to Corrain, that leaves us free and unobserved to keep a weather eye on Caladhria's real saviour.'

Jilseth knew that Planir meant this Mandarkin wizard whom Corrain of Halferan had somehow persuaded to come south and drive out those cursed corsairs.

The Archmage's tone was so chilling that Jilseth wouldn't have been surprised to see vapour rising from the water, like the mist from a pond in winter.

'Can you—' Kalion swallowed an obscenity as the water seethed and the magelight vanished.

At least Jilseth could be sure it wasn't her unruly magic disrupting the spell.

Planir drummed his fingers on the table. That, or some unguarded resonance from his frustrated wizardry, stirred the stubbornly unreflective water.

'Have you made any progress at all in finding a way through these veiling spells?' he demanded of the Hearth Master.

'Not as yet.' Kalion flushed unbecomingly. 'But I have been refining a new nexus working with Ely, Canfor and Galen.'

'Galen is cautiously optimistic,' Ely insisted.

The Archmage glanced at her with a thin smile. 'I would rather hear that you are optimistic, since scrying is a water magic. You should have as much confidence in your abilities as you do in Galen's.'

Ely couldn't meet the Archmage's eyes. She looked at Jilseth instead. 'Has your nexus been considering this challenge?'

Jilseth wished she could say yes. That she was weaving her elemental affinity with the earth into Merenel's fireborn wizardry, to be further enhanced by Nolyen's talent for water magic and Tornauld's grasp on the elusive air.

A single mage could add the other elements' magics to their own affinity with sufficient study and application. A nexus of four wizards could double and redouble each other's power to summon up quintessential magic. Such wizardry was far stronger and more durable than anything a solitary mage could achieve.

Or so the Element Masters and Mistresses of Hadrumal had always thought. Now the whole city was speculating how this unknown northern mage could sustain such impenetrable magic all on his own.

'We are considering it.' That much was no lie. If she couldn't join them in a nexus, her friends insisted that Jilseth share her gleanings from years of reading in Hadrumal's libraries, in case something could possibly hint at some answer. Nolyen in particular was obsessing over the puzzle, like every water mage from Flood Mistress Troanna down.

'We have no insights to offer.' That was, alas, also the truth.

'Have you learned anything from the Soluran Orders?' Kalion asked the Archmage without much hope.

Planir's lip curled. 'All the Elders whom I have sought to contact refuse to acknowledge my spells.'

There was so much that the mundane populace didn't understand about magic, Jilseth thought inconsequentially. A wizard's ability to bespeak another across a thousand leagues was truly marvellous. It was also only useful if the bespoken mage deigned to reply.

'Have you explained to the Solurans that we never invited this Mandarkin wizard to our waters?' Kalion demanded. 'That it was this Caladhrian ruffian Corrain who chose to travel beyond the reach of Hadrumal's edicts to find a wizard prepared to sink the corsair ships? That it was only when the wizards of Solura rebuffed him that he allied with a Mandarkin mage?'

'You think I should throw some blame their way?' Planir raised a quizzical eyebrow. 'When looking for co-operation?'

'Why won't the Solurans share what they know of Mandarkin magic?' Ely looked from Archmage to Hearth Master. 'They have been at each other's throats for generations.'

Planir shrugged. 'Silence is their prerogative. Happily there are others we can ask, who know something of those northern mountains and the magics used there.'

Kalion narrowed his eyes with sudden suspicion. 'Suthyfer?'

'Artifice?' Ely couldn't hide her disbelief.

Jilseth suddenly guessed who the Archmage meant. 'Aritane has aetheric magic to use against the Mandarkin?'

She should have remembered that Planir liked to consider challenges from unexpected angles and the Mountain woman had been born and raised in one of the scattered settlements in the valleys among the peaks separating the Kingdom of Solura and the Mandarkin realm. Aritane had also been one of the *sheltya*, the teachers, law-makers and judges governing the Mountain race's miners and trappers. Until some folly that even Ely's curiosity couldn't discover had seen her banished from those uplands, forced to accept Hadrumal's shelter.

'You think that mumbled enchantments can prevail,' Kalion scoffed, 'where the united magecraft of Hadrumal cannot?'

Loath as she was to agree with the Hearth Master, Jilseth found that equally hard to believe. For all that the mainland scholars who studied Artifice claimed that its adepts could influence and even invade another person's thoughts, those whom Jilseth had encountered could do little more than listen through a distant person's ears or see through their eyes.

The marvels once wrought with Artifice were as long lost as the Old Tormalin Empire. Indeed, didn't those same scholars say that the Old Empire had fallen because Artifice had failed them? That and the arrogant folly of the emperor known to history as Nemith the Reckless.

'Perhaps, perhaps not.' Planir shrugged again. 'But Aritane knows far more of Mandarkin wizardry than we do, though she herself followed the uplands' aetheric tradition of magic. She has shared what she's seen of Mandarkin magecraft with Usara and Shivvalan.'

Kalion grunted. 'Have your pet malcontents some revelation to share?'

Jilseth knew that the Hearth Master disapproved of the Suthyfer settlement. If he were Archmage, he would never have allowed those mages who chafed at Hadrumal's customs and traditions to set up their own haven of wizardry in the distant eastern ocean.

Kalion warmed to his theme. 'How can an adept of Artifice contribute anything to an understanding of Elemental wizardry? They have no more hope of mastering the antipathy between the two magics than we have.'

Jilseth knew that some mages felt personally insulted because no mageborn could grasp the most trivial aetheric enchantment. Kalion merely saw it as proof that Artifice was beneath his notice. Very few wizards like Usara and Shivvalan were fascinated by the challenge of understanding why.

Kalion waved all this irrelevance aside. 'What do you intend on doing about this Mandarkin mage?'

'Until he does something that requires me to act, nothing.' The Archmage looked expectantly at Kalion. 'So I need to see what he's doing, Hearth Master, and as soon as possible. Don't let me detain you from further refining your new nexus.'

'As you wish, Archmage,' Kalion said testily as he rose to his feet. 'Good day, and to you, Jilseth,' he added as an afterthought.

'Good day, Hearth Master.' Jilseth echoed Planir's farewells. 'Ely.'

As the door swung closed behind them, Planir gestured to the vacated upholstered chair. 'Why don't you have a more comfortable seat?'

Jilseth stayed where she was, struck by an unnerving possibility. 'Archmage,' she said hesitantly. 'If my magic has truly deserted me, do you think that I could learn something of Artifice?'

She had never visited Suthyfer but Merenel had spoken highly of the stone mage Usara and the Tormalin magewoman was not easily impressed.

Jilseth would gladly flee to those remote islands in the eastern ocean, certainly before she returned to the placid village on Hadrumal's southern shore where her parents farmed their small-holding, proud that their mageborn daughter had left them to hone her talents in the wizard city just as her mother's brother and her father's sister had done.

'Your magic has not deserted you,' Planir assured her.

Jilseth stared at the hearth rug. She didn't want to see pity in his eyes, or worse, false kindness.

'Look at the fire,' he chided her.

'Archmage?' She was surprised into looking up at him.

He pointed at the hearth and she saw that the coals had been utterly consumed.

'That was your magic stirring,' Planir observed. 'Somewhat erratically, I must say, but Ely was being particularly provoking. Wild magic is not unusual in such circumstances so I tamed it. I didn't think you'd relish the Hearth Master's advice, however well-meant,' he added drily.

'Archmage—' Jilseth couldn't doubt Planir but she still couldn't feel any wizardry within her.

'Your magic has not deserted you,' he repeated, unexpectedly stern, 'but recovering it will be neither easy nor swift. If you can master this upheaval, you may well find yourself a far more powerful mage than you ever were before. Otherwise,' he said with brutal frankness, 'you will find your affinity as much of a burden as the rawest apprentice for years to come. You may even have to leave this city, for your own safety and that of others.'

Now Jilseth was wholly lost for words. She could only stare wide-eyed at the Archmage. He looked steadily back at her.

'Do your utmost to hone your affinity afresh,' he advised her. 'I don't think that we need look for omens and portents as the Aldabreshi do, to know that Hadrumal will need wizards of your insight and ability to curb this Mandarkin mage's ambitions, when he finally decides what to do with this island he has claimed for his own.'

— CHAPTER FOUR —

Black Turtle Isle
In the domain of Nahik Jarir

Was it the turn of the season from Aft-Summer to For-Autumn? Hosh looked at his tally marks scratched in this sheltered angle where the black stone steps ran up to the broad terrace that served as the deserted building's foundation.

If he'd recalled the Caladhrian almanac correctly. If he'd kept his own count right. Was it tomorrow? Maybe yesterday. He frowned and recounted on his fingers before abruptly giving up.

What was the point? The Aldabreshi didn't consider the solstice or the equinox as any more significant than any other day and they certainly paid no head to the divisions between the seasons framing those days, as decreed by the different mainland authorities, so often differing by a day more or less.

Hosh gazed up at the darkling sky. Why should the Aldabreshi heed the mainlanders with their almanacs and calendars constantly needing adjustment when their count governed by the moons slipped out of true with the sun's aloof tally? The Archipelagans could trace and predict the path of every constellation as well as of the solitary coloured stars charting their own course through the heavens, named for the jewels which their colours recalled.

An Aldabreshin compass was an intricate marvel; an engraved disc overlaid with a pierced swirling lattice dotted with enamels and gemstones and revolving around a central pivot. Navigating the hundreds of domains in the Archipelago, the thousands of islands, barren islets and hidden reefs, was simplicity itself to a ship's master who knew how to read one.

A Caladhrian compass was a box with a single needle pointing north. That was all the aid any traveller could hope for, from the Tormalin Empire in the east, where the mainland met the ocean, all the way to the Great Forest in the west, a trackless sea of trees by all accounts.

Every Aldabreshin child grew up watching the skies. This wasn't only the business of scholars. Everyone from the lowliest slave to the Archipelago's fabled warlords with the power of life and death over thousands knew where the stars and the heavenly jewels would be and how to read the portents seen in the different arcs of the heavens.

The best that Hosh could do was scratch marks on a wall and the mainlanders had the arrogance to dismiss the Aldabreshi as shoeless barbarians. He looked down at his toes squelching in the black mud. Didn't anyone on the mainland know that going barefoot in these Aft-Summer rains was the only way to avoid foot rot? That could cost a man his leg if it didn't kill him outright?

He looked warily around the anchorage to reassure himself that all the pavilions were truly deserted. No movement caught his eye and he breathed a little more easily.

Once the luxurious dwellings for some Aldabreshin noble family, the houses offered wide windows to catch the sea breeze in the punishing dry season heat and broad eaves offering shelter from the torrential rains which swept back and forth across the island since just after the Summer Solstice.

Then corsairs had seized this anchorage, slaughtering any who didn't flee before them. Hosh had seen the splintered bones in the scrubby woodland. But now the corsairs had fled, abandoning both the pavilions which their galley and trireme masters had claimed and their rough-hewn settlement of huts built from driftwood, sailcloth and crudely shaped branches.

Hosh looked at his tally marks again. It was seventeen days now since he'd seen any of the raiders or their slaves. At first they had retreated to the trees, watching fearfully as the glow of magic showed them this unknown wizard searching their abandoned dwellings.

Some had tried to summon up the courage to attack that magical barrier. Such daring had rapidly failed for lack of encouraging omens. Some had waited, tense, for the wizard to send some word.

Nifai, Hosh's former overseer at his slave oar aboard the *Reef Eagle,* and Ducah, the sword-wielding brute who backed him, had stayed close to Hosh at first. The wizard must be a mainlander, Nifai had reasoned, and so they would need a mainlander to act as their go-between. Whatever else he might be, Nifai was no fool.

But no summons had come and some portent or other had deterred Nifai from sending Hosh to open negotiations. So one morning, the overseer and the swordsman had simply been gone.

Slowly at first, and then more and more of them day by day, the Archipelagans had crept away. Because for all their wisdom in mathematics and alchemy and so many other skills, the Aldabreshi were as terrified of magic as some infant crying for fear of the dark.

At least Hosh knew better than that. Granted, wizards were frightening and certainly not to be trusted. He had learned that lesson in the hardest fashion imaginable from his one encounter with that treacherous bastard, Minelas, the renegade mage who'd so vilely betrayed Lord Halferan.

But he'd heard enough barrack hall tales before that to know that the mages were men and women much the same as any other. Except for their uncanny talents with air, earth, fire or water. Was that blessing or curse? Hosh had never really considered the question with the wizard isle so comfortably remote. There hadn't been anyone mageborn in Halferan village in his lifetime.

But he certainly didn't share the Archipelagan conviction that even a wizard's presence irrevocably contaminated and corrupted the natural order and thus all the portents, from the flights of birds to the rhythms of the sea, that so wholly governed their lives.

That said, Hosh had to admit that the view down the long anchorage offered intimidating evidence of wizardly might. First there was the ravaged heap of stones that had once been the corsair leader's pavilion. The terrace, the walls, the shutters and doors of oiled wood, the tiled roof, everything had been reduced to splinters and flinders by a single strike of magical lightning. The seething cloud of dust that followed had reached out with tendrils crackling with wizardry to murder any survivors trying to flee.

Then there was the impossible wave rearing up between the distant headlands of the anchorage's entrance. Hosh had had no notion that a wizard could do such an astonishing thing. Taller than the baronial tower back in Halferan Manor, that curve of green water was topped by an ever-changing flurry of foam but the wave itself had remained constant for the past twenty-seven days.

It confined every ship within the anchorage; every raiding galley rowed by chained and lashed slaves, as Hosh had once been, and every fighting trireme with its oars manned by those eager to prove themselves worthy to join the ranks of the corsair swordsman and share in their plunder, as Hosh had sworn he never would.

Surely the incredible sight of that wave was proof that Captain Corrain had truly found his way back to the mainland? More than that, it showed that the captain had somehow secured a wizard's aid even if the Archmage of Hadrumal was too callous or too cowardly to defend innocent Caladhrians.

Only wizardry could hold that watery barrier firm and no Aldabreshi could ever have woven such spells. Archipelagan superstition condemned any mageborn to being skinned alive, so Hosh had heard. Only their spilled blood could wash away their taint.

So Halferan must be safe at last and every other village along the Caladhrian coast who had suffered the corsairs' raids this past handful of years.

Sweet as that consolation might be, Hosh couldn't set aside his bitter self-castigation. If only he'd kept his wits about him, when Corrain had provoked such chaos on that Archipelagan trading beach, starting a brawl along with that Forest man, Kusint. If he'd only been that bit quicker on his feet, maybe Hosh could have reached home too.

Then he'd be celebrating the turn of this season with his beloved mother. It would be the two of them as it had been for so long but there'd be roast pork and foaming ale on their humble table at For-Autumn's sunset. The turn of each season had its special meal. Sweetcakes and flower cordial with the For-Spring sunrise. Bread fresh from the oven and creamy cheese at For-Summer's noon. Though Hosh had never been too keen on salt beef and pickles at midnight, he always welcomed the token of Maewelin's pledge to see prudent households through For-Winter's hunger.

If today really was the turn of the season, Hosh guessed his mother would be praying to the Winter Hag, even if For-Autumn was rightly sacred to Dastennin— and that was a good question, wasn't it? What did the god of sea and storms make of that impossible wave?

But Maewelin was the goddess of mothers and of widows and Hosh's father had died so long ago that he barely recalled him.

His throat ached with the threat of tears. He couldn't set aside his fears and doubts. His mother would be praying for him only as long as she still lived. If the Halferan barony hadn't been utterly laid waste by the vile corsairs who'd murdered their lord in the For-Spring of the year before, who had enslaved the few guardsmen who survived that slaughter.

Hosh gazed desperately at that wave. Had Corrain truly managed to escape and steal a boat, as he had sworn he would? Or had some other twist of fortune brought a wizard here while Corrain and Kusint's bones lay mingled on the seabed, to be stripped bare by fish and crab claws and washed this way and that by the swell of the waves above? How long did it take for a drowned man's mortal remains to crumble into sand? To release his shade from the torments of Poldrion's demons, preying on all those unable to pass through Saedrin's door?

His stomach growled. He heaved a heavy sigh, the breath rattling through his broken nose. If he could do nothing about anything else, at least he could do something about his hunger. While there was life, there was always something to thank at least one god or goddess for. That's what his old mum always said.

He climbed warily up the steps leading to the terrace surrounding the pavilion. With the swift dusk of the islands deepening, he could hope he wouldn't be seen. Better yet, he could see the tell-tale glow of magelight that showed him the wizard was safely ensconced in the furthest pavilion over towards the far shore of the thrusting headland. But he needed to be quick, before the impenetrable darkness made foraging impossible without a lamp that could so fatally betray him.

On this face of the building, the door of slatted wood opened into the kitchen. He crossed the room, careful where he put his feet since the tiled floor was littered with broken pots which the panic-stricken Archipelagan slaves had let fall as they fled.

The building was a hollow square with a garden at its heart and the jealously guarded well for sweet water. Hosh looked through the shutters. Sufficient daylight lingered to show him a few birds idly pecking at weeds sprouting in the gravelled paths before fluttering up to the shrubs growing ragged for lack of tending. After the islands' brutal dry season, plants flourished astonishingly once the rains returned.

So he was still alone here. Hosh had guessed that he would be but it did no harm to be sure. Especially when all those countless folk, corsairs and their slaves alike, must surely be growing so desperately hungry wherever it was they had fled.

Even if anyone had bothered to plant crops or properly herd the feral goats, this little island would have been hard put to support the modest fleet of corsairs lurking here when Hosh and Corrain had first been captured. Through the year and a half of their imprisonment, the corsair leader's successes had drawn ever more ships to sail in the wake of his trireme.

Old, grizzled, blind, the man held every ship master in thrall, apparently infallible as a soothsayer. Hosh grinned in the shadowed kitchen. The old blind bastard hadn't foreseen this unknown wizard burning his warship to the waterline with sorcerous fire or blasting his chosen pavilion to the bare rock of its foundation with lightning ripped from a cloudless sky. Hosh relished remembering that.

He reached up for one of the lidded pots standing up on a long shelf. It was sealed with wax so he found a knife and ran its point around the edge of the lid. Not for the first time, he considered taking the blade away with him. But no. If some desperate corsair did come searching for food, Hosh couldn't fight off a sword with a kitchen knife. Being found with a blade would surely get his throat cut. Unarmed, he could hope to surrender.

The pot held dark fish flesh preserved with brine and herbs. That would do well enough. Hosh opened the next jar. Some leaves, leathery and pickled. He dipped a cautious finger in the vinegar and touched it to his tongue. Sometimes the islanders spiced their food so fiercely it felt like eating a mouthful of the sticky fire their triremes flung in battle. But this proved mild enough.

Hosh set the pots on the table and crossed to the

waist-high crock in the corner. Recoiling from the reek as he lifted the cover, he didn't bother looking inside. Mould grew as swiftly as any plant in the rainy season and whatever cloud bread had been left in there was well beyond eating.

A small box tucked behind the crock caught his eye. He stooped to pick it up and twisted it open.

Dream smoke. It was a handful of days since Hosh had last found some of the fine-ground herbs which the Aldabreshi scattered on hot charcoal. Breathing in the fumes soothed mental and physical pain through the solace of waking dreams. So Imais had told him, one of the slave cooks to the *Reef Eagle*'s master, the galley where he and Corrain had been chained.

Hosh had tried the smoke once in the depths of utter despair after Corrain and Kusint had escaped. But returning from that temporary surcease had only made his miseries harder to bear. Worse, the acrid fumes had seared his broken nose and inflamed the whole imperfectly healed side of his face, where his cheekbone had been smashed by the pommel of a slaver's brutal sword.

He missed Imais. She had saved him the pick of the ship master's scraps in return for him scrubbing her pots clean. With her knowledge of healing herbs, she had given him leaves to chew and tisanes to drink that had reduced the intermittent swelling and perpetual pain from his injuries.

It wasn't her fault the dream smoke hadn't helped him. Hosh tossed the box back into the corner, the contents scattering across the tile.

'Is that not good to eat?' A voice sounded behind him, intrigued.

Hosh whirled around but there was no one to be seen.

Pale light flared in the dimness. A pallid blue flame dancing on the palm of a man's outstretched hand.

The mage chuckled. 'Do you think that I will kill you?'

Hosh guessed his face must have given away his shock and dread. But he couldn't guess what manner of accent that was, rasping deep in the stranger's throat.

Though he spoke the Tormalin tongue. Hosh frowned, puzzled.

'You are from the same land as him,' the mage said confidently. 'I see it in your hair and skin.'

'Who do you mean?' Hosh demanded.

'Corrain.' The mage stepped closer and the light brightened to fill the room with soft radiance.

Hosh recoiled. Not from the flame but from the stranger's breath. The man's mouth reeked worse than a hound's that had been eating deer shit.

'Why did he leave you here?' The mage folded scrawny arms across his chest. He wore a sleeveless white silk tunic adorned at hem and neck with gold beading and stained down the front with reddish sauce. His blue cotton trews had been cut for a much taller man so he had rolled the cuffs up into ungainly bulges.

I could take him in a fight, Hosh though, incredulous. He had been so used to being the skinniest among the Halferan guards that it was a wonder to face a man half a head shorter than he was and surely a generation older, his face was so deeply lined.

Perhaps I could take him in a fight if he wasn't a wizard, Hosh reminded himself.

'Corrain didn't leave me.' He swallowed hard. 'We were supposed to flee together, only there was a fight and then I had to run—'

Because his nerve had failed him so utterly amid the chaos engulfing the seaside market. So he'd fled back to the dubious sanctuary of the anchored *Reef Eagle*, and Nifai the overseer had stepped in to save his neck from the furious vengeance of the Khusro warlord's swordsmen. Hosh had paid a heavy price for that boon. The Archipelagans might know nothing of coin but they knew the price of every traded service or bartered good.

'He said nothing of you when he and I came here together,' the mage said silkily.

'Corrain came—?' Hosh floundered.

'Once we had killed all of these vermin we found in your homeland,' the mage explained comfortably.

'He must think that I'm dead,' Hosh realised, desolate.

'What is your name?' The mage angled his head, dark eyes glinting in the eerie light.

'Hosh.'

'You are from—' the skinny mage paused before speaking carefully '—Hal-far-ain.'

'Halferan. Yes.'

'I am Anskal.' The mage struck his bony chest with an oddly flamboyant gesture. 'Once I was of Mandarkin but I now rule this island!'

Hosh nodded warily. Mandarkin. He'd never heard tell of the place before Kusint the Soluran had arrived here to be chained with them as one of the *Reef Eagle's* oar slaves. After he'd told them of his own distant homeland, the red-headed man had explained that the realm of Mandarkin lay still further north. A cruel and barren land ruled by still crueller men, their tyranny upheld by magic, sworn enemy to Solura and its kings.

By all that was sacred and profane, what had Corrain done?

'But I do not rule this island's people?' Anskal looked at Hosh, clearly waiting for an answer.

'No,' Hosh ventured.

'They fear me.' Anskal nodded with evident satisfaction. 'But you do not. Good.' He reached for the jar of soused fish. 'Let us eat and talk as friends.'

'Thank you.'

Politeness costs nothing, so the priests at the village shrine would say. Hosh's mum always said that forgetting it could cost the common folk everything.

The skinny wizard plucked a long fillet from the pot and ate it from his fingers. He offered the jar to Hosh but he couldn't bring himself to take anything which the Mandarkin had touched, not given the unwashed stink of him. It was hard to think of a greater contrast with Master Minelas, so elegant in his dress and so meticulously groomed.

But not eating might be an insult far away in the north. Hosh hastily scooped up a handful of pickled leaves. Then he all but choked on a sudden realisation. If this wizard had killed whatever corsairs infested Halferan, then Master Minelas must be dead. Corrain would never have come here unless he'd left the treacherous wizard's head on the spike of Halferan's gibbet.

'They have no chairs.' Anskal the Mandarkin looked curiously around the kitchen.

'What?' Hosh hastily gathered his wits. 'No, they sit on cushions.'

Anskal chewed another piece of fish, contemplating Hosh in a way that made him horribly uneasy.

'You do not fear me,' he repeated, thoughtful.

'I do fear you,' Hosh protested. 'You could kill me as soon as look at me!'

'True,' Anskal allowed. He picked at some fragment stuck between his chipped and stained teeth. 'Tell me, why do these dark-skinned men not bury their dead? I have seen them leaving corpses to be eaten by the vermin of this isle.'

Hosh wondered what else the wizard had seen, wandering around the island under whatever spell of invisibility he'd used to sneak up into this pavilion and surprise him. When he wasn't foraging for food Hosh laired up in a fringe tree thicket, barely venturing out to piss behind a rock for fear of encountering some returning Aldabreshi. Some Archipelagan like Ducah who could have decided he'd mistaken whatever portent had persuaded him to leave Hosh alive.

'Tell me!' The Mandarkin demanded, peremptory.

'They wish to become part of their home or at worst, the place where they died,' Hosh said hurriedly. 'Some domains favour burial, others are content to become one with the living creatures.'

Imais had explained all this, when Hosh had been repelled to find a dead corsair laid out for the land crabs and palm rats in a charnel grove on the far headland. She had tried to explain where practice varied among the domains but the endless litany of unfamiliar names had only left Hosh dizzy.

'The Archipelagans believe that everything they have been in life will influence the omens that guide those who survive them.'

Hosh found the eerie notion a coldly comfortless alternative to the hope of rebirth in the Otherworld. Imais had been appalled to think of any body being burned on a pyre, reduced to ashes to be swept away on the wind or stowed amid a shrine's funeral urns.

'This is a strange place with very strange customs.' Anskal sucked on a pickled leaf. 'Tell me, why are all the men and women cowering on the far side of this rock?' He gestured vaguely eastwards. 'They are right to fear me but why have they not come to yield to my rule? They are starving,' he continued, incredulous, 'yet you are the only one to come here, though these cellars are full of food.'

'They—' Hosh desperately tried to find an answer that wouldn't cause offence. 'They couldn't eat any food taken from a pavilion so close to your magical wave. They'd fear it has been touched by your sorcery.'

Anskal pursed his lips. 'It is good that we met. You are born of Halferain so you know enough of magic to know that you cannot challenge me and live. Yet you also know of these islands and their customs. Do you know their tongue? Will you be of use to me?'

'Yes.' What else could Hosh say?

'Then what is this?' Anskal tossed something from his pocket at Hosh.

He fumbled the catch and the glittering thing went rolling across the floor. He dropped to his knees and went scrabbling after it.

Anskal growled what could only be an oath in his harsh tongue. A shimmer of sapphire magelight scooped the object from the floor and slammed it into Hosh's cringing hands.

He grimaced as he opened his stinging fingers. It was one of the gaudy ornaments which the Aldabreshi coveted, men and women alike. This arm ring was a trifling piece by local standards, studded with rock crystal and with silver showing through the gilding rubbed away on the inner face.

Getting to his feet, Hosh unclasped it, ready to refasten the trinket above his elbow. 'It's worn—'

'I see that.' Anskal clicked his tongue, irritated. 'Where is it from?'

'I have no idea.' Seeing Anskal's expression darken, Hosh looked more closely at the shining piece. 'I don't think it's islander made.' It reminded him of some of the ornaments that Lady Zurenne or other fine visiting ladies in Halferan wore; heirlooms of their baronies.

'It must be plunder from the mainland.' He offered it back to the mage.

'Keep it.' Anskal waved his hand impatiently. 'Is there more such loot? Men who can tell me where they stole such things?'

Hosh wondered which was more perilous; refusing a wizard's gift or accepting it? He fastened the arm ring and slid it beneath his ragged sleeve. Maybe he could lose it later. If he lived so long.

'They won't talk to you.' There was no point in lying.

Anskal shrugged. 'But they will talk to you.'

'Me?' Hosh stared at the Mandarkin, horrified. 'They'll kill me as soon as look at me.' He tried desperately to explain. 'They will be afraid that some miasma will cling to me, after I've been so close to your magic.'

Now the Mandarkin was smiling, making Hosh more and more nervous. He braced himself for the mage's next words.

So he wasn't expecting Anskal to snatch up the knife from the table. He was utterly unprepared for the Mandarkin's swift step around the table to drive the shining blade into his belly.

Hosh screamed. Then he felt something painfully hard fall onto his bare foot. It hurt. But his toes were all that hurt. Where was the agony of murderous steel ripping through his guts? He looked down to see the snapped-off knife blade on the floor.

Anskal tossed the broken hilt onto the table. 'They cannot kill you.'

How? Hosh bit down hard on that most stupid of questions. Magic, obviously.

Smiling slyly, Anskal reached forward to push up Hosh's tattered sleeve. 'As long as you wear that. They cannot kill you.

'Now you will go and find someone who commands these people's obedience. You will tell them I wish to know the origin of that piece and of others like it.'

'I can ask.' Hosh chewed his lip. 'But—'

'If they oblige me,' the mage gestured westwards, towards the impossible wave blocking the anchorage, 'I will allow them and their ships to leave. They may take food from these cellars, if they dare brave my presence.'

Once again, Hosh saw how much the thought of the corsairs' terror pleased the skinny wizard.

'I can take that offer to them,' he said hesitantly.

Would Nifai be willing to make a deal with the wizard? For the sake of escaping this island prison? If the *Reef Eagle*'s erstwhile overseer was even still alive.

'I will go now.' Hosh ducked his head obediently and stepped back from the table.

If Nifai was alive, could Hosh possibly find something in one of the deserted pavilions to trade for a seat back at his old oar on the galley? He would row until his hands bled to get away from here. So would every Aldabreshi, slave or corsair.

'In the morning.' Anskal raised a grimy hand. 'Tonight you will tell me of your homeland.'

'Of course. Please—' Hosh's palms were sweating '—
Captain Corrain? Where is he? You said he came here
with you—'

'I sent him away when he displeased me.' Anskal
leaned forward, his dark eyes unblinking and menacing.
'You will also tell me all that you know of the wizards
in your southlands.'

'I don't know much,' Hosh said, frightened.

If this Mandarkin mage had sent Corrain away, where
had he sent him? Home to Halferan or somewhere else?

— CHAPTER FIVE —

Ferl, Caladhria

3rd of For-Autumn

IF THIS WAS a normal parliament, this would be the high day of a festival. If Corrain was still a guard captain, he and his men would be at liberty to go out and get drunk after their lord had attended the day's debates by the parliament. With a little blessing from Halcarion, he could hope to find a girl willing to let his hand feel her frills.

Well, this was no normal festival and Corrain no longer believed in the goddess of love and luck. He wasn't a guard captain. He was the new Baron Halferan, even if he was currently lodging in this rancid tavern.

With the likes of Lord Karpis hiring entire inns for themselves and their retinue, only the meanest accommodations had been left for latecomers to the parliament. Not even the Archmage's coin could buy him some more dignity. Corrain sighed and drank the sour small beer that the tapster had offered for breakfast. He chewed on a slice of bread so full of chaff it was more fit for horses than their riders.

Voices grew loud outside the empty taproom's door. He threw the bread down and hurried outside.

In the morning sunshine in the yard, Fitrel was glowering at a handful of Karpis men.

Corrain didn't waste any time on courtesies. 'What do you want?'

He could see all the rest of the Halferans coming down the wooden stair from the stable loft where they had been sleeping. Karpis men and Halferans alike bore the bruises from their earlier encounter.

'We have a letter for you.' The Karpis sergeant proffered a sealed parchment with bored insolence.

'Linset!' Fitrel jerked his head at the nearest Halferan trooper.

It took Corrain a moment to place the boy. Of course. The son of that new blacksmith who'd come to Halferan while he'd been a corsair prisoner. The lad had some growing to do, if he was ever going to match the breadth of his father's shoulders. Linset might be tall enough for his head to reach the required measure on the old manor shrine's door but he was thin enough to hide behind the stable yard's hitching post if he turned sideways.

The instant before the boy's fingers touched the letter, the Karpis sergeant let it fall to the straw-strewn cobbles.

'Too slow,' he mocked.

Corrain saw Linset's face turn ugly, his hand going to the short sword at his belt.

'You don't want to soil your hands, boy.' Fitrel stepped between Linset and the Karpis man and smiled as merciless as a mantrap. 'How about you? Got a new blade yet? Not going to crumble away, I hope? You lads need steel the likes of ours.'

All the Karpis men recoiled. The panic on their faces was almost comical.

It took Corrain a moment to realise that the Karpis

troopers were ready to believe the Halferans were still carrying ensorcelled blades. Weapons deadly with that same black enchantment which the lady wizard Jilseth had sent sliding along every Halferan sword to cut down the corsairs.

And these Karpis men had more reason than most to fear the meek and mild lady wizard, as modest as her plain grey gown. Corrain had heard that tale the evening before in this very tavern.

Their fat baron had heard, back in the spring, that Master Minelas had abandoned Halferan. Karpis hadn't bothered with legalities, arriving instead with a troop of his guards and relying on force of arms to seize control of Lady Zurenne, her children and the household.

Before a chime had sounded, the Karpis troop and their baron had retreated, humiliated and defeated. Wizardry had rusted their blades and chainmail away in an instant, their sword scabbards warping and splitting.

That was all very well but Corrain didn't have such magecraft to back him now, whatever the rumours troubling this parliament. He also didn't want to attend the day's session with news of another brawl following hard on his heels.

'Enough!' he snapped. 'Halferans, you're dismissed, all of you. Karpis, you may go!'

The sergeant had the grace to look guiltily down at the letter lying on the ground. He didn't pick it up though, hastily marching his men away instead as Fitrel drove the Halferans on into the tavern for bread and sour ale.

The Karpis troop's pace was ragged and their posture worse. If Corrain was their captain, that lad so completely out of step would win an extra day of stable duty. That duffer twisting his head to look back at the Halferans would be washing up the whole troop's dinner plates for three days.

Once he was satisfied the Karpis men were out of sight, Corrain drew a deeper breath and went to pick up the dropped letter. He might as well see what their noble baron had to say for himself, before he headed for the parliament hall.

A man stepped out from behind the stable yard gate. The white linen of his shirt and the black broadcloth of his sleeveless summer jerkin echoed Tallat's chequered standard.

'Captain Mersed.' Corrain bowed as one equal to another since there were no censorious barons around to see.

The wiry, long-limbed man was much his own age and with similar experience of life as a baron's guard captain. Up to the point when Corrain's liege lord had been murdered, he himself had been enslaved, and all his struggles against that fate had sunk him deeper into this mire.

'Baron Halferan.' Mersed looked warily at Corrain. 'My lord would speak with you in private. Since you have the Archmage's ear.'

Which Lord Tallat believed because Mersed, this loyal and honourable captain, had dutifully told him Corrain's bare-faced lies; that the Archmage Planir was secretly helping Halferan despite all his insistence on that ancient edict forbidding magecraft in warfare.

Corrain swallowed an urge to explain and to ask for Mersed's forgiveness. But how else could Corrain have convinced the guardsman that they could successfully lie in wait and slaughter a whole boatful of corsairs?

Halferan had needed allies and the Tallat captain

would never have believed the prosaic reality; that Corrain and his one-time friend Kusint had scoured their recollections of life chained as oar slaves in the galleys. The two of them had identified one of the inlets in the marshes where the prowling galleys took on fresh water and calculated the likeliest tide for the raiders' next assault. Then simple luck had brought them their victims in timely fashion.

Not that Corrain would be thanking Talagrin, lord of the wild places and the warrior's god. After all that he had endured, Corrain had abandoned his belief in all such deities, just as they had abandoned him. Since he need not fear answering for his life's misdeeds to Saedrin, he need not ease his guilty conscience by confessing to his deceits now.

Corrain looked steadily at Mersed. 'I will be at Lord Tallat's disposal after today's debate.'

He owed the guard captain a debt of honour but he had no such obligation to Mersed's lord. If Tallat hadn't looked on Halferan with the same greedy eyes as Baron Karpis, he had been as ready to believe in Master Minelas's forged grant of guardianship.

Fitrel had already reported what Tallat men were saying in the taverns in their lord's support. It was ridiculous to suppose he should have consulted Lady Zurenne when Minelas had already told the parliament of his dealings with her late, lamented husband.

Everyone, from highest rank to humblest knew that a lord's duty was to protect his family, his home and his loyal tenantry while it was his lady wife's duty to ensure his comfort, to manage his household, to nurture his children. No woman had a voice on questions of business, governance or law. Why should she, when wise and loving husbands, brothers and fathers stood ready to take on such burdens?

Lady Zurenne should have sent word to her sisters if she was unhappy. Their husbands would have judged if she had any real cause for complaint, over and above a woman's usual fancies.

If only Corrain could have cut that bastard Minelas's throat and saved everyone all the grief that followed. It was no consolation to think that the villainous wizard had died an agonising death, betrayed by his own black-hearted greed as he sought to profit from Lescar's interminable wars. Or so the lady wizard Jilseth said. Assuming she could be trusted. Could any mage be trusted?

Captain Mersed was still standing in the yard, looking at Corrain. 'He would like you to convey his gratitude to the Archmage, that Tallat was spared the worst in the most recent spate of attacks.' Mersed looked a trifle embarrassed.

'So I heard.' Corrain managed a curt nod, much as he disliked to lie to the man. 'I can do that.'

After all it wasn't as if Lord Tallat was likely to uncover the falsehood by talking to any wizards himself. Last night, Corrain had also heard the story of Jilseth wrapping the whole Kevil market place in magical silence when Tallat had somehow insulted her. A couple of years ago he'd have scorned such a story as chimney corner embellishment. Now he knew better.

'Then let us thank Talagrin for his mercy to Tallat.' Corrain smiled too briefly to convey any real meaning. 'Now, if you will excuse me, I must attend the parliament.'

'Until this evening then.' Mersed bowed and retreated.

Corrain watched him go. He would far rather spend the evening drinking ale with that straight-forward man rather than sipping wine with his weasely master. He would also welcome Mersed's thoughts on that particular puzzle. Why had that final onslaught been so ferociously intent on Halferan?

Granted, Tallat's villages and crops had been trampled underfoot as the raiders swept across their barony but the Archipelagans hadn't lingered to indulge in the wholesale destruction which they had inflicted on Halferan.

Three chimes rang through the morning air. Corrain cursed. He should already be at the parliament hall. He headed out of the yard at a trooper's jog keeping to the back alleys.

He felt at home here, as he did in market towns across Caladhria. There was little difference in the sizes and styles of the modest dwellings, the merchants' houses and workshops, beyond variations forced on local builders by the materials to hand. More building stone was found in the north and more thatch across the breadbasket fields of the midland plains compared to the brick and tile of the coast which Corrain had grown up with.

As his route took him on to the main thoroughfares, he passed the weathered remnants of Tormalin Imperial grandeur here and there. In the biggest towns like Ferl, a grand house or a merchants' exchange could endure through successive rebuilding over the twenty generations since the Old Empire fell into the Chaos.

Later grand edifices stood as testament to some long-dead baron's pretentions when Caladhria had sought to challenge Ensaimin's great trading cities. Embellished with carved stone canopies and fussy garlands such buildings were as outdated as a dowager's frayed furbelows. Sterner lines and clean-cut facades in the Rational style now appeared as heirs returned from their education in Vanam, Col or Toremal to declare their independence in architecture, while abiding by the established consensus in the parliament.

Arriving at the central square, Corrain was forced to slow, to approach the parliament itself at a more sedate walk. Only as he reached the steps to the portico did he recall that unopened letter from Karpis left lying in the horseshit.

No matter. Whatever cutting words the fat baron had come up with, Corrain was used to fighting in the gutters with harsher tongues and real knives. These noble lords would do well to recall that.

As he entered the hall, he braced himself to meet the censorious gaze of the already assembled barons. His arrival prompted a murmur that swept through the gathering like a breeze through a wheat field.

'Captain Corrain.' Baron Ferl acknowledged him with a curt nod.

'My lord.' Corrain bowed politely as to an equal. 'Kindly honour the barony of my birth and my lady wife's inheritance with my present title.'

Every movement within the hammer-beamed hall stilled. Good.

Over his rudimentary breakfast that morning, Corrain had decided to make it plain that he wasn't some suppliant desperate for the parliament's approval. Nor would he satisfy those expecting a common trooper's bluster and belligerence. Not after that first day's scuffle contrived by Karpis had stirred all their noble lords' prejudices.

Nor, by all that was sacred and profane, was he going to sit through another day of tedious head-shaking and hand-wringing over each and every barony's summer travails, even of those towns and villages two hundred leagues from the sea.

Baron Ferl's fleshy lips thinned. 'My Lord Halferan.'

On the bench opposite, Baron Karpis snorted with audible contempt. 'That remains to be seen.'

'My lord?' Corrain bowed to Baron Karpis with precisely measured courtesy. 'You have some doubts as to my marriage? After you and your household guard heard Lady Ilysh of Halferan declare it, gladly and unprompted? When you have seen the contracts for yourself, signed and sealed all according to proper form? You have heard firsthand witness that Lady Ilysh and I were wed with every necessary rite observed before Drianon's altar.'

Corrain surveyed the rest of the assembled nobles, challenge in his eye if not in his tone. 'We married with the full consent of Lady Zurenne and with her husband dead, a mother has the right to give her daughter into wedlock under Caladhrian law. In accord with tradition and precedent, in the absence of any male heir of the bloodline, I am now Baron Halferan.'

As he raised his voice to make that final bold declaration, he noted which lords were staring down at him with frank, sometimes prurient, curiosity.

Sure enough, Baron Karpis satisfied them with his next question from the comfort of his seat.

'You may have married Lady Ilysh of Halferan according to law. Have you made her your wife in fact as well as in name?'

Corrain could see plenty of other lords were repelled

by the thought of a rough-hewn swordsman a full generation older bedding a girl who had only just seen her thirteenth summer solstice.

'My lord,' he said mildly, 'should you not honour this assembly by rising to speak?'

'What?' Baron Karpis was visibly taken aback as he realised his contempt for Corrain had betrayed him into such discourtesy. He was halfway to his feet before he realised he had nothing more to say.

'Answer the question,' he snapped, sinking down again.

Corrain could see some lords wondering if he had challenged Karpis's incivility in hopes of avoiding an answer. Far from it. He had known from that first summons to this unprecedented parliament that he would face this question.

Just as he knew making such a reprehensible admission would guarantee their assembled lordships' enmity quicker than spit could hit the floor. On the other hand admitting that he hadn't claimed his rights as a husband would give Karpis grounds to attack the validity of this scandalous marriage.

Corrain had been in enough knife fights to know when to sidestep to avoid an over-confident thrust.

'That question has no bearing on the legality of our union. If I was dissolving a marriage for lack of an heir of my body, then this parliament would be entitled to ask for such intimate details. If Lady Ilysh was seeking redress on account of non-consummation, the same would be true. Since neither case applies, Lord Karpis, how and when my wife and I share a bed is no one's business but our own.'

Hopefully the honourable men on these benches would see the tacit denial beneath his refusal to answer. After all, a rank scoundrel wouldn't shrink from boasting of his conquest to put the matter of the marriage beyond doubt. As for the others, especially those few betraying an unwholesome interest at the thought of deflowering a child?

'I don't suppose any of your lordships would welcome such impertinent enquiries into the business of your own bedchamber.'

Corrain's life as a common guardsman might be over but there was more than a hint of a retainer's livery in his sternly cut doublet and breeches of pewter linen, with dark red collar and cuffs to recall the Halferan standard.

Let these noble men consider what scurrilous gossip they learned from their own loyal servants. Let them wonder what he might have heard around the taverns and stable yards whenever their parliament had assembled these past twenty years.

Baron Karpis rose to his feet, though. Whatever else might be said of him, his devotion and fidelity to his noble lady was beyond reproach.

'Whatever a wife might expect in the bedroom,' he said with some distaste, 'a more pressing question in the current season is what she might expect by way of protection. The Halferan barony has been ravaged by corsairs yet again and the demesne guard is reduced to greybeards and unshaven boys. Granted, these black-hearted raiders have retreated for the present, but there's no knowing when they might return.

'Karpis is the largest barony to border Halferan lands.' The plump lord took a step forward and turned to address the whole gathering. 'I have a fighting force of proven worth sworn to my service. We yield to no one in our resolve to defend Halferan's worthy tenants as well as the widowed Lady Zurenne, and her two young daughters. Thus I propose myself as their most suitable guardian. This so-called marriage is an irrelevance.'

Wheeling around, he looked Corrain up and down with open contempt. 'When you and I last met, you were weeping like a dairymaid who had dropped her cream dish. I would be failing in my own duty if I were to leave defenceless women in the care of such a vagabond so clearly seen to be unmanned.'

He made a point of staring at Corrain's unwarrior-like plait of hair.

Corrain took care not to clench his fists. It wouldn't do to punch the baron's face so hard that the fat bastard spat out a mouthful of teeth.

Besides, there was no denying his collapse after he had been hurled back to Caladhria by that villainous mage Anskal. Halferan men and troopers from Karpis and Licanin had all been witness to it. Now Corrain saw that those few barons unaware of his humiliation were being quickly informed by avidly whispering neighbours.

'I was exhausted, my lord Karpis, when you and I last met,' Corrain said with hard-won composure. 'I had been searching the coastal marshes for days, for any sign of those fleeing the destruction of Halferan Manor. In hopes of rescuing any who had been enslaved by the corsair raiders.'

Until he had finally returned, walking league upon endless league, as drawn by unthinking instinct as any courier dove to its nest. Where else could he go but back to Halferan?

Where Baron Karpis and his household guard along

with Lord Licanin and his own troopers had escorted Lady Zurenne and her daughters back to survey the ruination of their home.

They had all seen Corrain reduced to helpless tears as he saw so many of those he'd thought dead had somehow been saved. Even if they didn't know the full burden of the guilt that had driven him to his knees.

Corrain's only consolation was he remembered so little of that dreadful day himself. With the seemingly endless anguish shredding his wits, his recollections were like glimpses through a distant window as shutters opened and closed.

Halferan Manor's roofless buildings, half-consumed by fire. Lady Zurenne, so gaunt and pale yet stiff with resolve to protect her daughter's inheritance. Lady Ilysh, looking so excruciatingly like her dead father whom Corrain had so grievously failed to protect.

'You were talking of defending Halferan, Lord Karpis.' Corrain fixed the baron with a penetrating stare. 'Yet the manor and its village lie in ruins, along with countless hamlets and farms between the demesne and the sea. You singularly failed to prevent that destruction.'

Baron Karpis spread lavishly beringed hands. 'I had no authority to stand between Halferan and the raiders. I had sought it, last Aft-Spring, after I had learned that Master Minelas had abandoned his responsibilities, and then again at this summer's parliament, only to be denied in favour of Lord Licanin. Alas, entrusting Halferan to the care of a barony so far away proved a sad mistake.'

Lord Licanin sprang to his feet. 'You were happy to entrust Halferan to a scoundrel and a thief. You stood before our summer's parliament last year and gladly assented to Minelas of Grynth's guardianship on the basis of documents which we now know to be base forgeries.'

His voice shook with fury and for the first time Corrain realised Lord Licanin was as angry with himself as he was with Baron Karpis, for taking so long to realise Zurenne's true distress.

Licanin strode forward, walking in a wide circle to command the whole parliament's attention. 'If we are to consider who has safeguarded Halferan, my faithful guardsmen fought and died when those corsair raiders last attacked, intent on razing the manor to the ground.'

'While my men helped burn their ships when they came to shore.' Lord Tallat rose slowly from his seat, sweating despite the thick stone walls shielding the hall from the lingering heat as summer turned to autumn. 'Though this is little enough to set in Raeponin's divine scales against my most grievous error in not questioning Master Minelas's claims. To see him revealed as a fraud and a thief and worse—'

As he broke off with a shake of his head, Corrain tensed. Had Tallat somehow discovered Master Minelas's wizardry?

Could the Halferan barony weather that storm, if the parliament learned that Master Minelas hadn't washed up on Caladhria's shore by accident? That Baron Halferan himself had suborned the man's magecraft, both of them defying the Archmage and Hadrumal's edict. Until Minelas had betrayed Halferan for the sake of the greater gold the corsairs had offered him. And Corrain had been one of the few men who'd known the baron's secret.

But that wasn't what Lord Tallat was struggling to say.

'I owe you a considerable debt, Lord Licanin, for rescuing the Widow Halferan from the unintended consequences of my dishonour. I can only beg forgiveness of the current Baron Halferan.' The dark haired lord bowed awkwardly towards Corrain. 'And if we are to consider who has defended Halferan most faithfully, there can be no doubt of his loyalty. His devotion has proved stronger than Aldabreshin slave chains!'

As unexpected voices acknowledged that with loud approval, Lord Tallat's nerve failed him. He sat down with a jarring thump.

Baron Karpis wasn't bested yet. 'Yet Captain Corrain was nowhere to be seen when the corsairs last attacked. He had long since vanished on some mysterious journey which he still has not accounted for. Nor has he ever explained his miraculous escape from the southern slavers.'

'More questions which have no bearing on the validity of this marriage.' A soberly dressed lord rose from one of the middle benches.

Corrain recognised him, as well as the barons to either side raising their hands to support his contention. Baron Saldiray, with the lords of Taine, Myrist and Blancass.

They had been his dead lord's allies. They had supported Corrain's bold plan to demand aid from Hadrumal's wizards, renewing Caladhria's appeals to the Archmage themselves after the former Baron Halferan's death.

Even after the Archmage's unwavering refusal had hardened the barons' unease about dealing with wizards into outright dislike, it seemed they believed Corrain had somehow secured magic to defend Caladhria. So if they helped give him Halferan, he would be honour bound to give them such help if the corsairs returned.

He could only hope they never discovered the true disgrace of his debt to wizardry.

Baron Karpis snorted, this time with outrage.

'My lords?' Baron Ferl was on his feet, swift to read the mood in the hall. 'Shall we vote? That will at least tell us if there is anything more to be gained by debate.'

'I agree,' Lord Licanin said promptly. 'Let those approving this new Baron Halferan show their assent!'

Corrain raised his head and squared his shoulders, standing in the middle of the flagstones. He looked at that far window as the lords muttered and argued among themselves. He dared not look as the first few hands were raised. He didn't want anyone to look into his eyes and see how wholly unworthy he was to take his dead lord's place.

He had failed his liege lord utterly. His desperate efforts to make some recompense had come at the cost of further failure. He had abandoned that fool boy Hosh, even though he was one of Halferan's own, all for the sake of escaping from the corsair slavers. Even though he knew full well the lad could never survive a slave's brutal life without Corrain to defend him.

It was almost enough to make him wish that he still believed in the gods, even at the cost of answering to Saedrin for all his sins. Then Corrain could have hoped that the wretched lad was already safely reborn in the Otherworld with all his injuries healed, every hurt that Corrain had failed to save him from soothed.

But there were no gods and Corrain had failed Hosh. As badly as he'd failed Kusint, after all that the Forest-born lad had done. Helping him to escape the corsairs;

Corrain couldn't swim much less sail a boat. Telling him of Solura's mages who owed nothing to Hadrumal. Taking him north in search of just such a mage. Then Corrain had repaid him by allying with the Mandarkin, no matter what Kusint had told him of that wicked race's villainy. No wonder Kusint had abandoned him in disgust.

The bright colours of the distant window blurred.

'Very well,' Baron Ferl said in measured tones. 'We have our answer, my lords.'

Corrain blinked hastily and looked to see what that might be. He felt abruptly weak with relief as he saw more than half the assembly's hands were raised, though some of the lords were already heading for the door.

'Good.' A nameless, exasperated noble said to his companion. 'Let's hope we can get on the road before the fifth chime of noon.'

Corrain didn't care who had only voted in his favour in order to go home. He pushed his way through the shifting throng. He had to sit down.

Lord Licanin caught his elbow and pulled him roughly to one side.

'Have you bedded Ilysh?' he hissed in an undertone. 'I won't betray her shame but I have a right to know! I know your reputation.'

Corrain should have expected that. After he had joined the guardsmen's barracks, he had rarely bothered to hide his dalliances with tavern girls and village maids. Why should he? They were willing and old Fitrel had shown him the uses of alum and beeswax so none ever arrived at the manor's gatehouse with a swelling belly.

He had grown a little more discreet in later years but

only because his tastes inclined towards married women. Not discreet enough, when it had come to Starrid's wife. Corrain had grown too used to cuckolded husbands too busy with their own pleasures to notice a straying wife or to play the hypocrite if they did.

Halferan's former steward had rolled the third side of that rune. He had beaten his hapless wife black and blue. There was no hiding that scandal so Corrain had lost his captaincy to ride as a common trooper. Of course Lord Licanin would have heard of that through his man Rauffe's letters to his former home.

So the grey-haired lord wasn't about to stand idly by and allow Corrain to abuse a defenceless girl. Not when he had already failed Lady Ilysh once.

All the same, Corrain owed Lord Licanin some measure of honour for the Licanin blood shed in Halferan's defence. The truth was fit repayment.

'No, I have not touched her, nor will I,' he said low-voiced, 'until and unless she is of an age and of a mind to make that choice for herself, and I don't see that ever happening. Saedrin's stones, my lord, I'm old enough to be her father.

'Besides,' he added frankly, 'even if Lady Ilysh were ever willing Lady Zurenne would cut off my manhood before I laid a finger on her daughter. I've sworn to dissolve the marriage whenever Ilysh asks it and she will go virgin to a worthy husband.'

He didn't see any need to add that his manhood hadn't so much as stirred at the sight or thought of any woman since he had returned to Caladhria. The corsairs might as well have gelded him as brutally as the Aldabreshin warlords who reputedly cut stick and stones entirely from the slaves attending their wives.

Lord Licanin looked at him for a moment, his expression impenetrable. Then he rose without a word, to stalk away not looking back at Corrain.

Corrain rubbed his hands over his face and wondered how soon he and his men could be on the road back to Halferan where so many fresh challenges awaited him.

And there was no magic for him to call on, to lessen that distance or lighten those burdens.

— CHAPTER SIX —

'GOOD MORNING, JILSETH.'

'Archmage!' She stiffened, sitting upright on the weathered bench as she opened her eyes.

He took a seat beside her and contemplated the neatly tended beds of herbs and other potent plants. Some had already been harvested, others were waiting out the season. A few wouldn't be touched until For-Winter brought the first possibility of frosts to the island along with swathing mists which owed nothing to the concealing sorcery that habitually hid the wizards' sanctuary.

The whole garden was surrounded by the high walls supporting the densely fruiting canes and the artfully shaped trees whose boughs were laden with pears, apples and quinces. Those would supply syrups to sweetly disguise the apothecaries' harsh nostrums.

'Do you find a cure for what ails you here?'

Jilseth didn't imagine that Planir thought that she hoped 'for some pill or potion to miraculously restore her magic.

'To some degree.'

What she had particularly come in search of was peace and quiet and a complete absence of curious eyes. Whenever she went from her rooms in the Terrene Hall to one of the city's libraries, she felt the weight of so many gazes; some sympathetic, some barely concealing their callous amusement, all avid to know if her affinity showed any signs of returning.

Even when she closed her door on them all, to sit alone at her workbench littered with tools and spirit lamps, with cracked or molten specimens of rock and ore, she was painfully aware of the wizards living in the accommodations beside her own and up on the floors above.

Calm and self-control was essential to the proper exploration of magic. Jilseth had been told that by every mage who had ever taught her. Any excess of emotion threatened precisely the untamed and damaging eruptions of affinity that saw the mainland mageborn so hastily sent to Hadrumal.

That was all very well but what lay on the reverse face of that particular rune bone?

'Archmage,' she said abruptly. 'You told me to be wary of chaotic magic as my affinity returns. But what if I am too wary? What if my apprehension is stifling my mageborn instincts?'

She wouldn't have imagined such a thing was possible when she had been an apprentice but that was before she had encountered that Mountain Man Sorgrad. His magebirth had gone unsuspected by the disapproving *sheltya*, the Aetheric adepts and lawgivers of the uplands, because the scoundrel had been able to keep his affinity in check through sheer unadulterated stubbornness.

Planir nodded. 'That is, unfortunately, possible.' He shifted on the bench, resting one elbow on the carved back as he looked at her. 'Perhaps a complete change of scene might help take your mind off your troubles. I want to visit the Widow Halferan.'

'Archmage?' That certainly startled Jilseth out of her preoccupations. And explained why Planir was dressed as soberly, in long-sleeved black tunic and breeches, as some Ensaimin merchant's head clerk. A very prosperous merchant's clerk.

He looked easterly, as though he could see through the artisans' houses surrounding this garden, all the way down the road leading to the harbour and across the seas beyond. 'I suspect it would be considered more seemly if you accompanied me.'

'But Archmage—' Jilseth began, somewhat hesitant.

She had heard the increasing whispers of friction among the Council of Wizards' higher echelons, for all that she was currently spurning Hadrumal's wine shops and cook houses in favour of scouring musty archives for any mention of past mages who'd suffered something of her calamity. Tornauld, Merenel and Nolyen were proving their worth as her friends as well as fellow seekers into the intricacies of quintessential magic, bringing her food and drink spiced with the distractions of the latest gossip.

Surely the Archmage himself should be leading the search for some way to break through this impertinent Mandarkin's veiling. So the wine shop sages said to each other. How was sustaining such a spell possible for a wizard from such an obscure and impoverished tradition? How dared the Soluran Orders hold themselves so infuriatingly aloof? What was the Archmage doing to answer these questions?

Planir's face hardened as he smiled. 'I am at no one's beck and call, not even the Flood Mistress or the

Hearth Master. Shall we go?'

'Yes, Archmage.' Jilseth was suddenly filled with longing for some time spent where no one could find her, not even those with the very best of intentions.

Planir's smile softened as he took her hand and the garden disappeared in a soft white haze. When the mist cleared a moment later, Jilseth found herself standing in front of a sprawling, ornate building, most notable for the severely Rational wing added at a sharp angle to the end, its harsh orange brick barely softened by winter weathering.

'Taw Ricks hunting lodge.' Planir grinned.

Jilseth nodded, unable to speak. Their translocation had been so smooth and swift, woven of air and fire in a fashion any Cloud Master would envy. Yet again, this evidence of the Archmage's mastery both astonished and oppressed her. Would she ever regain command over so much as her own inborn affinity for the earth?

'Oh! My lady! That's to say, Madam Jilseth!'

'Good morning to you, Doratine.' Jilseth startled out of her preoccupation at being so abruptly addressed by the Widow Halferan's cook, hurrying out of what must be the door to the servants' hall.

'I am Planir of Hadrumal.' The Archmage offered a courteous nod.

'Saedrin save us.' The woman twisted her bony fingers around each other. 'Is there news? From Ferl?' Then she clapped a hand to her mouth, horrified. 'But that's not for me to ask. My lady Zurenne—'

'Is she receiving guests?' Planir began walking along the dusty path where hobnailed boots had worn away the grass separating the lodge from the carriage way that cut across the front of the building before curling around to the stable yards. 'Perhaps you could ask? We can wait.'

'Of course.'

As the cook hurried away through the floridly carved porch, Jilseth was reminded how awestruck the mundane populace were by magic. Though of course Doratine had seen the wizardry that saved Halferan and few on the mainland would ever have seen the like of that. Then again, Jilseth mused, those magics which she had wielded had been simple enough spells compared to the magecraft within Planir's reach. Did these people have any idea of wizardry's true scope?

As she concluded that, no, they really didn't, Zurenne's personal maid appeared.

'Raselle.' Jilseth smiled at the girl.

'Madam mage. Archmage.' Raselle looked wide-eyed at Planir.

Jilseth noted the maid was clenching her jaw tight shut, presumably to keep herself from asking if there was any news from Ferl. Hadn't Planir realised that's what everyone would ask, as soon as they appeared here?

She took the opportunity to study the Archmage's expression as they followed Raselle through the lodge's entrance hall, so cluttered with boxes and bundles that the aisles crossing it from front to back and from side to side were barely wide enough for two people to pass each other. Planir's face gave nothing away.

The maid opened one of the two doors side by side in the hall's rear wall and ushered them into a sitting room not only crowded with original furnishings and salvaged chattels but also boasting a startling selection of frivolous new accoutrements.

Planir inclined his head courteously to the slightly-built, dark-haired woman standing by the fireplace. 'Lady Zurenne.'

Jilseth had noted the maidservant's apron and cap were recently hemmed from a bolt of new linen. Lady Zurenne was wearing a fine silk lavender gown trimmed with fresh lace. The widowed noblewoman had been quick enough to spend the Archmage's coin, whatever grudges she might hold against Hadrumal. Grudges she had good reason to bear, Jilseth reminded herself.

'Archmage.' The Halferan noblewoman wasn't precisely unwelcoming but she couldn't hide her surprise swiftly followed by apprehension. 'Madam Jilseth.'

'I was wondering,' Planir stepped forward before she could continue, 'have you had any news from the parliament?'

'From Ferl?' Zurenne stared at him. 'You haven't come to tell me...?'

Her words trailed off in confusion.

'We have no business with Caladhria's parliament.' Now it was Planir's turn to look mildly puzzled.

Zurenne was provoked into an uncharacteristically sharp retort. 'Then why are you here?'

Planir looked around the room before answering. 'Lady Ilysh tells me that you'll be dedicating a shrine today.'

'Lysha?' Lady Zurenne's hand went to the silver rune sigil on the black ribbon around her neck.

Had she not realised, Jilseth wondered, that the girl would use the pendant which she too had been given, for her own purposes? In the next breath she wondered what else the child had told Planir.

Zurenne's dark eyes, shadowed with weariness, promised a reckoning with her elder daughter. 'She should have told you that is to be a purely household affair.'

'She did,' Planir assured her. 'However I realised that I can do you a particular service in advance of those rites.'

'What service?' Now Zurenne was wary as well as mystified. Before Planir could speak, she turned to Raselle who was hesitating in the doorway.

'Tisane for our guests, if you please!' she snapped.

The girl shut her mouth, bobbed a curtsey and shut the door. Jilseth heard her boots pattering away on the flagstones. She'd half expected the girl to listen at the keyhole.

Planir looked steadily at Zurenne. 'I was most grieved to learn that your husband's ashes are now mingled with those of his ancestors.'

Distress creased Zurenne's forehead. 'We swept everything into a new urn and set it before Saedrin's statue. We had no choice—'

Jilseth recalled how the barony's shrine at Halferan Manor had somehow escaped the destruction levelling the rest of the buildings but funeral urns toppling from shelves had smashed and scattered their pale contents across the tiled floor.

'I can draw your husband's ashes out of all the rest,' Planir said quietly. 'To be enshrined separately once again. I know what it is to lose the love of one's life. It is a comfort to me to have her funeral urn close by.' The unmistakable shadow of grief dulled his own eyes.

Zurenne stared, open mouthed. Jilseth was as utterly dumbfounded as the noblewoman. Separating the blended ashes would be a challenge for all but the most expert earth mage. Jilseth realised she was grinding her teeth and forced herself to stop.

'I—I shall have to give it some thought.' Zurenne turned abruptly away and walked towards the wide bay window.

Not quickly enough. Jilseth saw the shine of tears on the noblewoman's rose-petal cheeks.

The door opened but the new arrival wasn't Raselle.

'Archmage?' Lady Ilysh hurried into the sitting room, ignoring both her mother and Jilseth. 'Do you have news of—of my husband? Of Halferan's new baron?'

Jilseth wondered if the girl's father had always been so direct, so reckless? Perhaps that explained his fatal readiness to trust Minelas.

'A little decorum if you please.' Zurenne rounded on the girl.

'No, I have no news,' Planir apologised to Ilysh.

'Mama?' the girl demanded. 'Do you?'

Jilseth saw Zurenne make a visible effort to keep her temper in check. So it wasn't only her father who had bequeathed the girl her spirit.

'How?' Zurenne asked bitingly. 'We have barely a handful of courier doves raised from the nest and that nest was in Halferan Manor—'

Now Ilysh's hand went to her own rune sigil pendant. 'Archmage—?'

Zurenne interrupted before the girl could demand Planir's magecraft to assist them.

'I sent a pair of troopers to wait by the ruins of the manor's dove loft. As soon as Corrain sends word, they will catch the bird and bring it here with its message. Saedrin willing, we'll have word by the end of the

92

following day, whenever the parliament comes to a conclusion.'

Whatever that conclusion might be. Jilseth noted that Zurenne laced her fingers tight together to still her trembling hands.

She wasn't prepared to grant the former guardsman the honour of her dead husband's title. Not yet anyway. But she would have to, if the noble lords acknowledged Corrain as the new Baron Halferan. And this whole contrived marriage had been Zurenne's idea.

'My lady, your tisane.' Doratine hurried in from the corridor as Raselle opened the door, crystal chiming on the tray in her hands.

The cook must already have been preparing such refreshments when Raselle arrived in the kitchen, Jilseth realised.

'Thank you, Doratine.' Zurenne made her way towards the spindly silk-cushioned chairs on the incongruous carpet before the fireplace.

'There you are, my lady, my lady mage, my lord Archmage.' Doratine curtseyed briefly before retreating and ushering Raselle out through the door.

'Madam Jilseth? What would you like in your tisane?' Zurenne asked with a determinedly cheerful smile. 'We have lime blossoms, gathered this very season, as well as raspberry leaves, camomile and elder flowers.'

She gestured at the bowls on the tray, along with the glasses in their polished holders, the pierced silver balls to hold the steeping herbs and the tall jug of hot water, a wisp of steam escaping from its long spout.

'Lime blossoms, thank you.' Jilseth took a chair opposite Zurenne.

Both women looked expectantly at Ilysh. After an

instant of indecision, the girl took a seat.

'The same, thank you, mama,' she said curtly.

Zurenne busied herself spooning pale dried petals into the hinged silver balls, dropping each one into a tall glass and pouring on hot water. 'Archmage?'

'Raspberry and a little elder, if you please.' He walked to the window to look out at the broad sweep of grassland bounded in the middle distance with a paling fence overhung with trees.

'Archmage.' Ilysh looked up from stirring her tisane. 'Do you play white raven?'

'White raven?' Planir turned from the window. 'Yes, I play.'

'It was one of my father's favourite pastimes.' Ilysh set down her glass. 'I am the heiress to Halferan. I intend to honour my father's legacy by learning the game. I don't care if it's not considered *seemly* for women.'

Jilseth trusted that Planir had also seen the challenge in Lysha's eyes as the girl glanced at her mother. So this was another bone of contention between them.

'Will you teach me?' Ilysh was on her feet and heading for a side table. The round board was set ready with the carved wooden pieces assembled on either side. 'Do you prefer to play the forest birds? Or to set out the trees and play the raven itself?'

Planir considered the question. 'I find different challenges in playing either side.' He smiled as though struck by sudden inspiration. 'The most suitable person to teach you would be Merenel. Don't you agree, Jilseth?'

'Indeed, Archmage.' Sipping her tisane, she wondered what game Planir was playing here.

Her Tormalin-born friend would seem as exotic as

a Derrice songbird among the dowdy hens of the Taw Ricks' household with her warm olive skin and curling black hair. She would overtop Lady Zurenne by a head though, more handsome than pretty, Merenel shouldn't prompt the Widow Halferan's envy on any other score.

At least Planir hadn't suggested that she teach the girl white raven herself. Jilseth had never found the game particularly engaging. The intellectual challenge of devising tactics within the game's constraints couldn't outweigh the essential triviality of the opposing tasks; capturing the solitary white bird for the player marshalling the forest fowl or evading them amid the wooden thickets which the raven's player arranged on the board at the outset.

'Provided that your lady mother agrees, of course.' Planir came to accept his own tisane glass from Zurenne's shaking hands.

'We'll see, Lysha.' Whatever she saw in the Archmage's eyes seemed to calm her nerves as she looked up. The hot water's agitation in the glass stilled.

'May I ask?' Planir nudged the pierced silver ball with the long spoon and red tendrils spread through the hot water. 'Where is the new shrine to be?'

Zurenne sipped her own tisane before replying with some ill-grace. 'There is a window bay in the great hall, much like this one. The shutters have been locked and there's enough room for a shrine table. For the present we've hung a curtain and the Taw Ricks carpenter and some men from the manor say they will carve a proper screen.'

'Come and see it,' Ilysh urged.

'My lady Zurenne?' Planir raised his dark brows as he

fished the steeping ball out of his glass and laid it in the waiting dish on the tray.

The noblewoman took another drink. Jilseth expected her to say no. Then Zurenne shrugged in a fashion that reminded Jilseth irresistibly of encounters with Ilysh on her previous visits to Halferan.

'If you really wish to.'

Ilysh was already half way to the door. Jilseth set down her glass and dutifully followed Zurenne and Planir after the girl, through the cluttered entrance to the great hall.

She wondered what the long-dead baron who'd found the original lodge so inadequate would have made of this use of his proud addition. The once-polished floor of the vast room was invisible beneath rolls of blankets, heaps of clothing, wooden boxes and wicker baskets. Thankfully the Halferan villagers who were bedding down in here were currently all out and about. Jilseth still had no notion what the Archmage sought here so this lack of an audience was surely preferable.

Zurenne hurried towards the shallow dais, along the wavering aisle between the clusters of salvaged belongings marking each family's claim on a patch of floor. Presumably that was where the high table had stood, to benefit from the bay window's light. Now the smaller shrine table stood in shadow, thanks to the locked shutters supporting pale new shelves. Small effigies stood on each one.

'We have recovered some unbroken statues from village shrines.' Zurenne turned to explain, her tone bitter. 'A few of those ungodly barbarians were more interested in loot than in wanton destruction.'

'And you recovered this.' Planir rested his hand on a

storage jar; dull ochre and undistinguished but the only vessel large enough to contain all the ashes which had been scattered across Halferan Manor's sanctuary. The lid was sealed tight with wax as well as tied on with twine, a further gloss of wax coating the knots.

Ilysh bit her lip. 'It was all such a horrid mess.'

In that moment, to Jilseth's eyes, the girl looked as young and as vulnerable as her little sister Esnina. Was Planir truly here, she wondered, to offer Lady Zurenne this service or to soothe this facet of the girl's intolerable grief, shared through her own ensorcelled pendant?

The Archmage was also, Jilseth realised, far too skilled at playing these games, to provoke Zurenne by repeating his offer. Drinking his tisane, Planir had turned from the jar to examine an archaic statue of Racponin. The god of justice's hood hid the direction of his gaze as he held his scales in one hand and a bell in the other.

The noblewoman cleared her throat. 'Archmage, if you please—'

'I am honoured to do this for Halferan.' As Planir spoke, pale golden magic threaded itself through the overlapping strands of twine securing the jar's lid. The wax disappeared and the string fell away. With a soft grating sound, the lid rose up and removed itself to the linen-draped shrine table.

'Lady Ilysh?' Planir held out his hand. 'I need your assistance.'

Zurenne moved to stand between her daughter and the wizard. 'How can she possibly help you?'

Jilseth didn't imagine the noblewoman meant to sound so accusing but once again she reflected how little the mainlanders truly knew of magic.

Planir didn't seem offended. 'Lysha is born of your lost husband's blood and of his bone. Her touch will enable me to find his ashes among the rest.'

Wordlessly, Ilysh walked around Zurenne and to the Archmage. As she extended a trembling hand, he touched his fingertips to hers.

The great diamond of the Archmage's ring blazed with rainbow-hued fire. Lysha gasped and snatched her hand back.

'Don't worry, my dear.' Planir smiled though his gaze was remote, his attention all on the storage jar.

'It's all right, mama!' Before Zurenne could move, the girl pressed her fingers hard against Planir's, her face now adult in its determination.

The Archmage's ring caught fire a second time, this time sparking an answering glow in the gems set around it.

Amber magelight burned in the neck of the storage jar. A brighter light kindled in the heart of it, golden as candle flame. A thread rose upwards, gossamer fine. Insubstantial though it was, Jilseth could see motes dancing within it. The dead Lord Halferan's ashes.

More than that, she could feel the gentle wizardry sifting through the pale contents of the jar. She could feel the infinitesimal resonances between the dead fragments and the living girl. On the very edge of her wizardly instincts, Jilseth could sense the earthborn connections between parent and child and this land that had nourished them; the minerals carried into blood and bone by their shared lives here.

That was all that she could feel. She couldn't begin to see how Planir was working this magic, much less attempt it. But it was more comfort than Jilseth could have possibly imagined; to feel her own affinity outstripping the reach of her own hand once again, her wizardly instincts going beyond the paltry evidence of her own eyes and ears.

'Thank you, my dear.' As Planir withdrew his hand from Ilysh's, the radiance in his ring subsided.

He was still carrying his empty tisane glass in its silver holder. The pale thread rising from the storage jar came to coil inside it. The humble vessel glowed as though it came fresh from the glass-blower's hearth. Then between one heartbeat and the next, the magelight dimmed from a furnace glow to the dullest of embers.

Planir set the glass down on the altar table. It was no longer a plain tisane glass. Straight sides rose from a broad foot shod with silver leaves. The vessel was adorned with incised lattice work framing crystal teardrops. At the top, the glass folded over to cover the veiled contents with a crystal blossom. It was as exquisite an artefact as the most skilled glasswright might produce in a lifetime.

Ilysh knotted her trembling hands behind her back as she bent to study the five-petalled flower. 'Mama? Is it a periwinkle?' Tears shone on her cheeks, burnished by a stray shaft of light from the window at other end of the room.

'It is,' Planir confirmed.

Movement at the far end of the room caught Jilseth's eye. The doorway was now crowded with men and women, servants and villagers. She could make out the maid Raselle holding little Esnina up so the child could see.

How many of these Halferan folk had just seen the Archmage's magic? What would they make of that, and whatever else would local rumour make of his visit here today? What did Planir intend them to make of it? He was after all, a skilled player of games such as white raven.

'My thanks, Lady Zurenne,' Planir bowed low, 'for allowing me to do you this service.'

Zurenne could only nod and reply with a curtsey. Jilseth could see she was far too close to tears to risk words.

'We will leave you to your devotions.'

Planir bowed a second time and Jilseth expected him to take her hand to translocate immediately back to Hadrumal.

Instead the Archmage stepped down from the dais and walked serenely down the length of the great hall. Jilseth was quietly amused at how fast the throng managed to melt away given the clutter choking the entrance hall.

The first whispers of awe-struck speculation were beginning among those now pressed back down the corridor to the kitchens as she and Planir left through the front porch, both doors hastily opened by the steward.

'Master Rauffe,' Planir acknowledged him politely.

'Good day to you,' Jilseth made sure to greet the lean man too, 'and thank you.'

Not merely for opening the door. She owed him a lifetime's gratitude for his skilled handling of their carriage and its team of panicked horses in that nightmare retreat from Halferan Manor's destruction.

A hand plucked at her elbow before she could follow Planir out onto the threadbare grass.

'My lady.' Doratine the cook was proffering a napkin full of glazed ochre sweetmeats. 'Eryngo toffee, my lady.

Merely a token of my thanks. Eryngo's a restorative.' Doratine peered closer, all solicitude. 'Are you quite recovered, my dear—that's to say, my lady mage? From your swoon?'

A swoon. Of course. That's what these Caladhrians would think had laid her low. Mage or not, she was a woman and thus subject, in their eyes, to vapours and hysterics at the slightest provocation.

Jilseth managed something approaching a smile. 'Thank you.'

There was no doubting the cook's sincerity and it was hardly the Caladhrian woman's fault that she knew so little of wizardry. Or that it would take far more than some sweetmeats to restore a mage in her predicament.

'You must excuse me.' Jilseth hurried after Planir.

He was waiting beyond the carriage sweep. 'What have you got there?' He peered curiously into the napkin.

'Eryngo toffee apparently.' Jilseth wrapped the linen tight as Planir laughed out loud. 'What's so amusing?'

She had intended to ask something quite different. Why was the Archmage proposing to send Merenel to teach Lady Ilysh how to play white raven? What did he think the Tormalin magewoman might learn here? Or was she simply to be his spy? Before Jilseth could decide what to ask, that same pale haze swept them away.

The translocation spell didn't stop the questions going through Jilseth's head. Did Planir truly think that was the best use of Merenel's considerable talents? Surely every mage of Hadrumal should be focusing all their attention on finding some magic to defeat the Mandarkin's infuriating veiling magic.

Who knew what he might be getting up to, while they couldn't see him?

— CHAPTER SEVEN —

'THIS IS ALL very strange,' Anskal pronounced.

'Yes, it is,' Hosh agreed, 'but they believe in this heavenly compass absolutely, and in its earthly counterpart.'

Anskal walked around the beaten earth circle with the twelve stones equally spaced around the ditch that ringed it. He paused to study the symbols carved on each one. 'These are for the stars?'

'For the particular constellations that the Aldabreshi follow, yes.' Hosh nodded.

He wouldn't have brought Anskal here given a choice but his first attempts to explain how and why the Archipelagans traced such intricate patterns in the sky had ground to a halt in utter confusion.

As the Mandarkin had angrily berated him, Hosh didn't need any omens to tell him how perilous his situation was. He was a dead man if Anskal concluded he was either lying or that he was simply too ignorant to be of continued use as a source of information about these islands.

So he had brought the wizard here this morning, to this sacrosanct hollow beyond the line of ironwood trees some way inland from the pavilions and the hut settlement. To his profound relief, these ancient stones had finally enabled the Mandarkin to grasp his meaning.

'Each also marks an arc of this earthly compass, where they look for omens of any kind; birds, clouds, some unforeseen occurrence. To give them some answers as to questions of partnership, death, travel?' Anskal marked out the first quarter of the circle with his pointing finger before cocking his head at Hosh. 'But these stars are not anywhere close to these stones at the moment. What of that?'

'I don't know.' Hosh hated to say so but there was so much he didn't understand about the Archipelagans' philosophies.

'This is also where they test their slaves?' The Mandarkin had lost interest, returning once again to the dark stains marring the trampled soil.

'Yes.' Hosh swallowed stomach-churning recollection of the slaughter he had seen here, when newly-chained captives had been set to fight each other. The corsairs had both wagered and read portents into who lived and who had died.

There were days when he still couldn't believe that he had survived being hurled into such deadly combat. Followed by nights when he dreamed of the half-starved, half-witted unfortunate whom he'd had to kill to live. Hosh kept telling himself that the dead man must surely have been reborn, all unknowing by now. That Saedrin would understand he'd had no choice at all. That was scant consolation when he woke sweating, his heart pounding, his stomach heaving.

'That is good.' Once again Anskal was nodding.

Hosh couldn't decide which was more disturbing; that the wizard so clearly approved of such brutality or that he had recognised these blood stains for what they were before Hosh had begun to explain. What was this distant homeland of his like?

'All the same, very strange.' Anskal shook his head in wonderment before turning back to Hosh. 'Now you will go and talk to those who fled across the island.'

The Mandarkin nodded and turning his back, began walking back towards the shady trees, heading for the huts and the pavilions beyond overlooking the curve of the beach at the head of the anchorage.

Hosh watched him go. The bastard clearly didn't doubt for an instant that he would be obeyed.

Because the wizard wasn't wrong, he thought unhappily. As wretched as his life was, Hosh wasn't yet so tired of life that he'd defy the Mandarkin outright and die in some magical agony before he'd so much as closed his mouth on the words.

But wouldn't that happen regardless, if he came back from the island's far shore with some message of rejection from the corsairs and their slaves? Because Hosh couldn't think how he could possibly persuade them to listen to any wizard's proposal.

He contemplated the stained earth. The blood shed here wasn't only from captured slaves. The corsairs had clustered in the hollow, seeking desperately for omens in the first terrified days after Anskal's arrival. Fear and anger had seen them turn murderously on each other. Hosh had seen Ducah kill a double handful of men and more, for no reason beyond his own impotent fury.

He felt for the silver-gilt and crystal arm ring hidden under his tunic sleeve. It seemed a horribly flimsy protection against a corsair horde's fury. He could only trust that it was proof against however many blades he might face. Surely Anskal wouldn't knowingly send him to his death? Hosh wished he could be sure of that. He began walking regardless.

As he left the bloody hollow, he looked up at the blue sky streaked with the clouds of the rains that would come shortly after noon. He had bought himself a few days by insisting to Anskal that if he was to get any hearing at all, they must wait for the most favourable alignments of the heavenly jewels.

Just at present, as any Aldabreshin would know, day or night, all the most significant coloured stars and both the moons were in the same quarter of the sky. Apart from the Sapphire which took seven years to traverse a single arc, if Hosh had understood Imais the slave cook correctly, and the Topaz which crossed those invisible boundaries only once a year, thus marking the calendar for the Aldabreshi some time in For-Spring by the Caladhrian almanac.

Hosh shoved his way through a flourishing thicket of fringe tree saplings. It was remarkable how the island's greenery had returned without the corsairs' greedy blades hacking everything down for firewood and after half a season of the island's drenching rains.

The Amethyst for calm and humility floated serene with the Pearl that supposedly soothed unruly emotion and promoted intuition. It was also a talisman against magic and with the Lesser Moon waxing, Hosh could only hope all that would count against these jewels being in the compass arc for omens of death. The stars there were the Mirror Bird and that was another talisman against magic, wasn't it?

Didn't that mean they could at least listen to him without being stained by wizardry's corruption? Hosh only hoped he'd get the chance to make that argument. If he could only find Nifai.

Of all the *Reef Eagle's* crewmen, the overseer had been the keenest to trade his share of their loot to maximum advantage. That was one reason he'd saved Hosh's life; to learn more of the Tormalin tongue, in order to deal with mainland merchants in person without losing a portion of his gains to some more fluent middleman.

A thicker tangle blocked his path and Hosh had to cast back and forth to either side before he found a gap he could squeeze through without risking the knotted vine's vicious spines. The slightest scratch from those could fester so vilely in this place. He'd seen enough men die to know, deliberately lashed with the things for some corsair ship master's entertainment.

Perhaps he should have asked Anskal if he could have a hacking blade, to cut himself a path? No, Hosh concluded with a sigh as he retraced his steps yet again to avoid a wall of red canes with razor sharp leaves. Asking the wizard for anything that might be used against him was surely as good as cutting his own throat.

Besides, was there anything else here that he might need to defend himself against? Hosh paused and listened but could barely hear a trill of bird song. There hadn't been much by way of animals left on this island with the corsairs' ever-hungry slaves ready to catch anything that moved. Now he guessed that the raiders themselves had been driven to eat that same poor fare in place of their plundered feasting. Well, Hosh supposed he could thank Raeponin for that small measure of justice.

He toiled up a long, long slope, rehearsing yet again the arguments which he hoped to make. He could point to the Ruby, jewel for courage and moreover in the arc of Travel and Learning alongside the Opal for truth and good faith. And if the Greater Moon was unhelpfully waning, that gemstone was also another talisman against wizards and the stars of the Bowl in that same arc advocated sharing. Surely that should mean he should at least get a hearing?

After a tiresome struggle to find a way through the broken gullies marring the island's highest ridge, he eventually realised he had begun the gradual descent towards the far shore.

Hosh began to feel increasingly nervous. He was much less certain about the Diamond. Granted it was a sign for clarity of thought and purpose and currently rode alongside the slow-moving Emerald, token for growth and peace. But those gems were together in the arc on the eastern horizon where omens for marriages were most commonly sought. Hosh vaguely recalled Imais saying that omens there also counted for any dealings between two individuals and no more, but mostly he remembered the more brutal corsairs joking about whatever they saw there as a guide to the women whom they'd seize and violate when they were making ready for a raid.

He was horribly thirsty by now. He took his time finding a stream running down from the higher ground. It had to be swift running and clear. Captain Corrain had taught him that, when neither of them dared risk the gut rot that saw men driven from the anchorage to die inside a handful of days if they were ashore or taken from their oar to be tossed to the sharks at once if they were aboard.

Sitting to cleanse his hands as best he could with the

particular leaves which Imais had shown him were best for the purpose and then cupping the refreshing water to his mouth, Hosh wondered uneasily how the corsairs were faring on this side of the island. This was the furthest they could flee without a vessel to brave the waves. Surely they must have had sufficient water to drink with these streams running down to the shore.

But what had they had to eat? They must be starving now, raiders and slavers alike, standing shoulder to shoulder on the barren sands. Unless they'd started eating each other. The darkest rumours of Aldabreshin customs back in the Halferan barrack hall had hinted at such atrocities. Hosh's own insistent hunger after his long morning's exertions turned to hollow nausea.

He hugged his knees close, burying his face. He didn't want to go on. But what choice did he have? He couldn't go back and admit his cowardice. Were there any lies that he could tell that could possibly deceive a wizard? Miserably wiping his face, Hosh had to admit that was unlikely. He'd never been able to fool anyone, not once they'd seen their tenth solstice anyway.

He forced himself to his feet and crept reluctantly onwards. Now his fate surely depended, one way or the other, on who he encountered first.

As the gradual slope smoothed out towards the water, Hosh saw the first traces of the fleeing corsairs. Dead bodies sprawled amid nut palms stunted by the fierce winds blowing constantly along this shore. He buried his face in his sleeve to counter the worst of the stink, brutal even through his broken and snuffling nose. Abandoned cloud bread wasn't the only thing rotting in this season.

He moved hastily upwind. The light through the

trees brightened and he realised he was getting close to the rocky beaches. He'd only been over this way once before, when the oar slaves had been left to their own devices for days at a time over the winter, when storms made all but infrequent voyages to neighbouring domains too perilous.

As soon as he'd realised it could be done, Captain Corrain had insisted on making a complete circuit of the island. They had been forced to acknowledge that the old blind corsair Grewa had chosen this hideout well. No other island was visible from any point on the shore and they hadn't seen a single ship even hull down on the far horizon. Not from some triangular-rigged fishing skiff to any great square-sailed galley with a triple bank of oars.

So what, Hosh wondered, were the corsairs hoping to find here? He peered up through the nut palms' burgeoning crowns of leaves but could see no column of smoke from any signal fire. There must be fish to be caught, he supposed, but if there was any scent of cooking, it couldn't penetrate the lingering stench of the dead.

He saw movement ahead. Hosh dropped to his hands and knees. His heart pounded. Remembering his magic arm ring did nothing to slow his panic. Then he realised the slowly moving figure was a woman. She was cradling something in one arm. As he watched, Hosh realised she was plucking leaves from the tips of a sprawling shrub's branches and dropping them into a fold of cloth.

She was looking cautiously around, in all directions but most often towards the sea. Doubtless she feared being robbed of her foraging's spoils. Or perhaps she feared the man with the sword shadowing her, for all that he was supposed to be protecting her. Hosh noticed the raider just in time to crouch behind a dense cluster of spiny-tipped leatherspears. Like the woman, the swordsman was most concerned with some threat from their seaward side.

Hosh didn't recognise the woman or her guardian at all. But just perhaps if he followed them, he would find someone whom he knew?

As best he could judge, peering up through the trees, midday had come and gone before the unknown woman turned towards the shore, her shadow trailing after her. Hosh followed, his guts knotted with apprehension. Finally he followed her to a makeshift shelter of nut palm branches laid across the gap between two black and broken boulders.

Drianon, goddess of hearth and home, of women and wheat be blessed now and for ever more. Among the assorted slaves clustered close to the rocks, Hosh could see Imais using a roughly shaped wooden pestle to pound something into mush inside a basket woven from green palm fronds.

But how could he hope to approach her with a double handful of gaunt swordsmen prowling the edge of this crude encampment? Hosh found himself a fringe tree thicket to hide in and pondered that challenge as the first drops of rain began to fall.

Within a few breaths, the rain was coming down in cupfuls as was customary hereabouts. Hosh was soaked to the skin, something he'd also grown well used to. He watched the roaming swordsmen head back towards the black boulders. They didn't need to use their blades to claim what little shelter the makeshift roof of palm branches offered. The slaves hastily yielded to sit out in the rain.

Hosh watched Imais walk to a nut palm where he'd already noted a patch of clean-swept earth at its base. She carefully nudged aside the few wind-blown leaves with a stick. She had been one of the first to warn Hosh of the Archipelago's countless venomous spiders, insects and snakes.

Satisfied, she sat down and leaned back against the tree trunk, closing her eyes as the rain streamed through the tight dark curls dotting her scalp like peppercorns and on down her rounded coppery features. Though Hosh saw she wasn't nearly as comfortably plump as she had been when she was living in the anchorage as the *Reef Eagle*'s pavilion's cook.

He looked at the black rocks. The raider swordsmen were nowhere to be seen. The other slaves were sitting close by, heads hanging, heedless of anything beyond the rain hammering down on their heads.

Edging carefully along behind the fringe tree thicket, Hosh moved as close as he dared to Imais. He was much too far away to risk calling out though and she still had her eyes closed. He wrestled with a sappy twig until he managed to break off a short length.

He stripped off the leaves but for a few at the end. Would that help it fly like an arrow? Breathing a desperate prayer to Talagrin, god of hunters and wild places, Hosh hurled the stick at Imais.

It landed a little way short of her foot. But when she shifted her position, Hosh saw her toe catch the twig. He already had another ready. He threw it as hard as he could. Imais stiffened as it flopped onto the dark earth a handspan away from the first one.

Hosh could see her peering in his direction. He looked hastily towards the black rocks. There was no sign that anyone there had noticed. Desperately hoping the fringe thicket hid him from view, he rose from his painful crouch, waving a cautious hand.

Imais hid her face in her hands. Was that some signal? If so, Hosh had no notion what it might mean. Before he could worry about that, he saw Imais get to her feet. Unhurried, tugging at the drawstring as though to loosen her grimy trews, the woman walked towards the fringe trees.

Now Hosh understood. Hopefully anyone watching would assume she was going to find some hollow to piss in.

Imais had originally come from the Archipelago's southernmost reaches, if Hosh had understood her markedly different dialect correctly. She had been born and sold anything up to a thousand leagues away, before being bought and sold again across more domains than he could comprehend. He didn't know if she'd been slave-born or captured in some warlord's raid or traded away by her own family in their desperation to save her from starvation or disease. Had she ever had children? Hosh had never dared to ask, for fear of learning that some dreadful fate had befallen a once-beloved son or daughter.

She rounded the thicket and halted, to stare at him in disbelief. 'Both died, mouse and scorpion.' Mystified, she shook her head. 'But no sting to kill the mouse and with the canthira leaves still green.'

It took Hosh a moment to realise what she was talking about. The glass jar. It had repelled him, though he'd taken care not to show it.

With the Canthira Tree stars on the horizon, Imais had taken a spray of leaves from the earthly tree and put them in a jar with one of those deadly creatures, a scorpion, as well as a little mouse captured in the kitchen. As long as the mouse clung to the leaves in the top half of the jar, it could stay out of reach of the scorpion's sting.

She had been looking for an omen, as she had done the time before, when she'd trapped a spray of vizail blossoms with the jar's lid. That time the mouse had lived. Hosh didn't understand why but Imais had said that the portent promised good fortune for him.

He didn't want to know what she thought this second result of her cruelty might mean. He spoke before she could tell him.

'The wizard, he wants to speak to someone. I need to find Nifai.'

'His taint kills all.' Imais spat on the ground.

Hosh knew from that gesture that she was talking about the wizard, not the overseer. Did she blame Anskal's presence for whatever had gone wrong with her carefully prepared jar?

Hosh could think of any number of reasons why the mouse had died. Terror alone could have killed the poor little beast, trapped in a cloth-covered jar with a scorpion scuttling around the bottom.

'I need to find Nifai,' he repeated. 'The wizard says he will let you go—there are terms,' he added hastily as he saw desperate hope dawn in Imais's dark eyes. 'A bargain to be made.' Surely the Aldabreshi would understand that?

Imais stared at him for a long moment. 'Have you seen Grewa?'

The rain rattled the leaves all around them.

Hosh blinked water out of his eyes. 'Grewa?'

The blind corsair who had previously ruled this nest of thieves? Surely the only question was whether he had been inside that pavilion, shattered when Anskal struck, or had he burned alive along with his crew and hapless oar slaves when magical fire consumed his trireme.

Hosh shook his head. 'He's dead.'

Imais shook her own head. 'He was seen, after the mainlander came.' She spat on the ground again. 'His skiff was seen sailing away from its hiding place. He must have seen a portent.'

Hosh refused to believe any of this. 'You say he was seen? You say he had a hidden boat. Did you see any of this yourself?' He stepped forward, ready to seize her, to shake the truth from her.

Imais warned him off with upraised hands. 'I only know what I hear. They say that Grewa will return to have his vengeance.'

'Do you truly believe that? Have you seen any omens to tell you that's true?' Hosh demanded. 'Wouldn't you rather go now than wait and hope? He says he is ready to bargain.'

He remembered to spit on the ground as he gestured back towards the anchorage side of the island. Then he swept his hand towards this rocky, hungry shore.

'What debt would these people owe you, if you helped them make a trade for their freedom?'

If they didn't kill her first, for daring to suggest such a thing, Hosh thought with sudden terror.

'Help me find Nifai. He can make the deal. He can risk the taint.'

Imais ran a hand over her sodden hair. Hosh could see

rainwater trickling down the side of her neck.

'I must think on this.' She turned abruptly and hurried back to her chosen tree.

Hosh shrank back behind the fringe thicket. He dared not follow her and risk capture by those swordsmen.

But he dared not return empty-handed to Anskal. Not that Hosh had much idea what the wizard might do, if he thought he was being defied or betrayed. But he guessed there would be a lot more corsairs dead at the end of it. More than had already died in that obliterated pavilion and the trireme where Grewa had surely burned.

And he would die along with them as likely as not, and his poor beloved mother would never know how he died and his bones would lie and moulder into the dead leaves on this island, with Poldrion's demons tormenting his shade till the last dissolution of his body in this world allowed him to finally cross Saedrin's threshold.

Hosh sank to his knees and wondered by all that was holy, what was he supposed to do now? If only he had managed to escape with Captain Corrain. Tears stung his eyes and trickled down his face to mingle with the raindrops. If only he was safely back in Halferan.

— CHAPTER EIGHT —

WAITING FOR NEWS from the parliament had become intolerable. Zurenne had decided that she must do something or she would surely go mad. So she had begun with a few roughly sketched plans. Now those were overlaid with much-amended lists of all that would be needed to rebuild the manor. As best she could guess, anyway. Zurenne's pen nib hesitated over an estimate of the tiles needed to reroof the great hall.

'Mama?' Ilysh looked up from the pile of maps which she was studying at the far end of the sitting room's long table. 'What do you suppose is happening in Ferl?'

Esnina looked up from her copy book, her little face anxious. Zurenne saw the little girl's hand shaking and stifled a groan. That would mean another page of blots to prompt a tantrum when Neeny realised what she had done, without anyone so much as venturing a criticism.

'Try to cultivate some patience, Lysha,' Zurenne advised in the mildest tone she could summon. 'What are you looking at there? Why don't you show Neeny?'

Ilysh hesitated but as Zurenne had hoped, her desire to show off what she had learned got the better of her.

'See, Neeny? Madam Merenel says that these mountains are called the Southern Spurs. The Gidestans mark the close of their mining season as the year turns to For-Autumn and head back to the Dalasorian side of the mountains—'

Zurenne had only the haziest idea of what the Tormalin magewoman had been talking about. Come to that, she'd had no idea that her husband had amassed what Madam Merenel assured her was an outstanding collection of charts and travellers' journals.

Lysha had unearthed them in a search through her father's chests to find a second white raven set for Neeny to play with, to stop her screaming that she wanted to learn like Lysha and snatching game pieces out of Madam Merenel's hands.

'Some of the Gidestans take the western pass to spend the winter in Wrede but that's a hazardous journey.' Ilysh's finger traced the Dalas river running east towards the coast before she tapped a void in the mountains above it.

On the map it was a modest distance though Zurenne had no notion what that might mean in terms of travel on the ground. These sweeping charts were incomprehensible compared to the strip-maps she was familiar with; each page depicting a single day's journey and showing the halts and landmarks along the way. What more did a traveller need?

'The Ushaltena pass is the widest path to the ocean and Madam Merenel says that its trails have been well maintained for generations,' Lysha was explaining. 'Most of the miners take that route to winter in Inglis and the villages thereabouts.'

Esnina leaned closer to study the neatly inked dots tracing the great roads' routes through the mountains and the forests. 'Trees,' she said brightly, one plump finger pressing on the parchment.

'That's right.' Ilysh smiled. 'And these little marks mean marshland, like our own saltings back home.'

Zurenne had never realised there were marshes in Tormalin. All she knew of that land and its Emperor was what her father had told her. That the noble princes of the Empire's great houses were forced to surrender a yearly tithe of all their profits to support his legions. Legions which would march west to reclaim their lost Empire, given the slightest excuse. But her husband hadn't believed that and if half the rumours of the past year's upheavals in Lescar were true, her lost beloved would be proved right yet again.

If her husband had been so interested in these distant lands, that surely made them a fit topic for Lysha to study. That was surely preferable to her daughter learning how to play white raven. Zurenne shuddered to think what any prospective husband might think of such a pastime. Such strategy games fell solely within the purview of the men who might one day have to lead men into battle, not that a Caladhrian baron had done so for generations.

Her pen shook and now she saw she had blotted her own page. Ilysh already had a husband and he would be coming back within a handful of days, for good or ill.

'Home?' Esnina echoed her older sister, looking anxiously at Zurenne once again.

'Soon,' she promised, hating herself for lying to the child.

'Perhaps the Archmage will have some news—' Ilysh's hand went to her own silver pendant.

Zurenne was sorely tempted to rip it from the girl's neck, if only to assert her authority over her daughter. She clenched her fist beneath the tabletop and spoke as calmly as she could. 'What makes you think he'll tell you, if he wouldn't tell me?'

'But I am—' Ilysh flushed red as she bit off her words.

The Lady of Halferan? Zurenne couldn't face that quarrel again.

'We expect Madam Merenel shortly after noon, don't we? You should get some air before nuncheon,' she said crisply. 'Take Neeny for a walk around the deer paling.'

'Mama—'

'Come on, Lysha.' Esnina closed her copy book on a glistening page, her discarded pen leaving a smear on the table. She hurried into the bedchamber.

'Go and find Raselle,' Zurenne ordered Ilysh before the girl could argue any further. 'I don't think it will rain but you should both wear a cloak.'

Ilysh's expression remained mutinous. Before she could speak a knock sounded on the door.

'Enter,' Zurenne called out briskly.

'My lady?' It was Master Rauffe, holding a ledger.

'Is that the final reckoning of all that's been salvaged?' Zurenne held out her hand. 'Ilysh, take your sister for her walk.'

'Come on, Lysha.' Esnina had already found her own cloak and was standing in the bedchamber doorway, her sister's in her arms.

Ilysh accepted the garment with ill-grace. 'Don't you go tugging at my skirts and asking me to carry you back.' As she fastened the clasp, she glanced at her mother with veiled eyes.

Zurenne had seen her fingers brush that silver pendant once again. Had Lysha only agreed to the walk in order to pester the Archmage without any witnesses but Neeny?

There was no point in accusing her. The girl would only deny it. Anyway, if the Archmage yielded to Lysha's entreaties, they would finally know their fate.

'Master Rauffe?' She invited the steward to show her the ledger as the girls departed.

The wiry man set the book on the table and turned the pages one by one to reveal his neatly inked entries.

'My oath to Saedrin, my lady,' he concluded at last, 'I believe we have now recovered all that's worth having from Halferan's ruins.'

'Indeed.' Zurenne blinked away a sudden mistiness of grief. She didn't have time for weeping if the manor was to be rebuilt. Though it was hard to imagine they'd have any use for *seven serving platters, red-glazed earthenware, chipped.*

Rauffe closed the ledger and picked it up again. 'If we are to see the rubble cleared and the brickwork begun before the onset of winter, we will need to start at once and to summon every strong man from across the barony, aye and any women and lads who can be spared. And my lady, Madam Merenel, when she was here the other day, she did say a second time, there are wizards who've offered to help.'

Zurenne recalled a Caladhrian-born mage making that same offer, that first and last time when she had seen the ruination of her home.

She also wondered if Master Rauffe realised how the tightness in his voice betrayed him, along with the way the tall man hugged the ledger to his chest, as though leather-bound boards could protect him from magecraft.

She wished she could find some way to tell him that she understood his apprehension. That she still shivered whenever she recalled the successive waves of wizardry wrought in their defence as he had driven the baronial carriage away from the howling barbarians intent on destroying Halferan. Who could have imagined such things were possible? After seeing such a thing, asking a mage to help shift beams and bricks seemed ludicrous, not to say insulting.

'My lady?' Master Rauffe prompted her for an answer.

The door to the entrance hall flew open.

'Oh my lady, he's back!' Raselle was so torn between excitement and uncertainty that she was barely coherent. 'The captain— that's to say, the baron—unless—'

'Tell Corrain to meet me in the great hall, in the new shrine,' Zurenne ordered. 'At once! He is to talk to no one until he has spoken to me!'

She could only pray to Trimon, god of travellers, that Lysha and Neeny were already well away on their walk, their backs turned to this bustle of new arrivals in the stableyard. She needed to know Corrain's news before she had to deal with her daughter.

How insufferable would Ilysh be, if he had indeed been confirmed as baron? Making his wife the pre-eminent lady of the demesne? Well, if Ilysh thought that raised her above a mother's discipline, she would learn different. Zurenne lifted her chin as she hurried through the cluttered entrance hall.

The new shrine was still only hidden by the curtain which Evrel the seamstress and her daughters had sewn from a tapestry formerly decorating the kitchen corridor. In keeping with the lodge's purpose, the cunningly woven wool showed a hunting scene and that was surely no impiety with Aft-Autumn sacred to Talagrin.

As Zurenne approached, she saw the flower-studded grass along the bottom edge was already half obscured by pinned scraps of cloth, tokens of the household women's heartfelt prayers.

Drawing the tapestry aside she found the curtain was rattling. Copper cut-pieces pierced with hammer and nail had been stitched to the linen backing. Of course; men were accustomed to nail copper pennies, sometimes silver ones, to their local shrine's door to mark their entreaties and vows to the gods, for their friends to witness and their foes to fret over.

Though what measure of devotion was this? Halved and quartered pennies were common currency among the poorest of the poor. Then Zurenne rebuked herself. In such uncertain days, the dispossessed villagers were surely wise to hoard their whole coin.

'My lady?' A booted footfall on the floorboards was lost in the thud of the closing door.

'Corrain.' Zurenne gripped the edge of the tapestry. 'What news?'

'What is this?' He was walking slowly up the hall, his eyes fixed on the statues of the gods now half-revealed. The rest of the great hall might have been echoing emptiness for all the heed he took of that disorder.

'We made a shrine—' Zurenne broke off as Corrain's gaze fixed on the table shrouded in white linen.

'Rosemary for remembrance.' Corrain was looking at the green sprigs framing the silver leaves of the urn's base. 'For my lord?'

Zurenne nodded. She had found the herbs there just after dawn when she'd brought her own wreath of bay laurel to garland the new urn. She didn't know who had laid them.

'The Archmage,' she began to explain. 'He drew my lord's ashes out of all the rest and—'

'Planir?' Corrain's scowl accused her. 'What bargain did you make with him for that?'

'None,' Zurenne protested.

How dared Corrain speak to her in such a manner? He wasn't her husband and he was Ilysh's only in name for the sake of defending the barony. Let him conduct himself as befitted a guardsman.

'Could you not have sent word for us to expect you?' she demanded with some heat.

'I rode as fast as any despatch rider.' Corrain shook his head. 'I am Baron Halferan, confirmed by the parliament's decree.' He sounded as if he didn't believe it.

'Saedrin be blessed.' Zurenne's euphoria was short-lived. She contemplated the heaps of belongings all around the hall and wondered how long it would take to return all these people to their homes. If they had any homes to go back to.

'Now you are confirmed as baron we must rebuild without delay,' she said slowly, 'if we're to have the manor and village fit to live in before the winter weather bites.'

How long would that be? Could they hope for any more boons from the gods? Would Maewelin hold off the first frosts for the sake of the widows and orphans?

As she turned her back on the silent demands of the household goods piled up in the hall, Zurenne looked for the Winter Hag. Seeing the rough-hewn representation carved from twisted bog oak and rescued from some ransacked shrine, she was shocked by a sudden memory.

Zurenne had promised the holy crone a new statue if her children were rescued from Minelas. The ancient goddess's most sacred duty was a secret passed from mothers to daughters; the Crone was the righter of women's wrongs at the hands of men. But Zurenne had never made good on that pledge. She must do so and quickly, with the Archmage's coin.

'We will need wizardly aid.' Zurenne raised her hand to her rune sigil pendant with sudden resolve. 'Madam Jilseth will surely advise us, or Madam Merenel. Do you recall her? She's been teaching Lady Ilysh—'

'No!' Corrain reached out as though to physically stop her before drawing his hand back into a clenched fist.

Shocked, Zurenne retreated a step. 'Why not?'

The misery in his face sent a sick chill through her.

'The Archmage.' Corrain twisted the broken slave shackle around his wrist. 'I will have to answer to him now. As long as he swears to keep Halferan safe—'

'What are you talking about?' Zurenne swallowed growing misgiving. 'The barony is safe from Karpis if the parliament has confirmed you as Lysha's lawful husband. The corsairs have given up after their ships were sunk in the retaliation which you contrived with Tallat. If you couldn't find a mage to help us in Solura, Jilseth was there when those last raiders arrived, Halcarion be thanked.'

Though Zurenne couldn't think of a greater contrast than those scenes of slaughter and the light-hearted tales of games and dalliance usually involving the beauteous goddess of love and luck.

Corrain was staring unblinking at the crystal urn. 'I did find a mage.'

'What?' This made no sense to Zurenne.

'Planir must know.' Corrain almost sounded relieved. 'I'll take whatever punishment he decrees as long as it doesn't threaten Halferan.'

'I don't understand what you're saying.' Zurenne's unease was deepening to dread.

'When we sailed for Solura, we didn't find a mage to help us, not as Kusint hoped.' Corrain stumbled over the name of his lost companion

'As you told me,' Zurenne reminded him. 'When you finally returned to Halferan!'

Long after she and everyone else had given Corrain up for dead. Everyone save Ilysh.

'That was no lie.' He grimaced. 'But it was far from the whole truth. We did find Soluran wizards pursuing a Mandarkin mage—'

'Mandarkin?' It took Zurenne a moment to recall the barren mountainous realm to the north of Solura. Its easternmost fringe had been marked on that chart where Madam Merenel had shown Lysha the barren wastes of Gidesta.

Kusint, the Soluran who'd escaped slavery with Corrain had said the Mandarkin tyrants had been foes of the Soluran kings for generations beyond memory. That Solura's wizards were accustomed to wield potent magics to defend their land and its people. Kusint had sworn such magecraft would defeat the corsairs. Soluran wizards weren't hamstrung by the Edict of Hadrumal.

Zurenne had given Corrain her blessing when he'd sworn to secure such aid for Halferan. She had used his devotion to safeguard the barony as far as she could. If he had died on that improbable quest, the protection of his marriage contract with Lysha would have given her a case to argue against Lord Licanin's claim or Baron Karpis's. If no one could prove that Corrain had died, she could have delayed submitting to a guardian with all manner of stratagems. Maewelin forgive her. She glanced guiltily at the Winter Hag.

'I rescued him, the Mandarkin mage, from the Solurans since they wouldn't help us.'

Zurenne realised that Corrain was addressing her dead husband's ashes rather than talking to her.

'He's a starveling wretch—' but the contempt in Corrain's voice warred with fear '—he only wanted gold and food to fill his belly, fine clothes on his back. But he had magic the likes of which—'

Corrain shook his head, eyes closing on some lacerating memory. 'The Soluran wizards called up dust storms to blind him and set their own guards' swords on fire to cut through armour like it was wax. He still cost them two of their own before escaping all unseen.'

Now Corrain was pleading with the funeral urn. 'The Solurans wouldn't help us. I couldn't come home empty-handed. We have no quarrel with Mandarkin—'

His face twisted with anguish. 'He killed all the corsairs plundering Halferan Manor. He used his magic to find their anchorage through my ties to that cursed place. I thought he would kill them all, I swear it!'

Zurenne struggled to recall their conversation, when she had still been reeling from the shock of Corrain's reappearance amid the ruins of Halferan. He had walked back in through the manor's gates like the shade of a dead man fleeing Poldrion's demons.

What was it the old wives said, as in the sewing circles sharing their wisdom of age with newlyweds? Be careful what you wish for. Eldritch Kin lurking in the shadows might hear and send that very thing, to spite the gods who know far better than you do.

'You said that the corsairs had enough loot to satisfy ten mages.' She grasped at a fugitive memory. 'If this Mandarkin sought gold—'

'He said he was claiming their whole island and would take all the corsairs for his own slaves.' Corrain seemed oddly bemused. 'He didn't sink their ships. He just closed up their harbour with a wall of water. Then he sent me back to Halferan.'

'What does all this mean?' Zurenne's voice was shrill with confusion and apprehension.

'I don't know.' Corrain finally looked at her. 'But you should know that I defied Planir of Hadrumal, like my lord. And I was betrayed just as he was.'

His voice was harsh though Zurenne couldn't tell if he was condemning her dead husband or his own folly.

She seized on a far more vital question. 'Are you saying we must still fear corsairs?'

Corsairs with a mage to call on? Magic such as Jilseth had used to slay those last raiders? That prospect was so truly dreadful that further words froze in Zurenne's throat.

Corrain twisted the shackle around his wrist. 'He swore there would be no raids on our shores as long as he ruled their island.'

'You trust his word?' Zurenne frowned at abrupt recollection of something her husband had once told her, of the southern barbarians' ignorance and superstition. 'But the Aldabreshi abominate magic. They kill all wizards on sight.'

Corrain nodded. 'Perhaps that's what we should pray for, my lady.'

'That they kill him and reclaim this island you speak of? When that would leave the corsairs freed from his oath and his rule, to sail north and attack us again?' Zurenne cried. 'Corrain, what have you done?'

What manner of man had she shackled her innocent daughter to? What bargain could she possibly strike with the Archmage now, to save them all from the corsairs' return?

What would Planir do, to punish Corrain? What could he do beyond that, to curb this unknown wizard's ambitions, whatever they might prove to be?

— CHAPTER NINE —

'JILSETH?' NOLYEN'S KNUCKLES rapped on the oak.

She hurried to open the door. 'Keep your voice down!'

Living cheek by jowl was convenient for wizards eager to share their knowledge but it could prove cursed awkward with a close neighbour who was a light sleeper.

Jilseth looked warily across the quadrangle as Nolyen pushed past her into her study. Thankfully she saw no sign of Simne stirring. The austere mage would be like a bear roused from its winter torpor to be woken so soon after dawn. He rarely closed his own shutters before midnight.

'What has you coming here so early and in such haste?'

She opened the shutters to allow the pallid daylight through the ivy cloaking these walls and encroaching on her windows.

Nolyen paused in loosening the drawstring of the leather sack he had dumped on her table. 'What's keeping you from your sleep?' he asked, looking at her critically.

'Apart from your arrival?' Jilseth snapped. 'Excuse me while I dress.'

At least her current incapacity hadn't reduced the privileges her wizardry had already won her. She enjoyed one of the Terrene Hall's most coveted apartments with a separate bedchamber as well as a spacious study well supplied with bookshelves.

She closed the connecting door with an emphatic snick of the latch rather than a slam to relieve her anger and to annoy those still asleep above her. Pulling her linen nightgown over her head, she found the chill in the air raised gooseflesh on her naked skin. Summer was definitely passing.

Nolyen had arrived too early for her to ring for one of the hall's resident maidservants in hopes of a kettle of hot water. Well, a swift wash in the cold water of her basin's ewer chased away some of her weariness after another broken and troubled night. She dressed swiftly in a fresh chemise, stockings and a plain grey gown. Perhaps Nolyen had brought something to distract her from more fruitless musing.

Returning to the sitting room, she saw that he'd lit the lamps in the sconce by the door and on the table by the fireside chair where she was accustomed to sit and read. Their glow burnished the carved stone figurines arrayed along the front of every bookshelf; animals, buildings, men and women, as varied in style and craftsmanship as the rocks they had been made from. Every line had once told Jilseth some secret of their substance or of their shaping.

She contemplated the items which Nolyen had laid on the table; a shallow silver bowl and lumps of black rock seamed with sandy stone. Bitumen. The hardest, purest kind from a ravine in remotest Gidesta kept a close secret by the miners who profited from it.

Jilseth didn't need her mage senses to recognise such a specimen so intriguing to any earthborn wizard.

Nolyen's amiable face reflected his chagrin at his foolish question earlier. 'I would have asked you to join me in my chamber but I thought we would do better with more space.'

Jilseth judged that was the closest she would get to an apology. She decided to accept it. 'That's true enough.'

Nolyen had only recently quit the room which he had shared as a lowly apprentice. Now he had a cramped chamber in the noisy courtyard where the Seaward Hall ran alongside Hadrumal's high road. Flood Mistress Troanna did not believe in cosseting her pupils with featherbeds and hip baths like Hearth Master Kalion.

Nolyen grinned. 'I've been wondering how to go scrying for the Mandarkin without actually scrying for him.'

'All night?' Jilseth queried. His eyes looked as shadowed and heavy as her own felt. 'It's too early for riddles. Let me make a tisane.'

She crossed the room to the small fireplace, reaching for the mantel where she kept her glasses and herb jars.

The small blaze she had lit for comfort the evening before had long since died. Cool though the morning was, no one would cover their embers to keep them smouldering overnight until the turn of For-Winter.

Jilseth could not countenance reaching for steel and flint, not with Nolyen in the room, for all that his back was so tactfully turned. Throwing a handful of kindling onto the ashes, she concentrated all her wizardly strength on summoning a spark of elemental fire. To her profound relief, a cheerful yellow tongue licked at a frayed twist of bark.

Jilseth set the kettle on its hook and turned to ask Nolyen what herbs he'd favour in a tisane. As she did so, she caught sight of the muslin bundle from the Taw Ricks lodge. She had left it on the windowsill, well away from the fireplace in case of undue stickiness.

Nolyen was Caladhrian, from some northern barony, and noble born besides. A third or fourth son, if Jilseth recalled correctly. Not the eldest and heir anyway, which must have made the revelation of his magebirth and the necessity of sending him to Hadrumal easier for his parents to bear. With his quick wits and love of learning he would surely have been destined for the university at Col regardless.

'Nol, what do you know about eryngo?' She made sure to pronounce the curious name as Doratine the cook had done.

He was wringing water out of the empty air to fill the scrying bowl. 'Eryngo? Why do you ask?'

'Why are you blushing?' Jilseth couldn't decide if she was more entertained or perturbed by that.

'It's a—' Nolyen stroked his neatly trimmed beard to a point '—restorative herb.'

'So the Halferan cook said, when she gave me some sweetmeats,' Jilseth informed him drily.

'Eryngo toffee?' Nolyen looked relieved. 'Yes, that's a treat for convalescents.'

'And for those who haven't been ill?' Jilseth wasn't about to let him off this hook.

A splash of emerald magelight bounced back from the brimming bowl as Nolyen set his hands on the table. 'Men losing their potency between the bed sheets favour the candied roots,' he said without looking up at her. 'Any man whose wife is seen buying them can expect to be the butt of a good many jokes in his local tavern.'

'Oh.' Jilseth was surprised into a laugh.

'Shall we discuss bitumen?' Nolyen asked pointedly.

'Not commonly used in scrying.' Jilseth sat at the table.

'No,' he agreed, 'but widely used for caulking ships, along all the mainland coasts and right through the Archipelago.'

'Quite so.' Jilseth supposed that a mage with a water affinity would know what barriers might be used against it.

'We found Corrain in Solura because you thought of scrying for that metal shackle which he wears.' Nolyen looked intently into the water though no magelight glowed in its depths. 'I wondered if we might find the ships trapped within the corsair anchorage in similar fashion. Why should the Mandarkin mage veil those from our sight? Once we know where the anchorage is, we can direct a scrying there and see what's afoot without encroaching on his own magic.'

'How are we to find some corsair galley among all the countless hundreds that ply the Archipelago's sea lanes?'

Jilseth felt a thrill of anticipation all the same. Nolyen wouldn't have roused her so early if he didn't think he had an answer. Or the possibility of one. He couldn't be certain of his magecraft though, otherwise he'd have taken this to Flood Mistress Troanna or Archmage Planir.

'We need something specific to draw our magic to those particular ships,' Nolyen gestured at the lumps of bituminous rock, 'which is precisely what we have here.'

'Not so very specific, surely?' Jilseth was puzzled by his certainty.

His smile widened with satisfaction. 'According to Mellitha Esterlin, this particular pitch comes from the very shipyard in Relshaz where a ship known to have joined these corsairs was laid up for repairs and refitting the winter before last.'

'Along with how many others?' Jilseth protested.

Nolyen shrugged. 'A good few, doubtless, but if we have to search through them all, we'll be closer to finding this Mandarkin mage than if we scryed after every ship afloat.'

Jilseth was sorely sceptical. 'These shipwrights haven't replenished their stores? A boatyard must get through sacks of this stuff.'

'Mellitha had her man scour the corners of the storage bins,' Nolyen said stubbornly. 'She's confident that these are the remnants of that season's deliveries.'

If that assurance had come from anyone else Jilseth wouldn't have given it a moment's credence. Mellitha Esterlin offered an entirely different quality of information. In addition, her understanding of scrying magic was acknowledged as second to none. It was widely whispered in Hadrumal's wine shops that she could have been Flood Mistress, had she chosen to challenge Troanna.

There was no such agreement on the far more puzzling question of why she had chosen to leave Hadrumal and had established herself in Relshaz as a tax contractor for the Magistracy which ruled the port city. What was the attraction of such a humdrum life when she could have been a pre-eminent mage of Hadrumal?

Did she use her magic to spy on the myriad merchants, to read their ledgers through shuttered windows and inside locked storage chests? Opinion on that was as sharply divided, though apparently the Relshazri all believed it and thus saw no point in trying to cheat her.

That must make life easier for Mellitha, so the wine shop sages nodded over their goblets, both in delivering the revenue which she was contracted to deliver to the magistrates and in securing a handsome profit for her own coffers.

Jilseth wondered why it occurred to no one that Mellitha must surely be one of Planir's chief sources of information about mainland affairs. News from every nook and corner of those lands formerly ruled by Toremal came along the roads and rivers with all the goods which the Relshazri bought and sold. The city also handled more trade with the Archipelago than any other port, so Aldabreshin news and rumour landed there, first and freshest.

She stroked a piece of the bitumen with a fingertip. Her wizardly senses, dull as they were, felt the rock's distant kinship with the ivy growing around the windows.

Like coal, this curious substance had been formed from plants growing in some remote age far beyond hope of memory. Before it had been sunk deep into the earth by the shifting mountains and sinking seas, to be transformed over aeons through slow and subtle alchemical processes born of crushing and heat.

That elemental understanding gave her affinity mastery over it. That was to say, it always had done. After so many recent failures and disappointments, Jilseth was growing reluctant to try the simplest magecraft.

She handed the lump to Nolyen. 'Can you feel the essence of the plants within this?'

Mages with a water affinity were by far the most adept at manipulating growing things. Even wood felled generations ago remembered the sap that had once flowed through it, offering a conduit for their emerald wizardry.

'I can.' He grinned.

If Jilseth's elemental senses had been blunted, she had her wits. 'You're hoping to weave your hold on that essence into your scrying.'

Nolyen nodded. 'Just as you combined the lodestone fragments in the shale oil into our scrying for Corrain's shackle.'

'That was a very different working.' Jilseth frowned as she recalled using the unseen magnetic fragments to direct the searching magic for that singular piece of metal. Could she ever hope to craft such wizardry again?

'What would you like in your tisane?' She rose and went to the fireplace to swing the singing kettle away from the flames.

'Whatever you're having.' Nolyen peered closely at the lump of bitumen in his palm and it began to crumble.

By the time she returned with two glasses of hot water and steeping lemongrass, she had herself in hand. 'Surely an enhanced scrying would be better tried with a full nexus of mages?'

Saying so nearly choked her but the search for the renegade Mandarkin was too important to risk her own inadequacies hampering Nolyen.

'If you can light that fire under your kettle, you can melt this stuff for me,' he said firmly. 'I can't, not once it's in the water, not and have any hope of scrying.

That's all I need from you. Once the bitumen's melted, we can see if it's sufficiently distinctive to be worth pursuing. Then I can direct a nexus in a quintessential search for the ships trapped in that anchorage.'

'I see.' Jilseth nodded.

Of course he wouldn't be trying to work the full spell with her unreliable assistance. Of course he would find any fire magic nigh on impossible to work within his own element of water. Jilseth found the volatile magics of Air the most elusive and challenging of all, so far removed from her earth-bound instincts.

And if this all proved to be a delusion born of desperation, only she and Nolyen would know of it and he could trust in her discretion for the sake of their friendship.

'Let me melt the pitch.' She cupped her hands around the cool scrying bowl.

The pure metal's familiar touch soothed her fraught emotions. Jilseth realised she had forgotten how calming silver could be. That was a worthwhile reminder, whatever else might come of this dawn experiment.

Nolyen dropped a few chips of bitumen into the water.

Jilseth searched for the memory of heat born of crushing deep within the black essence while denying the water's desire to drain all such warmth away. To her delight, that proved easier than she had expected. Bitumen in its natural state was a liquid after all, albeit one that commonly flowed more slowly than the thickest treacle.

Its vapours would be far more insidious than the scent of Lady Zurenne's cook's toffee. Jilseth took care to keep the lead and quicksilver seeping out of the melting blackness contained within the scrying water. Painters might choose to poison themselves with orpiment for the sake of vivid yellow in their sunsets but mages tolerated no such hazards.

She looked across the bowl to Nolyen. 'Can you feel the metals leaching out and their alchemical balance within the bitumen?'

His chances of success through the quintessential scrying would depend on that. If Mellitha was correct and the caulking the corsairs had used on their boats had truly included pitch from this particular source.

Any earth mage could distinguish between candlesticks wrought from silver from two different mines though they might be identical to the non-wizardly eye. Had Nolyen learned enough of such wizardry? Jilseth could hope so; water magic had more sympathy with earthborn spells than with either of the other two elements.

Nolyen laid his hands carefully on the rim of the bowl and concentrated. 'Yes, I have it.'

Green magelight suffused the water. Oils escaping the oozing pitch shone iridescent.

'You're scrying?' Jilseth was surprised.

He grinned across the table at her. 'We might as well see if any ships in Hadrumal's harbour used that Relshazri shipyard around the same season.'

Jilseth withdrew her hands and the liquid bitumen yielded to its natural desire to drift upwards in sluggish gobs.

Nolyen hissed as the emerald radiance faded to a jaundiced hue. 'This is no good.'

'Never mind.' Jilseth tried to offer encouragement as well as consolation. 'Perhaps with a nexus—'

'I don't need a nexus.' Nolyen shook his head, impatient. 'I need you to keep the bitumen pooled in the bottom of the bowl.'

'As you command, master mage.' She cupped her hands around the bowl again and herded the black blobs together.

Nolyen was too intent on his scrying to notice her sarcasm. As the bitumen slid back down to the bottom of the bowl, the green magelight grew clearer. Then it grew brighter, taking on a golden hue. The radiance strengthened inexorably.

Jilseth felt her own magic surge upwards from the swirling pitch to weave itself into his wizardry. Even with only Nolyen's magic to bolster her own, this sensation was akin to working within a nexus. Every elemental instinct told her that this scrying could go far beyond her usual reach. Only she wasn't directing it.

'What are you doing?' Nolyen demanded, alarmed.

'It's your scrying,' Jilseth protested.

Images slid across the surface of the water, like reflections glimpsed by someone running down a street of windows. Oared galleys patiently followed wooded coastlines. Fat-bellied merchant galleons wallowed out in the open seas, plump sails hauling their cargo onwards. A flurry of fishing vessels were rigged with the Archipelago's distinctive triangular sails.

'Jilseth!' Nolyen stared at her and then back down at the bowl.

Golden magelight burned deep inside in her hands, bright enough to outline the bones within her flesh. The unbidden magic flowed from her fingertips, gilding the scrying bowl completely.

Pale haze cloaked Nolyen's hands. He grimaced and

tried to pull away. He couldn't. The haze darkened to an amber nimbus.

Now the floating reflection showed them a narrow strip of sand crowded with Aldabreshin traders. Galleys were beached in the shallows while watchful triremes prowled off shore.

Jilseth couldn't withdraw from the magic. She could no longer tell where her flesh ended and the silver bowl began. It was as though she cupped both water and liquid bitumen in her own hands. Her wizardly senses showed her every secret that would unlock the spell which Nolyen had groped for. She could find the elemental essence of this bitumen as surely as a compass needle could find north.

'There!' Nolyen gasped, as the scrying shifted again.

'Yes.' Jilseth had no doubt of it.

The stretch of water was longer than it was wide. It stretched inland between two headlands towards a spread of expansive houses built of coarse black rock and tiled with green ceramic. Ramshackle huts had been built all around them though all the dwellings from highest to humblest looked as deserted as the listless ships swaying at anchor—

They had found the corsairs' anchorage. There couldn't be another harbour in the Archipelago blocked by such an unnatural wave.

'Please stop—' Nolyen broke off with an agonised whimper.

With a shock of horror, Jilseth realised that this unbidden magic was reaching deep into Nolyen's bones. She could already trace its path as far as his wrists.

She fought to draw the wizardry back into the silver of the bowl. That was a struggle in itself but after a long, tense moment, Nolyen was able to pull away with a heartfelt oath.

'Talgrin's hairy arse.' Grimacing, he curled his red and swollen hands against his chest.

Jilseth was striving to feel her own flesh and bones again. At present she couldn't distinguish them from the silver of the scrying bowl. Her elemental affinity thrummed with every unique resonance of the metal. The effect was so unexpectedly sensual that she was reluctant to withdraw her hands. Never mind that some remote, dispassionate voice of reason was telling her this unknown magic could do her irreparable damage.

'Jilseth!'

Standing to lean over the table, Nolyen slapped her face with stinging violence. He reeled away, yelping at the pain he had inflicted on himself.

That shock of physical sensation ran through Jilseth like and yet unlike pain. It gave her an instant of realisation of her body's boundaries. With all the strength that she could muster, she forced a division between her hands and the scrying bowl. She cried out with the agony of it. It would surely have hurt less to take a knife to her own flesh.

The amber magelight dulled. Emerald scrying magic brightened briefly before it was snuffed out by the rising gobbets of molten pitch. The golden magelight suffusing her own hands was far slower to fade.

'What did we do?' She stared across the table.

'We found the Mandarkin's lair,' Nolyen said roughly.

That wasn't what Jilseth had meant and she could see that Nolyen knew that.

But they had done it all the same; found a way through the renegade's veiling magic.

Only Jilseth wasn't at all sure that she would ever try working such a scrying again.

Planir had warned her about unruly magic. Like every other apprentice Jilseth had learned the names of those wizards who had succumbed to obsession and intoxication with the untamed element of their affinity. Those wizards who had died in disgrace, their stories a dreadful warning.

Jilseth had been so scared that her wizardry wouldn't return. As she gazed at the scrying bowl, she realised she was far more fearful now that it had.

— CHAPTER TEN —

NO WONDER LADY Zurenne had been so easily convinced that wizardry offered Halferan's only hope of recovery, however rough and ready, this side of For-Winter with Aft-Winter's even greater travails to come after the solstice.

Corrain contemplated the burned ruin of the gatehouse, not one wall left standing higher than a short man's belt buckle. Where an archway had once admitted honoured guests, now a tangle of charred rafters perversely blocked his horse's way into the manor's courtyard without offering a defence that a curious rat couldn't scramble over.

The lingering smell of burning was still strong enough to disconcert his fractious mount. Corrain soothed the horse with a firm stroke of its glossy chestnut neck as he considered the manor's encircling wall.

Once it had been a solid bulwark of sturdy brick capped with ruddy tiles. Now it was scabrous inside and out with patches of plaster fallen away to reveal the brickwork beneath. Ominous cracks ran all the way down from the coping tiles to vanish into the foundations beneath the ground. If the corsairs were to attack with their grapnels now, Corrain judged that their ropes could bring down whole stretches of Halferan's defences.

He closed his eyes, rejecting abrupt recollection of the scavenging hordes whom he and Anskal had discovered looting the abandoned buildings. Though that enabled him to picture more clearly the brutal blast of azure magic which had killed some corsairs outright and levelled buildings to crush the rest.

Corrain opened his eyes. That bell couldn't be unrung. Wizardry was the Archmage's concern and until Planir of Hadrumal chose to exact some retribution for his crimes, Corrain must turn this wasteland of broken brick, burned wood and shattered plaster into the reassuring, imposing heart of a barony. How could Baron Halferan command any respect from his noble neighbours as long as he was crammed into an inadequate hunting lodge with servants cooped up in store rooms and half the demesne folk sleeping on floors?

And coming here, Corrain himself would be relieved of Zurenne and Lady Ilysh's constant questions. The physical trials and personal anguish of camping in a guardsman's tent amid the ruins of his dead lord's former honour was a small price to pay.

'Ca—' Master Rauffe managed a creditable pretence of a cough. 'My lord baron? What are your orders?'

Corrain wanted to ask the man why he had not returned to Licanin once the parliament had decided Halferan now lay beyond his liege lord's purview. Was Rauffe's status as steward here so much better than whatever he might return to? Or was he still Licanin's spy as the grey-haired baron played a longer game of white raven?

Such questions were currently moot. Rauffe was a most capable and efficient steward and no one else in this household could do nearly so good a job.

'Clear this entry.' Corrain gestured at the choked gatehouse. 'We must be able to get wagons in and out. Then establish our accommodations.' He nodded at the dray which had rumbled along at the rear of their ramshackle column, carrying bedding and food for their journey, tents and tools for their stay here.

'My lord.' Rauffe nodded and twisted in his saddle. 'Sirstin! Gartas!'

Corrain urged his balking horse aside with insistent hands and heels as the blacksmith and the erstwhile reeve of the Halferan demesne answered the steward's summons. The rest of the men and boys who had trudged across the barony from their Taw Ricks refuge spread across the unkempt grass between the manor and the brook.

The weariest dropped to sit slumped, heedless of lingering dampness after the night's rain. Others were wound too taut by grief and outrage to stand still, walking instead in aimless, frustrated circles. A few stood motionless some distance downstream. They were looking at the broad black scar on the turf where funeral pyres had burned for all of those killed amid the manor's destruction.

All of the Caladhrians, Corrain reminded himself. The corsairs executed by Anskal's magic had been thrown into fellmongers' wagons, driven to the edge of the marshes and dumped in a charnel pit.

Their flesh would be slowly eaten by the silver reed lizards, their eyes pecked out by the crows, their bones stripped by the brindled marsh kites. Their shades should suffer a generation's torment at the claws of Poldrion's demons, so the Halferans told themselves with satisfaction, until that long-delayed day when no last scrap of their earthly bodies remained to tie them to this world.

Corrain had considered telling them that the Archipelagans didn't believe in Saedrin or his judgement or his door to the Otherworld. But what good would that do anyone?

He watched as Sirstin and Gartas passed on their so-called baron's orders. Some of the skills he'd learned as a guard captain served him well in this new role. He had learned long since that a wise commander let competent men get on without unnecessary interference

Corrain knew Gartas of old; a diligent man well respected by those who laboured in these fields surrounding the manor and supplying its needs.

Those families had lived in the village on the far side of the brook along with those of the manor's servants who didn't live within the encircling wall. It was now a pitiful sight; every thatched cottage burned, workshops and tithe barns ransacked, their doors and windows swinging on broken hinges. Rebuilding those homes and re-establishing men and women in their livelihoods was as important as restoring the manor. A baron's honour was reflected in the prosperity his tenants enjoyed.

Corrain still didn't know Sirstin beyond a passing wave of acknowledgement but his lad Linset was proving his worth to the guard troop. While a reliable hound could sire a troublesome whelp, it was far more uncommon to get a good-natured pup from a tainted bloodline. Besides, the blacksmith wouldn't have been offered the manor's forge if he hadn't proved his skills with hammer and anvil. Nor would he have become so proficient in his craft without a good measure of common sense.

The physical contrast between the two men was marked. Sirstin's shoulders and neck were thickened with the muscles of his calling and he strode ahead with the vigour of a man in his prime. Gartas had grown bald and stooped amid his ledgers and followed at a pace husbanding his strength.

The Halferan men gathered. Corrain knew most of their faces and could probably separate the craftsmen from the labourers but he would be hard-pressed to put a name to each and every one as his own dead lord had done. Though there was one face he couldn't see.

'Master Rauffe?' He summoned the steward politely. His dead lord had been scrupulously courteous to his servants down to the humblest lackey.

'Where's Astirre?' he asked with foreboding.

'The mason?' The steward shook his head with regret. 'He died in the attack. May Saedrin see him safe to the Otherworld.'

'I'm sorry to hear it.' Corrain contemplated the encircling wall and thought about winter's approaching storms. If rain and frost got into the weakened brickwork to crumble the mortar, a gale sweeping in from the sea could all too easily bring down a calamity on someone's unsuspecting head.

'Did he have an apprentice?' he asked. 'When did he last send a journeyman out to another village?'

'I will find out,' Rauffe assured him.

Corrain nodded but wondered how many skilled craftsmen the barony had lost along with all the knowledge they hadn't yet found time to teach their apprentices. He realised with growing misgiving that such deaths were likely to be all the more devastating as the most proficient in every skill naturally headed to a barony's manor in hopes of their liege lord's personal favour.

'Captain!' An alarmed voice hastily corrected itself. 'My lord baron!'

Corrain turned his horse to see a small troop of horsemen emerging from the woodland framing the high road northwards.

Those men with swords or daggers drew them. The rest readied prybars and mallets.

'Halferan colours!' Corrain yielded to temptation and gave his chestnut mount its head.

The beast sprang forward, eager to escape the scent of burning. He let it gallop down the well-made track towards the curve of the brook, following the shining stream for a few plough lengths before veering away towards the high road.

Fitrel was at the head of the horsemen already cantering to meet him.

'Sergeant!' he called out as he reined in the eager steed. 'Report!'

Fitrel was always the first to remind Corrain that he must keep his distance from his former barrack-room equals.

The old man rode forward, his weather-beaten face deeply lined with weariness. It had been many a long year since he'd last ridden the barony's boundaries and that was a demanding task for younger men; long days in the saddle followed by comfortless nights with the ground softened only by the blankets rolled behind his saddle.

'My lord baron.' Fitrel saluted smartly nevertheless.

'What's the news from the east?' Corrain braced himself.

'Herdsmen from Wanflest and Antathele.' Fitrel scowled. 'Well inside our borders and all saying that they were searching for their own stock lost in the panic over the corsairs.'

Corrain was prepared to give the Antatheles some leeway. That barony flanked Halferan lands away to the south and east and if the marauding corsairs hadn't reached that far inland, the populace could hardly be blamed for fleeing ahead of the fearsome threat. He had judged Antathele's guard captains to be honourable men over the years.

'How many of our own cattle and sheep were they driving home?'

'A handful or so mingled in with their own.' Fitrel glowered. 'We checked the beasts' brands, you may be sure of that. They swore to Ostrin they'd made an honest mistake and readily surrendered the animals,' he allowed grudgingly.

Which explained the absences which Corrain had noted in the troop's muster. Reclaiming livestock also meant losing men to herd them to the closest village.

'And where our lands march with Wanflest?' Corrain was much less inclined to give any benefit of the doubt there. With his lands north and inland to the east, only touching Halferan thanks to a long finger reaching past Karpis, Baron Wanflest hadn't seen a single corsair set foot within his borders.

That hadn't stopped his guardsmen brutally repelling those fleeing from Halferan, so Fitrel had heard around Ferl's taprooms. Add to that, while Lord Antathele had abstained in the vote in parliament, Baron Wanflest had apparently been loud in his support of Baron Karpis.

'We found plenty of his men's traces.' Fitrel's

expression grew more grim. 'Half the standing crops in our fields have already been cut to stubble. Our tenants said they were penned up in their villages for a handful of days at a time. Anyone venturing out was beaten senseless by howling men with soot-blackened faces dressed in motley-coloured rags.'

Corrain scowled. 'A festival masquerader's notion of the Aldabreshi.'

'We're supposed to believe that these island barbarians carefully harvested those crops and carted them away in wagons leaving the tracks we found,' Fitrel spat with savage sarcasm.

'So it'll be a hungry winter.' Corrain rubbed a hand over his chin, feeling the stubble of his days on the road. The shackle around his wrist snagged a strand of his untidy hair.

He had sworn an oath on both those tokens, to himself and his dead lord's memory. He would see this land and its folk safe from the cursed corsairs, or so he had spat at Talagrin's statue.

He knew exactly how to make these thieving Wanflests pay. He would lead a guard troop inland and follow those wagon tracks all the way to the barns where those bastards had stored their plunder. They'd reclaim Halferan's winter stores, aye and use the flat of their sword blades on anyone who tried to stop them.

But of course, Corrain couldn't do any such thing. He wasn't Halferan's captain of guards, trained for such duty since he was a beardless boy. Halferan's baron couldn't lead such a raid. And he couldn't send this troop to reclaim the stolen harvest regardless. These guards were all too old or too young to prevail against Wanflest's handpicked ruffians.

But Halferan's entire populace was relying on him, as surely as they had once relied on his dead lord and the guard troop who had died in the marshes.

Corrain was beginning to fear, very seriously, that he could not measure up to their expectations. Oh, he was confident that he could meet any one of these challenges; commanding the guard troop, taking charge of rebuilding the manor, even running the household once that was done, should Master Rauffe and his wife return to Licanin.

Though playing the part of Halferan's baron remained a daunting prospect, he had bested the other noblemen in their parliament once, so as long as he stepped carefully, he should survive the next gathering.

But how was he to manage all these things, with so many constant and conflicting calls on his time? He could barely address one problem before a handful more came clamouring.

'My lord baron,' Fitrel prompted.

'I will write to Baron Wanflest.' Not that Corrain had any notion of how to frame such a letter.

Could Lady Zurenne advise him? She was currently sorting through the remnants of the barony's archive back at Taw Ricks. Perhaps she would find something to guide them?

'Yes, I know how feeble that sounds,' Corrain snapped before the old sergeant could speak. 'But it's the first step to laying the matter before the Winter Solstice Parliament.'

By which time, those harvested crops would have been eaten or Wanflest would claim they had been lost to damp or rats.

'No, my lord baron.' Fitrel sounded as exasperated

as he had been long years ago, whipping the callow Corrain into line. 'On the eastern road!'

Corrain stood in his stirrups, unable to believe his eyes. 'Get the troop down to the manor and see the horses watered and groomed,' he ordered through gritted teeth.

Furious, he spurred his mount into a startled gallop. The three riders on the eastern road slowed, their horses shying at the chestnut thundering towards them. Two horses anyway. The donkey bringing up the rear regarded his approach with stubborn indifference.

'What are you doing here?' Corrain didn't know who to berate first; Lady Ilysh or young Reven.

'My place is by your side.' For all her bold words, Ilysh sagged in her saddle.

'Your place is at your lessons and heeding your lady mother!' As hotly as Corrain spoke, his blood ran cold at the thought of this trio of fools unaccompanied on the road.

What would become of the barony if Ilysh were to be killed or worse? Little Esnina would be the next heiress and prey to all those claimants Corrain had only so recently faced down. There was no way under the sun, both moons and all the stars that those noble lords would stand for him and Zurenne contriving a second marriage of convenience.

'My mother is no longer Lady Halferan.' Ilysh's defiance returned as she thrust a shaking finger toward the shattered buildings. 'It is my duty to see my manor restored!'

That dramatic gesture provoked her ill-tempered grey mare into a buck that could have well unseated her if the beast hadn't been so tired.

Reven's firm hand was there in an instant. 'My lady—'

The lad gasped, his words cut short. The gleaming point of Corrain's sword pressed against his throat.

'What were you going to do if you stumbled across a band of corsairs?' he snarled. 'Or freebooters from Attar or Claithe, prowling on the nod from Lord Karpis? You only carry one blade. Were you relying on Abiah to defend your open side?'

Though he supposed he should be grateful that one or other of these idiot children had appreciated the necessity of a chaperone.

Corrain's hand shook as he remembered how he had also sworn never to honour Talagrin again until he saw the lad Hosh safe at his old mother's fireside.

Reven yelped, but seeing the bloody scratch was no worse than a razor scrape, Corrain swallowed his impulse to apologise. That soreness could keep the lad mindful of the possible consequences of his folly.

He turned his anger on Ilysh. 'How dare you defy your lady mother? She will be frantic with worry!'

At least until Lady Ilysh returned with a fitting escort. But that was a new thorn in Corrain's shoe. He didn't want to send Fitrel's hard-pressed guard troop back to Taw Ricks. Once men and horses alike were rested, they must travel south to wave Halferan's colours in Tallat faces.

Ilysh's voice rose to something perilously close to a wail. 'I left her a letter!'

'My lord baron.' Old Abiath spoke.

'What have you to say for yourself?' Corrain wasn't about to spare the frail old woman, even for Hosh's sake. For one thing, she looked the least travel-worn of the trio. Not so frail then, for all her slight stature and her shawl-wrapped grey head.

She ignored his question. 'Look to the manor, Lord Halferan, and to the demesne men.'

Corrain wasn't about to be distracted. 'You can rest here till I can find you fresh horses. Then you'll be on your way back to your mother.'

'I won't!' Ilysh teetered on the brink of tears. 'I am the lady of Halferan!'

'You will. I am your husband and your liege lord and you will do as I command!' Corrain reprimanded Ilysh as harshly any rebellious recruit to the guards' ranks.

He couldn't think what else to do. Corrain had no experience of dealing with barely blooded maidens, noble or common born. Truth be told, he had scant experience of living with women of any age. His mother had died labouring to deliver the babe who would have been his sister before he'd seen his tenth summer. When his father had died not long after, Fitrel had taken him in and the old sergeant-at-arms had lived his whole life unmarried. While Corrain had enjoyed plenty of female companionship, he generally left his lovers sleeping before their bed sheets had time to cool.

Those tears trickling down Ilysh's cheeks unnerved him horribly.

'Ca—' Reven's tongue stumbled in his anger. 'My lord—' His words were drowned out by rising cheers from the ransacked manor's compound.

Corrain turned to see what was afoot, thankful for an excuse to pretend not to hear the boy's insolence and not have to punish him for it.

He saw the work gangs had all halted, along with

Fitrel's guardsmen picketing their horses in the rough pasture along the brook.

The men were all hallooing. Some waved their shirts, stripped to save the linen from sweat and dirt. As he watched, he saw them realise that their lady had seen their greeting. They returned to their labours with alacrity, calling out encouragement to each other.

'They'll work all the harder for their lady's sake,' Abiath remarked, 'and they'll take it hard if you don't trust them to keep her safe and comfortable here.'

'Reven was only doing my bidding.' Ilysh scrubbed the tears angrily from her face. 'You cannot whip him on my account.'

Corrain would much rather deal with her angry than weeping but he wasn't having that. 'I will discipline my guardsmen as I see fit, my lady wife.'

Satisfied to see Ilysh bite her lip, he glared at Reven and jerked his head towards the picket lines between the manor and the brook.

'Report to Sergeant Fitrel and see to your horse. I'll deal with you later.'

Corrain took Ilysh's bridle from Reven and felt the tremors of the grey mare's exhaustion. 'You've ridden this poor beast to her knees, you silly girl.'

'You can't—' Ilysh bit her lip again as evidently she recalled Corrain could now speak to her exactly as he wished.

'Abiath.' He looked at the old woman. 'Tell Master Rauffe to set up a tent for you and Lady Ilysh in the most sheltered spot he can find. Set up my own tent beside it.'

'As you wish, my lord baron.' With a look he had no hope of interpreting, she urged her donkey forward.

Corrain dismounted with a curt nod to Ilysh, gathering both horses' reins in one hand. 'We'll walk.'

Ilysh opened her mouth, thought better of it, and slid from her saddle in a flurry of dusty skirts and begrimed petticoats. As her boots reached the ground, her knees buckled.

Corrain barely managed to wrap his free arm around her waist to keep her from collapsing completely. 'Didn't you rest at all last night?'

'We had to stop when the moons set.' Ilysh wriggled free before thinking better of such independence and threading her hand through his elbow as a compromise.

Corrain could feel how heavily she was leaning on him and curbed his long stride to her maidenly pace. The horses were content to walk placidly behind them.

Ilysh heaved a sudden sigh.

'What is it?' Corrain asked warily.

'All… that.' Ilysh gestured helplessly at the devastation ahead.

Corrain was sorely tempted to sigh himself. 'I know.'

'Why won't you let the wizards help us?' Ilysh looked up and her hand went to the rune sigil pendant around her neck. 'The Archmage has offered. He has already helped us. My mother, my sister and I would all be dead in a ditch if it wasn't for Madam Jilseth's wizardry.'

But the Tormalin magewoman Merenel had not come to give Ilysh her white raven lesson, as she had been supposed to, on that day when Corrain had returned to Taw Ricks, or since.

'There are considerations you're not aware of.' Though Corrain couldn't think how to explain his fear of wizardly retribution to the girl.

When would the Archmage demand that he answer

for bringing that Mandarkin mage southwards? How much could he achieve for Halferan before that happened?

He cleared his throat. 'You can rest here overnight, then—'

'I swapped marriage vows with you at Drianon's altar for the sake of keeping Halferan safe.' Ilysh's intense expression reminded Corrain irresistibly of his dead lord. 'Why won't you allow me a say in the barony's future, when it's my bloodline that makes you its lord? I know my father did something which my mother wishes to keep a secret and I believe it has to do with his appeals to Hadrumal but I'm not interested in such tangles. I want to see Halferan restored.' Now she was pleading with him. 'Why can't the wizards help us?'

'Because they have other concerns,' Corrain said harshly.

By all that was sacred and profane, that was surely the truth. What was happening in the corsair's anchorage? Was that why Merenel hadn't returned?

He watched Abiath on her plodding donkey approaching the gatehouse ruins. What had become of her beloved Hosh?

All the questions besieging Corrain tormented him like gadflies.

— CHAPTER ELEVEN —

Black Turtle Isle
In the domain of Nahik Jarir

HOSH RUBBED HIS eyes, gritty with lack of sleep. He glanced up at the sky, wondering how long it might be before the rain began to fall today.

'Have you seen some omen?' Anskal instantly demanded.

'No.' Hosh yawned so wide that he felt his jaw crackle.

'Where are they?' The Mandarkin's patience was wearing ominously thin.

They had been sitting waiting since first light on the terrace by the kitchen steps of the pavilion formerly claimed by the *Reef Eagle*'s master. Even though Hosh had explained how long it would take Nifai to cross the island.

He could only trust that Anskal wouldn't kill him now that the meeting the wizard had sought was so close. After all, the Mandarkin hadn't skewered him with some bolt of lightning when he had finally returned to relay Imais's message; Nifai would come when the stars offered him most protection and not a day before.

Perhaps it would help to remind him. 'The Ruby has moved into the arc of Honour and joined the waxing Pearl. They're with the stars of the Vizail Blossom for this one day. Those are all omens promising your good faith.'

Anskal's sideways glance silenced Hosh more effectively than a slap in the face. The boy looked down at the ground below the terrace. He couldn't read anything in the wizard's hooded gaze, certainly not good faith.

But there were other stars which should surely persuade Nifai to run this risk. The Diamond had shifted into the arc of Death and now rode with the Amethyst for new inspiration with the Mirror Bird whose feathers supposedly turned magic back on those who used it. Two jewels in each of those arcs made for a powerful portent, all the more so with the Opal for truth waning in the arc of Foes, tangled in the stars of the Net.

As long as Nifai hadn't seen some other omen to dissuade him. Seeing a mothbird in the daytime. Seeing a spider's web between two trees of different kinds. A pattern of crosses left on the sand at low tide. A lamp flame dividing into two, if any of the fugitive corsairs had such a thing to light their nights. And those were only some of the portents promising bad luck. Hosh didn't doubt that the Aldabreshi had a handful more for each one he knew of.

He looked up again as he heard rustling leaves. There couldn't be anything large enough left uneaten on the island for that to be an omen. It must be Nifai.

As he saw the overseer appear amid the undergrowth now choking the path through the ironwood trees, Hosh froze. Ducah had come with the overseer.

He was an Archipelagan straight out of a mainlander's nightmares. Half a head taller than even Corrain, he was the tallest man whom Hosh had ever encountered and far more heavily muscled than the wrestlers who travelled Caladhria's markets and festivals. He had overseen *Reef Eagle*'s master's affairs here ashore whenever the raiding vessel was voyaging.

His ebony back was ridged with whip scars. Ducah never sought to hide them, going bare-chested however cold and insistent the rain. So everyone could marvel at the strength that had seen him survive such a flogging. They could wonder in awed whispers what feats he must have accomplished to escape an oar slave's chains and rise to such a privileged position.

Hosh reckoned that the villain judged a day when he didn't kill someone was a day wasted. The slightest provocation, or often none that Hosh had seen, ended with Ducah's curved blade slicing off someone's head or hooking out their entrails.

Yet now, the instant the brute saw Hosh and the wizard waiting, he balked like a packhorse scared by some shadow. That was hardly good news. If Ducah was terrified, his first instinct would surely be to lash out with the swords thrust through the sashes wound around his hips.

Hosh fought not to touch his arm ring for reassurance, settling for a silent prayer that it would truly save him from one last glimpse of the damp earth coming up to meet him as Ducah's blade swept his head from his shoulders.

But who should he pray to? Hosh realised with a shock that his mother had never spoken of any god or goddess having an interest in magecraft.

If Ducah could have been a wrestler, Nifai had the build of a runner likely to win prizes in every festival's foot races. He betrayed less obvious nervousness, though he kept fiddling with the four large pearls he wore in each ear. Hosh could see the last holes still bleeding where the overseer had driven the silver hooks through his lobes that very morning.

His coppery forearms were weighed down with mismatched silver and gold bracelets all studded with lesser pearls which skilled craftsmen had halved on account of some flaw. These were highly prized here at this northern end of the Archipelago, as far as it was possible to get from the pearl reefs of the most remote south.

Ducah wore ropes of pearls around his neck, a double handful of strands iridescent against his dark chest.

Anskal smiled broadly. Hosh guessed he was pleased to see such proof that the corsairs had indeed fled with a good haul of their loot. He would have no idea of their trust in the pearls' talismanic properties.

'Good day to you.'

The Mandarkin spoke in his strongly accented Tormalin. Nifai looked guardedly at Hosh, who saw that though the Archipelagan had understood, he had no intention of answering.

Ducah's expression was too thunderous for Hosh to tell if he had understood Anskal or not. His lip curled on the brink of a sneer as a gust of the shifting breeze from the sea carried the rank stink of Anskal's unwashed body to them. Like all the Archipelagans, the corsair was scrupulous about his personal cleanliness.

Hosh didn't imagine he was impressed by Anskal's yellow tunic either, or his gauzy white trews embroidered down the side seams with scarlet sprays of vine blossoms. Hosh guessed that the garments had been sewn for some corsair's whore but he'd kept his mouth shut about that.

The Mandarkin mage pursed his lips as though

coming to some conclusion. 'I do not speak your tongue and I have no magic to do so,' he said to Nifai. 'That is the privilege of the Mountain enchanters.'

Nifai looked helplessly at Hosh, lost as to the wizard's meaning, for all that he understood the words.

Hosh quailed at the thought of trying to explain whatever it was called. Artifice? Aetheric magic? He had barely believed half the tales tossed around the barrack hall, of adepts speaking to each other across a thousand leagues and seeing through each other's eyes. Corrain had dismissed all the stories as nonsense.

Then again, Hosh had barely believed in wizardry until he'd seen Master Minelas's murderous spells and Corrain had been proved so wrong about so many aspects of Aldabreshin life.

He cleared his throat. 'There are different magics on the mainland. Master Anskal is only master of one.'

'Then we will speak as the broken-face slave does,' Nifai said warily. 'He can help us understand each other.'

Anskal looked up as the first drops of rain pattered onto the terrace's stones. For one appalling moment, Hosh though he was about to ward off the shower with some sorcery. If he did, this meeting was over before it had begun.

Instead the Mandarkin mage gestured first to the steps and then to the pavilion's broad eaves overhanging the terrace. 'I would offer you shelter. I would offer you food but Hosh says that my touch would taint it for you. Still, the boy brought those up from the cellar. I have not touched them.'

He gestured with his filthy hand towards a basket of wax-sealed bottles.

Well, that was a lie and a half to shame Trimon the teller of tales, as Hosh's mother would say. He had done no such thing. Why had the Mandarkin told such a falsehood?

He set that question aside as he hurried under the eaves to escape the strengthening rain. After a long moment's thought and glances of unspoken debate, Nifai and Ducah slowly climbed the steps to join them.

Whatever Anskal sought, Hosh saw his well-hidden satisfaction as the corsairs yielded to their thirst after toiling across the island.

Ducah twisted the wax off a bottle neck and drew the protruding cork out with his teeth. Downing half the contents in one swallow, he tossed a bottle to Nifai and as an afterthought, lobbed another one to Hosh. Nifai already had a knife in his hand to lever out the cork.

Hosh looked at the bottle in his hand. He had no way to get the cork out without a blade. Trying to work the stopper out with his teeth was out of the question. Hosh had lost most of his upper teeth where his cheekbone had been broken and the rest were none too securely rooted in his lower jaw these days. He wasn't about to risk condemning himself to starving to death.

'Boy!'

Looking up, startled, Hosh's hand instinctively snatched at the gleam of silver flying through the air. Anskal had thrown him a small folding knife.

'Drink,' the Mandarkin urged with a grin.

Hosh managed a grateful smile. He would rather have cursed. Now he could see fresh mistrust in Nifai's eyes as well as Ducah's.

And it wasn't as if he liked this fermented sap which the Aldabreshi tapped from one particular stubby tree.

They would cut off a dull greeny flower spike and lash a gourd over the oozing stump. Corrain had always said the stuff tasted like a stagnant puddle that a pig had pissed in. But Hosh wasn't about to give offence by refusing so he worked the cork free with the knife.

'You wished to speak with us.' Refreshed, Nifai challenged Anskal more boldly.

'Indeed,' the Mandarkin agreed. 'I wish to do you a service.'

Hosh's heart sank. Hadn't the fool wizard understood the Archipelagan loathing of magic?

He took a long drink of the reeking brew and thought of Corrain drinking Halferan's finest ale and regaling the tavern with tales of his exploits amid the Archipelagan slavers. The captain would explain how he had made the most of whatever opportunity had come his way. So Hosh folded the finger-length blade into its bone handle and slipped it discreetly into his trews pocket.

'You can do nothing—' Ducah took a step forward before recoiling as Anskal raised a warning hand.

As Hosh narrowed his eyes against the expected flash of magelight, he wondered why Ducah was here. To defend Nifai against any other corsairs wandering the island? Or had the brute come here to kill the mage himself?

Did Anskal realise the danger he was in? If the evil of elemental magic touched him, there could be no doubt that Ducah would attack. He could have nothing left to live for beyond spending his life to kill the wizard. Where would that leave Hosh?

There was no sign of magic. Ducah halted, eying the Mandarkin suspiciously. Hosh breathed a little more easily.

'The boy has told me of your people's hatred for magic,' Anskal said calmly. 'So I will take all the gold and silver and gems which I have found in these cellars and you will all deliver up whatever wealth you managed to carry off when you fled from my magic. You may consider this your payment for the service which I have rendered you.' He nodded airily towards the enchanted wave. 'Then I will allow your ships to sail away.'

Hosh didn't really think he needed to remind the Aldabreshi of his power and their plight.

'What is this service that you speak of?' Nifai asked, desperate.

'Ridding you of the magic which you don't even know you have here.'

Anskal's secretive smile made Hosh's blood run cold. In the next instant, his heart leaped in his chest from pure terror. Ducah's sword was flying towards his head. Not wielded by the bare-chested brute but whipped from its scabbard by sapphire magic.

Hosh was too shocked to duck or even to close his eyes, until his vision was seared by the brilliant glow erupting from the gold and crystal arm ring. Ducah's blade fell away as though it had struck a physical barrier.

'Your people—'

Whatever Anskal wished to say was lost beneath Ducah's venomous curses. The big man was ripping the looped sashes from his waist, hurling away the sword scabbard thrust through them. His curses rose to a deafening pitch as hatred for the wizard blazed in his eyes.

Nifai shouted something. Hosh didn't catch what the overseer said to silence Ducah but it worked. A good thing too, given Anskal's next menacing words.

'If you cannot curb your tongue, I will wrap you in silence and you may live with that taint on your skin as best you can.'

Ducah took a step backwards, something Hosh had never expected to see. The corsair's dark face was ashen with dread. Anskal nodded with malicious satisfaction before addressing Nifai.

'There is magic in these islands, though you do not know it. The wizardry that can be bound in trinkets such as the boy wears.'

Hosh looked down to see the magelight had shrunk to an amber radiance ringing his upper arm, visible through his sleeve. Well, there was no hope now of trading the gold and crystal for passage on an Archipelagan ship. Nifai's appalled expression told him that much.

'I have found several such artefacts among the treasures here,' the wizard continued. 'There will be more among the loot you have hoarded. I will take them off your hands and you may purify yourselves as you see fit.'

His smile curved like the mouths of those sharks which Hosh had seen following the galleys to eat the sick slaves who were thrown overboard.

'Or I can use my magic to hold you all in thrall as I search for them at my leisure,' Anskal offered, as Nifai and Ducah failed to answer him.

Hosh saw their shudder of revulsion. So the wizard had been paying attention when he had tried to explain the Aldabreshin dread of magic's miasma.

'Allow me to do you this service,' Anskal urged, 'and I will give you your ships once again.'

Were the Aldabreshi so desperate that they would make this deal? When the alternative was starving and worse, now with the unsuspected taint of magic among them? When as soon as they had rowed to some refuge, every galley and trireme, every oar and spar and scrap of rope and sailcloth could be taken to some deserted reef and burned into oblivion to rid them of the curse of sorcery.

Then Hosh would be safe, or as safe as he could be, imprisoned by this venal wizard. It wasn't as if the corsairs would ever sail back to this harbour, not after Anskal had released them. Once word spread along the sea lanes and through the neighbouring domains, no Archipelagan would ever set foot on this shore again.

'What say you?' Anskal invited Nifai. 'I will make good any damage which your ships have suffered.'

The overseer dragged his gaze from the magelight encircling Hosh's arm to look hollow-eyed at Anskal.

'No!' Ducah bellowed, fists impotently clenched.

'You mustn't touch the ships,' Hosh said urgently, 'or no one will be able to set foot on them.'

'I will put all this to the ship masters,' Nifai said hoarsely. 'I cannot answer for them.'

Even after all he had suffered, whatever Nifai's guilty part in all that torment, Hosh's gut twisted with unexpected anxiety. Would the overseer be able to explain before the half-crazed raiders killed him out of hand for merely talking to the wizard? Even weak with hunger enough of them attacking would overwhelm even Ducah's fearsome strength. Especially now that the brute didn't have a sword.

Anskal nodded, satisfied. 'You may go.'

Nifai and Ducah stumbled down the black stone steps. Within a few paces they were running headlong from the deserted pavilions.

Anskal laughed as the fleeing corsairs vanished amid the burgeoning scrub on the path to the bloody hollow and the far side of the island beyond.

'Let us eat and drink in more comfort.' Not waiting for an answer, he went into the pavilion's kitchen.

Hosh noticed faint cerulean radiance crackle through the falling rain. He recognised the magewrought defence that always enclosed whichever pavilion Anskal chose to sleep in.

So despite his show of confidence that he would get his way, the mage wasn't taking any chance that the trapped Aldabreshi might look for a third side of the rune bone which he had just rolled for them and try killing him instead.

Hosh sighed. At least he was inside the wizardry, if Ducah decided to vent his spleen by trying to kill him instead of the wizard.

He contemplated the brute's abandoned sword belts, scabbard and blade, before fingering the arm ring under his sleeve. Could the raiders have sorcerous weapons amid their unsuspected ensorcelled trinkets? Even if they didn't know what they were or how to wield them? If they did, could Hosh get his hands on one? If he did, what good would that do him? There could be no way off this island for him short of some magic.

So he had better make himself useful to the only wizard he was likely to find in the Archipelago. 'Master Anskal? Can I—' Hosh walked through the door only to find the pavilion's kitchen empty.

He went to look in the garden but there was still no sign of the Mandarkin. Puzzled Hosh searched the rest of the building; the kitchens at the rear, the audience chambers at the front and the bedchambers along the corridors that linked them.

He still couldn't find the wizard. Finally he returned to the terrace outside the kitchen. He looked at the faint haze of magic shimmering in the rain. He would wager all the treasure the Aldabreshi had stolen that he wouldn't be able to pass through it. So much as trying would most likely infuriate Anskal. What would be the point, anyway? Once Ducah and Nifai had told their tale, Hosh knew he would be considered irretrievably tainted by the Mandarkin's magic.

All the same, a sword might come in useful, some day. Thoughtful, he looked around. If anyone had followed Ducah and Nifai to spy on what they were doing, Hosh could see no sign of them among the ironwood trees.

So Hosh stowed Ducah's sword behind a long earthenware trough catching the rainfall from the roof. Imais had planted it with potherbs, now running riot for lack of tending.

Saedrin send he was unobserved. Was Anskal scrying on him, wherever the wizard had gone? Why should the mage bother? It wasn't as if Hosh could go anywhere.

He grimaced at a sudden fearful thought. Wherever the wizard had gone, what would happen if he was killed? Would his magic die with him? Or would Hosh be trapped here, to starve slowly to death once he'd eaten whatever remained unspoiled in the pavilion's cellars beneath the terrace?

Saedrin save him from such a fate, or Dastennin, god of sea and storm, or Talagrin the warrior's guardian or any other god or goddess who might hear his prayer, or his mother's entreaties in Halferan Manor's shrine.

— CHAPTER TWELVE —

FOR AN INSTANT, she didn't know where she was. Then Zurenne felt the carriage body sway on its leather straps and opened her eyes to see the trees thinning on either side of the road. Now she knew they were heading down the final slope towards Halferan Manor. Soon they would reach the junction where the high road headed inland, marked by the barony's gibbet so seldom used by her beloved husband.

She had hoped that they would reach Halferan the previous evening but the full of the Lesser Moon alone couldn't make the roads safe enough to drive the horses on into the clouded darkness. They had been forced to stop, though Neeny hadn't finally yielded to sleep until well after midnight's chimes. No wonder all three of them had fallen asleep in the carriage this morning.

Rubbing at the vicious crick in her neck, Zurenne looked out of the window to see the gaunt hanging tree approach. No bodies swung there to amuse the crows and to warn off miscreants. There had been no rule of law in Halferan since her husband's death. Master Minelas had shown no interest in such things and Lord Licanin had been arguing his case to stand as the manor's guardian at the last summer parliament.

Would Corrain have cause to condemn anyone at

the Autumn Equinox assizes? What would he sit on, to sit in judgement on those who had been so recently his equals? Zurenne tried to stifle an unexpected, almost hysterical laugh. Her husband's great carved and canopied chair, the hereditary barons' formal seat, must have been reduced to splinters and charcoal as the corsairs' raging fires gutted the great hall.

Opposite, Raselle stirred and opened her eyes. 'My lady?' She hurried to sit up straight.

'No—' Zurenne held out her hand.

Too late. Esnina's eyes snapped open. She wriggled free of Raselle's comforting embrace and scooted across the velvet upholstery to peer out of the carriage's window.

'We'll be seeing Lysha today, Neeny,' Zurenne said brightly. 'Won't that be nice?'

For a long moment, Esnina's plump lower lip quivered. Zurenne braced herself for a fresh bout of screaming.

Back at Taw Ricks when Zurenne had told her their destination, Mistress Rauffe had been forced to carry Neeny, kicking and sobbing, to the coach. There had been tantrums whenever they had halted on the road and every single time they resumed their journey.

Now, Drianon be blessed, Esnina simply looked defeated. Drawing her half-booted feet up onto the seat, she curled into a ball, burying her face in the crook of one elbow to deny everybody and everything.

'She's so tired.' Raselle looked guiltily at Zurenne, patting the child's rump in a helpless attempt at comfort.

'As are we all.' Zurenne managed a smile to reassure the maidservant.

It wasn't as though Raselle had anything to feel guilty about. Zurenne had no doubt that everyone they had encountered on this unwelcome, unnecessary journey had been looking straight at such an unruly child's mother.

The goodwives in those villages were doubtless passing judgement on her as they hemmed and embroidered in their sewing circles. They would be telling each other till midwinter that they had never realised what an ineffective mother their late baron's lady had been. Perhaps that explained her elder daughter's scandalous flight from Taw Ricks to her unsavoury husband's side.

They passed the mercifully empty gibbet. Zurenne noted by the hanging post's shadow that the sun had not quite risen to mid-morning. They had made very good time. Then again, the recent days had been mercifully free of rain blowing up from the south and the sea. So they had travelled speedily along dry roads between the wheat fields full of diligent men and women reaping whatever could be salvaged for harvest.

Now the road curved towards the devastated village. Zurenne caught sight of the manor. She sat up straighter. 'Oh!'

'My lady.' Raselle twisted to try and see without disturbing Esnina's stubborn immobility.

'They have cleared so much already.' Zurenne saw the gatehouse had been reduced to a footprint of knee-high walls. Salvaged bricks were stacked to one side and a circle of old men and young boys were busy with trowels, knocking away the last fragments of old mortar and plaster. As the coach drew nearer, Zurenne saw a diligent pair attacking a more stubbornly intact lump of fallen brickwork with hammers and chisels.

Older youths on the verge of manhood were at work

outside the manor wall and within, alongside their fathers and uncles. Robust grandsires trundled barrow loads of hopelessly broken rubble to a growing mound on the other side of the entrance.

Beyond, blackened and broken timbers had been laid out on the turf. Carpenters were shaping freshly felled trees to the original measure of the wreckage, to rebuild the guards' barrack hall or perhaps the stables. The cracking of wood riven by wedges and mallets offered a counterpoint to the rhythmic ringing of trowels and chisels. The fresh scent of newly sawn timber rose above the lingering stink of char.

A rider appeared alongside the coach window. Zurenne unhooked the strap to let the glass slide down into the body of the door.

'Where to, my lady?' Reven called out wearily. Well he might, after riding this road thrice in barely twice that count of days.

'Inside the walls.' Zurenne could see the creamy sailcloth of tents through the gaping void where the gatehouse had stood.

Cheerful hails greeting their carriage were raised ever more loudly. Esnina shifted her crooked arm, revealing her flushed, perplexed little face.

'Now, Neeny,' Zurenne warned hastily, 'there's a great deal of work to do, before we can come home.'

'But we will come home, my pet,' Raselle insisted, unbidden.

Esnina silently uncoiled herself from her sulk and went to look out of the window.

The coach rattled over the cobbles, halting beside the windowless shell of the baronial tower, beside the gutted great hall. The coach rocked jerkily as the horses fought with the coachman's reins, displeased at confronting so much commotion.

Zurenne welcomed the moment to compose herself. If Corrain had been furious at Lysha's arrival, as the letter he'd sent back with young Reven had made so icily plain, she didn't imagine he'd be much happier to see her and Neeny.

So she would explain, she told herself firmly, that Master Rauffe was needed back at Taw Ricks to manage that household's affairs, if only to stop his wife and Doratine from finally coming to blows. Since Lady Ilysh insisted that her place was at Halferan itself, Zurenne was here to show her how a manor should be properly run. And to offer whatever assistance she might with the business of rebuilding.

And who better to chaperone Ilysh than her own mother? Zurenne clenched her fists. She would dare Corrain to challenge her on the grounds that he was Lysha's husband.

'Raselle, if you please.' She nodded at the coach door.

The maid secured the window and opened the door. Unfolding the step down to the dirty cobbles, she got out of the coach and opened her arms to Esnina. 'Come on, my pet?'

For a tense moment, Zurenne thought the little girl would refuse and start wailing again. To her relief, Neeny stepped forward to be lifted out of the carriage.

The toiling men cheered in greeting. Raselle struggled for a moment but the child would not let herself be put down. She settled Neeny on her hip and the men all laughed indulgently as the little girl buried her face in the maid's shoulder.

Zurenne gathered up her skirts and stepped carefully

out of the coach. She looked around, startled by the fervour of her welcome. Just as it was dying away, Ilysh's appearance at the flap of her tent prompted a fresh hurrah.

With the devastated kitchen, brew house, bakery and laundry now all levelled, Zurenne could see the household's temporary accommodations stood on the laundresses' drying ground, between the manor's storehouses and the encircling wall.

Zurenne was pleased to see that Ilysh's tent was separated from the rest by an emptied wagon and still more pleased to see Lysha's apprehension. It was only right and proper that she should shrink from the prospect of facing her mother after such disgraceful defiance.

Then she wondered if the girl was merely hesitating over the uncertain footing. Her path was littered with the shards of broken tiles.

'My lady mother.' Well short of the baronial tower, Ilysh sank into a low and apparently dutiful curtsey.

Zurenne curbed her first impulse to chide her for dirtying her petticoat on the ashy ground. There was little point. Despite what must have been Abiath's best efforts, the girl's skirts were sadly creased and grubby.

Zurenne offered a measured curtsey of her own, hitching her hems rather higher than was dignified. She had noticed the ground glittered with splinters of glass, for all the sweeping brooms propped against the great hall's steps. 'My lady of Halferan.'

She held her tongue as Lysha's eyes widened with surprise. There would be time enough when they had some privacy to explain that her forbearance didn't mean that Lysha was forgiven, not in the slightest. But Zurenne knew what was due to the Halferan barony's dignity even if Lysha had that to learn. Along with so much else.

'Where is your lord and husband?' she asked her daughter with the remote politeness she would once have used to greet a previously unknown guest.

Even Neeny was so surprised at her mother's tone that she raised her head from Raselle's shoulder and stared, open mouthed. The maid seized her chance to put the child down.

Ilysh raised her chin, folding her hands together at her waist. 'He is consulting with Master Vachent, on the far side of the hall.'

Zurenne had no idea who this Master Vachent might be but nodded calmly all the same. She wondered what to say next. She could see that Lysha had no idea.

Abiath stepped into the awkward silence amid the bustle resuming all around them.

'My ladies both, shall I arrange a tisane tray?' She stooped to offer a hand to Neeny, though that was no great effort given her short stature. 'Would you like some blackcurrant griddle cakes?'

As Neeny nodded mutely, Zurenne saw Corrain come round the corner of the tower. He was accompanied by a man she wasn't familiar with, his voluminous workman's tunic heavy with stone dust.

'The first statue in your shrine after Saedrin's should be Misaen,' the man insisted, 'and you'll go down on bended knee to thank him before you start rebuilding.'

Ilysh asked before anyone else could. 'Why should we be so grateful, master mason?'

'My lady.' Master Vachent ducked his head in swift obeisance and then bowed lower to Zurenne. If she didn't know him, he clearly recognised her. 'My lady.'

'The walls of the great hall are sound!' Corrain declared this news to the assembled men rather than answer Ilysh directly.

Zurenne had seen them all slow in their labours. Some had been looking hopeful; others braced for bad news.

Corrain grinned at the workforce's cheers and exultant whistles. It was the first time that Zurenne had seen such an unguarded expression relieve his severe countenance.

'The topmost course of masonry gave way—' Master Vachent was determined to explain to Ilysh '—when the joists tying the roof together across the width of the hall burned through. If the stonework had held firm, then the whole weight of the roof would have borne down straight through the rafters right onto the wall beams.' He shook his head, his expression dour.

'That would have pushed the whole wall out of true, maybe brought it down, both walls front and back. But when those topmost stones gave way, the wall beams were shoved over the edge and the rest of the roof fell down to the hall floor.'

He nodded with what struck Zurenne as unwarranted satisfaction before his mouth turned down at the corners.

'Of course, all that wood fuelled the fire. There was no hope of saving the glass once the leading started to melt. So that all needs replacing. But the roof is the real challenge. We need wagonloads of seasoned timber. We can rebuild the barrack hall with green wood, since needs must but with Baron Karpis refusing us—' He shook his head.

Zurenne raised a hand. 'What has Baron Karpis refused us?'

'Seasoned wood, my lady.' Master Vachent girded

himself for further explanations. 'We cannot use fresh-felled timber. The sap—'

'Enough.' Corrain cut him short, addressing the men in the compound once again. 'Now that we need not fear the walls falling in on us, start clearing the hall's interior.'

Ilysh moved to stand in front of Corrain. 'This is surely something that wizardry could help with.'

Zurenne recognised that tone of old. So Corrain remained firm in his refusal to seek wizardly aid and Ilysh was still refusing to take no for an answer.

Corrain's expression turned severe. 'My lady wife, I suggest that you see to your lady mother's comforts.'

Seeing rebellion flare in Lysha's eyes, Zurenne intervened. 'I would like to visit the shrine. Will you accompany me, Lady Ilysh?'

She held out her hand, ignoring Master Vachent's assurances that the shrine was structurally sound.

Corrain was already walking away, shouting loudly to summon the blacksmith and the village reeve. Lysha had little option but to salvage her dignity by acquiescing to her mother's request.

'Of course.'

As they walked to the shrine at the other end of the stricken great hall, Zurenne noted the newly polished pennies nailed to the outer face of the door. When she had last been here, she had seen that the plundering corsairs had stripped away every last token in their godless greed.

Ilysh's barely repressed fury got the better of her after barely a handful of paces. 'Mama—'

'A moment.' Somewhat to Zurenne's surprise, Ilysh heeded her until they entered the low-roofed building.

The emptiness within silenced them both for a moment. When they had last been here together, the floor had been covered with broken statues, shattered urns and spilled ashes. Now all that destruction had been swept away to leave only hollow emptiness.

The structure had not escaped entirely unscathed, whatever Master Vachent might say. Narrow shafts of sunlight struck drying puddles on the patterned floor where roofing tiles had fallen away overhead. That must have happened when the Mandarkin mage killed all the corsairs. Zurenne shivered at the thought of the slaughter which Corrain had confessed to her.

'Mama.' Ilysh wasn't to be denied any longer. 'If we must have seasoned timber for the great hall's roof, can't wizards turn green wood into whatever we need?'

'Perhaps.' Zurenne had been wondering what Corrain had told Ilysh of the part he had truly played in the manor's destruction. 'Or perhaps we could simply purchase seasoned timber?'

'Why spend good coin when we have the Archmage's goodwill?' protested Ilysh.

'Why be beholden to any wizard?' Zurenne countered. 'Why not let Halferan's populace restore their own homes and livelihoods and regain some measure of pride? Let them throw their achievements in the teeth of the Karpis folk or whoever else might mock them.'

Since Zurenne had learned the full story of Corrain's dealings with the mage he had found in the distant north, she had agreed that Halferan should have no more dealings with wizards than was strictly necessary. The less they had to do with Hadrumal, the less chance there was of the corsairs' true fate becoming known in Caladhria. The barony needed no more scandal.

'The master mason is right.' Zurenne sought to turn the conversation as she contemplated the empty shrine. 'We must set up new statues and beseech every god and goddess's blessing on our new beginning. That's a fitting task for you as Halferan's new lady.'

A crash from inside the great hall startled them both. Before Zurenne could stop her, Ilysh ran to the interior door leading from the shrine onto the wooden dais. The high table had stood there, raised above the hall's flagstoned floor, along with the great canopied chair, as a visible symbol of the barony's authority.

Ilysh hauled open the door, intact though its frame was ominously charred by the fires which had raged beyond it.

Zurenne hurried to hold Lysha back on the threshold. She saw that her fears were justified. The dais was burned black with gaping holes where plummeting rafters had smashed through the boards.

'Mama?'

Zurenne looked up, expecting to see men opening the main entrance at the far end, ready to make a start on clearing the charred remnants of the fallen roof timbers.

'Who is that, Mama?'

Zurenne watched dumbfounded as the man walked across the wreckage. Because he was not clambering across the burned beams, nor cowering lest some perilously balanced truss tumble down to crush him.

This unknown man was walking across the top of the debris as easily as he might stroll along the highroad. Granted, he was undersized but Zurenne doubted that a mouse could leap so nimbly from one scorched foothold to the next without prompting some catastrophic collapse.

'Where is Corrain?' the stranger demanded.

As the man crossed the distance between them, Zurenne saw that his bare feet barely touched the charred wood.

'Who are you to ask so familiarly for the Baron Halferan?' Ilysh demanded incredulously.

'Hush!' Zurenne couldn't think how to warn her daughter.

This must surely be the Mandarkin mage. Corrain had described Halferan's saviour with unsparing accuracy; a dark-eyed man, his blond hair matted with filth, half a generation older than he was. Wretchedly stunted by lifelong hunger, he was so accustomed to privation that living unwashed and unkempt didn't trouble him.

Yet he spoke the Tormalin tongue, the language of all scholars and it seemed, most especially wizards. Though he looked nothing like Hadrumal's mages, dressed in an overlarge blue silk tunic belted with a length of dirty rope over baggy orange trews.

'Where is Corrain?' The Mandarkin cocked his head to study Ilysh. 'I am Anskal.'

His courtesy unnerved Zurenne. 'What do you want with us?'

'You might offer me some thanks for clearing your house of vermin.' The Mandarkin's red-rimmed eyes narrowed. 'I will take that silver trinket which you wear to begin with.'

'You received recompense.' Zurenne fought to keep her voice level. 'All the corsairs' loot!'

Threading her fingers through her daughter's, she squeezed hard enough to make Lysha gasp. Better that than risk her speaking.

'Your business with Baron Halferan is concluded.'

For the second time that morning, Zurenne summoned up the disinterested courtesy of a noble lady.

'Our agreement was based on trust and now I know that he lied.' The Mandarkin looked unblinking at Zurenne. 'I see that you know it too.'

'I have no notion what you mean.' Zurenne trembled. Was her ignorance to be the death of her and Lysha?

The Mandarkin's harsh laugh startled them both into a backward step.

'You lie to my face with the evidence hung around both your slender necks? Enough!' he continued impatiently, jabbing a dirty finger at Zurenne's pendant. 'I have searched but I cannot find where he has hidden more such treasures as those. So tell your man to deliver up all such magic that you have.'

His face hardened, more menacing. 'Or I will bring my corsair ships north to take such treasures, along with anything else that my raiders desire.' He looked Lysha up and down, blatantly lascivious.

Then he smiled, as sudden as a lightning flash. 'I'm willing to trade something that he values. I have his boy, the one taken with him.'

'Hosh?' Ilysh gasped. 'Abiath's Hosh?'

'He is safe—for now.' There was no mistaking the Mandarkin's threat.

'I will—' Zurenne stammered.

'Oh, no, pretty one—' The Mandarkin lunged forward, his hand clawing at Lysha's rune sigil.

In the blink of an eye, Zurenne saw that the girl had been about to touch the silver pendant. To summon the Archmage's help?

Lysha screamed and recoiled, tearing free of her mother's grasp. Quick as a whiplash Zurenne slapped the Mandarkin mage's face. She staggered backwards, her hand stinging. She wondered frantically what had possessed her to do such a foolhardy thing.

The mage stood motionless for a moment before bursting into chilling laughter.

'I should know better than to threaten a mountain cat's kitten. Very well, my pretty one,' he said to Ilysh, 'keep your guardian's trinket for the moment. I will know how to find you when I want it and I can fathom its secrets once I have taken you both.'

He rounded on Zurenne. 'Tell your man Corrain to give me what I seek or I will seize every last thing which he values and leave him ruler of a wasteland strewn with his dead.'

In the next instant, the terrifying man vanished.

'Mama?' Lysha whispered fearfully.

Before Zurenne could answer, the outer door to the shrine flew open. Young Reven stood there, Sergeant Fitrel behind him.

'You cried out?' Reven only had eyes for Ilysh.

'My lady?' The grizzled guardsman searched the room before pausing by the open door to the dais.

'Something fell and startled my daughter.' Zurenne had herself ruthlessly in hand. She shot a warning look at Lysha and was pleased to see her daughter obediently silent. 'Where is Baron Halferan? I will speak with him now.'

'He's seeing what's to be done with the forge.' Reven explained as though that meant Corrain couldn't possibly be interrupted.

'Kindly tell him that I must speak to him without delay. I will be with Lady Ilysh in her tent,' Zurenne said firmly.

'At once.' Fitrel ushered Reven through the outer door.

'Mama?' Ilysh asked in a small voice. 'What did that man want? Where did he go?'

'I don't know.' Zurenne hastily corrected herself. 'That's to say, I think I may know but we need to talk to Corrain.'

She gazed through the open door into the ruined great hall. 'I think we may need the Archmage's assistance with more than clearing fallen timbers.'

If the price of her daughters' safety was surrendering Corrain to Hadrumal's justice, so be it.

— CHAPTER THIRTEEN —

Trydek's Hall, Hadrumal
14th of For-Autumn

'THAT IS ALL very well, Archmage,' the Hearth Master said testily, 'but there is only so much we can infer from what this pestilential Mandarkin has not done or where he hasn't been. We need to know what he is doing on that island. Then we might have some hope of divining exactly what he seeks.'

'It must be something significant,' Cloud Master Rafrid murmured, 'for him to threaten Lady Zurenne so. How long do you think he will wait before he returns to Halferan?'

'Or before he makes good on his threat to send the corsair raiders north again,' Troanna added grimly.

'What do you suppose he might do, when he realises that Captain Corrain cannot give him what he's seeking?' Kalion demanded. 'Because he has no more notion what that might be than we do! Archmage?'

As the Masters and Mistress of Element fell silent, Jilseth and Nolyen stood as motionless as those statues of the Archmage's predecessors set in the niches around this spiral stair. Only motes of dust moved in the shafts of sunlight falling through the deep-silled windows.

Above them, through the open door to the spacious sitting room, they heard Planir's voice.

'I don't believe that the corsairs will do any wizard's

bidding,' the Archmage said thoughtfully. 'I don't think we need fear more raids.'

'I'm sure that will comfort Halferan,' the Flood Mistress said acidly, 'when the Mandarkin vents his spleen by levelling their rebuilding and kills them all for good measure.'

'Do we know what interested him so about Lady Ilysh's pendant?' Rafrid asked, more perplexed than hopeful.

'Have we had any word from Solura?' Troanna asked.

'From the Elders of Fornet?' As Planir paused, Jilseth could picture him shaking his head. 'Alas, no.'

'I have heard something from the Order of Raine, through the good offices of a mutual friend in Col, a mentor at the university.' Kalion's irritated sigh floated down the stairwell. 'They might be willing to share something of what they know of Mandarkin magic, if we are willing to share our insights into quintessential magic.'

Rafrid's loud objection met Troanna's outrage in a rare moment of accord between the two pre-eminent mages.

Jilseth looked at Nolyen to see if this meant anything to him. He could only shrug his shoulders in mute mystification.

In her apprentice and pupil days, Jilseth had often imagined presenting some notable discovery to Hadrumal's most senior mages. To prompt their congratulations and to persuade them to share fresh insights into her magic drawn from their far greater experience. She hadn't envisaged eavesdropping on them like some sly-faced maidservant.

Planir laughed wearily. 'We should admire their audacity.'

'Have we had any word from Suthyfer?' Now Cloud Master Rafrid sounded uncharacteristically impatient. 'Any insights from Usara or Shivvalan?'

'Any revelations from their Aetheric adepts?' Kalion asked waspishly. 'Any Mandarkin mysteries uncovered by the Mountain woman Aritane?'

'Not as yet,' the Archmage answered over Troanna's tsk of irritation. 'So let us see what we might learn from scrying across the corsairs' anchorage.'

He raised his voice. 'Nolyen, Jilseth, please join us.'

That left them with no option but to climb the remaining stairs.

'You did ask us to come here at the sixth chime,' Nolyen began explaining as they crossed the threshold.

'Indeed,' Planir reassured him. 'There was an unexpected occurrence in Halferan this morning.' His gesture explained the presence of the other senior mages accordingly.

Troanna turned all her attention to Nolyen and Jilseth. 'The Archmage says that you may have devised something to help us scry for the corsair anchorage where this renegade Mandarkin has his lair?'

Jilseth reminded herself that the thickset, gap-toothed woman habitually looked and sounded so stern that newly-arrived apprentices had been known to burst into tears and flee her audience chamber in the Seaward Hall.

'We're at your disposal,' Planir said easily.

Jilseth might have been more reassured if the Archmage wasn't dressed in a high-collared black doublet and broadcloth breeches. Had he come from some formal gathering or was he to attend one later in the day?

Speculation along Hadrumal's high road was growing ever more avid. The senior wizards of every hall and elemental discipline wanted to know what was to be done about this northern mage so insultingly and so improbably hidden away in the Archipelago.

Planir's face gave nothing away. He sat along with Kalion, Rafrid, and Troanna around the polished table big enough to accommodate the twenty or so other chairs set back against the walls. This sitting room took up the whole breadth of this tower below the private rooms traditionally granted to the Archmage. Planir was accustomed to teach his own pupils here, to instruct or to admonish those sent to him by the principal mages of Hadrumal's other halls.

There were also comfortable upholstered settles closer to the hearth. The Archmage generally preferred to welcome envoys from the island's merchants and yeoman, or from the mundane populace of the mainland, in less daunting surroundings than Trydek's Hall, that most ancient sanctuary of the mageborn.

Nolyen was setting out their scrying bowl and summoning water to cover the slick of bitumen already melted in the base.

As Nolyen nodded, the water glowed a heartening green. 'We have managed to tie this pitch to several ships in the corsairs' anchorage and now we have that link, it's far easier to find them a second time.'

'Show us,' Troanna commanded.

Jilseth took a chair from beside a window and sat opposite Nolyen. He didn't dare look at her and risk losing his focus on his spell. She rested her fingertips lightly on the rim of the bowl and concentrated on channelling his scrying through the alchemical pull of the bitumen; like calling to like in the black pitch sealing the wooden seams of those distant ships.

These past two days of concentrated application had enabled them to craft this magic without undue incident, she reminded herself firmly.

'We have it.' Nolyen's voice cracked with relief.

The image of the anchorage floated across the ensorcelled water.

Kalion was on his feet at once. As he stood beside Nolyen, he clasped his hands behind his back to avoid any temptation to touch the bowl. As he bent for a closer look Jilseth saw the tension in his rounded shoulders.

'Can we identify this place? How deep does this island lie within the Archipelago?'

'We cannot draw the scrying sufficiently far from the shore to find any other islands which we might recognise,' Jilseth was forced to admit. 'Though we believe that it's little more than sixty or so leagues from Cape Attar and on the westerly side of the Archipelago's northernmost string of islands.'

'These raiders must lair with reasonably easy reach of the mainland coast and ideally where they can navigate uncontested sea lanes.' Cloud Master Rafrid came to stand at her shoulder. 'The more warlords' domains they must cross, the greater their chances of losing their loot to some affronted ruler's triremes.'

Kalion was calculating distances. 'Then this renegade could be no more than a hundred leagues from Hadrumal!'

'Which domain was giving the raiders sanctuary?' Planir looked thoughtful as he remained seated at the head of the table. 'Was the warlord coerced or is he somehow complicit in their thievery?'

'Either way, he'll rue the day he chose not to stand firm against such parasites.' Rafrid's face hardened as he hitched up his midnight-blue tunic to shove his hands in his breeches pockets.

The Flood Mistress circled the table to stand on Nolyen's other side. If Rafrid was dressed like any merchant on Hadrumal's high road, Troanna's mossy gown suggested some briskly practical grandmother.

She leaned forward to study the emerald-framed vision of that foaming tongue of water curling up between the headlands. 'You've managed to work this scrying despite such intense water magic at work there.'

Jilseth guessed that was as much congratulation as Nolyen could hope for. Did the Flood Mistress have any idea of his struggles these past few days, to assert control over the scrying when that wave continually sought to compel his affinity like a lodestone skewing a compass? Jilseth could only hope so.

Troanna was still studying the ever-shifting, unyielding wave. 'We must unravel his spells in such a way that we can learn exactly how they are wrought, not merely smash through his wizardry.'

Kalion nodded firm agreement. 'Absolutely.'

'We mustn't try any such thing until we're certain we will succeed,' Rafrid said firmly. 'Evidently this new scrying doesn't impinge upon his own magic so we must not do anything to prompt him to foil us with more as yet unknown magecraft.'

'First we must master this new working,' Planir pointed out, rising unhurriedly to his feet.

Troanna had already laid her calloused fingers over Nolyen's. 'Let your spell flow through my affinity.'

Jilseth saw Nolyen's eyes widen. He smiled and she

barely felt a tremor in the scrying as he drew his pale hands out from beneath Troanna's. The Flood Mistress settled herself in the chair as Nolyen slid sideways to stand beside Kalion.

Planir walked around Rafrid and laid his long-fingered hands on top of Jilseth's. The great diamond of his ring of office glittered green with reflected magelight.

She felt the warmth of his fire magic spread through her own magecraft, blending seamlessly with his innate dominion over rare earths, ores and minerals to claim mastery over the molten bitumen.

'Excuse me, Cloud Master.' Withdrawing, Jilseth discovered how very awkward it was to swap seats like this.

Kalion flexed impatient fingers, the ruby on his own ring kindling. 'Shall we strengthen the working with a nexus, Archmage?'

'We are only testing the principle here.' Planir contemplated the emerald glow, thoughtful. 'The Mandarkin magefolk, like the Solurans, know little or nothing of quintessential magic but there's no assurance that this wizard wouldn't somehow feel such greater strength. It's not as though we're any great distance away. Let's fry the fish we've caught rather than use it to bait a hook and risk losing any chance of dinner.'

The intensity of his expression was at odds with such homely wisdom.

'I agree,' Rafrid said promptly.

Troanna was silently concentrating on the bowl. The emerald of the scrying flickered as a mist of magelight rose from the water. It shone bright with rainbow hues shifting on the very edge of sight. The mist cleared and the floating vision slowly began to drift along the anchorage towards the tree-fringed shore.

Now they saw the corsair ships abandoned by their terrified crews. A handful out in deeper water had dragged their anchors, presumably caught in the swell prompted by the Mandarkin raising that ensorcelled wave. Two galleys pressed close together, their oars tangled. Another was noticeably listing at the prow. Several triremes rode ominously low amid floating oars and spars.

'Their bilges are awash,' Troanna explained, though no one had asked.

'Can the vessels be salvaged?' Rafrid asked.

'Most likely,' Troanna replied after a moment's reflection. 'If someone goes aboard to pump the season's rains out of their bilges, and whatever's sloshed in through the oar ports.'

'That's hardly our concern,' Kalion said, dismissive.

'That depends on how much goodwill we might wish to secure from the Archipelagans,' Planir observed.

Jilseth saw the other three wizards look at him, surprised. The Archmage glanced up from the scrying.

'Goodwill is as readily traded in the Archipelago as foodstuffs, cloth and cooking pots, and worth far more than any mainland coin which they value only for the sake of its metal. How much stronger will our bargaining hand be, if we can offer those who've been trapped here a seaworthy means of escape.' He grimaced nevertheless. 'Always assuming that they're willing to risk taking passage in a vessel touched by wizardry.'

'They're at liberty to refuse and stay there till they starve,' Troanna said coldly.

'Perhaps we should consider devising the necessary omens to persuade them,' Rafrid mused.

Kalion was far more interested in the scrying than in any Archipelagan's fate. 'That trireme was mage-burned.'

Troanna sent the scrying to examine a blackened hulk half submerged in the shallows.

The other warships had fared better, especially those already beached when this calamity struck. As the scrying spell circled each one, Jilseth could see rope ladders dangling on either side of their upcurved stern posts, in contrast to the fixed wooden steps which the galleys favoured.

Kalion folded his arms, his expression grudging. 'This Mandarkin has considerable skills with fire, for all that his affinity is with the air.'

'One of his affinities,' Troanna corrected him. 'The magecraft underpinning that wave shows equal talent with water magic.'

A double affinity. Jilseth exchanged a wide-eyed glance with Nolyen. Such a thing was so rare in Hadrumal that the rawest apprentice damp with sea spray became the Archmage's personal pupil the moment they set foot on the dockside.

'He can only work with one element at a time,' Rafrid observed, 'for the most part and certainly for any significant spell crafting. I see nothing to indicate he has anything beyond the most basic understanding of quadrate magic.'

Kalion nodded. 'Much like the Solurans.'

'I don't believe we've seen enough of his wizardry to draw any firm conclusions.' As Planir spoke, the green magelight in the water shifted to a more yellowish hue. 'Let us not forget,' he added, 'that whatever their deficiencies in quadrate or quintessential magic, Soluran mages are very well versed in the aggressive wizardry which Hadrumal has long forsworn.'

'Indeed.' Troanna's face hardened.

The scrying left the beach to search along the shore. Moving inland from the debris strewn beach, the spell circled each of the abandoned pavilions. Through open doors and windows they saw furniture shoved askew or knocked clean over as the corsairs fled in utter panic.

Jilseth's hands began to tingle. It felt as though she had slept with one arm pinned beneath her and woken to the rush of returning sensation. But there was no such numb heaviness in her fingers. Quite the opposite. She could feel every bone, every sinew, the blood in her veins and the skin enveloping all.

'Archmage?' Kalion frowned.

Jilseth saw the amber hue of earth magic dulling the emerald magelight more and more. She could also feel Planir's long fingers laid over her own, just as he had done when he and Troanna had taken control of the magic. That was ridiculous. She was standing an arm's length away and she could see his hands resting lightly on the silver bowl's rim.

'Is that the Mandarkin?' Troanna snapped. 'Has he sensed our spell?'

The water in the bowl was seething like a pot come to the boil. Ripples of every hue of magelight skidded across the roiling surface.

Jilseth looked down at her hands. They glowed as though she had laid her palm over a lantern's glass. But such light would be red like the flesh that eclipsed it. This was the unmistakable amber radiance of earth magic.

'No, it's—' Planir broke off with a hiss of surprise.

Troanna had sent the scrying creeping, circumspect around the pavilions. Now the spell sped inside, diligently quartering every room.

Evidence of looting was plain for all to see; locked cupboards broken open, floor tiles pried up, scrolls and gold-embossed books swept from a shelf in search of... what?

The scudding visions left Jilseth nauseous. Her heart was racing with this urgency of the search, her palms burning with cold fire. Searing white light rose from her clawed hands. A burst of radiance darted across the room and enveloped the scrying bowl.

Now her affinity had control of the scrying though Jilseth had no hope of restraining her magic. Her wizard senses searched out every shard of shattered ceramic strewn across the floors, every stolen pewter bowl or silver spoon, every bronze pot, every splintered casket with twisted lock and hinges.

Now only one pavilion remained unsearched, on the south side of the anchorage, overlooking the open water where the headland narrowed. The building was veiled in azure light.

'No.' Planir spoke with soft, incontestable authority and the great diamond in his ring of office glowed.

The silver bowl rang like a bell, heedless of the water within to dampen such a note. The scrying veered away from the sapphire-warded pavilion.

'Who is that?' Rafrid's finger jabbed at the spell.

Unerring the spell shot forward until a slightly built young man filled the vision. He was walking back from one of the other deserted dwellings.

The youth dropped to his knees, the jar he'd been carrying spilling across the ground. He clapped his sword hand to his opposite arm with a scream of silent agony twisting his already distorted face. A fingerwidth above his elbow, white light flared, bright as burning quicklime.

The light died as the youth ripped at his tunic's tattered sleeve. The cloth yielded, rotted by sweat and seawater, though it hadn't so much as been scorched by that fierce light.

'Who is he?' Kalion was outraged.

'What is that?' Planir leaned forward, his grey eyes intense.

The youth wore a gilded arm ring ornamented with rough-hewn rock crystal. Amber magelight glowed in the heart of each translucent gem.

'He's not mageborn.' Rafrid shook his head in absolute denial.

'That trinket,' said Kalion with profound disgust, 'is ensorcelled.'

The youth was breaking his fingernails in his haste to unclasp the arm ring. He threw the gaudy trifle away. The scrying sped after it, only halting as the arm ring came to rest.

Jilseth could feel the spells resonating within the ornament. She couldn't begin to explain though how the strongest, most arcane warding spun from the volatile element of air had been confined within metal and gemstones in defiance of elemental antipathy.

Not yet, she couldn't. If her affinity could get a little closer. She took an involuntary step towards the table.

'That's enough of that.' Planir's ring blazed and Troanna's emerald magelight reclaimed the scrying.

The magic luring Jilseth towards the table shattered. Her hands ached as though they'd been slammed in a door.

'Archmage,' Rafrid warned.

'I see him.' As Troanna answered, the scrying retreated so far and so fast that the figures on the distant island looked like pieces on a game board.

A second man had come running out of the warded pavilion. Scorning the stone steps, he stepped in the empty air at the edge of the terrace and floated down to the ground as gently as a feather.

The youth was still on his knees. He flinched away from the newcomer like a dog expecting a whipping.

The Mandarkin didn't touch him, though his gestures spoke eloquently of a violent scolding. The menace was palpable, even at this distance, even with the man so ridiculously and gaudily dressed.

Rafrid scowled. 'If we could only hear—'

'No,' Planir said sharply. 'A clairaudience spell would brush against his air affinity.'

The Mandarkin's hand stilled. He stood, expectant.

The youth rose to his feet, tangled head hanging and bony shoulders hunched. He went to retrieve the arm ring, every step unwilling.

The Mandarkin watched him clasp it back around his arm, nodding with satisfaction before returning to the pavilion he had veiled with glittering azure magic.

The youth trailed after him, climbing the steps to sit on the terrace, hugging his knees. Though his face was hidden from view, the shivering rats-tails of his unkempt hair showed the distress wracking him.

'A mainlander, enslaved.' Troanna remarked, dispassionate. 'See how pale his skin is, where the sun hasn't touched it? And his hair hasn't seen shears in a year or more.'

'Some mother's son.' Planir withdrew his hands from

the sides of the silver bowl. The image trembled as the emerald magelight dulled.

Troanna removed her hands and the floating reflection faded to nothingness, leaving only the ungainly blob of the bitumen in the water.

Jilseth couldn't sense any of its properties, mundane or magical. Her affinity was as dulled as it had been when she'd first woken to discover that she hadn't died at the hands of the corsairs ransacking Halferan.

She blinked away tears. Could she leave the room before any of these wizards noticed her distress? But taking a step would surely draw all their eyes. At the moment they were still looking intently at the empty bowl.

'Do you suppose he knew,' Rafrid wondered, 'that there were ensorcelled artefacts to be found there?'

'How could he?' Kalion disputed. 'The wretched things hardly announce their presence, even to a mage, unless they're close enough to touch.'

'As far as we in Hadrumal know,' countered Rafrid. 'Who knows how far Mandarkin magic might reach?'

'The Solurans have always had a taste for crafting the tiresome things.' Troanna's lips thinned. 'The rot may well have spread further north.'

'We have no reason to think this Mandarkin's arrival on the island is anything but chance,' Planir asserted. 'Captain Corrain wasn't seeking him out, any more than the Mandarkin went looking for him. Their meeting was pure happenstance just as the Mandarkin discovering these artefacts was a random roll of the runes.'

'But now he's wondering what other such treasures he might find in Caladhria.' Rafrid looked at the Archmage. 'And he's scried out those pendants which you gave Lady Zurenne and Lady Ilysh and he believes there are more to be had.'

'Quite so.' Planir nodded, exasperated.

'By your leave, Archmage.' Nolyen couldn't restrain himself. 'Why do Soluran wizards instill magic properties into artefacts?'

'To leave their pupils some legacy of their wizardry,' Troanna answered, disdainful. 'Since their Orders come and go and they have no tradition of libraries or scholarship.'

'Crafting such trinkets has always been the lesser Orders' way of ingratiating themselves with the nobles who shower them with gold.' Kalion spoke with equal scorn.

'How do you suppose that arm ring ended up in the Archipelago?' Rafrid was fascinated.

Kalion continued instructing Nolyen. 'Magecrafting such a thing is no easy task. You would want the recipient to value it accordingly—'

'Make it from precious metal and gems and anyone will value it, whether or not they know its true nature,' Troanna interrupted, impatiently.

'The Archipelagans have an eye for such trinkets to rival a pied crow's.' Planir observed. 'That artefact could have passed through a hundred Aldabreshin hands. There wouldn't be any mageborn among them to realise what they held.'

'What will this Mandarkin do with it?' Rafrid wondered.

'He has a whole hoard of other such artefacts stowed in that house.'

Jilseth hadn't meant to say that out loud. She looked down at her aching hands.

'What precisely were you doing?' Troanna asked icily, 'when you turned our scrying into your seeking spell?'

'Jilseth?' Planir prompted. 'What happened?'

Her mouth was dry as dust. 'Forgive me, Archmage. I simply don't know.'

He smiled. 'I didn't ask you to explain. Simply tell us what you sensed, with your affinity and in yourself.'

With everyone looking at her, if Jilseth had still had the most tenuous hold on her wizardry, she would have risked it all in an attempt to shift herself away. But she didn't think she could take a step across the room without her knees giving way.

'There will be answers for us to find,' Rafrid assured her kindly.

Troanna looked down at the scrying bowl. 'I am rather more concerned to know if the Mandarkin realises we've found him.'

— CHAPTER FOURTEEN —

Black Turtle Isle

In the domain of Nahik Jarir

HOSH WONDERED WHICH god he had offended. Talagrin reputedly had a cruel sense of humour. It was a truly a savage joke that Anskal was nowhere to be found now that Nifai and the ship masters had finally found their resolve and come back to the anchorage.

Or had Poldrion's demons finally found a path through whatever Aldabreshin omens had been saving him from their claws? When the sunset marked the start of a new day by the topsy-turvy Aldabreshin reckoning, the stars of the Hoe would rise on the eastern horizon and the shifting heavenly jewels left nothing in the arc of Death but the stars of the Canthira Tree.

Imais had told Hosh that the plant epitomised the eternal, seasonal and unceasing circle of life and death, its seeds only sprouting after fires killed the parent tree. Did that mean Hosh should look forward to his own funeral pyre? The god of the dead was unrelenting, so chimney corner tales back home said, sending his minions in pursuit of anyone who should have already been ferried to the Otherworld. Surely Hosh should have been dead long since.

Except he reckoned it was Ducah who was most likely to kill him, not some taloned fiend from the Eldritch realm. The brute had got a new sword from somewhere, killing its former owner most likely. When he'd come to bellow from the path through the ironwood trees, yelling that the ship masters were ready to bargain for their freedom, the bare-chested raider looked more than ready to try testing whatever luck he'd read in some portent against whatever vile sorcery had saved Hosh.

Hosh did his best not to catch the fearsome man's eye as he tried to appease the men assembled in the stone encircled hollow. He ducked his head, his expression as humble as he could possibly make it.

He had considered bringing the sword that Ducah had discarded before concluding that his first instincts were correct. Carrying a blade risked provoking a challenge. He was better served by humility and trusting in the arm ring. Even if the cursed thing had behaved so oddly the other day. Anskal hadn't explained and Hosh doubted the wizard ever would.

'The... visitor will be here shortly.'

Hosh wished he could have asked Imais how best to refer to Anskal. Was there some Aldabreshin form of words to show he was the Mandarkin's most unwilling lackey?

Surely the rising stars of the Hoe promised reward for honest endeavour as long as the Diamond shone bright alongside the constellation? That should hold good for the next thirteen days, if Hosh's reckoning was correct. The moons alone would continue their dance round the sky until the Diamond shifted into the arc of Death. Hosh guessed that the Archipelagans would want to be long gone from here before that particular portent.

He quaked with fear as he saw the ship masters exchanging looks of outrage. Had he somehow just insulted them? Or was Anskal's absence the offence?

Who could tell with these men maddened by hunger and fear?

Hosh could only rely on his arm ring to protect him if they attacked. And he had to keep them here. Something had put Anskal in a truly foul mood. If the corsairs' nerve broke and they fled, Hosh wouldn't wager goatshit against Tormalin gold on the Mandarkin not killing him outright. And he had no doubt that the wizard could kill him, arm ring or not.

Nifai stepped forward from the glowering huddle. The copper-skinned man glanced nervously from side to side, only to meet threatening glares from the other ship masters. That worried Hosh still more.

'If there is one who would speak to us, let him come before us beneath the open skies.'

Nifai spat copiously on the bare earth.

Hosh hoped that Anskal wouldn't take offence, if he had seen that apparent discourtesy through his spying magic, wherever the bastard was.

If he hadn't, so much the better. Hosh didn't relish the thought of explaining that even referring so obliquely to the wizard left a taint on Nifai's tongue.

'I take it that spittle means that our friends won't accept refreshments on this visit?' Anskal sounded amused.

How long had he been standing in the deep shadows under the shade trees ringing the hollow, before strolling out to stand behind Hosh? That must have been where he'd been. If the Mandarkin had simply appeared out of thin air, the raiders would have turned tail and fled.

For one awful moment he feared they still would, if Anskal stepped across the shallow ditch to set foot inside the circle. He breathed a little more easily when he realised the Mandarkin had no such intention.

'No, they will not eat or drink anything that you offer them.' Hosh stared down at the ground, his shoulders hunched. Hopefully the corsairs would see how reluctantly he served this mage.

Except, he realised, they weren't looking at him at all. So Hosh could study them discreetly, his uncut hair hanging over his eyes.

The ship masters should have all looked ridiculous. Every man was armed and armoured as though for battle and then draped with all the pearls they had found in their plunder for talismans against magic. One thick-set and ebony-skinned man had a brass hand-claw bristling across his knuckles with delicate silver pearl-studded rings jammed onto his fingers beneath it.

But they didn't look absurd. The ship masters looked as dangerous as a pack of feral dogs. Hosh had once seen Corrain and brave, murdered Captain Gefren whip such a pack from the manor's gatehouse. Like those dogs, these ship masters might be cowed but given the sniff of a chance, they would rip out Anskal's throat and Hosh's too, for good measure.

None wore opals though. Then Hosh realised this night was the dark of the Greater Moon. What else might that mean by way of an omen?

'Mainlander!' Nifai snapped his fingers. 'There is one here whom you say wishes to offer us a trade?'

'They won't talk to me today?' Anskal was still more entertained. 'Never mind.' He waved a dismissive hand before Hosh could try to explain. 'Are they willing to hand over their treasures? In return for me releasing their vessels?'

'Are you willing—'

The corsairs were shouting their agreement before

Hosh finished speaking, including those who barely spoke a word of the Tormalin tongue.

'Very well,' Anskal approved. 'Tell them to follow me for proof of my good faith.'

He didn't wait for Hosh to explain, heading down the path through the ironwood trees towards the beach.

Hosh waited in fearful suspense. Nifai was the first to step out of the circle, Ducah at his shoulder. The rest followed, slowly at first and then treading on each other's heels as no one wanted to risk being left behind.

Anskal was waiting on the shoreline. As soon as half the ship masters had reached the top of the beach, he thrust out a hand towards the incessant wave.

More than half the Aldabreshi dropped to their knees, some wrapping their arms around their heads, faces pressed in the dirty sand.

Anskal's laughter was lost in the deafening noise of the impossible wave collapsing against the sunset. Every island bird which the starving corsairs hadn't managed to eat erupted from the fringe trees along the shore, screeching in panic. Hosh saw them tossed around by a swirling wind, as helpless as the feathered lures used to train Lord Halferan's hawks.

The pent-up water surged out of the anchorage into the open sea beyond. The ships wallowed, masts flailing and oars slipping from their rowlocks to bob uselessly amid the roiling waters. One trireme which had been safely beached was dragged into the shallows to crash ominous into the skeletal blackened ribs of blind Grewa's ship.

A foaming crest of water swept back in between the headlands, rearing up as the inlet narrowed. Some of the ship masters fled. Others, too terrified to move, froze where they were kneeling, pale sand smudging their ashen faces.

Two of the severely listing galleys were overwhelmed. The groans of the surviving vessels' abused timbers mingled with the Archipelagans' answering cries of distress.

The surge of water rose up the beach, only to retreat as the foam moistened Anskal's leathery feet. The tide line was left freshly marked by a glistening slew of wreckage.

'I have upheld my end of this bargain!' Anskal's voice echoed loudly around the anchorage. 'You will not depart until you have done the same!'

The *Knot Serpent*'s master wasn't listening. He was already splashing through the debris in the shallows.

A bolt of lightning from the cloud-streaked dusk sky struck the man's shaven head. The ship master toppled forward, dead, into the water. The skin of his back was split and blackened like an overripe plum, revealing seared flesh and the creamy bones of his spine.

As Hosh tried to blink away the smear of yellow scarring his vision, someone screamed closer at hand. The *Scarlet Fern*'s ship master had drawn a dagger intent on murdering Anskal. The man dropped the blade, pressing his hands to his own throat instead.

A shard of ice was stuck deep in the side of the corsair's neck. It was already melting in the Archipelagan heat, water glistening on the gurgling man's hands. Bloody runnels slipped down his forearms, writhing like veins. Inside a breath more blood than water flowed to stain the man's yellow tunic ochre. Unable to staunch the wound as the ice shrank away, the ship master died on a blood-choked curse.

'You will not depart until you have fulfilled our agreement.' Anskal looked at the motionless corsairs.

Hosh reckoned the ship masters would have swum for it and risked the sharks regardless if they didn't fear Anskal's sorcery dragging them back out of the sea.

'Bring all of your treasures to that pavilion.' Anskal pointed to the dwelling closest to the path, once the *Reef Eagle*'s master's pride. 'Once I have taken what I seek, you may board your ships and go, leaving all taint of magic behind. Tell them,' he ordered Hosh.

The ship masters stood motionless as he repeated the Mandarkin's ultimatum, groping for the most courteous phrasing in the Aldabreshin tongue.

When Hosh stumbled to a halt, no one spoke.

'Well?' Anskal betrayed the first hint of impatience.

Those who had first followed him to the shore retreated as swiftly. Those who had been slower were still lingering amid the deserted huts. Some withdrew while others dithered. Then a handful broke into a run and the rest followed in an utter rout.

'Very well,' Anskal said briskly, 'fetch me food and drink. It will be some while before they return.'

The Mandarkin's satisfaction revolted Hosh. But what else could he do but obey?

So he fetched some of the pickled roots that the wizard liked and strips of the goat flesh that Imais and the other women had rubbed with some fiery blend of spices to keep off the flies as the meat dried in the hottest season's sun.

Anskal settled himself on the pavilion's terrace and dined.

Ostrin send that the filthy swine died of some stomach rot, Hosh prayed silently. The god of hospitality was also the god of healing and demanded cleanliness in each undertaking. But Anskal never washed his filthy hands and never seemed to suffer any ill effects.

Perhaps magic kept the swine safe from the bloody flux that Captain Corrain swore always followed such bestial behaviour. So poisoning him would be a waste of effort, even if Hosh had any idea how to go about it.

He longed to talk to Imais. She knew intoxicants as well as pot herbs. Could she tell him how to stupefy Anskal with the dream smoke powder? Not that Hosh had any idea what he might do after that. He could hardly row a galley away on his own.

'No.'

Anskal waved away the bottle which Hosh offered as the wizard had finished eating. It was the finest white brandy, a Tormalin noble house's stamp on the wax sealing it. The mage had already drunk his way through half the basket of the liquor.

'Fetch me water.'

Hosh went through the kitchen to the well in the garden. He filled a multi-hued glass goblet for himself, a luxury whose cost would have given the wealthiest Caladhrian baron pause. Anskal didn't give such things a second glance. Did he not know what such wares were worth or did he simply not care? Hosh was beginning to think that the only things which the mage valued were silver, gold and gems. And magic.

'Eat, if you wish.' Anskal waved a hand at his leavings.

'No, thank you.' Hosh stood in the shadow of the eaves watching the *Knot Serpent*'s murdered master's corpse rocking back and forth in the shallows.

He couldn't imagine the Aldabreshi would be burying the bodies of those killed by magic to become one with the soil. Not and corrupt all the omens for an island's inhabitants for as long as memory of their fate endured. Though that hardly mattered here. Anskal had blighted this whole island with his sorcery.

'Here they come.'

Anskal's triumphant words startled Hosh out of his reverie. He hadn't expected the Aldabreshi to return before dawn at the earliest. If they returned at all.

But now it was apparent that the Archipelagans were so desperate, they had already followed the ship masters across the island, prepared to make any deal to escape the wizard.

Scores of men and a lesser number of women were picking a wary path through the shadowy ironwoods. Trireme crews flanked their ship masters, the steersmen and the flute players whose notes governed the rhythm of their oars.

Scarred galley slaves cowered away from overseers who had armed themselves with fresh-cut reeds in place of their lost whips. Young and old, favoured slaves and whores of both sexes straggled after them.

Hosh looked in vain for Imais but couldn't pick her out of the jostling throng in the rapidly failing light. He couldn't see Nifai now nor Ducah.

Most were carrying something; a box or a bundle of silk or sackcloth. Hosh was surprised to see how much the Aldabreshi had managed to seize before they fled after that first magical onslaught.

'Good.' Anskal threw the peerless drinking goblet away to shatter on the stones. 'Come!'

'Shouldn't we wait for the rest?' Hosh set his own glass carefully down.

'There are no more to come.' Anskal was already at the

top of the steps. 'So many have already died. So foolish.'

Corsair swordsmen amongst the crowd hurried to the fore, as though they believed that their gleaming blades could be a match for the wizard's lethal magic.

'You will each stand before me,' Anskal said crisply, 'and place all that you carry on the ground. I will know if you are concealing anything that is rightfully mine beneath your clothes,' he added with naked menace.

As Hosh relayed the wizard's words, he could see plenty of those who understood Tormalin speech were already passing on this news to those further back.

Anskal still didn't understand, did he? No Aldabreshin would risk taking away anything that might carry the taint of magic.

'Once I am satisfied, you may go to your ships and depart.' Anskal concluded.

As Hosh conveyed that assurance, he saw urgent conversations between ship masters, overseers and crews as they peered into the dusk, trying to see which galleys and triremes might be seaworthy and which were beyond salvage.

'When you leave,' Anskal smiled, 'carry these words wherever you go. This island is now mine and my reach is long. Any ships wishing to pass within a hundred leagues must pay me my due. I will accept a tithe of each vessel's cargo. Any ship master who will not pay will be wrecked on unforeseen reefs no matter what his course.' He nodded towards the entrance to the anchorage. 'You have seen how strong my hand is, when I choose to command the waters.'

As Hosh repeated those cruel words he could see the blank disbelief on the faces of the most fluent in the mainland tongue.

'Tell them again,' Anskal instructed.

Hosh obeyed. Nobody moved. The silence was absolute.

'You may stay or you may go.' Anskal's voice hardened. 'The choice is yours but make it quickly.'

Hosh couldn't tell if the first corsair to stumble forward was volunteering or if he had been caught unawares and shoved. Those behind certainly raised their swords against any attempt to retreat.

The dark-skinned man with the paler eyes of mixed blood flung a small basket on the ground. A scatter of rings and bracelets spilled out with some tarnished silver coins. He threw his rings and a heavy gold necklace down before stripping off his tunic to show the wizard the old faded scars of a lifelong slave.

Anskal raised a languid hand. 'Very well, you may take your coin and go.'

Not stooping to take a penny piece, the man ran for the water's edge and waded in. The trireme he sought was close at hand and he hastily climbed the dangling rope ladder.

Another man stepped forward. Anskal nodded as he dropped a leather sack beside the basket and waved him on. Once again, the Aldabreshi left his loot lying by the terrace. He proved to be a shipmate of the first man and joined him in anxiously surveying the vessel from prow to stern.

A handful followed more readily but the next trio hesitated, all unwilling to be the first. Once they were seen to pass safely past the wizard though, the remainder grew less reluctant. Hosh saw some jostling to get more swiftly to the front.

They were abandoning a barony's purchase in treasure

as they went. Hosh noted that pearl-studded ornaments were prominent among the discarded plunder. Had the islanders lost their faith in such talismans against magic? He could hardly blame them.

What was going to happen when they had all rowed away? Did Anskal honestly think any vessel would sail willingly into this harbour to pay him what he demanded? What could he do with all these tenth-shares of cargoes? No Archipelagan would trade for goods that had passed through a wizard's hand. Did he expect Hosh to barter for him?

'No.'

Anskal's firm voice startled Hosh out of his wandering thoughts.

He saw the remaining corsairs and their slaves were just as shocked. Though nothing equalled the abject terror of the slave rower stood at the base of the steps.

'I have nothing!' He began ripping off his ragged clothing. 'I have nothing!'

'But you have.' Anskal offered his hand with a welcoming smile. 'My friend.'

The sizeable heap of abandoned treasure stirred. Anskal held out an open hand and a tangle of silver chains writhed. An amulet carved from dark veined jade sprang up into the wizard's palm.

He tossed it to the slave rower. The man's fingers closed instinctively around the jewel. Emerald light glowed inside the man's fist. He screamed and dropped the swirl of jade. It lay on the sandy soil, inert. The radiance clung stubbornly to the man's fingers.

'You have mage blood in your veins,' Anskal told the horrified rower.

'No.' The man dropped to his knees to scoop up a

handful of soil, frantically scouring his glowing hand. 'No!'

Anskal didn't seem overly perturbed by the man's abhorrence. 'You now have a choice to make.'

The slave looked up, sick with fear.

'You may go,' Anskal assured him. 'I keep my word. But of course, everyone has now seen your true nature.'

He nodded towards the waiting boats. 'You may take your chances out there, though I believe they are less than promising. Or you may stay and I will give you all the boons of your birthright.'

The rower peered fearfully over his shoulder and recoiled from the loathing on every face he could see.

Once again, Anskal was offering a choice that was no choice at all. Even if Hosh guessed that the corsairs would think better of killing the slave immediately he tried to rejoin his ship. Surely they wouldn't risk offering the wizard such a blatant insult?

But the mageborn man faced a lingering and agonising death as soon as the corsairs reached some other beach. Imais had told Hosh of the bounties that warlords paid for any wizard's hide. Word of anyone suspected of magebirth circulated around every trading island, travelling as far and wide as the courier doves that carried their descriptions from warlord to warlord.

The rower staggered to his feet. Hosh had never seen such ghastly desolation on any man's face.

'Wait over there!' Anskal clapped his hands impatiently. 'Who else wishes to leave?'

The next galley slave stepped forward, empty hands spread wide. As the wizard waved him towards the shore, the man so unexpectedly condemned collapsed into a sobbing heap.

Hosh couldn't find any comfort to offer. All he could do was wait and watch as Anskal somehow found more mageborn among the island's survivors.

He surreptitiously tallied them up as the night wore on. Eleven corsair swordsmen. A triple handful of slave rowers and a double handful of women.

Hosh was both devastated and delighted to see that Imais wasn't among them. She didn't meet his eye as she dropped the twisted cloth she was carrying to spill bronze plates and cups on the ground.

Nifai and Ducah both escaped as well, stripping themselves all but naked in their haste. Hosh lost sight of them as they raced for the shore. Regardless, he was glad to see the back of both of them.

The first lanterns lit on the wallowing ships glimmered in the darkness like fireflies. The most distant galley was already edging towards the southern headland.

By the time the last of the Aldabreshi had braved Anskal's scrutiny, the first trireme had already departed. The Archipelagans were more willing to risk the hazards of night rowing under the solitary Lesser Moon than to stay here any longer.

Hosh studied the mageborn sitting on the damp ground below the terrace. The Aldabreshi among them were still appalled, either silently distraught or wailing in incoherent terror.

Anskal looked down at them, exasperated. 'When they have come to their senses, tell them to find food and shelter as they please.'

He vanished in a shimmer of azure light before Hosh had time to answer.

Hosh was watching the remaining mageborn; in particular the group of nine men sitting quietly thoughtful with their backs together, conversing in low tones as they kept a watchful eye on the distressed Aldabreshi. They were speaking in Tormalin.

Mainlanders, enslaved as he had been. They weren't Caladhrians; that was too much to hope for. But Hosh guessed that a handful were from Ensaimin, judging by their accents.

However their magebirth had gone undiscovered for so long, they would know something of wizardry. More than that, they would know it wasn't some all-encompassing evil, as the Archipelagans believed.

Was there any hope of them proving useful allies against the Mandarkin? Hosh couldn't sail away from the island alone but now there were enough of them to make up a crew. Though of course they would need a seaworthy boat.

And they would need to defend themselves against the other Aldabreshi. Hosh walked quietly to the herb trough where he'd hidden Ducah's discarded sword. Retrieving the blade, he walked around the terrace to go down the pavilion's front steps, the sword pressed against his side. He had already decided where to hide it on the furthest pavilion's terrace.

— CHAPTER FIFTEEN —

The Esterlin Residence, Relshaz
16ᵗʰ of For-Autumn

'SO WHAT DO we think he is doing with these wretched mageborn today?' Mellitha studied the scrying spell floating on the surface of the water.

Jilseth didn't answer. She had become used to the comfortably plump magewoman's habit of asking such questions as she worked her magic in this luxurious salon looking onto the carefully tended garden of her well-appointed home.

Would they ever see some clue as to what the Mandarkin intended? Jilseth had no more idea what the mysterious northern wizard was up to than she had when she had first arrived here.

Any more than she had fathomed why Planir had sent her away from Hadrumal so abruptly. Had Troanna been so grievously offended by Jilseth's unbidden magic invading her scrying? Though, granted, Jilseth knew she was the obvious person to explain the trick of blending the bitumen into a scrying to Mellitha—

'Madam mage?' Mellitha looked across the silver bowl, her expression as serene as ever. 'Your full attention, if you please?'

Jilseth realised that the glob of bitumen was threatening to escape her frighteningly erratic affinity. She quickly brought her full attention to bear on the molten pitch and the reflection brightened.

'How many are missing this morning?' Mellitha's dark eyes darted this way and that as her generous mouth twisted wryly. 'Two more lost lambs. Your scrying, madam mage,' she said lightly.

Jilseth summoned up all her resolve and the emerald spell darkened. The touch of Mellitha's wizardry was as gentle as a mother's caress as the older magewoman relinquished the scrying but Jilseth's mage senses were still as raw as scalded flesh.

A heady scent rose from the ensorcelled water to vie with the fresh-cut flowers in the vases by the long muslin-draped windows.

Mellitha had been among the first mages to experiment with perfumery essences in scrying and she was wont to release their oils by warming the water beneath them. Jilseth marvelled at her ability to command elemental fire while working water magic. Had there ever been another wizard born to this affinity so skilled with the antagonistic element? Yet again, Jilseth had to wonder why this elegant magewoman wasn't given the credit she was due among Hadrumal's halls.

A sharper note underlying the fragrance cleared Jilseth's head with all the efficacy of a blademint tisane the morning after too much wine. She had noticed that before. What else might Mellitha be doing with her magic? Something she didn't want Hadrumal to know about?

'The missing mageborn?' Mellitha prompted.

Jilseth concentrated once again. This dismal search offered some balm for her bruised pride. Only a necromancer could scry for the dead. Only an earth wizard could master such eerie magic to pursue and to commune with the dead. Jilseth was one of the very few born to her affinity who chose to pursue the little known discipline in recent years.

Though like any winning rune, such expertise had its grim reverse. Jilseth would much rather not be looking for the fresh corpses of those captive Aldabreshi mageborn. But so many had chosen to flee beyond all recall from whatever fate they feared the heavenly compass predicted. Or whatever they feared the Mandarkin mage intended for them.

Jilseth sent the scrying magic in search of cold and clotting blood; that unique combination of elemental water infused with so many aspects of essential earth. Immediately the spell was drawn to the corpses littering the far shore of the island where the corsairs had first fled.

She refined the magic further, spurning the ooze sinking into the sand beneath the deliquescing dead. Though her affinity hadn't nearly recovered its full strength, she was becoming ever more attuned to those subtlest of changes which inexorably followed once life and breath had left a body.

She sighed. 'The woman with furrowed hair.'

For whatever reason, she had come here to die; the woman whose hair had been her pride and ornament. Jilseth had never seen anything like it; tight black braids sculpted across her scalp in waves to gather in the nape of her neck.

'At dawn, as near as I can guess.'

Greedy flies clustered thickly around the gashes in the woman's forearms where she'd spilled her own blood rather than live cursed by her unsuspected magebirth. 'And the other one?' Mellitha queried.

Jilseth frowned as she sent the scrying skimming along the waterline. There was something on the very edge of her wizard senses.

'Is that—?'

Red-clawed crabs clustered thickly around something half buried in the wet sand but that sad remnant was much longer dead.

'There!' The scrying blazed vivid green as Mellitha's magic fought Jilseth's for an instant.

'I see him.' Jilseth yielded the scrying nevertheless.

Mellitha flung the spell right to the the far end of the charnel cove. A tall beardless man was stripping off his clothes and folding them into a tidy pile. They watched him tug a plaited band of silver from his wrist, the braided wire criss-crossing polished agate.

'The unscarred swordsman.' Mellitha grimaced.

No whip had ever marked this man's smooth skin. Even diminished after all this half-season's privations, his physique was impressive.

He waded into the sea amid the putrid carrion sucked into the shallows by the rise and fall of the tides.

'He's waiting for the sharks,' Mellitha realised with distant compassion.

'Is that bravery or cowardice?' Jilseth couldn't decide.

'Or something else entirely, to honour some Aldabreshin belief?' Mellitha shook her head, unable to answer her own question.

If only—

Jilseth let the unspoken words escape her lips as a soft exhalation. Despite all their command of magic, there was nothing which she and Mellitha could do short of plucking the man bodily from the water. She didn't imagine that he would thank them for that.

'Must we—?'

Before she could ask, the man scored a deep gash across his chest with a knife.

'It's as well to know that someone is truly dead.' Mellitha watched, unblinking. 'Especially a wizard.'

'But these are not wizards!' Jilseth looked away as the water seethed with the seemingly insatiable sharks. 'They are barely mageborn. If they had any affinity worth the name, they would have been discovered long before now.'

'And suffered the ghastly fate which Aldabreshin custom decrees.' Mellitha winced as the man vanished beneath a flurry of pink-tinged foam.

'Their magebirth may be stronger than we think. Don't forget that abject fear or sufficiently strong intent can suppress magebirth's manifestations,' she reminded Jilseth. 'We know of such constraint among the Mountain Men and the Forest Folk, for fear of being exiled by the Aetheric adepts who make their laws.'

She shook her head, regretful, as the screaming man's head broke the water's surface, silently vanishing a moment later beneath a pallid finned flank streaked with gore.

'These Archipelagans know nothing of wizardry so how would they know to fear their own nature? I cannot believe these mageborn have an affinity which Hadrumal would judge worth training,' Jilseth insisted stubbornly.

'That's a debate for another time.' With only one hand on the scrying bowl, Mellitha drummed her painted nails on the satiny fruitwood table set between their silk-upholstered chairs. 'We need to know what this Mandarkin intends for these remaining unfortunates.'

In the blink of an eye, the scrying returned to the pavilions by the anchorage. Mellitha drew the spell aloft to show them each of the three terraces where the remaining mageborn were usually found.

'Does he really think he can buy their loyalty?' This baffled Jilseth.

The Mandarkin had sent his Caladhrian slave with gifts of food and clothing and handfuls of his loot to his unwilling guests. Then he left them to their own devices; to hang themselves or take up a knife and end their miserable existence as they chose.

Mellitha was still absorbed in her own thoughts. 'Why has he been making them presents of those artefacts?'

Jilseth picked out the Caladhrian slave with the misshapen face on the terrace of the furthest pavilion. The one who wore that curious arm ring. She made very certain to ward her earthly affinity against the bauble's insidious lure.

How many ensorcelled objects did the Mandarkin have in his stolen hoard? Jilseth had felt curious earthly resonances several times as they had surveyed the captive mageborn. What of other elemental magics that didn't speak so directly to her affinity? What spells woven of fire, air and water had been locked into those artefacts once prized by unknown mages of ages past, now looted all unknowing by the Aldabreshi?

'We need to hear his cozening and cajoling. Until then we may as well be blind as well as deaf.' Mellitha withdrew her remaining hand and the scrying vanished. 'We need a clairaudience woven into this scrying.'

'Planir won't countenance it,' Jilseth protested. 'He says there is far too much danger of the Mandarkin sensing the working. Then he'll renew his veiling to hide from us again.'

'Not with Velindre weaving the air to listen in on him,' Mellitha assured her.

The magewoman crossed the sunlit salon and stooped to another polished table beside an upholstered daybed. She rang a silver hand bell. 'Do you wish to fetch a wrap before we take the carriage? There can be quite a breeze close to the docks.'

She picked up her own shawl, a lacy confection of knitted silk a few subtle shades lighter than her teal gown. Both might have been chosen to complement the leaf-green rugs on the dark wood floor and the watered silk wall-hangings.

'No, thank you, I'll be fine.' Jilseth had opted for long sleeves and a high neckline when Mellitha's favourite seamstress had visited to take her measure on her arrival, returning the following day with three gowns besides this one, its silk as iridescent as the inside of a pearl oyster's shell.

As she spoke, one of the household's well-trained lackeys opened the double doors at the end of the salon. He was another singularly well-favoured lad with the black hair and tanned skin that spoke of mixed Archipelagan and mainland blood.

'Tell Tanilo I want the carriage. Thank you.'

'Couldn't we bespeak Velindre and ask her to join us?' Jilseth looked at the fireplace for a spill or a candle but such humdrum necessities didn't sully Mellitha's mantelpiece. There were four miniature paintings there, the handiwork of the magewoman's artist son. Jilseth guessed that he and his brother favoured their respective fathers while their two sisters showed what a beauty Mellitha must have been when her chestnut hair was untouched by the white now frosting it.

'I see no reason to take Velindre away from her business.' Mellitha found her reticule and satisfied herself that the embroidered satin pouch held whatever she might need. 'Come on.'

She led the way through the cool, airy hallway. Naturally her coach was ready, waiting in the courtyard that separated the white stone house from the quietly prosperous street. Two more servants hurried to open the heavy gates in the high wall that sheltered Mellitha's residence from prying eyes.

Jilseth followed her into the light carriage with its single forward facing seat and Tanilo the coachman prompted the neatly made roan into a brisk trot.

Mellitha loosened the ribbons tightening the neck of her flower-bedecked purse and fetched out a silver memorandum tablet. 'There are some other matters I can usefully attend to.' She didn't explain further, as she unfolded the hinged tablet and took out a stylus to inscribe notes in the smooth beeswax.

Jilseth looked out of the window as the carriage turned into a wider road carrying them towards a busier quarter where taller buildings were plastered white rather than built of stone. Each balconied floor was a separate family's dwelling, four and five at a time set on top of each other. The women calling out to each other from their open windows wore dresses of bright coloured cotton, their only silk the ribbons and flowers in their hair.

She wondered if Mellitha owned a single cotton gown. On her previous visits to Relshaz, Jilseth had soon realised the magewoman was reckoned to be significantly wealthy, even for this river-mouth city of canals where generations of traders had amassed fortunes far beyond the greediest dreams of the destitute who drifted through its backwaters.

She was far richer than any other mageborn whom Jilseth had met, who had quit Hadrumal for life among the mundane. Their lives had all been in keeping with the wizard isle's opinions; that a mage of modest ability could live in unassuming comfort by assisting the mainland populace with their everyday tasks.

The light carriage had reached a more busily commercial district with the ground floors of each building given over to merchants. Each open frontage was flanked by eager apprentices trying to catch the eye or the elbow of potential customers hurrying past, and all the while keeping their own eyes open for sneak-thieves pilfering from the counters behind their open shutters. Goods were carried on strong men's shoulders or mules' sturdy backs between wharves and quaysides, workshops and warehouses.

The carriage turned into a street that was evidently the province of lamp sellers and candle makers. Warehouses offered everything from the finest Archipelagan glass lanterns to robust branches holding a double handful of candles and supported on stands as tall as a short man, all wrought from Gidestan brass.

The Relshazri craftsmen's custom of staying so close to their rivals must doubtless make shopping easier, Jilseth mused. Though she couldn't recall visiting another city where there would be so many competing artisans in any one particular trade.

At the end of the street, the rumble of the carriage wheels over cobbles changed to the quieter trundle of the iron tyres over flagstones. They had reached the far side of the city and a broad square where crowds clustered around the broad bowls of the fountains tiled with blue to reflect the sky.

'Make sure to carry nothing you value if you visit it. There are as many pickpockets as pilgrims hereabouts.' Mellitha looked up from her note-making and nodded towards the spotless white marble temple on the far side of the square. 'There are individual shrines to every god and goddess of the Tormalin Empire inside, and to deities and cults you've never heard of.'

Jilseth presumed their exploits were among those featured in the frieze of busy statues all along the temple's pediment, supported by the ornately carved pillars dividing the temple's bronze doors. She had no interest in such superstitions.

'What exactly is Velindre's business?'

Mellitha put her memorandum tablet back in her reticule. 'She sells her knowledge of sea states and incoming storms to merchant ships' captains.'

'Oh.' Jilseth was taken aback. While that was an entirely obvious occupation for a wizard with affinity for the air, it seemed singularly commonplace for a magewoman of Velindre Ychane's reputation.

According to Hadrumal gossip, she been considered a potential Cloud Mistress, after the former Master of her element, and her lover, Otrick, had died in some distant adventure. No two rumours agreed about that escapade but all concurred on the eccentric old mage's volatile nature.

'Here we are.' Mellitha tightened her purse's ribbons as the light carriage drew to a halt.

Jilseth stepped down as the coachman opened the

door. 'Madam Velindre does her business in a tavern?'

Though this was a superior inn. The taproom was well swept and well lit with wide shutters bolted open. Customers preferring the open air could find comfortable chairs and freshly wiped tables beneath a vine clad arbour reaching across one half of the building's frontage.

'Velindre!' Mellitha raised a gold-ringed hand.

A slender woman at a corner table acknowledged them with a beckoning gesture. The weather-beaten man sitting across from her rose to his feet, handing her a fat purse.

Velindre passed a hand over it and the coin pouch vanished in an ostentatious flash of sapphire magelight, doubtless for the benefit of any light-fingered onlookers.

Before they reached the arbour, as the mariner hurried away, Jilseth caught Mellitha's elbow. 'Has Madam Velindre been ill?'

The magewoman's pale golden hair was cropped as short as a fever patient's. The effect was as startling as it was oddly flattering to the woman's angular features.

'No.' Mellitha smiled with private amusement. 'She had it cut when she travelled through the Archipelago in the guise of a eunuch. She found growing it back to its former length so tiresome that she's gone shorn ever since.'

Astonished, Jilseth followed the older woman through the tables and chairs. She had never heard that particular detail about Velindre's rumoured travels among the Aldabreshi. She also noted that this business of selling weather guidance to mariners must pay handsomely. Velindre's periwinkle gown could have come from Mellitha's own dressmaker.

'Will you join me in a glass of orgeat?' The tall magewoman gestured at the opalescent glass jug on the table. 'Or would you prefer wine?'

'Orgeat will be very welcome.' Mellitha took a chair, settling her skirts decorously around her ankles.

'Please, sit.' Velindre's tone was more instruction than invitation as she glanced at Jilseth before signalling to the tavern girl to bring two more glasses.

Jilseth did as she was bidden.

'Do we have any idea what this uncouth Mandarkin intends to do with his new slaves?' Velindre asked Mellitha without preamble.

'Nothing as yet.' Mellitha didn't hide her frustration. 'Will you join us as we work our next scrying to see if you can blend a clairaudience into the spell?'

'Do you think that's wise?' Jilseth demanded. Perhaps this was why Planir had sent her here.

'That will depend on your part in the working.' Velindre looked straight at Jilseth. 'Have you felt any threat of wild magic when you've worked with Mellitha? Do you feel any excessive antipathy to elemental air?'

'No.' Jilseth poured herself a glass of the pale liquid and sipped it. The taste of orange-flowers amid the almond sweetness surprised her, though not unpleasantly. The revelation that Mellitha or Planir had told this stranger of her tribulations was far more unwelcome.

'I've seen no reason to doubt your control of your affinity.' Mellitha looked from Jilseth to Velindre. 'It's not as though we'll be working with a nexus and Relshaz doesn't have one tenth of the wizards to be found in a single hall in Hadrumal. There won't be any stray stirring of the elements to be caught in a vortex.'

Velindre was still looking at Jilseth. 'I've been

caught unawares by untamed wizardry. An unpleasant experience,' she observed dispassionately. 'The crucial thing is to learn from such calamities.'

'Indeed.' Jilseth set her glass down and studied the stencilled border on the painted table top.

Mellitha accepted the orgeat which Velindre poured for her. 'Is there any word along the docksides of the Aldabreshin warlords' thoughts on the corsairs' fate?'

'Not as yet.' Velindre shook her head. 'But the news is spreading barely half a day ahead of their ships. Until now, all anyone knew is the raiders had vanished from the sea lanes. There was speculation of course.'

She unfolded her thumb and fingers to count off the theories.

'Some hoped that the thieves had fallen out among themselves and cut each other's throats. Or some squall sweeping in from the western sea had sunk all their ships at anchor. If no one knew exactly where they laired, or wouldn't admit to it if they did, we've long known that their harbour lies in the northwest of the Nahik domain. The most optimistic guessed that Nahik Jarir had finally found his manhood stirring and sent his own triremes to drive them out.'

Jilseth resolved to play a part in this conversation. 'Why did he tolerate their presence in the first place?'

Velindre topped up her own glass from the glistening jug. 'A handful or so years ago, there were several raiding fleets prowling the northernmost sea lanes. They were small undertakings; perhaps three or four galleys following in a single trireme's wake. Crucially, they were only intent on raiding the mainland coast. So they traded Nahik Jarir a handsome share of their loot in return for their anchorages. Some scoured his outlying islands for runaway slaves and handed them over without asking for recompense. That suited him very well.'

She waved away the serving maid who would have taken the jug to refill it.

'According to Aldabreshin custom and law, neighbouring warlords have no interest in whatever mischief Jarir permits in his own waters, as long as it doesn't impinge on their own domain. Moreover, for those first few years, these corsairs were also killing the mainland pirates who lurked in the hidden coves between Attar and Markyate. Those pirates regularly attacked Aldabreshin galleys heading for Relshaz or Col.'

'Going unpunished by Caladhrian barons who saw no need to concern themselves with some shoeless southern barbarians' losses,' Mellitha remarked sardonically.

'Any more than a northern reaches warlord will have lost sleep over any Caladhrian's suffering,' Velindre agreed with a glint in her eye. 'The corsairs sank the mainland pirates' ships in successive bloody seasons, finally leaving those coves deserted. After that, the corsairs turned on each other but as long as they were only killing each other, the warlords saw no reason to intervene. Meantime, they took their pick from the defeated galley crews and swordsmen who turned up chained in the slave markets.'

'Jagai Kalu would have rallied a fleet against them,' Mellitha observed, 'and we tried to persuade the mainland ports to forbid anchorage to galleys sailing the Nahik sea lanes until the corsairs were driven out. We have been working against these corsairs for some years now,' she explained, 'discreetly of course.'

'Does the Council know?' Jilseth wondered why she'd heard no whisper of this in Hadrumal.

Velindre's careless shrug skirted a direct answer. 'We work at the Archmage's behest.'

'He must think highly of you,' Mellitha's dark gaze fixed on Jilseth, 'to send you here to join us.'

'I am honoured.' Jilseth had been fretting about dismissal from Planir's confidence. Now she worried about serving Hadrumal alongside these formidable magewomen with her own magic so untrustworthy.

'But the mainland port reeves wouldn't risk turning away trade which some neighbour would promptly welcome,' Velindre continued, sardonic.

'While the warlords from further south in the Archipelago weren't prepared to risk their galleys on the more perilous eastward routes for the sake of starving Nahik Jarir and his people into agreement.' Exasperation deepened the lines in Mellitha's face.

'Thus by the summer of this year, a single corsair leader had emerged with a formidable fleet and considerable force of arms at his disposal,' Velindre explained to Jilseth. 'Nahik Jarir would have been very ill-advised to try moving against him. Jagai Kalu would very much like to but he cannot hope to act without the full support of Khusro Rina on his own western flank and Miris Esul to the south of Nahik waters.'

She raised a hand and Jilseth realised her expression must have given away her confusion at this flood of unfamiliar names. 'I will send you a chart that shows all the detail of their respective domains.'

Mellitha sighed. 'The Aldabreshi may tolerate a corsair fleet master in their midst for a little while but as soon as they know there's a wizard lurking on that island, they will act. Whatever they do, news will come to Relshaz first and we must keep the Archmage informed.'

'And act in Hadrumal's interests, as we see fit.' Velindre's eyes glinted.

'Do we know where Kheda is?' the older magewoman demanded.

'In the southernmost reaches unfortunately.' Velindre grimaced. 'I've no notion when he plans to come north again.'

For the first time, Mellitha betrayed exasperation. 'If only we still had Sirince picking up slave trader gossip.'

'Sirince?' Jilseth was astonished. 'Sirince Mar?'

The grey-haired earth wizard visited Hadrumal every few seasons, though he spent most of his time in Tormalin. He would often invite prentice wizards and more senior pupils who shared his affinity to dine with him in Wellery's Hall where he maintained a suite of rooms. Jilseth had learned to value his insights casually offered in the course of such evenings.

Velindre surprised her with a mysterious smile. 'You think the old rogue's only ever enjoyed his present comfortable life in Toremal? He sailed the Archipelago for years as one of Planir's enquiry agents.'

'Buying up unjustly enslaved barbarians to see them returned home,' Mellitha added with a sigh. 'How much of this current trouble could have been avoided, if he'd been able to rescue Captain Corrain and those other Halferan captives.'

'No amount of lament will mend a cracked plate,' Velindre said, dismissive. 'Has Kerrit Osier found anything in the Temple archives that might offer some insight into these ensorcelled artefacts?'

'Not as yet.' Mellitha reached into her reticule for her memorandum tablet. 'I will send him a note.'

It took Jilseth a moment to place that name. If she was thinking of the right man, Kerrit was a scholarly mage who'd spent the last ten years or more searching out whatever hints remained of elemental magic in the Old Tormalin Empire. As a consequence, he had learned more than most in Hadrumal of aetheric magic's history, though Artifice's actual practise remained as closed a book to him as it was to every other wizard.

She was beginning to wonder who else, mageborn or mundane, might be about the Archmage's business on the mainland and elsewhere, unbeknownst to Hadrumal's insular wizards. Wasn't Kheda an Aldabreshin name?

Velindre looked at her. 'Has Planir heard anything more from the Solurans?'

Jilseth could only shake her head. 'Not as far as I know.'

'Apparently they will only share what they know of ensorcelling artefacts in return for our insights into quintessential magic.' Mellitha scowled.

Jilseth would wager a handful of gold that particular expression would prompt any Relshazri merchant to pay his taxes in full and quite possibly more, merely to stay in the magewoman's good books.

Velindre gnawed an already bitten fingernail. 'Let's hope he finds some way around their intransigence before this Mandarkin decides to make use of whatever he's found in the corsair hoards.'

— CHAPTER SIXTEEN —

The Hadrumal River Estuary
18th of For-Autumn

THE FAMILIAR SCENTS of a harbour at low water surrounded Corrain. The faint hint of decay as sea-soaked wood dried in the salty breeze. The stronger reek of seaweed left exposed and now crawling with jewel-backed flies. A taste of old tar from a weathered boat hauled up onto the mud. The sharp, clean bite of new hemp, creaking as a youthful sailor coiled a straw-coloured rope beside him on the wharf.

Corrain had been the last to disembark from the sleek-hulled Ensaimin two-master now tied up at the jetty reaching into the deeper channel to allow passengers ashore whatever the tide. The other men and women had already vanished into low-roofed buildings beyond the stout stone bridge some distance upstream from this placid harbour in the modest river's mouth, sufficiently far inland to be sheltered from all but the worst storms.

The sky was an unseasonal blue above the rolling downland of the island's interior stretching away serenely green. Darker smudges in the folds of the hills hinted at well-tended woodlands. Here and there he could see the distant white square of a cottage or cowshed.

The wizards' ancient refuge lay between this homely harbour and those placid pastures. Tall towers kept watch in all directions, thrust up among lofty halls themselves looking down on the humbler buildings in their midst. A better made road than Corrain had ever seen curved across the expanse of sere grass that separated these normal folk at the harbour from whatever mysteries the mageborn hoarded.

He cleared his throat. 'Where can I hire a ride to the city? I am Baron Halferan,' he added for good measure.

He half expected the lad to challenge him. The words still tasted like a lie in his mouth. The boy might even remember the true Baron Halferan's arrival, when his dead lord had come to appeal to the Archmage's better nature.

Dull resentment burned deep in Corrain's chest. Planir's refusal to help had been the beginning of all Halferan's misfortunes. But he couldn't dwell on what was past. He needed the wizard's help and he could afford no more delay.

The young sailor looked up from coiling his rope. 'The halls send a carriage for folk they're expecting. Else they walk—my lord.'

His belated courtesy didn't hide his complete lack of interest in some mainland noble's affairs.

'Very well.' Corrain hitched the strap of his leather travelling bag over one shoulder and followed the well-trodden path to the broad road.

Thankfully he travelled light as befitted a guardsman, and he was wearing the best boots he'd ever owned, thanks to the Archmage's gold filling Halferan's coffers. He fell into a comfortable stride.

What should he make of this though? He was expected, after all. He had told Zurenne to use her pendant to tell the Archmage he was on his way. After she had told Planir about Anskal's unexpected visit and his incomprehensible threats.

Planir had promised that his wizards would keep watch on the manor. That someone would be there to challenge Anskal if he appeared again. Corrain could only trust that Hadrumal's mages were quick enough to appear in the blink of an eye. He'd seen how swift the Mandarkin's malice could be.

As long as that bastard didn't realise where he was heading. Corrain was tormented by thoughts of the vengeance which Anskal might visit on Zurenne and her daughters for appealing to the Archmage.

He'd barely gone ten more paces when a round-bodied gig came hurrying up behind him.

The driver pulled up, a rough-coated bay colt tossing its head in ill-temper. 'Baron Halferan?'

The young man's well-born Caladhrian accents prompted unexpected recollection. 'Master Nolyen of Pardal Barony.'

Corrain could remember precious little else beyond the young wizard's name from that dreadful day when he had stumbled back into Halferan Manor to find so many of those he had believed were dead.

'Of Hadrumal; eight years since,' the mild-faced wizard said cheerfully. 'The Archmage's compliments, my lord baron.'

'And mine to you both.' Corrain slung his travelling bag into the space beneath the seat and climbed up.

Nolyen whistled up the bay colt and they started towards the city.

Corrain was still tense. Planir had said he was keeping watch for Anskal. What of other threats? Were courier doves carrying word across the length and breadth of

Caladhria; that the Widow Zurenne and her daughters were once more unprotected? Corrain ground his teeth. He had gone to the southerly port instead of to Claithe in hopes of taking ship here unnoticed. But someone might have recognised him on his travels.

Corrain stole a sideways glance at the Caladhrian born wizard. Could this Nolyen tell him anything useful? Or would asking questions risk Corrain revealing more than he wished to? He decided silence was the most prudent course.

Besides, the mage did have his hands full with reins and rebuke. The spirited colt took the open road as an invitation to break into a gallop. Corrain was relieved to see that Nolyen was no less a Caladhrian when it came to horsemanship.

The colt slowed obediently as they approached the city. Hadrumal had no walls to divide outlying artisans' lodgings from its older heart. In that it reminded Corrain of Caladhria. All across the baronies, the market towns would proudly boast that no marching armies had troubled the parliament's peace for twenty generations.

Ensaimin visitors sneered that was because Caladhria had nothing which anyone might want to take. The truth of that hadn't troubled Corrain until the corsairs had come to prove those Ensaimin wrong.

And now they faced Anskal's malice backed by those same cursed raiders and Corrain didn't have any notion what the Mandarkin wanted from them. But he'd wager that the Archmage did. So he was here to find out. Planir couldn't hide behind the infuriating evasions which Zurenne had repeated if Corrain met him face to face.

The gig advanced slowly up the gentle rise of the high

road. As far as Corrain could see, no two neighbouring buildings had been built by the same mason. Some had tall narrow windows defying any attempt to see what lay within while their arched, studded gates stayed stubbornly closed. Others extended a welcome with broad windows and wide archways opening into courtyard gardens, their invitation framed with carved birds and animals, leaves and flowers carved on their pillars and mullions.

Delicate stone tracery framed stained glass panels on one building. Boldly painted shutters were bolted back from deep sills on the next. The frontage beyond was a mathematical paragon of precisely measured windows and doors making subtle geometric patterns.

Only one thing was constant, as true of the substantial wizards' halls as of the prosaic shops and tradesmen's dwellings tucked in amongst them. All were built of the same fine-grained stone, softly golden in the sunlight.

Men and women, young and old, dressed in every mainland fashion, hurried up towards the heart of the city or down towards the harbour road, hampering each other and the few carts and gigs patiently threading a path through the throng.

Corrain had never imagined there could be so many wizards. That explained why this city on a remote island, exposed to attack from any quarter, felt no need for walls. If Madam Jilseth could defend Halferan Manor so doughtily, what couldn't this multitude do?

'Here we are.' Nolyen turned the horse through a square entry into a stone paved quadrangle.

An ostler appeared from a porter's cubbyhole to take charge of the colt while the mage jumped down. Gathering up his courage along with his travelling bag,

Corrain descended more slowly. He had come this far. There was no retreating now.

Behind him and to either side, ranges of accommodation faced onto the quadrangle. Ahead a great hall filled the fourth side of the square, far older, with high windows and a single door at one end reached by a tall flight of steps.

To Corrain's eye, it looked built for defence, wizardry notwithstanding. A solid square tower rose at the opposite end to the door, with tall pinnacles at each corner and parapets built to shield sentries keeping watch aloft. It reminded him of the very oldest halls he had seen across Caladhria's baronies. Though the lines of the lattice carving on the pillars supporting the pointed arch of the doorway were as sharp as if the stone mason shaping them had only then laid down his chisel.

Nolyen was quite at his ease, striding across the flagstones. 'This is Trydek's Hall, founded by our first Archmage.'

'Indeed.' Corrain's tongue felt like old leather, his mouth was so dry.

Nolyen led the way up the steps, lifting the latch to shove the heavy door open. It revealed a whitewashed passage with double doors leading into the main hall on Corrain's sword hand and a second way in or out at the far end.

He turned resolutely away from that illusion of a last-minute escape as Nolyen ushered him into the hall. The young wizard followed and closed the doors behind him.

'Good day, Baron Halferan.'

'Good day to you, Archmage.' Corrain bowed. He

had silently sworn not to be subservient but this was neither the time nor the place for arrogance.

Plain tables were framed with benches, running down the length of the hall. At the far end, the hall had the customary dais, though this one was raised much higher than Halferan's. A long table set crossways was backed by tall carved chairs. The Archmage sat in the centre, his seat no more ornate than the rest.

Corrain strode resolute down the length of the hall and he looked up at the wizard.

When they had met before, he could have taken the Archmage for some prosperous market town's reeve; neatly dressed in black broadcloth doublet and breeches, free of unseemly ostentation.

In this hall of wizardry, the lean-faced man wore a broad-shouldered black velvet mantle over an old fashioned tunic, buttoned high to the throat. Most of the portraits lining the whitewashed walls were dressed in the same style.

Planir leaned forward, elbows resting on the table, his chin on his interlaced fingers. 'Have you finally come to ask for wizardly aid in rebuilding your manor?'

'I—' Corrain hadn't expected this genial query. 'No. We wish to rebuild Halferan through our own efforts, my lord.'

Planir raised his brows, dark with no hint of the silver which shaded his temples and beard. 'Why?'

Corrain answered with swift certainty. 'To give every man, woman and child a stake in the barony's future. To teach them all that their surest defence is their neighbour.'

'Spoken like a true guardsman,' Planir observed. 'Then what do you want with me, and why,' he continued before Corrain could answer, 'have you spent the time, trouble and coin to come here in person rather than use my gifts to Lady Zurenne and Lady Ilysh to communicate your concerns?'

'You know that the Mandarkin mage Anskal believes that we are concealing further magic from him.' Corrain knew his voice betrayed his desperation. He didn't care. 'He says that I must hand this magic over or he will come north with a fleet of raiders. That he'll leave Halferan ruined. I saw what he did to the corsairs and I know that we cannot stand against him. But I have no notion what he wants—'

Corrain couldn't continue. The appalling recollection of the blind corsair's trireme burning and his pavilion's destruction was bad enough. The thought of such violence crushing Halferan's recovery was too much to bear.

Planir studied him for an interminable moment before speaking.

'I know what the Mandarkin seeks. He has discovered some stash of ensorcelled artefacts among the corsairs' loot. He believes that more such treasures remain on the mainland. Unfortunately my gifts to Halferan's ladies have convinced him that you possess some.'

'I know nothing of magical trinkets beyond chimney corner stories for children,' Corrain protested helplessly.

'Quite so,' Planir agreed drily. 'But I doubt that you'll convince him, especially now that he has discovered there are mageborn among the Aldabreshi, when you swore to him the islanders had no wizards.'

Corrain couldn't make any sense of that. 'But the Archipelagans abominate magic.'

'Indeed. Well now, the last time we met,' the Archmage

continued more briskly, 'you offered me a bargain, you and Lady Zurenne. Provided we helped you drive away those corsairs, you wouldn't disgrace Hadrumal. If we refused, then you would tell the world that Master Minelas was a wizard as well as a thieving murderer.

'Are you offering those same terms?' he enquired conversationally, 'for our help in rescuing you from the consequences of your own folly? You went seeking alliance with this wizard, Anskal. You brought him south.'

'I did.' The admission left Corrain feeling sick to his stomach. 'I will submit to whatever punishment which you think fit. Throw me from the top of your tallest tower if you must. As long as you keep Lady Zurenne and Lady Ilysh safe—' He broke off. 'Are they safe? I had to leave them to come here. But if I had stayed, I cannot fight this mage—'

'They are safe and sound,' the Archmage assured him, 'though the demesne folk are baffled, my lord baron, to see you abandon rebuilding your manor to go off on some jaunt without so much as your household guard troop.'

Planir leaned back in his chair, folding his arms. 'Please, continue with your demands. I see you have more to ask of me, even though you claim you're not offering me terms.'

'I ask nothing for myself,' Corrain insisted. 'But there was a lad taken captive with me and he's still a slave on that corsair island. I swear by all that's holy I would have brought him away with me if I could. I thought he must surely be dead but now Anskal says he'll return him to us if we surrender what he seeks. So we know that he's alive. But we have no magic to give him,' he protested. 'Since he doesn't believe us, he will surely kill the lad and he is innocent of all my follies, my lord.'

'So you wish me to save the boy, though you're making no demands?' Planir's eyes flicked past Corrain towards the back of the hall. 'Nolyen? You have a question?'

'When the Mandarkin mage, this Anskal, came to threaten Lady Zurenne, did he say anything to suggest what he might intend, once he has gathered these ensorcelled trinkets together?'

Corrain turned to look at the Caladhrian wizard, hearing frustration and apprehension equal to his own.

'No.' He shook his head, so desperately wishing he could say something else.

'It is for us to discover what the Mandarkin intends.' Planir laid his hands flat on the table. 'It is for you to make amends for your arrogance and your defiance,' he told Corrain ominously, 'and to lessen the burdens which Hadrumal now has to bear as a consequence of your follies.'

Corrain braced himself. 'Tell me what I must do.'

The Archmage leaned forward, folding his hands together. His ring snagged the edge of a sunbeam, throwing out a flash of light to dazzle Corrain. 'You must go to Solura.'

'What?' That made Corrain blink a second time. Whatever he had expected, of all the possibilities which he had debated with himself on the road and onboard ship, he had never envisaged this.

'You will go to Solura,' Planir repeated. 'You will find your erstwhile ally, the Forest born lad, who escaped from the corsairs with you. Kusint, wasn't that his name?'

'Yes, but my lord—' Corrain protested. 'He and I

parted as enemies. He told me not to strike a deal with the Mandarkin.' Regret strangled that admission.

'Then you will find him and humbly beg his pardon and tell him that he was right,' Planir said relentlessly. 'Then you will go and find those mages of the Order of Fornet whom you also so grievously offended and you will admit your guilt to them. You will submit to whatever punishment they decree for you. That may well cost you a flogging but as long as you tell them you're under my protection, it won't cost you your head.'

'I—' Corrain stared at the Archmage. 'Why—?'

'Kusint can bear witness that you did all this alone, without my knowledge or agreement. The wizards of Solura have friends among those adept with aetheric magic, who use it in the Soluran king's service. Artifice will prove the truth of whatever you tell them. I recommend you do not lie,' Planir advised, his tone cutting. 'You have significant amends to make for the strife which your foolishness has caused between ourselves and the wizards of Solura.

'Once you have convinced the Elders of Fornet that you alone are responsible for bringing this Mandarkin wizard southwards,' the Archmage continued, implacable, 'you will present my compliments to them and ask on my behalf, for whatever lore they or the Elders of other Soluran Orders might care to share about the ensorcelling of artefacts. I am particularly interested to learn if they know why this mage Anskal might find such things so intriguing. We will be indebted to them for any spells they may have for drawing the sting from such things. Do I make myself clear? Do you have any questions?'

'My lord,' Corrain protested. 'It took me the whole of For-Summer to reach Solura. I have no notion where to find Kusint. Who knows how long it could take me to track him down—'

Planir burst out laughing. Corrain reddened with furious humiliation as he realised an instant too late what the Archmage would say.

'I can send you there between one breath and the next,' Planir assured him, 'and we can help you find Kusint. We were following your journey this summer with keen interest, weren't we, Nolyen?' He glanced over Corrain's head again.

'You followed us?' Corrain looked around at the young wizard, disbelieving. Then he recalled Planir's earlier words. 'You say that you know what the Mandarkin has found among the corsair loot? You're watching him by means of some spell? Along with my lady Zurenne and her daughters?'

'Holding true to our edicts means that we do not intervene in mainland warfare,' the Archmage said, steely-eyed. 'That does not mean we do not observe and make ready to act in case our own interests demand it. Let us hope that we can deal with this Mandarkin before he causes too much commotion amongst the Archipelagans. Let us hope that you can secure the Solurans' forgiveness, so they will share the lore that will help us to safeguard Lady Zurenne and Lady Ilysh.'

Standing beneath the Archmage's withering gaze, Corrain felt a chill run down his spine. He raised his chin to answer the Archmage.

'I will go to Solura. I will admit my folly. I will take whatever punishment comes my way. I will do my utmost to return with the lore that you seek.' But he wasn't ready to surrender completely. Not yet. 'If you're keeping watch on Anskal, surely you can rescue Hosh? I can tell you what he looks like. I can tell you which galley we were chained in, which oar.'

'I'm sorry.' For the first time, Planir's expression softened. 'There would be no surer way of letting Anskal know that we are watching him, for us to pluck your friend from his grasp.'

Corrain wanted to argue but he could see that there was no point. Worse, he couldn't argue with the Archmage's reasoning. Antagonise Anskal and the consequences for Halferan could be deadly.

'We can warn the Mandarkin off any more visits to Caladhria without making our interest so obvious,' the Archmage offered. 'Allow us to help rebuild Halferan Manor. That will explain a mage's presence and whatever Anskal has planned, he won't draw attention to himself by challenging one of our own directly. Not yet.'

Once again, the Archmage glanced over his head. Corrain had no doubt that Planir knew far more than he was telling. So how much did the Caladhrian wizard Nolyen know and was there any way to get anything useful out of him?

Planir looked back at Corrain. 'Is that agreeable? Then you can be certain that Lady Zurenne and Lady Ilysh will be safe while you are in Solura.'

He nodded and the Archmage smiled with austere satisfaction.

'Nolyen will see you to an overnight lodging. We will find Kusint and send you on your way to meet him tomorrow morning.'

Corrain shook his head. 'Can you send him a letter

from me? Send me somewhere for him to come and find me? If he chooses not to answer, I will find these Elders on my own, I swear it.'

He owed Kusint that much; the chance to throw that letter in a fire and walk away without a backward glance.

Planir pursed his lips. 'If that's what you think best.'

'I do, my lord.' Corrain bowed to the Archmage and turned to follow the Caladhrian mage out of the hall, leaving Planir seated at his high table.

Despite the daunting prospect of an unforeseen journey back to Solura, Corrain felt unexpectedly relieved. He had always been used to following orders, albeit allowing for his tendency to interpret such orders as he saw fit, to secure the best outcome. Though he had better curb any such impulse to unsanctioned deeds on this journey.

As they went down the outer steps, Corrain tallied up the roll of these unexpected runes. Not be able to bring Hosh safe home was a bitter blow. The reverse of that loss was knowing that Halferan would be guarded by a wizard, keeping Zurenne and Ilysh safe from that Mandarkin bastard's malice.

Aye and Halferan Manor would be restored all the faster, maybe before the worst winter weather. Though Corrain would need to explain this about-turn to Zurenne and young Lysha would be insufferably smug to think that she had got her own way.

'Master Nolyen?' Corrain halted as the younger wizard turned, his amiable face expectant.

'Is there some way for me to send a message to my lady, to let her know what's passed between me and the Archmage? I should let her know that I won't be back for some while, and that she can expect Hadrumal's help with the rebuilding.'

Corrain guessed that Planir would send the magewoman Jilseth. She was a proven friend to Halferan and her magic was rooted in stone and earth. Who better to offer such assistance? And it would be far more seemly for a lady wizard to keep Halferan's ladies company while the manor's lord was away.

— CHAPTER SEVENTEEN —

MELLITHA OPENED HER letter with an ivory-handled knife and scanned the contents. She clicked her tongue in exasperation. 'Kerrit Osier's had no more luck discovering hints of ensorcelled items hidden in the Magistracy's archives, or in their strong boxes come to that.'

'That was a long shot at best.' Jilseth put the scrying bowl down on the table and went to fetch the tray of perfume vials. The crumbled bitumen looked incongruous in its white crackle glazed dish. She frowned to see how their supply had diminished. 'Is there more of this to be had?'

She wondered if some eminent mage would ever discover why searching wizardries could be worked only once using whatever was focusing the particular spell. At least they could still focus their scrying on the anchorage, thanks to one galley and one trireme which the fleeing corsairs had been forced to abandon as damaged beyond hope of repair.

'I'll see what can be done.' Mellitha made a note on the wax tablet beside her on the cushioned day bed. 'Until then, we may have to limit ourselves to fewer viewings.'

Now it was Jilseth who tsked with frustration. 'But they have stopped killing themselves. Surely he will make some move to bring them together.'

As relieved as she was not to be scrying out dead bodies, every passing day made her more apprehensive that the Mandarkin would do something unexpected. She was cudgelling her wits to think what any wizard might do with this rag-tag of untrained and distraught mageborn. What might they do while she and Mellitha were not watching?

'What will we learn from him simply bringing them together?' Mellitha's irritation sharpened her tone.

Jilseth didn't take offence. She knew it wasn't directed at her.

'We must work a clairaudience into the scrying,' the older magewoman said firmly. 'Unless we can hear what he has to say, we're wasting our time and that pitch.' She gestured at the crackle glazed dish.

Jilseth was sorely tempted to agree. 'We must put that to Planir,' she said by way of compromise.

Mellitha nodded as she read her next letter. 'We—'

Velindre's appearance in the salon startled them both. The tall blonde magewoman didn't give either of them a chance to speak.

'There's word of two galleys in sore distress coming into harbour.'

'Those corsairs who escaped Anskal?' Mellitha threw her correspondence aside.

Velindre nodded. 'The wharf rats say that they're raiders' ships fleeing whatever disaster befell them in the Archipelago.'

'Courier doves will be carrying that news all over the northern reaches.' Mellitha pursed her lips. 'Let's go and see what's to be seen.'

She held out a hand to Jilseth, who took it expecting to help the older magewoman up. Instead cool white mist enveloped her with the familiar sensations of translocation. As she felt firm ground beneath her feet, the mist cleared to show her the seaward face of the great white temple. All three of them stood in a sheltered nook between two massive buttresses. Barely five paces of marble paving separated them from the dark waters.

'There's never anyone here,' Mellitha said comfortably. 'This way.' Velindre strode on ahead.

The Aldabreshin quays proved to be no great distance away, built outwards into these deeper waters unsullied by the river mud carried down to the delta's shores. Lofty stone breakwaters embraced a calm expanse where Archipelagan cargo galleys were moored. These mighty ships were far bigger than any of those raiding vessels Jilseth had seen while scrying on the corsairs. Lean and predatory triremes were anchored between these great galleys, their stern platforms all manned by dangerous looking swordsmen.

More dark-skinned warriors leaned against the buildings lining the quayside. Each one seemed to have three times as many blades as he had hands to use them and they all wore the fine steel chainmail of the islands. The links were so small that the gleaming armour draped and flowed like cloth. Even their feet were encased in mail leggings, riveted to hobnailed leather soles.

It was very different to the riverside wharves which Jilseth had visited on her search for Minelas. The other side of the city offered rough-hewn warehouses and seedy taverns favoured by the Caladhrian and Lescari bargemen who plied their trade on the river Rel. Here substantial storehouses were built of smoothly sawn and darkly oiled wood with broad balconies on their upper storeys.

'Do we have an excuse for our presence?' she asked Mellitha in an undertone as one storehouse's guardian narrowed his dark eyes at them all.

'Trade.' Mellitha smiled serenely at the suspicious swordsman.

'The warlords who trade most regularly with the Relshazri like to build themselves a little piece of home.' Velindre gestured at the next building along the quayside. 'Their most trusted galley masters winter here, turn and turn about, and accommodate their visiting lords in the summer sailing season.'

'With their wives and children?' A high-pitched giggle drew Jilseth's eyes up to a balustrade where three small children leaned over to watch the scene below. A woman in vivid red silk scolded them away as the sunlight struck fire from the rubies in her high-piled long black hair and around her cinnamon-hued wrists.

'Concubines, more commonly than wives,' Velindre corrected her, 'but don't think that they're merely doxies looking no further than their bedroom ceilings. Every Aldabreshi woman will know all the ins and outs of the markets, looking to secure maximum advantage and profit through the trading season.'

'How much longer will this year's season last?' Jilseth contemplated the procession in and out of the nearest storehouse's wide doors.

Bales and chests and baskets, some open and others tightly corded, were carried to and fro alongside bolts of cloth sewn into sailcloth shrouds. Some were small enough to be managed one-handed; others needed two strong men to shoulder them.

Two strong slaves, Jilseth corrected herself, either Aldabreshin born or Relshazri ne'er-do-wells fallen into debt or paying for some crime against the Magistracy. So Relshazri slave merchants insisted, invariably and unconvincingly appalled when some hapless Lescari captured by mercenaries was discovered among their stock, or an unfortunate from yet further afield.

'We always see this last flurry of ships as the Archipelagan rains slacken off in the northern reaches in the latter half of For-Autumn,' Mellitha explained. 'But the gales from the western sea will strengthen as the equinox approaches.'

'The ships will stop sailing well before then this year,' Velindre said ominously. 'The Emerald moves into the arc of Death in eighteen days time.'

Before Jilseth could ask her to explain that baffling statement, a distant shout echoed across the water. More hallooing followed from the westerly breakwater. Velindre took a long stride forward, shading her eyes with one hand.

Two galleys appeared between the watch towers guarding the harbour entrance. One rode so low in the water that Jilseth marvelled to see it staying afloat without magical aid. The other looked more seaworthy but its oars flailed like some mortally wounded insect's legs.

The ships in the harbour cleared a path. The triremes' triple banks of oars hit the water with a disciplined splash. The massive galleys were slower to move but once their rowers were marshalled, a single stroke sufficed to haul the closest vessels out of the toiling arrivals' way. Coloured pennants flew up the masts of triremes and galleys alike.

Jilseth couldn't see any answering signals from the battered corsairs. She wondered how Velindre or

Mellitha proposed to learn whatever those aboard and escaping the Mandarkin wizard could usefully tell Hadrumal's mages.

'How soon—'

Velindre silenced Jilseth with a vehement oath in what must surely be the Aldabreshin tongue. Her words turned heads on all sides around them.

The hostility on the Archipelagans' faces sent a shiver down Jilseth's spine. She felt a warm glow of unexpected magic in the palm of her hand. Closing her fingers lest any magelight escape her grasp, she nevertheless kept hold of that instinctive surge of wizardry. 'Mellitha?'

The older magewoman laid a calm hand on her arm. 'They're not interested in us.'

Velindre contemplated the harbour scene guardedly. 'Let's be ready in case that changes.'

Sharp noises aloft sent seabirds perched on the roofs wheeling into the sky, squawking. Jilseth looked up to see all the balconies deserted; louvered doors and shutters being slammed.

A trio of armoured men rushed out of the closest storehouse's entrance. More Aldabreshin warriors emerged from the other buildings, right along the broad sweep of the quay. They were all heading for the only mooring left open to the labouring galleys.

The Relshazri were all departing, dragging their handcarts in panic. When several donkey-drawn wagons all tried to leave by the same alley between two storehouses, one muleteer abandoned his charges entirely. Ignoring cries of outrage, he vaulted an empty cart bed and fled.

As every face turned towards that uproar, the air around Jilseth shimmered although the day was nowhere near hot enough for the sun to strike haze from the stones. Magic wrought of elemental air rasped against her wizardly senses. Velindre's magic, concealing them all.

Jilseth would have preferred to be consulted but she couldn't deny her relief at being hidden. She looked in all directions, alert for anyone approaching. They might be invisible now, to anyone without both magebirth and wizardly education, but they were hardly intangible. The last thing they needed was some hurrying Aldabreshi barrelling into them all unawares. They could doubtless escape by means of a further translocation but that would cost them any chance of seeing what transpired here.

Invisible also didn't mean inaudible and despite this swelling clamour a disembodied voice might snag someone's ear. Jilseth looked to Velindre for some silent signal.

To her wizard sight, the tall magewoman looked like a charcoal sketch except that each feathered line and grainy shadow was wrought of vivid sapphire and the buildings behind her were clearly visible through her translucent form. Beside her Mellitha was similarly outlined in elemental air of a more muted hue. It wasn't her spell after all.

With both women now looking at her, Jilseth tapped her own ear and shaped a sphere with her cobalt hands, her brows raised in a question. Should she wrap a magical silence around them all so they could converse? She wanted to know what Velindre had read in those signal pennants.

Velindre shook her head in emphatic refusal. Mellitha was less adamant but clearly agreed with the tall magewoman. She cupped one gold-ringed hand hand to her own ear, like some festival masquerader showing the audience she was alert.

Jilseth nodded her understanding. They couldn't afford to risk not hearing some vital warning, cut off from the crowd by their own magecraft.

The ravaged galleys were approaching the quayside. Aldabreshi swordsmen raced along the open thoroughfare between the bollards and stone steps of the harbour and the storehouses. Gangs of slaves were now busy bolting and barring their ground floor doors.

The first vessel wallowed perilously, struggling to turn its stern ladders to the quay. Jilseth could barely hear the stuttering clash of oars being shipped above the harsh shouts from all those ashore. If the corsairs tried to answer, she had no way of knowing what they said or of asking Velindre.

The first of those aboard ship appeared. Ropes uncoiled through the air, tossed by gaunt men with haunted faces. Hands ashore caught the cables and hauled. With a shocking crash of splintering wood, the ship was irrevocably secured to the shore.

The crowd of armoured men on the dock rippled like a swarm of bees as the second galley struggled to make landfall. Those vessels already moored on either side of the new arrivals were now bristling with warriors. Every man was armed with the long curved swords or the simple short bow of the islands, arrows nocked and ready.

Jilseth's skin crawled with unease. Either that or the swathing elemental air was grating against her innate affinity.

Something by the waterside tripped the hovering

hostility into open aggression. Swordsmen stormed up each galley's stern ladders to overwhelm those on the raised decks. As they headed into the belly of each ship, loud alarm flew up from the rowers' benches.

Those first swordsmen reappeared with shocking speed to throw writhing bodies in ragged clothing down onto the quayside. The shifting mob ashore broke apart only to close on their victims in frenzied slaughter.

Heart-rending screams ripped through the roars of hatred. A few frantic corsairs struggled to their knees, momentarily visible before armoured men closed ranks around them. Blades gleamed in the sunlight, slicing downwards. Swords lifted dulled with blood to fling scarlet drops through the air. Lethal steel bit deep again and again.

Some of the murderous Archipelagans jostled so close together that they hindered each others' butchery. Jilseth saw one desperate corsair crawling between stamping feet as the men who sought to kill him threatened to turn their blades on each other.

He had no hope of escape. Two different Aldabreshi hacked him limb from limb. Jilseth's only consolation was that he must surely have been already mortally wounded, given the copious blood smeared behind him. One killer kicked the dismembered man's head, sending it bowling along the thoroughfare.

'Oh, dear.'

Jilseth looked hastily around but there was no one close enough to have heard Mellitha's dismay. Following the magewoman's silently pointing finger, she saw twin pillars of smoke rising. Fire burned in the waist of each galley.

Those Aldabreshin swordsmen who had swarmed

aboard were fleeing the ships. Some fell headlong down the ladders in their haste. Hauling themselves up from the stones, they limped away or clutched a broken arm across an armoured chest.

That disembodied head rolled back through the glistening pools of blood and the mutilated corpses. Relshazri watchmen had appeared in the alleys between the tall storehouses.

They wore Aldabreshin chainmail; the Magistracy could well afford to buy the finest armour. They did not favour Archipelagan swords though or the heavier, straighter blades more usual on the mainland. The watchmen all carried polearms with iron-shod hafts. Each one topped with a collar of spikes below a curved cutting blade which was tipped in turn with a piercing spike a handspan long.

'You put out that fire or you answer for it!' The nearest sergeant's outraged bellow fought the chaos spreading further along the quay.

More watchmen were yelling the same. Other detachments escorted frightened men hauling laden handcarts. Jilseth recognised the ungainly bulk of a fire pump; the squat apparatus framed by horizontal bars on either side.

The Archipelagans recognised the leather serpents looped on the tops of the pumps, waiting for quenching water to be forced through their coils towards each one's gaping brass head.

At first the Aldabreshi retreated, swords lowered, too bloody to sheathe. They shouted back at the watchmen, some in Relshazri dialect, most in the Archipelagan tongue. Jilseth couldn't make out what any of them said.

Then she couldn't hear anything at all. Her head pounded painfully in this magical silence.

'Fire-starting in any Relshazri dockyard is a capital offence.' Mellith looked grim through the blurring of Velindre's azure magic.

The tall magewoman repeated the shouted Archipelagan justification. 'But only fire will cleanse the stain of magic from this harbour which they consider as good as their own territory.'

Mellitha shook her head, in dismay rather than denial. 'We must stop this getting any worse.'

'And quickly.' Jilseth flinched as a handful of Aldabreshi attacked a hapless fire gang.

Several Relshazri reeled away clutching spurting cuts. One fell to his knees, mouth gaping in a silent scream as he clutched the stump of his severed hand.

Watchmen immediately raced to their aid. The first Aldabreshi to stand his ground was skewered by a pole arm's needle-point driven deep into his chest. The next was felled by a slicing blade sweeping low to smash his knees. The butt of the weapon finished him off, crushing one eye socket into bloody splinters.

Jilseth found the carnage all the more ghastly for unfolding in the utter quiet of elemental silence.

'No one must suspect magic,' Velindre insisted.

'There's no law forbidding us here,' Jilseth protested, 'and the Archmage—'

Mellitha cut her short. 'We cannot have the Archipelagans believing that the Magistracy let wizards loose on them.'

'Quite so.' Velindre's eyes were darting this way and that. 'Jilseth, blunt blades and offer some shield to those being attacked. I'll stifle the fires until the

Relshazri can get through to douse them.'

Before she could hear what Mellitha was supposed to do, Jilseth was deafened by the maelstrom of yells and abuse. She staggered backwards into the unyielding door of a building. To her relief, the other two magewoman followed her unintentional lead into that precarious shelter.

Hastily gathering her wits, Jilseth was relieved to see that most of the Aldabreshi had recovered their senses sufficiently not to attack the Relshazri without direct provocation.

Though the Archipelagans were adamant that the galleys should burn. They drew up into haphazard ranks all along the waterfront. Any attempt by the watchmen to force a path for a fire pump prompted savage retaliation.

Jilseth focused on the Archipelagans' single-edged swords, each one razor sharp. It was the work of a moment to smooth her magic along the metal. Now the blades would bruise and perhaps cut flesh but no longer slice clean through bone.

For an instant, she lingered, her affinity flowing through the intricacy of the weapons' steel. These layers upon layers of wafer-thin metal were quite unlike the watered silk patterns that she had felt in mainland swords.

She threw off the distraction, turning instead to the closest handcart. The fire gang cowered behind a handful of watchmen. Three Aldabreshi attacked; intent on destroying the pump itself. The first fell, betrayed by a slick of blood. As he sprawled headlong, the second lost his footing and then the third.

Jilseth's wizard sight caught fugitive glimpses of

emerald magelight all along the dockside as men were thrown off balance by the gore underfoot. Not so obviously as to look ridiculous or, worse, suspicious, but sufficient to rob their sword strokes of fatal effect if not deadly purpose.

A Relshazri sergeant drove his men forward to seize that breach in the Aldabreshin line. More watchmen rushed to support them, shoulder to shoulder with their pole-arms jabbing and stabbing, their longer reach defying Archipelagan swords.

The Relshazri wedge drove through to the edge of the quay. The men divided into two resolute lines, back to back and forcing the Aldabreshi to retreat step by step. The watchmen found firm footing while the islanders slipped and stumbled.

Now solid bulwarks guarded the fire pump's path to the waterside. The watchmen gave the fire gang no choice but to advance. Despite all the frantic Aldabreshin efforts, the handcart rattled to the water's edge.

A swift tug of Jilseth's magic and the water serpent's leather loops obediently uncoiled when the sweating pump master grabbed them. As the tail end fell down from the quayside into the harbour, she felt the surge of Mellitha's affinity sending seawater soaring up into the pump.

As soon as the gang started hauling the side bars up and down, Jilseth turned her attention to the brass valves between the pump and the serpent's gaping jaws. If the pump master ever wondered at how easily the stiff metal turned under his hands, he could put it down to his own strength born of terror.

Water spewed from the brass serpent's mouth, arcing upwards to fall down into the midst of the galley. Seeing

Velindre's sparkling magecraft cleave a path through the air for the jet itself driven on by Mellitha's wizardry, Jilseth had no doubt that the fires would quickly be quenched.

She turned her attention back to blunting the ire of those still intent on mayhem. She threaded her wizardry through the links of their armour. Though their chainmail had been wrought of fine steel, now it burdened the wearers like lead. Their swords weighed twice and thrice as much in their weary hands. Exhaustion would force the men to a standstill.

Once again, sudden silence left her momentarily dizzy.

'Those fires won't be rekindled.' Velindre's shimmering lips curved in a cold smile.

'We'd better make haste home.' Mellitha's water affinity had coloured the invisibility cloaking her almost turquoise after all her exertions. 'I'll be summoned by the Magistracy before the next chime.' She turned her glittering gaze on Jilseth. 'You had better come with me as Hadrumal's envoy.'

'I can't claim that office,' she protested.

'Why not?' Velindre challenged her. 'Planir sent you here and you've just proved your worth as a wizard. There's no need for any more nonsense about whether or not you can control your affinity.'

'I—' Jilseth stared at the hard-faced magewoman. There was no denying that she had forgotten all her doubts amid this chaos. That she had worked her magic with the ease and competence which she had truly feared was lost.

She also realised that she was rank with sweat and though translucent as she was thanks to Velindre's wizardry, she could see her gown was spattered with tiny dark stains. It was scant comfort to see the other two magewomen were equally dishevelled.

Velindre's iridescent eyes were unreadable through the veil of the magic. 'I know what it's like to have drained your magic to such an extent that you fear it will never return.'

'Enough.' Mellitha silenced them both with upraised hands. 'We must tell Planir what's transpired here as soon as the Magistrates are done with us.'

'I will be discovered in the gem-cutters' quarter,' Velindre announced, 'ready to be astonished by such tales of anarchy along the dockside. Bespeak me when you've placated the Magistrates. We should speak to Planir together.'

She vanished from the quayside between one step and the next.

— CHAPTER EIGHTEEN —

Black Turtle Isle

In the domain of Nahik Jarir

'GET THEM ALL together.' Anskal roused Hosh with a kick.

Hosh had already been rolling away. Sleeping in the furthest pavilion's entrance hall, he stirred whenever a sand-coloured lizard scuttled up the walls or a wind-blown leaf scraped along the terrace outside.

He had a comfortable bed now; a pile of three cotton-stuffed palliasses purloined from Archipelagan rope-strung bed frames. For the present, a single light quilt sufficed but come winter, he could have all the coverlets he might want. Not that he expected to be alive come winter.

'Yes, my lord mage.' He rubbed the remnants of sleep from his eyes with his other hand.

He winced at the insidious tenderness beneath the dent in his face. The toothless side of his upper jaw felt puffy and sore to his probing tongue and the taste in his mouth on waking grew more vile each successive morning. But there was nothing to be done about that without Imais and her herbal concoctions.

Hosh pulled his cotton tunic over his head and retied the drawstring of his trousers which he'd loosened for sleep. If something happened in the night, he wasn't going to Saedrin's door bare-arsed.

As he hurried down the terrace steps Anskal shouted an afterthought. 'Tell them to bring food!'

'Yes, my lord mage.' As Hosh raised his hand in acknowledgement, he saw movement at a window beneath the shady eaves of the closest dwelling.

Those shutters stayed wide open, day and night. Six Archipelagans had claimed that pavilion, all erstwhile swordsmen from the corsair triremes. Standing sentry turn by turn, they kept a close eye on Anskal from one sunset to the next.

Hosh headed for the steps, fringed with lush green grass where deep rooted tufts formerly crushed by trampling feet had been renewed by the rains.

'That's close enough, broken face.' A corsair appeared up on the black stone platform, more alert than hostile. 'What do you want?'

Hosh jerked his head back towards the furthest pavilion. 'He wants you all to join him. Bring something for breakfast.'

The corsair looked warily across the open space. 'What does he want?'

Hosh shrugged. 'I don't know.'

He would never have dared to answer the swordsman so carelessly without his magical arm ring. The Archipelagan wore two swords and three daggers which Hosh could see, never mind whatever lesser blades the man had surely concealed about himself.

These erstwhile raiders had scoured all the abandoned pavilions for weapons. Each man had probably amassed as many blades as the rest of these people trapped in the anchorage could have put together between them.

'We will come.' The raider squared his bare bronzed shoulders as though readying himself for the challenge.

Archipelagan born by his speech, he clearly had mainland forebears on both sides of his lineage to bequeath him that complexion. His new comrades' colouring ranged from ebony to a sallow tan.

'Thank you.' As Hosh headed for the next pavilion, he heard the bronzed swordsman calling out to rouse his allies.

There was no grass growing around this next set of steps. These five surviving women had scoured all encroaching vegetation away, just as they had thrown open all their chosen pavilion's shutters and doors when they claimed it. They weren't interested in keeping watch though, but in sweeping away the wind-blown dust and broken discards from Anskal's earlier plundering.

Of course there had been more of the women then. Nine, all told. One in four of the mageborn.

Was that usual, Hosh had wondered, on that other island of Hadrumal? He had so little knowledge of magecraft, though he did recall tavern tales which spoke of lady wizards.

This morning, their doors and shutters were tight closed.

'Good day to you!' As Hosh waited for a response, he looked over towards the other pavilions, beyond the blasted wreckage of blind Grewa's house.

A handful of Archipelagan slaves now squatted in the *Reef Eagle*'s master's home. He had seen them beseech the women or the swordsmen to give them some task to earn their favour.

Hosh could see the sense of staying on good terms with such heavily armed warriors. He wondered what the slaves thought they might get from the women. There'd been no sign that the remaining handful were willing to cook, clean or launder for anyone but themselves.

As for any other services, Anskal had shown no sign of interest in spreading their thighs—

'What do you want here?'

It wasn't one of the women opening a window up above. One of the mainlanders had appeared around the corner of the pavilion's broad stone foundation.

A second followed, growling. 'We get first split, shit-face.'

The third man simply leered, one hand already inside his loosened trews, trifling with his stick and stones.

At first Hosh had found these three men's behaviour as incomprehensible as their accents. Then he overheard the two Lescari lads condemning them as mercenaries. Lice sucking the blood of honest men in their homeland's recent strife. This last craven remnant of some defeated warband had evidently been captured in battle and sold down the river to the Relshazri slave markets.

Hosh backed away, empty hands raised. 'I came to tell you that you're wanted over yonder.' He gestured towards Anskal's pavilion. 'He won't like to be kept waiting,' he warned.

The first mercenary grinned. 'He can wait.' He brandished a fist at Hosh, a thick brass ring catching the morning light. 'What's he going to do? Flog us for being tardy?

The other two nodded in comfortable agreement.

Hosh took another step back. 'I'm only the messenger.'

'Then take him this message.' The first mercenary took a menacing step. 'We'll come when we're good and ready.'

'I will.' As Hosh continued retreating, the three

mercenaries went up the stone steps to contemplate the pavilion door.

Hosh looked frantically towards the pavilion where the other mainlanders had chosen to shelter; the two Lescari militiamen and four from Ensaimin with the weathered skin and hard muscles of lifelong seamen.

He heard splintering wood up above as a shutter was ripped open. A woman screamed. Another cursed.

Hosh turned tail and ran to Anskal's pavilion. He scrambled up the steps, slipping onto hands and knees in his haste.

The Mandarkin was standing in the doorway, an uncorked bottle in one hand.

'You must do something!' Hosh point a shaking hand at the women's pavilion, at the dark void of the broken window where the mercenaries had forced their way in. The women's shrieks and curses rang through the clear air.

Anskal smiled lazily. 'It is none of my affair.'

Hosh gaped at him.

The Mandarkin merely shrugged, taking a long swallow of his palm wine.

As Hosh whirled around, movement caught his eye on the terrace outside the Aldabreshin raiders' pavilion. All six men had emerged, armed and armoured, looking in the direction of the women's house. Even at this distance, Hosh could see they were appalled.

He ran down the steps and across the beaten earth. 'You must do something! This isn't right!'

He couldn't tell if they had heard him. Regardless, they were already making their way down their own pavilion's stair. Falling instinctively into step, every man drew a blade. They were all ready to defend each other, their instincts born of years of survival amid deadly peril.

Hosh hesitated. He had no sword, unless he recovered the one he had hidden. If he did, what help could he offer those women that a handful and more of expert warriors couldn't?

Before he could take another step, another scream soared above the muffled sobbing inside the women's house. Hosh only had an instant to realise that was a man's screech cut brutally short.

Surprise equal to his own halted the advancing Aldabreshi. They stopped, blades ready, as tense as hunting dogs.

Hosh saw a man inside the building stumbling backwards towards the broken-shuttered window. He was swearing in the vilest terms to ever soil a Tormalin tongue. The low sill caught him behind the knees and he fell out on to the terrace.

Two women leaped through the window after him. One landed to kneel on the mercenary's chest, beating him around the head and face with already bloodied fists. Hosh didn't need to understand her dialect to know she was cursing him to some unspeakable torment. The man flailed ineffectual hands, his retching indicating that she had already struck a mighty blow to his manhood.

The second woman seized the mercenary's ears. She lifted his head to smash it down on the unforgiving stones. Even after he went limp, Hosh expected her to continue until the man's brain began leaking out of his ears. Instead, the woman turned her attention to the man's hand. He had a melon knife. She took it and ripped it across the senseless man's throat. Springing to her feet, she vaulted the window sill with her sister in arms following her back into the building.

That spurred the Aldabreshin raiders to action. As they ran for the pavilion and up the steps, Hosh followed. As he reached the terrace, he saw the other mainlanders approaching, all open mouthed at this commotion. The former slaves dithered on the *Reef Eagle* pavilion's terrace.

One of the raiders kicked in the women's door with a well-practised foot. He immediately stepped backwards, throwing his sword away and raising empty hands. At his sharp command, all the other Aldabreshi sheathed their blades and spread their own arms wide. All the men retreated to the precipitous edge of the terrace.

Left alone at the top of the stair Hosh could see into the pavilion's entrance hall. The woman with the melon knife stood over the second man she had killed. The first mercenary who had ripped open the shutter lay sprawled on his back. His tunic was rucked up and his trews were bunched around his ankles. Loops of bowel protruded from the ragged gash across his naked belly.

Another woman stood in the inner doorway. She was all but naked, her bitten breasts bare for all to see. Her loose tunic had been torn from hem to neck by her attacker and her skirt or trews were nowhere to be seen. Her own violated blood trickled down her inner thighs. Tears from one swelling eye mingled with blood trickling from her split lip.

Undaunted, she took a step forward and brandished a knife at Hosh. 'You want to try your luck with us?'

Another woman appeared in the doorway, carrying a cleaver smeared with gore in one hand and a severed head in the other. Hosh recognised the man who'd been polishing up his stick in anticipation of beating these women into submission.

'Enter and be welcome.' Her smile was as friendly as one of the sharks who followed the galleys.

'If you dare.' The fifth woman emerged from a doorway to the rear of the hall. She carried a kitchen blade as well and looked just as eager to use it.

'I don't want—' Hosh took two steps back in hasty denial.

'Then leave us be!' The woman with the cleaver hurled the heavy steel at him.

Hosh was ready to jump and risk the drop rather than try escaping down the stairs. Instead, a shove of sapphire magelight sent the cleaver skidding across the black stones. Every man and woman recoiled from the brutal burst of wizardly radiance.

Anskal stepped out of the fading glare. 'So now you see.' He smiled with vicious satisfaction. 'Magebirth does not save you from attack. Yet working together, the weakest can defeat lustful fools.' He acknowledged the women with something approaching a nod of respect. 'Especially those brave enough to wait until such a fool is rutting like a fevered dog.'

Hosh looked aghast at the woman who'd been raped. Had she yielded to such violation for the sake of getting close enough to the mercenary to gut him with that knife? In order that his companions would be so rapt at the sight that her house sisters' attack could surprise them?

The implacable resolve in her unswollen eye convinced him she had indeed traded her body's immediate sufferings so that those three brutes could be taken unawares.

Mainland born brutes. Hosh could be certain that Saedrin would bar the door to the Otherworld while Poldrion's demons savaged them for an eternity. Though he decided against offering that consolation to these women.

'All of you, heed me now!'

As Anskal's words echoed oddly, Hosh saw the mainlanders and the slaves on their distant terraces stiffen. He guessed more magic was carrying the Mandarkin's words to their ears.

Anskal tossed an embroidered leather pouch to the woman with the melon knife.

She untied the drawstring and shifted the pouch in her hand for a better view of the contents before looking up at the wizard. 'Is this recompense?' Anger choked her.

'No.' Anskal gestured and the fallen cleaver spun through the air towards Hosh.

He couldn't help flinching as it rebounded from the arm ring's magic.

'You may be mageborn but you know nothing of magic. You cannot so much as defend yourselves against fools with knives. So I will give you a little such bound magic to protect yourself, for the moment.'

He gestured towards Hosh and smiled as the woman's expression turned to wary comprehension. She took a fine silver gorget on a chain from the pouch. Dropping her knife, she fastened it around her neck.

Anskal grinned and sent a twist of sapphire magic to hurl the cleaver at the woman. Hosh gasped along with everyone else as the heavy steel crumbled into rust before it came within a handspan of her cringing shoulder.

'I have more such valuable trinkets. Their magic differs in strength and effect.' Anskal's smile turned sly.

'The first to submit to me will be given the choicest. You know you need me to teach and guide you, if you are not to be as easily killed as these blind fools!'

As the Mandarkin gestured, contemptuous at the dead mercenaries, his challenge rang back from the walls of the distant pavilions.

Before anyone else could speak, he vanished in another blinding flash of light. An instant later the same bright blue radiance flared inside the furthest pavilion. No one need doubt where Anskal was waiting for their homage.

The women retreated into their pavilion, into the chamber beyond the entrance hall to close an unsplintered door on the slaughter. The raiders disappeared as promptly into their own bolt-hole and the slaves hadn't yet got half way so they scurried back to their lair.

The mainlanders stood gathered together below the pavilion's steps. Their conversation was too low-voiced and too swift for Hosh but their decision was soon apparent.

They came up the stairs and four went into the entrance hall to retrieve the headless corpse and the gutted rapist's body. The remaining two Ensaimin grappled with the dead man below the window. Throwing all three off the terrace to begin with, the men then went down the steps, retrieved the bodies and began carrying them away.

Hosh followed them to the headland on the southern side of the anchorage. He spared a wary glance for Anskal's pavilion as they passed by but there was no sign of the wizard.

As the mainlanders approached the headland, reef eagles and yellow-eyed gulls began wheeling overhead, eager to feast on the carrion. The sweating men threw the dead mercenaries into the breaking waves instead.

If they had been Aldabreshi, they would have waited to see if sharks or sea serpents appeared to feast on the windfall. Ensaimin and Lescari alike had no interest in such portents.

'What do you want?'

The last of the men to pass him as they headed back stopped to stare at Hosh.

'I—' Hosh didn't have an answer so he asked a question of his own. 'Do you want to be subject to that man?' He gestured towards Anskal's pavilion.

The Ensaimin mariner scowled. 'What choices do we have, trapped here?'

'You can sail a boat. We could escape,' Hosh urged desperately. 'If you are mageborn and from the mainland, the Archmage of Hadrumal is surely honour bound to help you.'

'Where is he? This Archmage?' The mariner cocked his ragged head. He and the rest had found some shears or knives to cut away the tangled locks that had marked them as slaves for all to see. 'Do you have a boat to sail away in?'

Hosh nodded towards the wrecked trireme in the anchorage. 'Surely we could make a raft?'

Though as he spoke, he wondered how they could possibly do that without catching Anskal's eye. Unless the Mandarkin was content for them to paddle off and drown. He had let so many of these mageborn kill themselves after all.

One of the Lescari militiamen had stopped walking to look back, his attention caught by their conversation. He retraced his steps.

'Hadrumal's wizards only help their own,' he sneered. 'My home has been plagued by the dukes and their bloody quarrels for ten generations. No Archmage ever spared us a tinker's curse.'

'What did he give you?' The Ensaimin mariner had a more pressing question now. 'To save you from harm?'

Hosh's hand strayed to the ring encircling his arm. 'A trinket,' he said slowly.

The Ensaimin mariner held out his hand. 'Give it to me and I'll help you make a raft.'

'Build the raft,' Hosh countered, 'and you can have it when we reach the mainland.'

As he spoke, the silver gilt tightened around his upper arm. Gasping, Hosh sank to his knees, clawing at the thing with his free hand. His arm was throbbing. His hand was swelling, visibly darkening. Hosh felt as though his fingers were about to burst like overstuffed sausages. He tried to force the ornament down towards his elbow but he couldn't get so much as a fingernail between the metal and his aching flesh.

The Ensaimin mariner muttered something under his breath and walked away. The Lescari waited for him and they went onward together, heads close in conversation.

Hosh slowly realised that the agony in his arm was lessening. The throbbing in his hand subsided and the terror twisting his bowels eased.

Reluctantly, he reached for the arm ring. The lightest touch left him whimpering, the flesh beneath was so viciously bruised. The only consolation he could find amid that dizzying agony was feeling the metal slip against the cloth. The arm ring was loose again.

Cradling the elbow of his aching arm eased the pain a little. As he contemplated the dull gleam of gold and crystal, he wondered blindly if this was Anskal's doing or some magical property of the cursed trinket? Not that it made much difference.

He staggered to his feet and made his way back towards the Mandarkin's pavilion. It was scant consolation to see that the mainlanders were all walking back to their own dwelling. They might not be ready to yield to Anskal without further deliberation but surely, as the mariner had said, what choices did they have?

As he climbed the steps to Anskal's pavilion, sudden rage swelled in Hosh's chest. He stormed through the open door and into the wide chamber beyond. If he was going to die anyway, he might as well court a swift and painless death.

The Mandarkin wizard was reclining on a heap of silken cushions, the bottle of palm wine in one hand as he laughed at the brightly coloured birds squabbling in a fig tree in the enclosed garden.

'Those women are mageborn like you!' Hosh shouted furiously. 'Why did you leave them undefended against such abuse?'

Anskal smiled smugly up at him. 'Magebirth is no measure of merit. I wanted to see who would be tempted to abuse the power which they thought they now possessed. Then the rest could see how such arrogance would betray them. Now they all know how much they need me to teach them, how much they all have to learn.'

'You could have told them—'

'Why waste breath warning a child against fire when the burned hand teaches best?' Anskal retorted. 'Now they will all come here, willing and eager to learn. Now they know that is the only way to save their own skins.

Now the women know that any men who would have abused them here are dead.'

'And if those women hadn't fought back?' Hosh demanded angrily.

Anskal shrugged. 'Then the men would have fought over who might claim the whores. But all turned out much as I expected,' he congratulated himself, callous. 'I have seen how fiercely women fight when they have no other recourse.'

As the Mandarkin's gaze turned inward, a shiver caught Hosh unawares. What had Anskal's life been like to leave him so pitiless? What was he truly capable of?

'See?' Anskal looked smugly towards the open door.

Hosh could hear the first of the mageborn warily approaching. The Aldabreshi swordsmen, judging by their voices.

— CHAPTER NINETEEN —

The Esterlin Residence, Relshaz
22nd of For-Autumn

Jᴉʟsᴇᴛʜ ʜᴜʀʀɪᴇᴅ ᴛʜʀᴏᴜɢʜ the marble-floored hallway. She didn't wait for today's handsome lackey to open the door to the salon overlooking the garden. 'Madam Mellitha? Oh—'

She stopped short beside a rosewood lamp-stand. 'Archmage? Good day to you,' she said hastily, 'and to you, Nolyen.'

'Join us,' Mellitha indicated the space beside her on the day bed.

Nolyen and Planir sat opposite on a silk cushioned settle with the low table between them.

'You have news,' the Archmage observed.

'I do,' Jilseth confirmed, 'and unwelcome.'

'You've been out since first light and it's long past noon. You should eat.' As Jilseth sat down, Mellitha handed her a gilt-edged plate.

With the tall windows standing open, the fine muslin curtains drifted towards the tray of savouries on the table. Smudged plates showed that the other wizards had already eaten their fill.

'The Archmage has sent Corrain, Baron Halferan, to Solura, as his envoy to the Elders of Fornet.' Mellitha poured her a lemon-scented glassful from the frosted jug.

Jilseth nearly dropped the salted almonds she'd helped herself to.

'You look as startled as he was.' Planir's smile came and went.

'Let's hope the Soluran Orders are similarly surprised, and sufficiently intrigued to give him a hearing,' Mellitha said tartly.

'Indeed. All the Hearth Master's efforts to explain recent events to them have come to naught.' Planir's expression hardened.

'Corrain agreed to go?' Jilseth reached for a batter cake topped with spiced mushrooms. 'What did he want in return?'

'Punishment.' The shadow behind Planir's eyes belied his lightness. 'Since his dead lord can no longer offer him redemption from all his calamitous mistakes by imposing suitable chastisement, I am more than happy to oblige.'

Jilseth had no idea how to answer that so settled for taking a roundel of cheese layered with pickled plums.

'We can see if his confession will help us to mend fences with the Solurans,' Planir continued more coldly. 'If they flay the skin from his back for consorting with the Mandarkin, so be it. If they think one of their Aetheric adepts can riffle through his thoughts and find the secrets of quintessential magic, they are welcome to try.'

Jilseth had never imagined she would feel such a pang of sympathy for Corrain.

'Halferan has neighbours who will make trouble,' she ventured, 'once they learn that the baron is absent again.'

'Not with Tornauld there as my personal envoy to assist in the manor's restoration,' Planir assured her.

'Of course.' Jilseth continued to fill her plate and

wondered what Zurenne and Ilysh would make of her brusque Ensaimin friend. He had probably already summoned up a whirlwind to scour Halferan clean for rebuilding.

The Archmage glanced at Mellitha. 'He will be keeping a weather eye out for any more visits from Anskal. Our Mandarkin friend has threatened the Widow Zurenne and her daughters,' he explained to Jilseth. 'He sees those pendants which I gave them both as proof of Corrain's deceit, and of some store of artefacts that he's concealed.'

'Tornauld should be a match for this Mandarkin,' Nolyen said stoutly.

Jilseth could only hope that he was right. She remembered what they had seen of the mysterious wizard's magic when three Soluran mages had been doing their utmost to kill him. Three mages well practised in using their magic with such lethal intent. Still, Tornauld had seen the same in the scrying nexus which she and Nolyen had worked with him and Merenel. Forewarned was surely forearmed.

'Hopefully, he won't have to prove that, though I'm sure he would like to try.' Planir shook his head as though remembering what Jilseth knew must have been a lively conversation.

Mellitha waved that away. 'What if the Solurans are content to quench their outrage in Corrain's blood without offering up any lore on ensorcelled artefacts?' However motherly her appearance, she clearly was more concerned about such an outcome than for Corrain's possible suffering.

Planir nodded. 'That's why Nolyen and I are heading to Suthyfer.'

Mellitha's precisely plucked brows arched. 'That thrice-cursed ring has given Usara or Shiv some insights into ensorcelled trinkets?'

Jilseth looked at Nolyen to see if he knew what this meant. Rather than returning her blank look, he narrowed his eyes, warning her not to ask.

She settled for eating another roll of vellum-thin pastry, filled with spiced meat, honey and raisins in the Aldabreshin style. Mellitha was right; she had spent a long and hungry morning with the coachman Tanilo taking her from one address to another in search of Relshaz's resident wizards, asking for any rumour which they might ever have heard about such artefacts, for any hint of lore that might have escaped Hadrumal's libraries.

'I've no idea what Usara has done with that ring, though Nolyen's naturally welcome to enquire.' Planir was answering Mellitha. 'I am more interested in talking to Aritane. All the more so if the Solurans insist that we've brought this trouble on ourselves and still refuse to help. This Anskal must surely be expecting some elemental challenge but perhaps we could surprise him with Artifice.'

'Aritane? She's the *sheltya* woman from the Mountains?' Mellitha looked thoughtful.

As Planir nodded, Jilseth looked at Nolyen and saw that, once again, he knew more of this than she did.

What little she did know chilled Jilseth. Not even Hadrumal's most scornful wizards could deny that an Aetheric adept of sufficient skill and malicious intent could invade a mage's thoughts. When the mage was intent on spellcrafting, such an assault could leave the victim comatose or dead. Hadrumal's finest scholars of affinity could not yet fathom that mystery.

'For the moment, how do matters stand in Relshaz?' Planir looked at Jilseth. 'You arrived like a hound with a hare in its mouth. What do you have to tell us?'

Jilseth cleared her throat with a swallow of the light metheglin. 'Ereweth, Fyrne and Senthal all say that they're being shunned by anyone doing significant business with the Archipelago though no one will explain why. Master Kerrit has been trying to find out—'

The salon's door flew open, once again without the help of Mellitha's well-favoured lackey. Velindre strode in. 'The Aldabreshi know that there's a wizard laired in the Nahik domain.'

The Archmage shifted to the edge of his seat. 'What do the Aldabreshi intend to do?'

'As yet, I don't know,' Velindre said grimly. 'But whatever they might do, I can tell you that they will act this side of the thirty-eighth day of this season. That's when the heavenly Emerald shifts into the arc of Death when the Diamond and the waxing Pearl will be waiting there to greet it. The Opal will be waning through the arc of Foes and then shifts to that of Life. Add the voids which that leaves in the heavenly compass and no Archipelagan will risk challenging a wizard under such skies.'

Jilseth saw Planir and Mellitha both understood how serious this was, for all that the blonde magewoman's words left Nolyen baffled as she was.

'The Emerald will linger in that same heavenly arc to weight every omen and portent until the third For-Spring from now,' Velindre continued, sombre. 'It's inconceivable that any warlord will tolerate such corruption staining the islands for so long, in a domain commanding such a vital sea lane. They will act, most likely when the Diamond shifts into the arc of Death though some will argue for waiting until the Amethyst joins the Ruby in the arc of Honour and Ambition.'

'When will those particular days fall, according to an almanac?' Planir queried.

'The Diamond shifts on the twenty-seventh of the season and the Amethyst on the thirty-first.' Velindre sat on the foot of Mellitha's silken day bed.

'Who will be the first warlord to act?' the older magewoman wondered.

'Jagai Kalu.' Velindre spoke without hesitation. 'I've no doubt he's settling his differences with Miris Esul as we speak. A crisis such as this should even get Khusro Rina down from his observatory.'

'His wives will already be busy,' Mellitha agreed.

Once again, Jilseth saw her own frustration reflected on Nolyen's face. There was so much they didn't fully comprehend here.

'If we hadn't been so cursedly thorough with that warding across the Archipelago, we could have summoned up a dragon to be the death of this Mandarkin.' Velindre ran a hand through her cropped hair, leaving herself crowned with golden spikes. 'No beast could resist the lure of so many ensorcelled artefacts. Doubtless the creature biting this Anskal's head off would cause commotion among the northern reaches but at least we'd have an end to this strife.'

'Otrick would be proud of you.' Mellitha smiled without much humour.

'Since that option's not open to us, shall we consider our other choices?' Planir invited tartly.

This time Jilseth saw that Nolyen could make more sense of those cryptic allusions.

'The Archipelagans might cut through this knot.' Though Velindre didn't sound overly hopeful. 'If they can kill this Mandarkin before the skies turn against them.' She sighed. 'Meantime all the Aldabreshi merchants here are refusing to do business with anyone whom they know to have dealings with wizardry. I have had a double handful of sea-captains send me sincere notes of regret, dispensing with my services. They would rather risk some unexpected squall than the certainty of Archipelagan hostility.'

'How long do we suppose this enmity towards us will persist?' Mellitha wondered.

'Once the Mandarkin Anskal is dead?' Velindre pursed her mouth. 'With good portents and a following wind, such fears should fade over a couple of winters.'

Planir raised a hand. 'Let's look back before we look forward. That might help us see our path more clearly. We know that the Aldabreshi here slaughtered the escaping corsairs. Had those ships made landfall anywhere between the Nahik domain and here? What word might have come from the Archipelago to prompt such merciless bloodletting?'

'We can ask.' Velindre shared a glance with Mellitha. 'Discreetly.'

'We will have to pass our requests from hand to hand and all round the city to disguise their origin.' The plump magewoman grimaced. 'Not a swift business.'

Jilseth studied the skirt of her mother-of-pearl gown. No trace remained of the mist of blood which had stained it on the dockside, thanks to those trifling cantrips that the rawest apprentices learned in Hadrumal.

If only she hadn't been so keen to relieve Mellitha's laundresses of the challenge of cleaning the costly cloth.

There were always hints of a man's travels in his blood.

She drained her glass of lemon metheglin and briefly wished it was the darker kind, brewed as much for intoxication as refreshment. A little courage born of liquor wouldn't go amiss.

'I might be able to learn something more useful more quickly.'

'How?' Velindre demanded.

'If we could recover some remnant of a corsair who died on the docks—' Jilseth couldn't restrain a shiver at the memory of that mayhem.

'—we can see what necromancy tells us,' Planir approved.

Velindre looked more doubtful. 'The docks have been scoured clean with salt and boiling water. A slave was accidentally scalded to death. The taverns and tisane houses are full of it.'

'The stones may have been cleansed but I saw more than one body fall off the dockside,' Mellitha observed.

'How—?' Before Nolyen could ask his question, the salon door opened a third time.

The lackey advanced with a silver tray bearing a twice sealed reed-paper letter.

'Thank you.' Mellitha snapped the wax discs, unfolding the letter to read swiftly as the servant waited for her instructions.

'I'm summoned to the Magistracy,' she said briefly as she rose from the day bed, 'in terms that make it unwise to delay.'

Velindre was shocked. 'They can't turn on you.'

'Not if they want the taxes to keep their watchmen paid,' Mellitha agreed as she smoothed her viridian gown over her hips. 'But I'd rather not give them pause for thought when they award next year's contracts.'

Velindre stood up too. 'I will set my own enquiries in hand.'

The Archmage looked at Jilseth and Nolyen. 'I take it you two can be suitably discreet retrieving some carrion from the docks? I will go on to Suthyfer.'

Mellitha addressed her servant. 'Tell Tanilo to take Madam Jilseth and Master Nolyen to the Pewter Rose fountain and then come back here to take me to the Magistracy. Naturally I will attend them today but they need not think that I'm entirely at their beck and call.'

As the salon door closed behind the lackey, she sketched directions in the air for Jilseth and Nolyen. 'Tanilo had better not take you all the way. If someone recognises him or my carriage, that'll be sufficient to associate you with wizardry even if no one knows who you are. Follow the Whitesmith's Lane towards the sea from the fountain square. Head westerly from the Cup of Secrets tavern and the main thrust of the road will bring you to the eastern breakwater of the Archipelago dock.'

'I understand.' Jilseth studied the glowing lines.

'Watch your step and use as little magic as possible,' Velindre advised. 'The slightest suspicion of magelight could draw unwelcome attention and not only from the Aldabreshi.' She looked at Planir and Mellitha. 'Shall we all meet here at sunset to see what we've learned?'

As everyone nodded she headed for the door without another word.

'Till later then.' Mellitha followed her.

Planir looked at Nolyen and Jilseth. 'Is there any further guidance you need from me?'

'No, thank you.' Nolyen sprang up.

Jilseth set her plate and glass down. 'Archmage.' She settled for a brief nod of farewell and followed Nolyen out into the hallway.

The door closed softly behind them. Naturally. Planir had no need of lackeys.

'Leave that,' she advised as Nolyen reached for his cloak hung on a branch of the carved ebony tree by the white stairs. 'Relshazri rarely wear them.'

Beyond that, his sober garb shouldn't draw curious eyes. A man's breeches and doublet only differed in the detail of buttons, collar and cuffs from Tormalin's ocean coast to Selerima in western Ensaimin. Every such variation could be seen on Relshaz's streets and thanks to Mellitha's seamstress, her own dress was of impeccably local cut.

She opened the outer door to see if Tanilo and the carriage were approaching.

'He can work that bitumen scrying alone now.' Nolyen was looking back towards the salon.

Jilseth recognised her friend's expression all too readily; admiration overlaid with urgent desire to emulate Planir's mastery, undercut by a hint of fear that his own affinity, his understanding, or both would prove unequal to the challenge.

'He is the Archmage,' she reminded Nolyen.

All the same, she wondered what Flood Mistress Troanna or Hearth Master Kalion made of Planir perfecting that spell for his own personal use. If they even knew.

Jilseth had always known that Planir kept a great many secrets closely guarded. That was an obligation of his office. But since she had arrived in Relshaz, she had come to suspect the Archmage did a great many things which Hadrumal's Council learned little or nothing about.

Did the Element Masters and Mistress know that Planir was here in Relshaz? That he intended going to Suthyfer?

Well, it seemed the Archmage had taken Nol into his confidence on some things. As Mellitha's coach horse appeared, Jilseth was glad to have this chance to talk to him.

She had barely pulled the carriage door closed before rounding on him. 'What does the Archmage hope to learn in Suthyfer?'

Nolyen hesitated, gathering his thoughts rather than trying to evade an answer. 'You know that scholars have found aetheric lore in the oldest shrine annals?'

'Of course,' Jilseth said impatiently as the courtyard gates opened to let the carriage leave.

Master Kerrit had been tediously eager to relate his researches among the archives tucked in the cubby holes behind Relshaz's great temple's altars.

'Some suspect there's more lore woven into chimney corner tales and tavern songs,' Nolyen explained, 'especially about the Eldritch Kin.'

'Truly?' That seemed a long step beyond sound reasoning to Jilseth.

Some shrines had endured through the generations since the Old Tormalin Empire had collapsed. It would be no surprise to find that devout priests and priestesses had hoarded their predecessors' wisdom.

The Eldritch Kin were wholly wrought from superstition. They supposedly lived in the shadows, so hard to see with their blue-grey skin, unmistakable with eyes that were pits of darkness. Some stories claimed them as Poldrion's envoys, warning those about to die, especially those with good cause to fear the wrath of his demons. Shiver for no reason? Eldritch Kin had stepped on your shadow, so mainland-born mages would joke.

She recalled an idle evening when Merenel and Tornauld had shared such myths with her and Nolyen, along with several bottles of wine. Some fables seemed to hold true though, however many hundreds of storytellers had passed them on across the thousand leagues that separated the furthest northwest corner of Ensaimin and the remotest tip of southern Tormalin.

Those stories told of a twilight realm between this life and the Otherworld. Of Eldritch Kin crossing from one to the other through shadows at dawn and dusk or under the fleeting arch of a rainbow. Some spoke of the Kin sharing arcane wisdom with those lucky enough to encounter them. More warned of their tricks and caprice, luring the greedy and gullible into their domain whence few would ever escape. Mainland mothers, Jilseth had concluded, kept such tales current to curb any impulse to stray among perilously adventurous children.

'The Archmage seeks such nursery tales in Suthyfer?' She asked, incredulous. 'Not this ring that Mellitha mentioned? And what do you know about that?' she asked pointedly.

Surely knowing more about these magically enhanced treasures was more likely to offer some insight into why Anskal was seeking them.

But Hadrumal's mages had turned their backs on instilling magic into artefacts for the past handful of generations. It had long been felt that offering the most paltry of wizardry's boons to the mundane born indicated very poor judgement in a mage. Jilseth recalled one of her early teachers rebuking a fellow apprentice asking for the truth of spell-casting rings in tavern tales. Such unworthy artefacts degraded every mystery of wizardry, so the Terrene Hall's former Mistress had said.

Nolyen leaned closer, lowering his voice though they were alone in the rattling carriage. 'Did you ever hear the full story of Larissa's death? Planir's lover a handful of years ago?'

'Not really,' Jilseth said slowly.

There had been plenty of speculation around Hadrumal's wine shops. Was Planir truly fulfilling all the obligations of his office when he was so clearly infatuated with this new pupil? Some openly and enviously wondered how soon Larissa might advance to a Council seat by way of the Archmage's bed.

When news spread that Larissa had died, those same wine shop sages wondered how badly the Archmage would be unmanned by what must surely be devastating grief? Jilseth had been far more interested in that debate than in piecing together Larissa's fate from the swirling fragments of gossip.

She had been relieved to see nothing to support such conjecture, any more than she'd ever seen reason to think that Planir would dishonour his office by handing a mage some unearned privilege, however dear they might be to him personally.

'Planir gave Larissa the ring which Mellitha was talking about. It had once belonged to Otrick and to Azazir before him, though I don't know who first ensorcelled it,' Nolyen whispered, wide-eyed.

Jilseth looked at him with equal astonishment. Cloud

Master or not, if half the tales told were true, Otrick had been one of Hadrumal's most unruly mages. Azazir had been far, far worse; always among the previous generation's wizards cited when conversation turned to those mages of legend driven to arrogance, madness and destruction by the intoxicating power afforded by their affinity.

Jilseth had been unpleasantly surprised to hear such tales, ancient and more recent, so commonly told in the mainland taverns, when she had been searching for Minelas last year.

'I'm sure the Archmage had good reason to give her such a ring,' she ventured.

Good reason beyond adorning his sweetheart with some token? Jilseth hadn't entirely believed that Planir and Larissa had been lovers; the woman had a dual affinity after all and any such wizard invariably became the Archmage's personal pupil. Discovering that Planir kept her funeral urn in his study had changed Jilseth's mind about their intimacy but she still had no reason to doubt Planir's integrity. Not so far, any way.

To her relief, Nolyen nodded. 'Very good reason. Larissa and other mages besides, along with other folk from Tormalin, Ensaimin and elsewhere between, were risking their lives in Hadrumal's service. Larissa wasn't the only one who died.' He looked faintly sickened and not by the swaying motion of the carriage through Relshaz's streets.

'Go on,' Jilseth prompted with some apprehension.

'There are Aetheric adepts of notable skills living in a swathe of islands in the northern ocean,' Nolyen explained. 'Akin to the Mountain Men and their *sheltya*. A handful or so years ago, they had ambitions to seize the Suthyfer islands and those new lands beyond the ocean besides.'

'The lands which the Tormalin Emperor had claimed?'

Tadriol the Provident had initially claimed the unexplored expanses, Jilseth recalled, on the grounds of some ill-fated Tormalin nobleman's expedition lost in the first years of the Chaos. Planir had intervened and invited the Emperor to think again, or so the story around Hadrumal went.

Whatever the truth of that, those unbounded lands were now open to anyone willing to risk the perilous ocean crossing. The vital stepping stones on that route, the islands of Suthyfer had become a self-governing fiefdom rapidly growing into a trading centre with ambitions to rival Ensaimin's city states.

Nolyen was nodding. 'Planir, Otrick and the Hearth Master led the first mages to defend the settlers—'

'Kalion?' Jilseth struggled to believe that. The Hearth Master was known to leave Hadrumal to be wined and dined by noblemen from Caladhria to Toremal but to suffer the indignities and discomforts of a settlement being hacked out of untamed wilderness?

But Nolyen was nodding. 'There were several clashes between those northern adepts and the other mages in Planir's confidence. Why else do you think he was so ready to allow Shivvalan and Usara to set up their new sanctuary for wizardry in Suthyfer?'

Jilseth frowned. 'But that was after Larissa had died. And what has any of this to do with an ensorcelled ring?'

Nolyen raised a placating hand. 'You know there are Aetheric adepts in Suthyfer, working with Usara and Shivvalan? Drawn from those who've studied medicine and other lore in Tormalin's oldest shrines as well as scholars and mentors from the universities of Vanam and Col? It seems that they found some way to use that ensorcelled ring to help shield the mageborn from aetheric attack by these northern adepts.'

'The adepts used the ring? But those who use Artifice cannot be mageborn any more than a wizard can learn these aetheric enchantments of theirs.'

Now Nolyen was shaking his head. 'You do not have to be mageborn to benefit from inherent magic instilled into an object.'

Jilseth leaned back against the carriage's velvet upholstery to consider this.

What was Planir thinking? If Artifice had somehow shielded those mageborn from aetheric attack, how might that rune land reversed?

She frowned. 'Is he hoping to find some way of using these artefacts which this Anskal is hoarding to render him vulnerable to an adept's assault, even when he's not actively engaged in magecraft?'

'I have no idea,' Nolyen admitted.

As the carriage rumbled on through Relshaz, Jilseth had to curb her envy of Nolyen, so much deeper in the Archmage's confidence than she was.

Deep enough to know something more of Velindre's excursions into the Archipelago? A handful of years ago, Hadrumal's gossip-mongers had peddled tales of dragons' devastating magic scouring Aldabreshin islands down to the bedrock before the creatures had apparently departed as abruptly as they'd appeared.

Otrick had long been rumoured to have an interest in dragons while Azazir had been widely condemned, according to legend, for actually summoning up such a beast in hopes of bending its innate magic to his wizardly will. It was generally agreed that the dragon had eaten him instead, unanimously judged to be a fitting and well-deserved fate.

'What did Velindre mean about crafting a warding against dragons across the Archipelago?'

'I've barely heard half that tale.'

That clearly frustrated Nolyen. Jilseth tried not to let it comfort her.

'Velindre definitely helped drive the beasts out of the islands,' Nolyen asserted. 'She learned that a dragon won't linger where one of its own kind has been killed. So she and some others in the Archmage's confidence spread soil stained with dragon's blood throughout the Archipelago on the winds and the tides.'

'So there really is no chance of a dragon biting this Mandarkin's head off.' Jilseth wondered if Planir would truly have resorted to such measures. Surely he was powerful enough to both summon up a beast and control it. But if that option was no longer open to them, there was no point regretting a cracked egg.

Still, it was reassuring to know that Hadrumal's mages had proved they could best the wildest and most devastating untamed magic bred into a dragon's very bones. The Archmage and the Council should surely defeat a single Mandarkin wizard.

The carriage trundled onwards. The two of them sat in silence.

Looking sideways under cover of her eyelashes, Jilseth watched Nolyen staring blindly out of the window. As he fiddled with the peridot studs at his shirt cuffs, she guessed he was contemplating whatever the Archmage truly expected of him in Suthyfer. Whatever he hadn't told her.

Jilseth could take comfort from knowing precisely what was expected of her and her necromancy. Though she didn't know how far they had to go to this fountain where the carriage would leave them.

— CHAPTER TWENTY —

Nadrua Town, Pastamar Province, in the Kingdom of Solura
9th of Grelemar (Soluran calendar)

'HAVE YOU SEEN him? His name is Kusint. He's of Forest blood, though not of the Folk, as I think the saying goes.'

Corrain hadn't realised until he'd started this quest that he had no idea of Kusint's family name. Nor if the Forest Folk used such courtesies.

'If you do see him,' he continued doggedly, 'tell him that I am here. That I will be waiting by the stone pillar in the market place every day at sunset.'

The bargeman nodded but he still didn't answer.

Corrain persisted. 'There will be silver coin for whoever gets my message to him.'

He didn't make the mistake of patting a purse to show where he carried his money, jerking his head back towards the town instead, to hint at a safely stashed coffer and perhaps associates, for the benefit of any watching would-be thief.

The man simply nodded again. Corrain was less and less convinced that the Soluran understood him. It was time to move on, he decided. 'Good day to you.'

The bargeman's face brightened. 'Good day,' he said in heavily accented Tormalin.

Now it was Corrain's turn to nod wordlessly before he walked away. He paused after twenty paces or so and looked up and down the wharves, searching for any ship whose crew he hadn't yet spoken to.

A morning sitting idle in the inn where he'd found a lodging to spend the Archmage's coin had been more than enough for Corrain. He'd spent these past four days, morning, afternoon and evening asking for word of Kusint. Asking as best he could anyway, not knowing any of the local tongue.

Regardless, he'd visited every merchants' warehouse and made the rounds of all the taverns. Awake before first light today, he had come down to the river in hopes of news. He was intent on sending messages far and wide.

Because Kusint must have ignored that letter which Planir swore had been delivered to him. The Archmage had said the lad was in some village whose name meant nothing to Corrain but it was supposedly within a day or so's travel of this town.

Well, Corrain wasn't about to give up. Perhaps the lad could be persuaded to come and find Corrain if enough people told him he was truly here in Solura. Even if the Forest lad only wanted to punch his treacherous face so long and so hard that he'd still be dizzy at Solstice.

He paused to take stock. As far as he could tell, Corrain had approached all the sail barges currently tied up alongside the extensive wharves. If this town was no match for the port city of Issbesk down on the coast, where this apparently endless river flowed into the Soluran Sea, Nadrua was as big as Ferl or Trebin and profited from twice or thrice as much trade as either of those towns.

So Corrain had guessed that plenty of the boatmen would speak some Tormalin. The crew of the barge which he and Kusint had ridden northwards earlier in the summer had done so. Now he was beginning to think that the red-sailed barge and its men were an exception, deliberately sought out by Kusint. None of the river-going Solurans whom he had spoken to today knew any more of the Tormalin tongue than they might need to conclude a trade deal or a fist fight with merchants bold enough to make the long voyage from the lands of the Old Empire.

He shoved his hands in his breeches pockets as he contemplated the river. The iron manacle around his wrist pressed into his thigh. He had taken care to shove it up his forearm, buttoning his shirt cuff tight. He didn't want the sight of the broken chain to deter anyone from helping him.

Maybe Kusint had done more than throw that letter into the nearest fireplace. This tributary, the Mare's Tail, wasn't even the main trade route hereabouts, for all that it could rival the river Rel on its own. It headed down from the mountains to join the still greater river of Solura's eastern boundary here at Nadrua and further bolster the town's wealth .

So there must be any number of boats which Kusint could have bought passage aboard, heading southwards, northwest deeper into Solura or northeast towards the mountains.

Or he could have crossed the river to go due east. Corrain looked across the fast flowing water, dark and mysterious, to the impenetrable forest running right down to the far river bank. Only a few grassy landings had been hacked out here and there for the flat-bottomed and shallow-sided ferries that hauled goods, animals and people back and forth, their ropes easily unslung to allow the broad-sailed barges to pass unhindered.

The Great Forest. Everyone called it that, here and in Ensaimin, each in their own tongue. No wonder. Selerima, the closest of Ensaimin's great trading cities was two hundred and sixty leagues away, at the far end of the single road that cut through the trackless trees from west to east. From the southernmost tip of the long thrust of land separating the Bay of Teshal from the Soluran Sea, Corrain had measured anything from three hundred and sixty leagues to four hundred, depending on where he guessed the Forest proper might end and the Mountains begin, on the map which he had asked the Archmage for, which Nolyen the Caladhrian wizard had promptly fetched from one of Hadrumal's libraries.

If Kusint had crossed this Great River of the East, as the Solurans called it, in search of some long lost relatives among the Forest Folk or in hopes of fighting more Mandarkin spies sent south to harry the Solurans' flank, as Anskal himself had been, Corrain had no hope of any message reaching the boy this side of winter solstice.

Then he would have to find some way to contact the wizardly Elders of Fornet himself, Corrain concluded. Though he couldn't deny that was a daunting prospect, after seeing three of their mages so efficiently slaughtering Anskal's henchmen over yonder in that very forest. And Kusint had said those Soluran wizards must be among the Order's lesser apprentices, to be sent beating such vermin out of the bushes.

After all, Corrain had outwitted the three of them, finding Anskal before the Solurans could execute the

Mandarkin mage out of hand, to promise him instead sanctuary and riches in Caladhria.

He ground his teeth in frustration. Were these mysterious Elders mages of sufficient proficiency to defeat Anskal once and for all? Or would they prove no match for the Mandarkin for a second time of asking? Assuming that they agreed to give him a hearing. Would they accept that Planir and Hadrumal had no part in Corrain's catastrophic folly without Kusint's word to lend weight to his contrition?

The doubts and fears that had gnawed at him as he lay wakeful in bed were continually snapping at his ankles, however briskly he walked these wharves and streets.

He was certain of one thing though. If Kusint's word was to have any value, then rejoining him must be the Forest lad's own decision.

The noon bell tolled and prompted an answering growl in Corrain's stomach. If the Solurans divided the full circle of a day and night into twenty equal hours, ignoring sunrise and sunset, midday remained the same fixed point as it was at home.

Home. Where he had left Zurenne to manage the rebuilding of Halferan Manor, so unseemly a task for a widowed baron's lady. Corrain set his jaw. She had Fitrel and Sirstin and Gartas and so many others to help her and now that burly Ensaimin mage, Tornauld. Halferan was safe enough for the present and if it was to be safe for his dead lord's children's future, they must be rid of Anskal. Only the Archmage could secure that for them.

He turned his back on the river. Careful not to fall foul of the laden drays and their labouring teams of horses heading for the wharves, he followed a broad

road towards the market square. He could see the tall stone pillar in the centre, rising above the awnings erected daily for the hucksters arriving in the town and willing to pay their copper pennies to Lord Pastiss's market reeve for a show of transient respectability.

The girl who'd brought Corrain his breakfast had explained there was always trade to be done in Solura as families made the long journeys from their remote farmsteads to these scattered towns where they could buy whatever finished goods, necessities and luxuries they could not make or raise for themselves. Especially in these last days before the autumn equinox as the harsher weather threatened to make the roads so much more of an ordeal until the following spring. Soluran life was very different from home.

As he approached, Corrain contemplated the illegible Soluran script on the broadsheets and lordly declarations pasted onto the stone pillar, as high as a tall man could reach. He remembered the landmark from their previous visit so he hadn't needed the tavern girl to tell him that's where everyone went for news or to meet by arrangement.

He would have preferred to meet Kusint in a shrine; ideally under Trimon's gaze, to convince the Forest lad of his sincerity. Though Kusint's orphaned mother had been raised by a Soluran family rather than out in the wild woods, she had taught her son to honour the Forest Folk's gods and goddesses, the Traveller most of all. Add to that, some priest or priestess's presence might curb Kusint's desire to cut his throat.

Corrain hadn't truly appreciated the Solurans' root and branch hatred for all Mandarkin. Not until he had seen the fury in Kusint's eyes, the loathing twisting his face at the notion of asking a Mandarkin wizard to fight the corsairs. Even after everything that Kusint himself had suffered at Archipelagan hands, fists and whips.

But the Solurans honoured no gods, not Trimon or Talagrin, Halcarion or Larasion. They had no shrines, not in the way that Caladhrians did. Kusint had told him that. So Corrain had to decide how many days he'd sit on those market steps. Until he became a joke for passersby, like a death's head on a mopstick at winter solstice.

He realised he was passing by an open door with a holly bush nailed above the lintel. That particular emblem served the Solurans instead of inn signs and within, he saw the tavern was busy. If that wasn't necessarily much recommendation at midday, the food being carried to and fro looked appetising enough and the kitchen maids all had decently clean hands and aprons.

He went inside and joined the line at the long deal counter separating the tavern's tables and stools from the wall of stacked and spigoted barrels. Rushes covering the beaten earth floor crackled under his boots.

'A nooning—' he began, half hopeful, half apprehensive lest he couldn't make himself understood.

'Sit, please,' the innkeeper said in swift, accented Tormalin. He thrust a foaming tankard at Corrain before looking past him to the next customer, their conversation a quick flurry of Soluran.

Corrain lifted the tankard out of the slopped puddle. Back home he'd have lamented that loss of ale and held back a copper cutpiece when he paid his reckoning. He wouldn't do that for the sake of this curiously scented brew. By all that was sacred and profane, whatever possessed the Solurans to throw spruce twigs into their tuns?

Besides, he wasn't spending Halferan coin. Planir had given him a fat purse of Soluran-minted silver. Had the wizards got such wealth in trade, he wondered, or summoned it up from the earth with their magic, like the gold that the Eldritch Kin supposedly stamped out of sunbeams? At least it didn't vanish after a day and night like Eldritch gold in chimney corner stories.

Moving slowly through the tavern, he seized his chance of a stool when a drover stood up to leave. One of the maidservants arrived with Corrain's laden wooden plate, wiped the table, swept up the previous customer's leavings and departed without a word.

Corrain ate quickly. Bread, but coarser and sprinkled with some pungent seeds which he'd never encountered back home. Cheese, pale as lard, not warmed to rich gold with the marigold petals which the Halferan maids used in their dairying. Its flavour hinted at goat's milk mixed with the offerings of the local rough-coated black cattle.

No bacon, but that wasn't surprising given the time of the year. Corrain had seen the herds of pigs being driven down to the wharves, to be ferried across to the woodland for final fattening on acorns and beechmast. There would be feasting hereabouts come autumn equinox. Meantime, Corrain was content to eat succulent venison, plump after summer's browsing.

He looked around the taproom as he ate, alert for any redhead coming into the tavern. He wasn't ready to give up on Kusint just yet and who better to carry his messages far and wide, than the lad's own Folk, so well known for their incorrigible wandering. They were the ones bringing the freshly killed deer, the raw, roughly cleaned hides and bundles of antlers across the wide river from the Great Forest.

He glimpsed a sun-burnished copper braid and a beaded leather-clad shoulder amid the shifting throng at the counter. Cramming the last of the food into his mouth, Corrain left the plate and half-drunk ale and eased himself through the crowd.

As he got closer, he saw why getting to the counter was proving so difficult. That shoulder belonged to a Forest lass wearing a tightly fitted and sleeveless leather jerkin ornamented with tiny bone beads dyed in myriad colours. Her plain hide leggings were as closely cut as that jerkin and cross-laced up the outside of the girl's thighs. The Folk might wear such garb to avoid snagging themselves on tree branches or brambles but the effect on feminine curves was undeniably alluring even in Solura where as many women as men went breeched.

Add to that the Folk's reputation for sharing their blankets, man or woman, and no wonder the Soluran drovers and traders were crowding around like bees round a honey pot. Not that Corrain had any inclination to casual lust.

The Soluran men suddenly backed away. One raised his hands in surrender and offered what sounded like an apology. Corrain didn't understand the local tongue but he could see the faint score across the man's grimy palm swelling into a thin line of blood. That was something else he remembered about Solura; the women mostly carried blades whether they wore breeches or skirts and used them as readily as the men.

The Forest woman looked around, her green eyes hard as agate. She was assuredly a woman, Corrain realised, now that he saw her face. Her sharp features were weathered and seamed with an old pale scar cutting through one sandy brow. She owed her slender figure not to girlhood but to scant foraging in the Forest through the lean summer seasons.

Corrain wasn't about to try fighting his way to her side and get a knife in his ribs for his efforts. He turned away and saw that a featherweight of luck had drifted his way. The seat which he'd left was still empty, his plate and ale untouched. He sat and lifted the tankard. Soluran brews might taste peculiar but he was thirsty.

Conversation swirled around him; the Soluran tongue, the speech of the Forest and the Mountains equally incomprehensible.

'Is this seat taken?'

He looked up, startled to be addressed in fluent Tormalin.

It was the Forest woman. Well, the Folk were as well known for their talent with unfamiliar tongues as they were for their skills with song, harp and flute as they wandered the highways and byways. Priests and nursery tales agreed that Trimon had given these gifts to his most favoured people.

'May I sit?' The woman looked quizzically at him.

'If you wish.' Corrain set his tankard down and gestured to an empty stool.

'You didn't want to try a roll of the runes with me?' She squared her shoulders to emphasise the alluring swell of her breasts.

'No.' Corrain took a drink. She would have to do better than that to get a rise out of him.

'What brings you so far from home?'

To his relief, she seemed honestly curious rather than

piqued by his lack of interest in bedding her. Regardless, Corrain took a moment to survey the taproom before answering. He had no time to waste on some Soluran buck who might hope to impress the woman by challenging this outsider straying onto Pastamar's turf.

Since the man with the cut hand had vanished and no one else was casting disgruntled glares his way, he looked at the woman. Dress her in modest Caladhrian garb and anyone would take her for Ensaimin born and bred with that accent, whatever her colouring.

'I am looking for one of your kind,' he said quietly. 'Of the Blood as I think you say. A young man called Kusint.'

Her sandy brows lifted. 'What is he to you?'

'A friend. No—' Corrain raised his hand in apology. 'I forfeited his friendship.'

'How?' She angled her head like a curious bird.

'Through arrant folly which, forgive me, I don't propose to discuss with you.' Corrain replied politely as he could. He still wanted this woman's help spreading word through her kith and kin.

But he wasn't fool enough to admit his stupidity here. The merest mention of Mandarkin would draw Soluran ears and one listener with a passable command of Tormalin could share his crimes with this whole tavern. Thrown into Lord Pastiss's dungeons with no one interested in his excuses? Corrain wouldn't wager goatshit against gold coin that Archmage Planir would rescue him to further enrage these Soluran wizards whose help he sought.

The woman pursed pale lips. 'What do you want with him?'

'To ask for his forgiveness.' Corrain found that

surprisingly easy to admit to a stranger. 'To ask for his help in putting things right. Not that I have any right to ask,' he acknowledged. 'He had no part in my folly.'

The faintest of smiles softened the woman's harsh face but only for an instant.

'What is that you wear?' She pointed at the link of chain protruding from his linen cuff. 'Are you some fugitive from lawful justice?'

Corrain was momentarily tempted to say yes. He certainly felt guilty for leaving Lady Zurenne and her daughters amid the chaos and dust of Halferan. But he was making amends for their sake as much as for his own and he was here because he had offered himself up to the Archmage's judgement.

'No,' he said firmly. 'I am no fugitive.'

Her slight smile teased him once again. 'Very well.'

Corrain expected her to say something further, to ask more questions. Instead she rose to her feet and walked away and left the crowded tavern without another word.

Would she share his message for Kusint with her people? Corrain had no idea. He looked at the dregs of his ale and couldn't face drinking any more of the stuff.

Someone spoke and he looked up to see two Soluran merchants with brimming tankards and expectant expressions. If Corrain couldn't understand them, their meaning was plain enough.

'Have the table and welcome.' He made his own way out to the street.

He should go the market square next, he decided. There would surely be more Forest Folk mingling with the peddlers and tawdry merchants.

'I could say well met but I'll settle for good day.'

Corrain spun around, breathless.

Kusint emerged from the shadows of an alleyway running alongside the tavern.

'You got my letter.' Corrain searched for some reply in the Forest lad's face.

'I did.' Kusint pulled the parchment from the unbuttoned breast of his tunic.

The abruptness of the gesture put Corrain in mind of a man pulling a dagger from a hidden sheath.

Kusint looked much the same as he had when the two of them had parted company. Copper-haired and lanky with the angular features of his mother's race. Though that rangy build would prove deceptive if anyone thought they would get the better of him. Kusint's stints at a corsair galley's oar had given him a formidable wiry strength.

Besides, the lad had new allies to save him from any attack. The Forest woman from the tavern stood a little further down the alley. A handful of other Folk stood with her; three men and two women, one couple in similar garb to the woman and the rest dressed like Soluran townsfolk. They were all looking sternly at Corrain.

He looked at the letter in Kusint's hand. Had the lad guessed how many blotted and scored-through drafts had littered the floor of his guest chamber in Trydek's Hall? Corrain had burned the Archmage's candles long past midnight striving to find the right words. Had all that effort been in vain?

'May I know your answer?'

Kusint chewed his lower lip. 'We should talk first.'

'You and I?' Corrain looked past him to the motionless Forest contingent, 'or with your companions?'

A brief smile warmed Kusint's cold green eyes. 'Ysant says that you can be trusted. That your repentance is sincere.'

Corrain looked at the woman in the beaded jerkin and considered just how easy he had found it to confide in her. He swallowed his annoyance. 'She has similar skills to Deor?'

Artifice. That eerie magic that enabled an adept to look into another's thoughts or to see through their eyes or hear through their ears no matter how many leagues apart they might be. That was the rumour back home as tavern talk insisted such enchantments had proved decisive in the recent Lescari strife.

Corrain should have remembered. That Forest man Deor had definitely had some aetheric magic at his command, helping those Fornet wizards to hunt Anskal. The *sheltya* of the Mountains shared such lore with the Folk, so he said.

'Ysant has some trifling aptitude.' Kusint coloured slightly beneath the freckles dusted across his face.

'Then you know I am truly sorry.' Hard as Corrain had found it to force his pen to write those words, it was harder still to repeat them facing Kusint. 'Truly,' he insisted.

'You say this Anskal has threatened Halferan?' Kusint demanded.

'He has, though he's made no move and the Archmage has sent one of his own to watch over the manor.'

Corrain realised it wasn't only hatred of the Mandarkin thickening the Forest lad's voice. After all that Kusint had endured in the Archipelago, the unexpectedly generous welcome he had received from the Halferan household had soothed more than his bruises.

'You say you have urgent questions for the Elders of Fornet.' Kusint contemplated the letter. 'You do not say what those questions are.'

Not when that letter could have fallen into anyone's hands, if Kusint had taken it only to discard it unread.

'This Mandarkin, Anskal found some hoard of ensorcelled artefacts,' Corrain said quietly. 'The Archmage doesn't know what he intends—'

'Mandarkin kill for the least trifle imbued with magic.' Kusint paled beneath his freckles. 'They will burn a village to the ground for rumour of an ensorcelled sword.'

'Hadrumal knows little of such things,' Corrain explained. 'The Archmage seeks Soluran lore.'

Kusint plucked at a beaded leather strap tied around one wrist. 'I don't know—'

'Anskal has Hosh,' Corrain said abruptly. 'He's alive. If we help the Archmage, Planir has promised to rescue him.'

As he spoke, he felt the first stirrings of hope. Guilt almost equal to his own darkened Kusint's eyes. The Forest lad also had to answer for leaving Hosh behind when the two of them had made their escape.

'I am ready and willing to do penance,' Corrain maintained, 'whatever these Soluran mages might demand. I will admit my guilt and my folly in asking for help from a Mandarkin. They can have my oath on whatever they hold sacred that you were not at fault, that you warned me against him.'

Kusint considered this for a long moment.

'This way.' The lad walked back down the alley without looking to see if Corrain followed.

As the woman Ysant approached, Kusint was already

speaking, swift and urgent, in the Forest tongue. Corrain could only wait and wonder what tale he was telling. It wasn't a long one.

The Forest woman took a step forward to address Corrain. 'You must go to Pastamar Town to deliver your petition for an audience with the resident wizard serving Lord Pastiss. That is the swiftest way to send your message to the Elders of Fornet since that wizard is of the same order. The Tower itself is a further seven days beyond and hard riding.'

'Pastamar Town is perhaps two days travel northeast of here,' Kusint explained, 'where the road that cuts through the Forest from Selerima and the west crosses the river. It's the only bridge over the Mare's Tail, guarded by Lord Pastiss's castle.'

'My thanks.' Corrain had hoped for swifter progress though. 'But what is this business of petitions?'

The man beside Ysant spoke up. 'If someone has some proposal, some request, a plea for justice or recompense to lay before Lord Pastiss, they must deliver their petition in writing to the castle gate. All such appeals are assessed and listed according to merit. A docket setting out the order in which they will be heard is nailed to the castle's outer door.'

Corrain raised a hand before the man could continue. 'We don't wish to see the noble lord. We only want to talk to the wizard.'

'You will need Lord Pastiss's permission before you meet with his mage.' Ysant's tone brooked no argument.

'How often are these dockets posted?' Corrain looked at Kusint. 'Daily?'

Ysant shook her coppery head. 'Two dockets are posted each month, the first at the Greater Moon's renewal and the second on the day after the full.'

Daylight or not, Corrain glanced up at the sky. 'The greater full is six days from now.'

Ysant nodded. 'That gives you time enough to make the journey and to present your petition before the next docket's drawn up. Then you must wait,' she warned. 'If a petitioner isn't present when their name is called, their name is struck off the list and they must submit their petition again to secure a place on the next.'

Like so much Soluran custom, this baffled Corrain. 'But if it takes two days to get to Pastamar and the next docket will be posted so soon, we'll be sucking hind teat after all those who've already made their plea. If we have to wait for the next docket after that—' he swallowed his frustration as he made the swift calculation '—we've no hope of being heard for twenty days, likely more.'

With the Equinox Festival a handful of days after that. How could he explain such a delay to Planir? What were the chances of Hosh surviving that long?

He shook his head. 'We should ride straight for the Order's tower.' And he would kick in the door if that's what it took to rouse a wizard to talk to him.

Ysant said something in her own tongue that raised wry smiles on her companions' faces.

'Kusint told you that I have some knowledge of Artifice.' She pronounced the unfamiliar word with care. 'I can ask one of my own blood who lives in Pastamar Town to present your petition. If you tell me what she should write, your letter can be delivered to the castle before sunset today.'

'My thanks for that.' Corrain tried to look suitably grateful though he wasn't sure how much two days would be worth so late in this game. He looked at

Kusint. 'Will you write this petition? You'll know best how to phrase it.'

Kusint hesitated, then nodded. 'What will you do?'

'Hire or buy two good saddle horses.' Corrain was ready to spend the Archmage's silver like copper to secure the best mounts he could.

One of the Forest men in Soluran garb raised a hand 'I know an honest trader,' he said in halting Tormalin.

'Then we'll meet you at the Half-barrel Tavern,' Kusint nodded, 'as soon as may be.'

The Soluran-born Forest man grinned at Corrain and beckoned for him to follow.

Corrain had to curb his long stride not to outstrip the man's pace down the alley. Two days, three at the most and they would be in Pastamar Town. This business of petitions and dockets was all very well but he would be looking for some other way to get a foot in that castle door, to put their case to this nobleman's sworn wizard once they arrived. To persuade that unknown mage to use his magic to relate their appeal to these Elders of Fornet, no matter how far away they might be.

Though these were only the first steps on this path. He and Kusint must convince these Soluran wizards to share whatever knowledge the Archmage might need to frustrate Anskal's plans. That was surely going to be a far greater challenge.

But he was not going to leave Lord Pastiss's castle until he had secured the Elders of Fornet's assistance. Not even if these Solurans chose to flog or imprison him for enlisting Mandarkin aid. Now that Corrain knew he could trust Kusint to hold Planir to his promise to rescue Hosh.

However powerful Anskal might be, one mage could

not hope to stand against Hadrumal. Not when a single magewoman like Madam Jilseth could drive off a whole band of corsairs.

— CHAPTER TWENTY-ONE —

The Relshaz Waterfront,
22nd of For-Autumn

MELLITHA'S CARRIAGE HAD finally arrived at their destination. Descending the step slowly behind Nolyen, Jilseth surveyed the broad square and recalled the magewoman mentioning pewter roses.

The fountain in the centre boasted a central column wreathed with silver-grey metal flowers. Black iron spikes ringed the base of that pillar and more fringed the rim of the fountain's outer bowl, in case anyone admiring the artisans' skills was tempted to try stealing a piece of such beauty. Those coming for the clean water supplied by the Magistracy could help themselves from troughs served by spouts marking the cardinal points of the compass.

A raggedly clothed crowd was thirstily scooping up water with their bare hands.

'Madam mage!' Tanilo jumped down from the carriage's driving seat. 'Master mage! Wait here!'

'Are those slaves?' Nolyen looked warily at the mob; all men and ranging from their first growth into maturity to those in their prime despite some grey or balding heads.

Jilseth had already noted their manacles and shackles as well as the watching Relshazri with whips lax in their hands.

What she didn't understand was the slave cohort's good humour. The men were smiling, nudging each other to ensure everyone shared in the joke. Even the Relshazri guards were teasing them, light-hearted.

'What are they saying?' Jilseth couldn't pick any meaning out of the clotted confusion of dialects.

A subtle swirl of enchanted air brought the voices to them, louder and more clearly. Tanilo was bemused.

'They have been sold to Khusro Rina's wives. But if they serve satisfactorily, they will be given their freedom and returned the mainland with as much silver coin as they can hold in their cupped hands.'

Nolyen cleared his throat. 'It is widely rumoured that Aldabreshin warlords' wives purchase mainland slaves to stand at stud.'

'Widely rumoured but with little evidence.' Tanilo shook his head, adamant.

Jilseth studied the contingent of slaves. In her frank opinion, few women in Hadrumal, mage- or mundane born, would give any of them a come-hither glance. Would an Aldabreshin warlord's wife, with all the riches of the Archipelago to buy the equivalent of a purebred stallion, opt for a wagoneer's whip-spoiled cast-offs?

'How many wives does Khusro Rina have?'

'Four,' Tanilo answered promptly. 'Debis Khusro, Katel Khusro, Patri Khusro and Quilar Khusro. They were born—'

'Never mind.' Jilseth had no need to know these women's origins. She tallied the heads of the slaves. Three score, near enough.

No, she refused to believe that any woman with the most prodigious appetite for bed sport would spread her legs for a triple handful of men risking every lover's disease from the Scald to the Itch. She couldn't believe it of one woman, let alone four together.

'Someone is lying,' she concluded.

'Can you find out which slave trader they came from?' Nolyen asked Tanilo.

The coachman nodded. 'When I've taken Madam Esterlin to the Magistracy.'

Jilseth noted that some of those bystanders who had been gawping at the chained slaves by the fountain were beginning to take an interest in this stationary carriage and the three of them standing beside it.

'We've lingered long enough.'

'Indeed.' With a brief nod to Tanilo, Nolyen began walking seawards.

To Jilseth's relief, the slave contingent was driven off down a different road, an incongruous spring in their step for all the chains hampering their feet.

She and Nolyen emerged on the dockside close by the eastern breakwater. Fewer than half the moorings around the curving harbour were occupied.

'There are different ships here today.' Jilseth noted the coloured pennants at their mast heads marked with the broad black strokes of an unknown script.

'The great galleys have all left.' Nolyen observed low-voiced as they strolled along the thoroughfare towards the swathe of quayside now gleaming starkly white. 'There are far more triremes.'

Each warship was tied up beside a smaller, swifter galley bearing the same domain's pennant. No rope ladders dangled from any trireme's stern and swordsmen stood guard at top and bottom of each galley's wooden steps. They had all lowered their round helms' sliding nasal bars and fastened the fine chainmail veils that protected face and neck. These warriors were ready for trouble.

More armed and armoured men stood watch in front of their warlords' storehouses. There were no families on the balconies today. As men and women arriving, all with armed escorts, were admitted through the doors, Jilseth could hear bars and bolts withdrawn and then quickly replaced.

Helmets shadowed the sentries' eyes, hiding any hint where they were looking. Regardless, Jilseth had no doubt that she and Nolyen were closely watched as they approached the scene of the slaughter.

'You'd never know what had happened here.' Nolyen was right insofar as there was no visible trace of blood. The unnatural cleanliness of this stretch of quayside suggested something awry however.

What might remain unseen? Jilseth allowed the merest trifle of her mage sense to brush across the tightly-fitted stones as she refined her earth affinity to the precise demands of necromancy.

Some blood lingered in the deepest cracks but the Aldabreshi hadn't only used salt and scalding water to clean these stones. She could sense some alchemical substance, somehow akin to rock oil and to bitumen. Something harsh and acidic, degrading whatever hidden blood it touched. Jilseth wondered how that unfortunate slave had really died.

The scoured whiteness extended from the waterside more than half way across the thoroughfare. Regardless, no Aldabreshi was walking across the pallid stones. The swordsmen outside the storehouses overlooking the bleached expanse were stepping back to allow Aldabreshi and Relshazri alike to encroach on paving safely soiled by ordinary occurrences.

Nolyen raised a hand as though to scratch his nose. Elemental air carried his muttered words to Jilseth's ear. 'How are we to get close to the water without drawing every eye to us?'

'Come on.' Jilseth slid her arm through his elbow.

Nolyen obediently escorted her around the curve of the harbour. When Jilseth calculated they had gone far enough, she released his arm to sit on a bollard conveniently free of any ship's rope.

She pressed the back of one hand to her forehead, as though fighting a swoon. Nolyen dropped into a crouch before her. His hands clasped her other hand, his expression all concern.

Jilseth looked at him through her fingers. 'Can you see down to the seabed yonder? Is there anything I can use?'

Nolyen edged sideways, taking care to seem intent on Jilseth as he looked across the arc of the harbour.

'They've scrubbed those stones down to the low waterline.' His gaze dropped, the opaque water no hindrance to his wizard eye. 'I can see a hand, several heads—'

'No heads.' Working necromancy with a dead person's face before her invariably disturbed Jilseth's sleep for days after.

Nolyen searched the unseen seabed. 'I see three hands and one foot. How shall we set about this?'

'Find a hand with shackle galls or similar Aldabreshin scars and raise it up to float just below the surface. I will take it from there while you make sure no splashes betray us.' Jilseth slid around on the bollard as though turning her face into the refreshing salt breeze.

She narrowed her eyes, focusing on the faint trace of his magelight arrowing across the water to the stark whiteness splashed like paint down the quay front.

This was a magelight only visible to another wizard. But the water seemed unduly hostile to Jilseth's affinity. She sent her own mage sense scurrying faster as Nolyen's wizardry vanished beneath a scum of nameless fragments caught between a moored ship's stern and the dockside.

Reaching the bleached quayside, she followed Nolyen's lead down into the depths. Before her mage sight reached the silt, a hand came groping upwards towards her. Obedient to Nolyen's magic, the water was resolutely rejecting this sad remnant of a lost life.

Crabs had nibbled at the fingertips. As the hand came closer, a fish tugged at a hanging fingernail before vanishing into the murk with its prize. Close to the choppy surface, the hand tumbled over to expose the clean cut through the wrist. Jilseth could see the remaining small bones of the wrist glowing golden amid the dull sea-sodden flesh.

'What are you doing?' Nolyen rasped, alarmed.

'Sorry.' Jilseth hastily thrust away both the earth magic and her necromancy. Too hard. The hand sank like a stone. Only Nolyen's command of the water caught it.

'Bring it right to the surface.' But as Jilseth spoke, she realised something was wrong. Granted air had always been the element most unreceptive to her magecraft. Now it was more elusive than ever. She struggled to weave a simple invisibility, never mind interleave the spell with a shield to contain the rank smell of the carrion.

Nolyen subjected her to a searching stare. 'Are you ready?'

'I am.' Jilseth thrust away all doubts.

Her shielding spell meshed with the invisibility and the dead hand rose, fish-belly pale. Lifting it free of the water, she saw Nolyen instantly smooth away the ripples where it had breached the surface. Falling drops of water dissolved into mist blown away on the breeze.

The hand weighed shockingly heavy on her affinity. All her earthly mage senses longed to explore the dead flesh and bone, to focus on the necromancy she intended.

No, she couldn't allow that. Jilseth drew on all her years of perfecting her wizard skills to bring the pathetic remnant scudding across the water towards them. She rose slowly to her feet, eyes fixed on the unseen hand.

Nolyen gripped her forearm with insistent fingers. 'Don't move.'

She dared not speak, still less look to see what had alarmed him until the murdered corsair's hand reached the stones where they stood.

Jilseth set it on the dock, swathed in magic. Now she could follow Nolyen's gaze. She saw what prompted such taut unease as he stood beside her.

Armed men had appeared, emerging from the broad road arriving at the waterfront half way between the east and western breakwaters. The sentries outside the substantial storehouses flanking the highway were ready, hands quick to their sword hilts. They stepped back, acknowledging these arrivals with measured courtesy.

'More slaves.' Jilseth saw that the marching Aldabreshin swordsmen flanked a double line of captives.

Once again, these men looked uncommonly cheerful for those condemned to the living death among the southern barbarians. By contrast, their captors looked like men facing the gallows. But men who would kick and spit and struggle up to the instant the noose tightened around their necks.

'Mellitha will want to know what ships these men are taken to.' Jilseth sank down to sit on the bollard again.

Cupping her hands over her face, as though once again overcome, she watched the column heading westwards around the harbour. They halted where two swift galleys flanked a predatory trireme. All three vessels flew the same pennant at their mastheads. Jilseth committed the angular symbol to memory.

As soon as the last stragglers of the slave column were being urged aboard, Nolyen's hand beneath her elbow forced Jilseth to her feet. 'Come on.'

She had no quarrel with his urgency. 'That way.'

Nolyen enchanted a swirl of air to carry the dead corsair's salvaged hand ahead of them as he took the closest route off the dockside. Jilseth looked steadily at it, making quite certain that no charnel stink escaped her tightly woven spell.

Nolyen ignored the yards on either side of the alley heading back towards the heart of the city. Longer, lower buildings framed these fenced enclosures. Some of these warehouses had narrow doors guarded by sharp-eyed Relshazri and windows criss-crossed with bars.

Elsewhere open-fronted barns sheltered tethered mules awaiting harness. From the grave faces of the men standing disconsolate around stacked packsaddles, the beasts' respite from burdens was likely to continue.

'One of the city's narrow canals arrived in a blunt-ended basin and Jilseth saw the watermen were similarly idle. They should be poling their flat-bottomed boats away from these docks loaded with Aldabreshin luxuries destined for the riverside wharves and the merchants trading onwards up the Rel to Caladhria, Lescar and Ensaimin.

'In here.' Nolyen dragged her into a lean-to hovel piled high with mouldy fodder. 'Take command of all the spells.'

Before she could object, his magic swept the dead man's fingers into her cringing grasp. The touch of a wizardly mentor's magecraft guiding an apprentice might be likened to a gentle hand as a child shaped letters with pencil and slate. This was akin to a slap in the face.

Jilseth gasped but before she could protest, Nolyen's magic wrapped her in smothering light. She landed with a thud that shook her from ankles to shoulders and sent her staggering across Mellitha's lawn.

Far too much of Nolyen's innate water affinity had mingled with the air and fire underpinning the translocation spell. Jilseth's lungs felt full of Hadrumal's thickest winter fog. As a coughing fit wracked her, it was scant consolation to see Nol struggling as desperately for breath.

Wiping tears from her eyes, Jilseth was relieved to see the dead corsair's hand lying at the edge of the lawn. However her magic veiling the noisome thing had unravelled in the shock inflicted by Nolyen's spell. The first blue backed flies were already converging from all directions. One more reason to be thankful for the high walls shielding Mellitha's elegant house from curious eyes.

Blinking Jilseth saw one of the household lackeys waiting by the open door. He looked unperturbed, either by their sudden appearance or their ghastly trophy.

Drawing a cautious breath so as not to start coughing again, she walked towards him. 'Could you find a lidded dish, to keep that from getting flyblown?'

She knew from gruesome experience that a single maggot's wriggling presence wreaked havoc with necromancy. She really did not want to have to go over the stinking thing with a darning needle heated in a candle flame before she could work her spells.

'Of course, madam mage.'

Jilseth wondered what the handsome lad had seen in Mellitha's service. What would it take to startle these servants?

Any impulse to smile died on her lips as a vivid sweep of sapphire magic propelled the courtyard gates open. Mellitha's carriage bowled through, the horse wide-eyed and lathered with sweat. Tanilo hauled the beast to a halt as mercilessly as he had driven him on. The coachman's fawn cotton jerkin was splashed with crimson blood.

'What's happened?' Nolyen demanded hoarsely.

No one answered.

Tanilo jumped down nimbly enough to indicate that the blood wasn't his own.

Velindre threw the carriage door open with another gust of sapphire magic. She stepped out backwards, her feet guided safely to the ground by the same azure radiance. All her attention was on drawing a sheet of woven air out of the coach. The spell supported an unconscious man.

Mellitha followed, her gaze never wavering from

the vivid green wizardry wrapped close around their charge. Both her silk dress and Velindre's long cotton tunic and flowing skirt in the Archipelagan style were as gruesomely bloodstained as Tanilo's jerkin.

'Master Kerrit?' Jilseth could hardly believe it.

She had left the stout mage safely on his own doorstep; an amiable man of middling years and middling height with the permanent pallor and stooped shoulders of a lifelong library denizen.

Now she could barely recognise him. Kerrit had been beaten bloodily insensible. His nose must surely be broken and bruises were swelling his jaw and cheeks. Blood oozing from a long gash in his thinning hair was rendered eerily discoloured by Mellitha's emerald magic.

Her wizardry was swaddling him from head to toe to make sure that no broken bones did further unseen damage. A dirty footprint was ground deep into the midriff of his linen shirt, his maroon doublet ripped open. One foot lay limp at an excruciating angle, stripped bare of its soft house shoe. Kerrit's other stocking had been torn by the buckle flapping loose at his breeches' knee.

'Sheyvie, fetch Master Resnada,' Mellitha said calmly.

As the lackey by the house ran for the gate, two more servants opened the doors to the hallway and to the salon beyond. By the time Velindre had coaxed her magical litter inside, a maidservant had spread a sturdy cotton sheet over the silken daybed.

'He needs more than an apothecary.' As her sapphire magic faded, Velindre looked at Mellitha. 'He has long held that aetheric magic offers the best healing.'

'Once we know how badly he's hurt.' The older woman was intent on her green wizardry shrouding the senseless wizard. 'Then we can send word to his friends at the Temple.'

Jilseth found her voice half a breath ahead of Nolyen.

'What happened?'

'Who did this?'

'Some Relshazri of islander blood have decided that all wizards must be driven out of the city,' Velindre explained icily.

'They can explain themselves to whatever warlord buys them for household slaves,' Mellitha observed with measured calm. 'Once the Magistracy has them arrested, they'll be sold at the next forfeiture auction.'

Velindre nodded with cold satisfaction. 'Once Kerrit's been tended, I will scry out their trail.'

'The Archipelagans are buying slaves by the boat load,' Nolyen remembered. 'We saw them being loaded aboard at the harbour.'

'Not only the ones we saw by the pewter fountain court.' Jilseth looked at Mellitha.

'Tanilo mentioned those, destined for Khusro Rina's wives.' The magewoman still didn't blink, all her attention on Master Kerrit.

'The galleys and trireme carrying them off bore this pennant.' Jilseth drew the sweeping strokes of the devices in darkly ochre magelight.

'Miris Esul,' Velindre said with satisfaction. 'What do we suppose the Miris warlord plans to do with them?' She absently scoured the blood stains from her clothing with a sweep of pale magelight.

'We need to know what's happened in the Archipelago to stir the local islanders into such a frenzy,' Mellitha said tartly. 'Jilseth, if you would be so kind as to address yourself to your necromancy?'

'Of course.' Though horror hollowed Jilseth's stomach as she realised she had no notion what had happened to the dead corsair's hand. The lackey she'd asked to pick it up had been sent for the apothecary.

'You'll need this.' Hoarse, Nolyen offered her the gruesome remnant, shrouded in turquoise magelight and hovering a finger width above his open hand.

'Thank you.' Relieved as she was, Jilseth looked at the carrion with some trepidation. This would be a gruelling test of her erratic magic.

'Take that to Hadrumal.' Velindre's tone brooked no argument. 'The Archmage himself must see whatever that man's fate has to tell us.'

'Quite,' Mellitha agreed. 'And tell Planir about this recent slave trading into the Miris domain and Khusro.'

'And about this attack on Kerrit,' Velindre added.

'But Planir has gone to Suthyfer,' Nolyen reminded them.

'Then bespeak him and call him back,' Velindre ordered curtly. 'Go on. We have our hands full here.'

Both the magewomen turned their attention to Master Kerrit's appalling injuries.

Nolyen offered his hand to Jilseth. She braced herself and focused on carrying the dead man's hand safely through the translocation spell.

As white magelight closed around her, she realised too late that they had left the last of the crumbled bitumen in Mellitha's salon. They must remember to retrieve that. Whatever this necromancy might show them of past events in the Archipelago, they still needed to keep a close watch on whatever the Mandarkin was doing.

The sooner the renegade wizard was dealt with, the sooner that harmless scholarly mages like poor battered

Master Kerrit could walk Relshaz's streets in safety again.

And she must remember to ask Nolyen and Merenel to help her scry for Captain Corrain. With Tornauld keeping watch over Halferan Manor, Jilseth was ready to invite Canfor to make up their nexus if that's what it took. She only hoped that the Caladhrian had persuaded the Solurans to share some scrap of their knowledge of ensorcelled artefacts.

— CHAPTER TWENTY-TWO —

Pastamar Town in the Kingdom of Solura
12th of Grelemar (Soluran calendar)

CORRAIN STIFFENED AS the tavern door opened only to slump on his stool a moment later.

The newcomer was merely another Soluran shaking his cloak to shed drops of the evening rain. The closest serving maid glanced down at his boots. Satisfied that the man had cleaned his hobnailed soles on the iron scraper, she gave him the nod to join his friends sharing dishes of stewed beef and freshly baked bread smeared with stewed apple at a corner table.

Corrain had long since eaten his fill of such dinner. 'How much longer are we going to have to wait?'

His elbows resting on their table, Kusint rolled a trio of rune sticks, far longer and slimmer than the bones which Corrain was accustomed to play with at home. 'Four days until the Greater Full sees the next docket posted. After that it'll depend how long the noble lord takes to deal with the pleas above ours.'

'But we don't need to see Lord Pastiss,' Corrain growled. 'We only want to talk to his wizard. You said we'd only need the noble lord's nod of permission.'

He couldn't help his exasperation. He had allowed himself to hope that they could somehow circumvent this rigmarole and meet with this unknown mage when they arrived here.

When Ysant had used her Artifice to set her sister writing out their petition, she had brought back word that very same evening. When the sister had taken their letter to the castle gate, her mention of the wizards of Fornet had seen the missive taken straight to Lord Pastiss's castellan. Then, better yet, Ysant's sister had received a message within the Soluran hour, instructing Corrain and Kusint to present themselves at the castle's gate as soon as possible and to be ready to be called for an audience.

So they had ridden here so brutally hard that their exhausted horses would be no use to them or anyone else before the turn of the season. They had presented themselves at the castle gate at dawn and been told to wait in this tavern until they were sent for. They were still waiting.

Kusint gestured at the three runes now landing upright. 'See? The Calm for contemplation and the Broom for the need to take care sit alongside the Fire for a trial. Meet this test and all will be well, you'll see.'

Corrain managed to resist the temptation to start snapping Kusint's rune sticks in half. He had no more time for this fortune telling which the lad had apparently learned from Ysant than he did for prayers to the gods and goddesses who'd so callously abandoned him and Hosh.

'How many people could be waiting to see this wizard?' he demanded

'Not nearly as many as will be wanting to beg some indulgence from Lord Pastiss.' Kusint cast another trio of runes and smiled at the symbols carved deep into the age-darkened wood. 'The Mountain for endurance, the Lightning for a fresh start and the Wellspring for a desire fulfilled.'

This time Corrain had to clench his fists unseen below the edge of the table. 'Then why—?'

'We haven't only sought an audience with the resident wizard.' Kusint gathered his rune sticks together. 'We have asked to lay a request from the Archmage of Hadrumal before the Elders of Fornet. You may be certain that those mages will be finding out all they can about both of us and of events beyond the Great Forest before we are summoned.'

'Do you supposed Orul will be there?' Corrain asked more soberly. 'Or the others?'

Kusint studied the smooth wooden stick showing the Sun, the Greater Moon and the Lesser on its three sides.

'If they are,' he said frankly, 'that rune definitely shows one positive face and one reversed by way of a warning. We won't have to waste time relating the details of our previous encounter in the Forest. But we can't expect to trade on any scrap of goodwill once that story has been told.'

His words were a clear rebuke and Corrain couldn't blame him.

If Orul the greybeard had seemed a fair-minded and mild-tempered man, Selista the woman had been hostile from the outset. Espilan, the youngest of the three Soluran wizards in Castle Pastamar's service, would surely be nursing the sorest grudge. Corrain had intervened when the Soluran wizard had been about to capture Anskal and doubtless return to accolade and reward. Corrain had cost him all that.

A new fear hollowed Corrain's stomach. 'What if they have used their magic to ask Planir about us?'

'I suppose they might have done.' Kusint sat up straighter, lashing his rune sticks together with a leather thong. 'How better to learn if we are honest messengers?'

'But if the Elders have done that, Planir could already have made his own case to them.' Corrain could have kicked the table over in his agitation. 'Leaving us with nothing to do here but stick our thumbs up our arses.'

If that had happened, since Corrain had not fulfilled his part of their bargain, how was he to force Planir to make good on his promise and rescue Hosh?

And all this while he would have abandoned Lady Zurenne and Ilysh in the midst of Halferan's rebuilding for no good purpose, he realised with belated guilt.

'You think the Archmage would just have left you here if that had happened?' Kusint demanded.

Before Corrain could take comfort from that, the tavern door opened again, admitting another gust of wind redolent with autumn rain.

'Here we go.' Kusint got to his feet, raised a hand and called out something in the Soluran tongue.

Corrain stood up so fast that his stool fell back against the wall. The newcomer wore the blue and grey surcoat of Castle Pastamar over a sturdy chainmail hauberk.

The pimpled youth cut through the tavern tables with all the assurance of a man with an armoured guard troop behind him. He offered a folded, unsealed leaf of parchment to Kusint with the briefest of words.

'What does it say?' Corrain ignored the youth who was already leaving, with men twice his age and a head taller hurriedly drawing their booted feet out of his path.

'That we are summoned to attend Gaveren Raso, wizard of the fifth order of Fornet.' Kusint spoke loudly enough for his words to reach those in the tavern now looking inquisitively at the pair of them. 'At once.'

Corrain was already heading for the door. 'Come on.'

Outside the gusting wind was now driving off the rain clouds. Only a spatter of cold drops struck their faces as they headed towards the castle.

It was a massive fortification, claiming a rise in the land which forced the river around in a wide muddy loop. The stepped battlements of a great square keep were just visible above the top of a curtain wall taller than any Corrain had seen. That outermost defence was guarded by numerous towers, each one substantial enough in its own right to withstand an army's attack. Though any enemy would be a fool to try an assault and would be a dead foe shortly thereafter. Corrain could see how each tower was well placed to give archers and crossbowmen a clear field of fire over all the fortifications that flanked it.

On this side of the castle, the turrets watched over the bridge crossing the river. Stone arches marched across dark water carrying a road wide enough for two wagons to pass abreast. The river was rising now with the season's rains but still flowed well below the high water stains on the pillars and the line of trees on the far bank that marked a safe foothold for saplings in all but the wettest years.

Lord Pastiss's boar's head crest was carved on massive stone shields above each span and the tusked beasts snarled on pillars at either end of the bridge. Barges anchored in the broad pool on the downstream side were disgorging their cargos to fill the wagons and to burden the mules waiting to head east and west along the road while the narrower boats able to shoot the bridge's spans waited to carry their share further upstream.

Corrain skirted a rutted puddle in the earthen track cutting between the low thatched dwellings. Wooden doors and shutters over glassless windows stood open to reveal Soluran craftsmen in their workshops even so late in the day. Goodwives and children too young to be put to work were busy in the yards behind. The yards in turn were flanked by buildings where scents of cooking here and laundry there suggested kitchens and other such domestic necessities. At the far end of each long plot reaching back from the road, Corrain could glimpse vegetable gardens, chicken coops, pig sties and here and there a house cow's byre.

It was as unlike a Caladhrian village or the good order of Halferan Manor as he could possibly imagine. He still felt a longing for home twist beneath his breastbone.

Corrain thrust that thought away, turning instead to something that irritated him like a burr beneath a horse's girth.

So much fine stonework evident in the castle and the bridge. So much trade filling this noble lord's coffers with dues and tariffs which he could see being collected by the bridge reeve and his lackeys in their livery. Yet the Solurans couldn't so much as lay some cobbles in their roadway to save themselves from the season's mud.

Corrain did his best to skirt the worst of the mire as he and Kusint crossed over the market place facing the bridge and hurried up the slope beyond. The pimpled envoy had already reached the outer gate of the brooding barbican.

Corrain braced himself for yet another delay. How better for this Gaveren Raso to prove that he was not subject to Hadrumal's Archmage than by keeping them waiting at the castle's very threshold?

To his surprise, when the young envoy waved towards them, the grimly-bearded guard signalled his men to raise the outer portcullis. He beckoned them on beneath the first iron-toothed lattice, hanging ready in its slot to drop and trap attackers foolhardy enough to charge across this first threshold in hopes of overwhelming the gatehouse.

Corrain noted the holes in the roof as they walked beneath the long vault separating that outer defence from the castle's inner ward. Any such trapped attackers could expect sharpened bolts fresh from the blacksmith's forge, scalding water or worse to come dropping on their heads.

'This way.' A lackey was waiting for them on the far side of the inner portcullis.

Corrain thought again. Everyone else he could see was armoured and surcoated like that first pimpled envoy. This lad wore a plain dun homespun tunic with no armour beneath it. His long sleeves were neatly bound with cuffs of scarlet broadcloth though the hem and the neck were only roughly sewn with coarse yarn. He didn't look like a household servant for a noble as mighty as Lord Pastiss.

Nor a man at arms and there were plenty of those to be seen by way of comparison. All but one of the castle's towers had a contingent of armoured men outside it. Some were honing their skills with swords and polearms, heedless of the spitting rain. Others were wrestling for wooden daggers, cheered on by their comrades sat mending gear and harness at trestle tables or on each tower's steps. All wore Pastamar livery except for one company in the plain flax cloth breeches and buff tunics which Corrain recognised from their earlier encounter with Lord Pastiss's mercenaries; men and outlandish as it seemed, some women, handsomely paid to risk their lives venturing across the river into the Great Forest to hunt down enemy scouts and spies.

The boy was leading the way across the grassy expanse of the castle's outer ward. He might be a within a year of Kusint's own age but his dark-haired head would barely reach the Forest lad's shoulder. He was a skinny youth too; whatever he was learning here, it wasn't sword play or anything else to put muscle on his bones.

Kusint gestured at the vast space. 'When the Mandarkin attack, everyone from the town takes shelter in here.'

Corrain nodded. He had guessed as much.

Their silent guide raised a hand as they arrived before the only tower lacking an armoured company outside it. The door at the top of the steps ahead opened obediently though there was no sign of a door ward. The boy stopped at the foot of the stone stair with a gesture indicating they should continue.

Corrain nodded and went on. He didn't speak. Either the lad was mute, so most likely he was also deaf. Or these wizards were trying to overawe the two of them, in which case that rune had two sides. Corrain could stay silent too.

The entrance led into a single round room taking up the entire lower floor of the tower. Lit only by narrow slit windows, Corrain would have expected it to be swathed in gloom as the autumn sun was setting. Instead it was filled with some radiance that had no obvious source.

Men and women, from those as young as their silent guide to a handful as old as Fitrel sat on stools and benches around tables little different from the tavern's furniture. Except these tables held books, inkstands, leaves of parchment and countless other trifles and trinkets presumably with some wizardly usefulness.

With all eyes on the pair of them, Corrain studied these unknown mages with equal frankness. All wore the same dun tunic as the lad who'd brought them here. Their sleeves were all bound with the different colours which Corrain knew denoted wizardry. Most had cloth of a second hue ringing the hem of their shapeless garment and a good few had a third colour neatly sewn to finish the neckline.

An inner door stood ajar to reveal a stair spiralling upwards. A woman rose from her seat close beside it. Corrain recognised Selista. She wore all four colours of magecraft, the last as a scarlet leather strap belting her tunic over a long black skirt reaching down to soft leather half-boots.

'Follow me.'

Though her words were calm Corrain felt the open expectation in the room harden into anticipation.

So he made sure to keep his expression as bland as Selista's words. He was pleased to see Kusint do the same.

'Thank you.'

Selista went ahead up the spiral stair. Corrain followed with Kusint close behind him. The next floor up offered another vast room though this one had the comforts of a broad fireplace built into the outward face and cushioned seats in the deep, wide windows on the inner side overlooking the castle's enclosure.

Seven cross-framed chairs made a half circle in the middle of the room. Four men and three women sat seated turn by turn. Corrain had no doubt that all were wizards, and evidently they had sufficient rank to shed those brown tunics for fur-trimmed mantles over costly robes and gowns in styles reminiscent of those favoured by the Caladhrian parliament's oldest barons and their ladies.

He followed Selista into the room. Kusint came after to stand at his side.

The wizard in the seat closest to a window raised a hand to the magewoman. 'You may leave us.'

'Sir.' Selista nodded briefly and turned back for the stair. Corrain couldn't read any clue on her face. He wondered briefly where Orul and Espilan might be. He hadn't seen either of them below and there was no one else in this room.

The wizard gestured again and the door closed obediently without need for anyone's hand. 'I am Gaveren Raso, wizard of the fifth order of Fornet,' he said briefly in fluent Tormalin. 'We are Wrothar Gardol, sixth order, Takten Mudis, sixth order, Strape Filstarra, seventh order, Peytel Roth, seventh order, Deule Lacrus, eighth order and Copin Eck, eighth order.'

So these were the Elders. Corrain found it disconcerting to see that whatever their rank or title, none of these wizards could be called old. Only the most senior man looked to be within a handful of years of Planir's age and Gaveren Raso was surely Corrain's contemporary.

Did Soluran wizards not live long enough to lay old bones on a funeral pyre? Corrain recalled the savagery with which Selista, Orul and Espilan had attacked Anskal in the Forest and the viciousness of the Mandarkin's retaliation.

'My humble duty to you all.' Kusint bowed low from the waist.

Corrain echoed both his words and his obeisance, though he didn't look away from the wizards. They all had eyes as hard as any battle-scarred warrior whom he had ever encountered. Corrain wouldn't want to turn his back on any of them.

The most senior of the women chuckled and said something to prompt laughter from the rest. Corrain straightened up warily. That had not been friendly laughter.

She smoothed the velvet of her golden gown. 'You keep a watch on us all while you offer us your submission.'

Like Gaveren Raso the resident wizard, the woman's Tormalin was fluent with the accents of Col. Corrain recalled the greybearded Orul saying that the Order had ties with the university in that Ensaimin city.

'I was taught that a swordsman should always stay alert.' Corrain decided against explaining that any newly-sworn Halferan lad looking at his own feet as he bowed could expect a punishing slap to the back of the head from Fitrel.

'So Planir of Hadrumal sends you to us to make his excuses.' The man granted the accolade of eighth order cupped one cobalt-clad elbow in a hand and rested his chin in the other.

'I offer no excuses, sir.' That was how Selista had addressed Gaveren Raso so surely that was sufficient courtesy. 'Not for myself, nor for the Archmage. He had no knowledge of what I intended,' Corrain insisted. 'I never planned on enlisting any Mandarkin's aid. I came north hoping to find a Soluran wizard willing to lend their magic to defending my home.'

He hesitated, seeing the seated Solurans exchanging glances. Corrain guessed they were recalling whatever

Selista and the other two had told them. He pressed on.

'My country has been ravaged by corsair raiders for this past handful of years. Men, women and children have lost their lives and their livelihoods. Those who survived have seen their homes plundered and burned time and again. If they have not been able to flee, they have been enslaved. They have been stolen away to be sold to the Archipelagans, their lives worth no more than an Aldabreshin's whim.'

He did his best to swallow his rising anger, brandishing the broken shackle around his own wrist instead.

'I was chained to a galley oar, flogged and only saved from starvation that I might help the villains attack my own kith and kin. My friends died aboard those ships. Only one survives and he won't live through another winter, my oath on it. I looked for magic to save him when Kusint told me of Solura's mages since the Archmage and Hadrumal's wizards would not help us—' he hastily corrected himself. 'They cannot, according to their laws.'

Kusint spoke up. 'I was also enslaved by the Aldabreshi after being taken prisoner in Lescar's recent battles. We hoped that a wizard practised in warfare could save more of Caladhria's people from such a vile fate. The Aldabreshi know nothing of magic and fear it to their very bones. We believed that a single season of seeing their ships sunk by wizardry would leave them too terrified to return to the mainland.'

Out of the corner of his eyes, Corrain could the red-headed lad deathly pale beneath his freckles.

'I was chained to those same oars. I would have lived and died as a slave if not for Corrain and his sword-mate Hosh. These corsairs are as brutal and as depraved as any Mandarkin.' Kusint's voice shook with hatred. 'When I found myself safe in Caladhria, Hosh's mother welcomed me as warmly as one of her own blood. I sought to repay her kindness by restoring their lost son, when I told Corrain of Solura's mages. Such debts cannot be left unsettled.'

'Yet this man whom you brought here to our king's realm offered gold to a Mandarkin,' the man in a sombre russet gown said harshly. 'He stands here before us and admits that he made this alliance with a lifelong enemy of all Solurans.'

'I did not understand what I was doing. Do not blame him for my folly, any more than you accuse the Archmage,' Corrain said quickly. 'Kusint did his best to warn me. He turned his back the moment he saw that I was in earnest. But I was too desperate to listen—'

'So you say.' The woman in the golden velvet gown cut him short. 'Where is Planir of Hadrumal now?'

'Where—' Corrain looked at her, uncomprehending. 'I don't know, if he's not in his own hall—'

'What help does he seek elsewhere?' A man in maroon demanded.

'I don't know.' Corrain could only repeat himself.

'What does Hadrumal make of these past few days' happenings in Relshaz?' The woman in the seat beside Gaveren wore a blue silk gown shot with green like a bankfisher's wing.

'Relshaz?' Corrain was entirely at a loss.

The assembled wizards exchanged trenchant looks.

Gaveren Raso pursed his lips. 'So you have admitted your folly to us and taken the blame. What do you want of us now?'

Corrain felt the suggestion of a headache rising from

the tension in his neck. 'This Mandarkin has claimed the raiders' island for his own. He seeks more wealth and threatens to plunder my home again. He will rob others regardless; I have no doubt of that.'

'Then you are well served for your foolishness.' The woman in the central seat drew her feet in beneath her leaf-green skirts as though ready to stand and leave. 'This is no concern of ours.'

'Tell Hadrumal's Archmage to kill this Mandarkin and that will settle accounts between us,' the woman in gold velvet said.

The woman in leaf-green looked startled, offering some protest in the Soluran tongue. The man in maroon added his voice to hers.

'Planir needs your help to kill the Mandarkin,' Corrain said desperately. 'The Aldabreshi know nothing of magic but their thefts have won them weapons and jewels with wizardry bound within them. The corsairs had no idea that they possessed such treasures but this Mandarkin knows ensorcelled artefacts for what they are.'

He drew a breath, seeing that piece of news had broken through the Soluran wizards' indifference. He pressed home his advantage.

'The Mandarkin will use these artefacts against us; I have no doubt of that. Planir says that Hadrumal has no great knowledge of such things. The Archmage asks you to share your own lore so he might put an end to this menace. Before this Mandarkin returns to threaten Solura.'

Surely these arrogant men and women had some concern for their own hides.

Half of the Solurans spoke up at once. The cobalt-robed wizard silenced them all with a glare. He twisted in his seat to look into the emptiness by the closest window.

'Sister Alebis?'

'Saedrin's stones!' Corrain took a swift step backwards.

Two women were sitting in the recessed seat which had seemed wholly empty before. One wore a charcoal gown with a creamy hooded cape hiding her face. The second wore dark breeches and a pale surcoat cut from the same creamy cloth as well as a gleaming chainmail hauberk. She stared at Corrain, leaving him with no doubt of her skills with the long sword belted at her hip.

The caped woman threw back her hood. She looked old enough to be her escort's grandmother or indeed mother to any of the wizards in the room.

'The Caladhrian speaks the truth. Planir of Hadrumal had no knowledge of what he intended.' She nodded at Kusint. 'This boy only sought to help. He would never have agreed to any alliance with the Mandarkin.'

'Has he any knowledge of Hadrumal's plans?' Gaveren Ruso demanded.

'No.' The caped woman gazed at Corrain. 'Nor of any of their secrets.'

Why did these Soluran wizards look so disappointed? Before Corrain could pursue that question, he saw the old woman's dark eyes fasten on him again.

'You're an adept of Artifice.' Now she wasn't merely seeing into his innermost thoughts. She was prompting him to speak them aloud.

The armoured woman laid one hand on her sword hilt. 'This is Sister Alebis of the House of Sanctified Repose.'

'He means no disrespect.' The caped woman raised an age-spotted hand to soothe her escort. 'He is merely ignorant.'

Before Corrain could breathe a sigh of relief, her wrinkled face hardened.

'The Caladhrian does not lie but he assuredly does not tell us all that he knows. Nor does he know all that we have recently learned of events in Relshaz. I cannot tell if that means Planir of Hadrumal does not trust him or that the southern Archmage has already abandoned hopes of this quest.'

The wizards looked at him with varying degrees of pity and contempt.

What hadn't he told these wizards that might have tipped the balance? A great deal, Corrain realised guiltily. He had said nothing of Minelas's treachery or of his own determination to see Hadrumal humiliated by way of return for their callous disregard for Caladhria—

'Ah.' Now understanding dawned in the old woman's dark eyes. Understanding and pity.

Corrain coloured furiously and tried to crush every fear and feeling of inadequacy at ever living up to his dead lord's example—

'No matter.' The aged sister folded her hands at the rope girdle knotted around her waist.

Corrain felt his faint headache ease. Artifice? If that's what it felt like, he'd know it again. He stared at the old woman. Let her know that for a certainty.

She studied him for a moment, a faint smile curving her withered lips before she looked at the woman in golden velvet, deadly serious. 'What he says of ensorcelled artefacts is also true.'

The assembled wizards exchanged glances, swiftly reaching some unspoken accord.

'Our business here is concluded.' Gaveren rose to his feet. 'We acquit you of malice and your stupidity looks likely to bring its own punishment down on your head so that will suffice. Return to Planir and tell him that we will deal with this Mandarkin as and when he should come north again. Hadrumal's travails and your own in the meantime are no concern of ours.'

'What—?'

Before Corrain could think what to say to this abrupt, disastrous dismissal, he was blinded by a brutal flash of light.

He found himself standing on the muddy turf outside the castle's gate where they had first entered. Kusint was staggering beside him.

'What—?'

Before the Forest lad could frame his question, azure magelight dazzled them both a second time and the burly Ensaimin mage stepped out of the emptiness.

'Let's get your gear and go home.' Tornauld said grimly.

'They gave us a hearing but—' Corrain began.

'We know.' Tornauld cut him off. 'We were watching.'

'Watching? From Hadrumal? Aren't you supposed to be standing guard over Lady Zurenne and Lady Ilysh?'

'They're safe and well,' Tornauld said testily.

'Planir cannot blame me,' Corrain asserted, 'for the Soluran wizards' refusal to help him.'

'No, he can't,' Tornauld agreed. 'Now—'

'I fulfilled my part of the bargain.' Corrain wasn't about to be brushed off by any more wizards today.

'Now the Archmage must keep his word and rescue Hosh.'

'All in good time.'

Before Corrain could ask what Tornauld meant by that, magecraft enveloped them a third time.

— CHAPTER TWENTY-THREE —

'I would not have thought it possible, my lady. It's a marvel, truly.' Raselle sounded a trifle uncertain all the same.

'Thanks to Master Tornauld.' Zurenne knew how the maidservant felt but would never be so discourteous as to betray her own misgivings regarding the wizard.

She scanned the courtyard but the sturdy Ensaimin man was nowhere to be seen. Reassured, she turned back to the Halferan gatehouse. It seemed like a dream, to see the entrance to the manor safeguarded once again.

It would assuredly not have been possible without Tornauld's magic. First he had lifted up the posts and planks for the scaffolding so that all the men had to do was lash them securely together. Then the outer walls had risen ever higher day by day with the wizard bringing stacks of bricks and buckets of mortar to those labouring to build them.

With that flick of his hand and a sapphire glimmer, the wizard did a gang of lads' work as easily as Esnina carried her little bag of wooden blocks from their tent to the shrine or wherever else Zurenne might be setting up her folding table and writing box, to tally up her accounts, to deal with her correspondence from the increasingly curious wives of the neighbouring barons, to manage all the demesne's affairs which inexorably continued amid all the bustle of renewal and rebuilding.

To her surprise, Zurenne found this daily round of ledgers and letters, mixing ink and trimming pens oddly soothing. The busyness all around proved far more heartening than the distraction she might have expected it to be. Sharing the tasks with Ilysh and explaining the true breadth of a noble lady's duties had brought Zurenne closer to her daughter than they had been since murder and treachery had first wreaked such havoc in their lives. Uncovering the intricacies of a noble lord's customary obligations had been an education for them both.

She looked down at her younger child. Esnina was standing in front of Zurenne, her shoulders pressed against her mother's skirts as they stood with Raselle contemplating the gatehouse.

To Zurenne's inexpressible relief, Neeny had proved content to sit quietly beside her mother's stool and build her own little walls to shelter the wooden animals which the village men had carved for her from scraps of lumber, so generous with the scant time they had for themselves and their own families.

The animals now had their own lidded basket which old Fitrel, the sergeant at arms, had woven as he sat supervising the Halferan guardsmen as they loaned their muscles to the rebuilding of their own barrack hall. The former wooden-walled building would be replaced with brick walls and a tile-hung roof and far greater comforts for the guardsmen within.

Zurenne could hear the incessant sound of sawing beyond the manor's wall. When she had taken Neeny out for a morning walk beside the brook, they had seen the sawdust lying thick as snow on the turf despite the swirling breeze. She must remember to write to Lady Antathele today, she reminded herself. To thank her for persuading her lord and husband to sell Halferan such a substantial stock of well-seasoned timber.

'Mama?' The little girl looked up. 'Where will mine and Lysha's bedchamber be?'

Crouching down, Zurenne encircled her daughter in loving arms. 'Up there, on the same side as the barrack hall. See?' She pointed to the roofless upper storey where the master joiner and his new apprentices were measuring the apertures for the window frames beneath the cloud-dappled sky.

Esnina nodded and smiled. Zurenne breathed that silent prayer of thanks which she must surely repeat ten and twenty times a day now; to Drianon, to Maewelin, to every goddess who might claim a share in the fragile peace of mind which Neeny had regained with each successive night's sleep here.

Though of course that rune had its reverse. Neeny's innocent assumption that she and her sister would continue to share a bedroom had carried clearly across the courtyard thanks to that penetrating tone Drianon had chosen to bless small children with. Zurenne didn't need to look around to see a handful of their household studiously avoiding her gaze, to avoid any hint that they might raise the awkward question that everyone was tacitly ignoring.

Where would Lady Ilysh sleep once her lord and husband had returned from his present journey about the manor's business, whatever that important though unspecified task might be precisely?

Zurenne would spin that wool when the sheep had been shorn. She was more concerned that Corrain would return with definite news of that vile wizard's death. It made no odds to her if the man died at the Halferan swordsman's own hands or if they ended up owing that debt to Planir.

She looked into the gatehouse's shadowed archway. The studded and banded wooden doors had been hung the previous evening, after days of the reek of hot iron from Sirstin's forge and the ringing of hammering echoing across the compound. Today she could see the blacksmith fitting the locks and bolts which he had made to secure the gateway more surely than ever before.

That might reassure the household's lackeys and maidservants and those villagers sheltering within the manor's walls while they doggedly rebuilt their homes over beyond the brook. Zurenne could not be so sanguine. Walls and gates were no defence against magic. As long as that vile wizard drew breath, he could step out of the empty air at any moment to threaten her and her children.

She hoped she need not fear him as long as Tornauld was here but what of the future when the restoration was complete and the wizard returned to Hadrumal? Zurenne looked around again. Where was the burly mage?

'Do you suppose we'll truly be able to move in there before the Equinox?' Now Raselle sounded wholly disbelieving, gazing up at the gatehouse.

'So Master Tornauld says,' Zurenne reminded her.

'Master Tornauld says so?'

Zurenne tensed at the sound of Master Vachent's voice behind her. It took a moment for her to compose herself with a suitably unrevealing expression. She turned her head to greet him with cool courtesy. 'Master mason, good day to you.'

She braced herself for yet another exhaustively detailed report on the progress of rebuilding the storehouses and servants' accommodations beyond the shell of the baronial tower. Vachent claimed her attention twice or thrice daily with such information, all of which he clearly expected her to dutifully convey to Corrain in his role as Baron Halferan. All delivered in a tone that somehow combined obsequiousness with infuriating condescension.

Instead the master mason wagged a reproving finger at Raselle. 'Master Tornauld has no business offering any such assurances. Those walls must be left to dry slowly and thoroughly.'

He glanced at Zurenne. This was, she noted, as close as he dared come to rebuking her along with her maidservant.

'Otherwise the mortar binding those bricks will shrink or crack,' Vachent continued. 'You must cultivate a little patience, my dear girl, no matter how eager you may be to quit your draughty tent. Because the lime—'

'Then let us ask Master Tornauld what he meant.' Zurenne interrupted before the mason's insatiable urge to air his knowledge overcame his conviction that such matters should not concern women, even those few capable of understanding a workman's mysteries.

'Or Madam Merenel,' Neeny piped up.

'My lady?'

Vachent's surprise turned to wary indignation as Esnina pointed to Sirstin the smith opening the porter's door that had been cut into one of the new gates. The amiable Tormalin magewoman had paused to exchange a brief word and a chuckle with Sirstin.

'You'll excuse me, my lady—'

'You are not dismissed.' Zurenne cut the mason's hasty bow short with implacable courtesy. 'Madam mage!' She raised a hand to greet Merenel.

As the wizard woman approached, she smiled at Esnina. Though the little girl pressed close to Zurenne, she didn't hide her face in her mother's skirts as she had done for the first handful of days after their arrival.

'My lady, good day to you.' Merenel brushed a drift of sawdust from her skirt and curtseyed with measured politeness.

Zurenne returned the compliment, at the same time relieved to see the magewoman in skirts rather than the breeches she had worn on her first visit to the half-rebuilt manor. She smiled brightly.

'Raselle hopes we can move into the gatehouse in time for the equinox. Do you think that is possible?'

Zurenne did her best to ignore all the other concerns which besieged her at the thought of the approaching festival. If she could have given every man, woman and child of Halferan village and the demesne five full days of feasting, that would still be inadequate reward for all their hard work. As it was, she couldn't see how she was to offer them anything remotely fitting for the season.

How was she to supply the richly flavoured and foaming ale to properly celebrate Ostrin's gifts of barley and yeast without a brew house? Where were the ovens to bake the plaited loaves of bread and the spiced cakes thanking Drianon for her gift of wheat? The manor's kitchens remained no more than an expanse of cracked tile where awnings sheltered the temporary open hearths providing rough and ready meals to fuel all this hard work.

'You will be hanging your garlands on your shutters well before festival eve,' Merenel assured her.

'I hardly think so,' Vachent protested in strangled tones. 'It will be days yet before we can think of burdening the walls with rafters. The walls cannot be plastered until the roof is complete and it will be well after festival before we can consider whitewashing—'

Merenel shook her head with a confident grin. 'I will have the mortar dry before this evening and we can make a start on the roof tomorrow. The plaster within will dry enough for painting inside a handful of days.'

Vachent looked as though he would like to dispute that but like everyone else in the manor or out in the village these days, he dared not challenge a wizard on matters of magic. Not now that tavern tales had proved to be such an inadequate and inaccurate source of information.

Not that such ignorance stopped certain of the maidservants muttering disapproval behind their hands of such unnatural goings on. Zurenne was sure that a number of the labouring men shared similar unease along with their meagre evening tankards of small beer.

'All the same, I take your point about the weight of the roof trusses on soft mortar.' Merenel inclined her head courteously to the mason. 'By your leave, Lady Zurenne, I'll go and see what's what before the first timbers are raised.'

She turned but before she had taken a handful of steps, daylight shone through the gatehouse arch. Sirstin the blacksmith had hauled open both doors, catching up his bag of tools as he retreated.

Horsemen rode into the courtyard.

'My lady?'

Zurenne was startled to see a crackle of white light edged with scarlet cupped in Merenel's hand.

'If this is some unwanted intrusion,' the magewoman offered, 'I can persuade these ruffians to turn tail as readily as Jilseth ever did.'

'No!' Zurenne spoke more sharply than she intended but she had felt Neeny shrink with fear and heard her daughter's whimper at the sight of Merenel's magic.

'No,' she repeated more calmly. 'Those men wear Lord Licanin's livery. My sister's husband is always most welcome here.'

All the same, she wondered who had betrayed Corrain's absence to Licanin. Master Rauffe was back at Taw Ricks but the steward had known of Corrain's departure before taking to the road himself. Had he sent some message to his supposedly former master? Zurenne was obscurely disappointed. She had truly thought that the steward's loyalties lay with Halferan now.

The Licanin troopers reined in their mounts in front of the half-built barrack hall. Halferans from all across the courtyard were laying down their tools and calling out heartfelt greeting to men whom they had fought alongside to escape the corsairs. Just as Lord Licanin had risked his own life for her sake and that of her daughters, Zurenne reminded herself. He had seen his own loyal swordsmen die for Halferan. Bonds of blood shed in common cause would link the two baronies for a generation.

'My lord, you are most welcome.' She stepped forward to greet him as he turned his horse's head towards the stable boy making haste to hold his bridle.

'My lady.' Before Licanin dismounted, his shrewd eyes took in every detail of the rebuilding. 'I am delighted to see that you're making such strides towards Halferan's restoration.'

Zurenne would have said that astonishment outweighed his pleasure by some margin.

'May I make known to you Madam Merenel of Hadrumal?' She gestured to introduce the magewoman to the baron. 'Wizardly assistance has been helping us make such progress.'

'Indeed?' After acknowledging Merenel with a courteous nod, Lord Licanin hesitated.

Merenel grinned before addressing Zurenne. 'If you will excuse me, my lady, I have mortar to examine.'

Lord Licanin surprised them both by raising his hand. 'May I beg a moment of your time, madam mage?'

'Of course.' She looked expectantly at the nobleman.

Licanin hesitated yet again before speaking. 'What can you tell me of the current turmoil in Relshaz?'

'What turmoil?' Zurenne demanded.

Once again Licanin apparently found the words which he sought elusive. Merenel explained instead.

'Aldabreshin hatred of magic has washed ashore in the city in the past handful of days,' she said, grim-faced. 'It's been spilling onto the streets.'

'How so?' Zurenne was confused.

'Wizards have attacked, their homes and their businesses threatened,' Merenel said curtly. 'Two mages have been killed by mobs.'

'Killed?' Zurenne was appalled.

Almost as swiftly, she was mystified. How could wizards be murdered with their devastating magecraft at their fingertips?

Fear crowded hard on the heels of that thought. If wizards could be killed by the non-mageborn, was Tornauld or Merenel's presence here truly the safeguard she was trusting her children's lives to?

Merenel cocked her curly head, eyes bright. 'What's your interest in this, my lord?'

'I—' The grey-haired nobleman looked away, a sweep of his hand taking in the courtyard. 'I would hate to see Halferan taken unawares.'

'You think to see such hostility here?' Merenel queried. 'When Halferan has such very good reason to value magecraft?'

'Let us hope not,' Lord Licanin said stiffly.

Merenel stood for a moment, expectant. When Lord Licanin stayed silent, the mage bowed to Zurenne with a smile so fleeting that she thought she might have imagined it.

'My lady, by your leave, I'll go and examine that mortar.'

This time Licanin said nothing to stop the magewoman leaving.

Once she was out of earshot, Zurenne rounded on the nobleman. 'What did you mean by that?'

Licanin looked startled and not a little affronted by her brusque demand. 'I simply wished to know that this wizard you have here is aware of recent events in Relshaz.'

'Did you have reason to doubt it?' Though as she spoke, Zurenne realised she hadn't spared much thought for Tornauld's communications with Hadrumal. He had received neither letters nor messages by courier dove, so she had assumed he conversed with his fellow wizards through some magical means. She assumed he was keeping the Archmage informed as to their progress rebuilding the manor.

Now she wondered what news Tornauld might have heard from the world beyond these walls. News which he had clearly not seen fit to pass on to her. She looked around again. Where was the burly wizard today?

'I have no knowledge of wizards' customary dealings with each other or anyone else,' Licanin said testily. 'How am I supposed to know how they stay informed?'

He glared around the courtyard. The folk who had been standing watching their noble visitor's encounter with the mage hastily resumed the tasks they'd had in hand or found something new demanding their attention.

Licanin looked back at Zurenne. 'Where is Lady Ilysh?'

'In the shrine, dealing with our correspondence from Taw Ricks.' Zurenne wasn't to be deterred. She repeated Merenel's question. 'Do you expect to see such hostility to wizardry in Caladhria?'

Now Licanin looked around to assure himself they were not overheard. He looked down at Esnina and then to Raselle. 'Might your maid take the child for some refreshment while you and I take a walk outside the walls?' he suggested pointedly.

'Of course.' Zurenne coloured, mortified to realise that she had neglected such basic duties of hospitality. 'Neeny, go with Raselle.' She urged the child towards the maid. 'Ask Abiath to prepare wine and cakes for Lord Licanin on our return.'

She accepted the grey-haired nobleman's arm and walked with him towards the gatehouse. He didn't speak until they were well clear of the manor's entrance, leading her in the other direction from the bustle of carpentry.

'How sound is this outer wall?' He squinted in the sunlight, tracing a crack upwards through the masonry to the crumbled tiles at the top.

'Substantial sections will need rebuilding,' Zurenne admitted. 'But we can tackle that once everyone has a roof over their head for the winter seasons.'

Licanin shaded his eyes with a gloved hand as he considered the clouds on the seaward horizon. 'Dastennin be thanked that the weather's stayed fair for Halferan's labours so far but the season will soon turn.'

'Quite so,' Zurenne agreed. She had been offering her own prayers of thanks to the god of sea and storms as well as to Larasion, goddess of wind and weather.

Licanin offered his arm to Zurenne again and they continued walking.

'Tell Master Rauffe to wait until For-Spring to start on these repairs,' he advised. 'Work will have to stop with the first frosts regardless.'

Zurenne had already decided to defer such work. For one thing, she and Ilysh had established how much further afield Halferan's wagons would have to go to find a ready supply of fired bricks. Their calculations had already proved that the salvaged building materials would fall far short of what was required.

She challenged Lord Licanin's assumption all the same. 'I imagine Madam Merenel will be able to keep the mortar from freezing.'

'I think that you will find it is time for all these wizards to return to Hadrumal,' Licanin said firmly. 'The corsairs are defeated—'

'They were driven off,' Zurenne interjected. 'Who knows if they will return?'

Licanin shook his head. 'Your household and the demesne folk cannot become reliant upon wizardry. A barony's men need to work to earn their bread and beer. Their sons must be apprenticed to master craftsmen to learn their own trades. Halferan cannot prosper if half the tenantry is left idle,' he warned her. 'Caladhria cannot afford to have malcontents and shirkers looking on with envious eyes and demanding magic to relieve their own labours, not if the country is to thrive. We hear that the Aldabreshi in Relshaz are refusing to do business with merchants who have any dealings with Hadrumal. How long before those same merchants spurn any Caladhrian barony indebted to their wizardry?'

'When did you hear this, my lord?' Zurenne interrupted. She had just realised the implications of Merenel's words. If unease about wizardry in Relshaz had erupted in the past handful of days, Licanin could not possibly have received such news at his home and then made the six or seven day journey here.

Licanin cleared his throat. 'I was paying a visit to Lord Darmenid. Since Halferan lay on my route home, I decided to pay you a visit.'

An unannounced visit. Zurenne forbore to point out that inherent discourtesy. That would be for Corrain to do when he returned, just as he would doubtless seek to discover what business Licanin had with the barony lying between Lord Tallat's southern boundary and the port city of Attar.

Of course, Corrain had taken ship for Hadrumal in Attar. Had Lord Darmenid got word of that? Perhaps Zurenne would write a letter to the noble baron's wife.

'Once Halferan is rebuilt, I imagine our association

with wizardry will cease,' she said carefully. 'I see no reason for the Relshazri to fret over magic's wider influence in Caladhria. There are not so many wizards even in the largest towns, as I understand it, and fewer still willing to trade their skills for coin and toil.'

Licanin shook his head once again. 'No one knows how many wizards there are in Hadrumal. We don't know if we can trust the Archmage's word these days. He swore for a year and more that his precious edicts forbade offering the slightest assistance to Caladhria's innocents, however grievously they suffered. Then as easily as rolling a rune, he changed his mind and sent magic to sink the raiders' ships and to repel the villains attacking Halferan. Not that he saw fit to tell our parliament, beforehand or subsequently,' he added with rising ire.

Zurenne wondered how much similar indignation was scorching the pages of letters criss-crossing Caladhria since the most recent parliament had been summoned out of season.

'Has this Master Tornauld let slip anything of the Archmage's intentions?' Licanin's arm tightened, pulling her closer.

Zurenne was certain that there was nothing to be gained by telling Licanin that Planir had no hand in the corsairs' defeat. Even if he believed her.

'I have no notion what the Archmage may be doing.'

'Once he has helped ensure your demesne folk have shelter for the winter, you may thank Master Tornauld and bid him farewell,' Licanin said firmly. 'I have no doubt that the present Baron Halferan will agree that is the best course for Halferan.'

Zurenne saw Licanin's lined face wrinkle further with

a grimace of distaste, though she could not tell if that was for Tornauld or Corrain.

She pulled her hand free of Licanin's elbow. 'The present Baron Halferan has deferred all decisions on the manor's renewal to me, out of respect for his former lord, my lamented husband.'

Licanin rounded on her. 'Where is Corrain? What is he doing now? Why has he permitted you and your daughters to stay here so inadequately chaperoned?'

Zurenne stared at him in disbelief. 'Is that what brought you here? Truly? You imagine that I would disgrace my beloved's memory with some sordid dalliance in the midst of all these onlookers? That I would turn a blind eye to Ilysh cuckolding a husband who has not even bedded her?'

Now it was Licanin's turn to colour with deep embarrassment. 'I would never believe any such thing, but you should know that some have wondered what the Archmage might seek by way of return for his assistance against the corsairs. For all the gold he has given Halferan to spend on this rebuilding.'

Zurenne was forced to keep her tongue behind her teeth a second time. She could hardly tell Lord Licanin that Planir only sought to repay her for all that the barony had suffered at the hands of the renegade mage Minelas. Not with such unforeseen unease at the notion of wizardry spreading among the parliament's lords.

Besides, now she had both the leisure and the ledgers to tally up Halferan's losses, Zurenne was uncomfortably aware that Planir's gift of coin far outstripped whatever Master Minelas could have stolen. Not that any amount could offer recompense for the loss of her husband.

'Who whispers such spite?' she hissed instead. 'Baron

Karpis? Lord Tallat? Will they dare repeat such things when Corrain returns?'

Once again, Licanin hesitated, searching for a fitting reply. Zurenne didn't give him the chance to find one.

'I take it this is all that you have to say? I cannot think how you might insult me, my daughter, Halferan's new lord or my beloved husband's memory further. Shall we return to the gatehouse? There will be refreshments ready. You are very welcome to enjoy wine and cakes before you continue on your way.'

Zurenne was surprised to realise they had made almost half the circuit of the damaged walls. She decided she might as well go onwards as retrace her steps.

Licanin's weary voice stopped her.

'I came here to invite you and your daughters to celebrate the equinox festival with us.'

Zurenne turned to see him standing where she had left him, half shame-faced, half indignant.

'Your sister, my lady wife, thought that you might welcome a few days of respite and comfort.' Licanin spread his hands in a helpless gesture.

She recalled an unguarded line she had written in her last letter to Beresa, longing for an easeful night's sleep in a feather bed in a silent, secure tower. She had admitted something of the sort to Celle and Danlie as well. Had all her sisters gone to their husbands with their concerns?

In the next breath she remembered Licanin's unexpected arrival when she was Minelas's terrified captive, though the renegade mage had long since departed. The noble lord and his troopers had driven off the hired ruffians incarcerating her. That had only been the first of his many actions defending her interests, irrespective of Corrain's return or any mage's intervention.

Zurenne felt a blush of shame warm her cheeks. 'That is a generous invitation, my lord. Shall we see what Lady Ilysh wishes?'

Did he understand what she was saying? If staying here was Lysha's decision, as Zurenne was sure it would be, he would know his offer wasn't being rejected because of this quarrel.

'As you wish.' Lord Licanin began walking, though this time he did not offer her his arm.

They concluded the circuit of the manor's outer wall without further conversation. As they reached the gatehouse, Sirstin held the porter's door open.

'Good day to you, my lady. My lord Licanin.'

Licanin merely grunted by way of reply but Zurenne saw more tiredness than anger in his face. Even with the recent good weather, this journey must have been taxing for a man of his years.

'We could offer you and your men tents and blankets and a meal this evening,' she said tentatively. 'Rough fare but satisfying. You could take tomorrow to rest before you take to the road again the following morning.'

'We've no wish to be a burden.' Licanin slid a sideways glance at her before continuing, more conciliatory. 'The demesne's folk must have first call on Halferan's resources.'

Zurenne nodded, judging this was as far as either of them need go towards an apology.

She could see Abiath beside the shrine door; the old woman's curtsey a clear summons. Zurenne led the way and they found Neeny sitting on the tiled floor putting her wooden animals inside the wall of blocks which

Raselle was building. Lysha was sealing the morning's letters.

'Lady Ilysh.' Licanin greeted her politely.

'My lord.' She stood and curtseyed dutifully.

Raselle scrambled to her feet, hurrying to pick up a plate of griddle cakes from the table where Abiath was pouring wine into two glasses which had survived the journey from Taw Ricks.

'Esnina.'

As Lord Licanin greeted her, the little girl stayed sat on the floor, looking up with wide, doubtful eyes.

'Neeny,' Ilysh prompted.

'No matter.' Licanin waved a hand before accepting a glass from Abiath. He looked around the shrine. 'So this is your muniment room now.'

'For the present.' Ilysh glanced at the chests of documents stowed beneath the lowest shelves where the manor's funeral urns had once stood. 'We mean no disrespect.'

'So I see,' Lord Licanin assured her.

No one could accuse Halferan of impiety. Statues of the gods and goddesses had been gathered from the closest shrines and each one stood on an embroidered cloth on the polished shelves.

Zurenne took her own glass of wine and a cake from the plate. It was a cup-cut round of flour, butter and dried apple rather than an elegant honey wafer but it was warm and golden from the griddle. Let Licanin scorn it if he dared.

Then Zurenne realised that Licanin was frowning, concerned, as he looked at the crystal urn before Saedrin's newly garlanded effigy. 'Have you suffered some new loss?'

Ilysh shook her head. 'We brought my father's urn here when we decided to stay as the manor is rebuilt.'

Licanin nodded. 'That is entirely fitting.'

Zurenne smiled at Lysha. Then she noticed that Neeny's plump lower lip was quivering. Mention of her lost father still prompted the little girl's tears. Zurenne spoke up quickly to distract her.

'Lord Licanin has come to ask if we wish to spend the equinox festival with your lady aunt Beresa and your cousins.'

'Mama?' Ilysh looked anxiously at her.

'You are the Lady of Halferan.' Zurenne spoke gently, to draw any sting from the echo of their earlier arguments. 'I could not make such a decision without you.'

Ilysh bit her lower lip and looked at Esnina. Zurenne was relieved to see that Raselle had successfully soothed the little girl with a griddle cake.

'That is a most generous offer.' Ilysh took a cup of watered wine from Abiath and sipped. 'But I would hardly be doing my duty as Halferan's heir if we were to accept. Forgive me, my lord, but I could not enjoy feasting and dances knowing that I had left my barony's people without any such pleasures. We have endured so much together. We should share this festival's celebrations, however meagre.'

Zurenne's heart warmed with love and relief despite Lysha's resemblance to her dead father twisting her heart.

Noise from the compound outside turned everyone's head. Esnina rushed to cling to her mother's skirts, frustrating any hope of Zurenne seeing what had happened beyond the shrine door.

'It's the baron.' Abiath was closest to the entrance and well able to see through the half-open door. 'With Master Tornauld.'

Zurenne scooped Neeny up and settled her on one hip. 'Then let us all go and greet them.'

As they approached the knot of men and women who had already gathered to besiege Corrain with questions, she saw Madam Merenel dragging Tornauld to one side. A chance gust of autumn wind carried their urgent words to her.

'Where is the Archmage?'

'Hasn't he returned to Hadrumal?'

— CHAPTER TWENTY-FOUR —

'ARCHMAGE. I WAS pleased to learn of your return.' Troanna swept into the study, a combative glint in her eye. 'I take it you have some compelling reason for cramming us in here?'

Planir looked down, as though he could see through the floorboards to the spacious sitting room. 'Herion, Ely, Sannin and Merenel are below collating lore on magecrafted artefacts gathered from our libraries. We should allow them some elbow room as they work.'

Troanna was unimpressed. 'I gather we can expect no help from the Solurans.'

Planir smiled. 'I thought I felt Canfor's touch in the second nexus that was scrying after Corrain. He is quite correct,' he continued briskly. 'Not that I had any great hopes of the new baron persuading the Elders of Fornet. But now they know for certain that neither I nor this island had any part in bringing the Mandarkin south, thanks to the good sister adept.

'More importantly they know without a shadow of doubt that this Anskal has amassed a hoard of ensorcelled artefacts from his Archipelagan treasure. They may yet change their minds, in the interests of defending themselves, or in hopes of securing such treasures for themselves. Hearth Master, you're very welcome.'

Kalion nodded, his colour unflatteringly heightened after the exertion of climbing up the tower's steps.

'If the Solurans will not help us, I will not see them rewarded with the most meagre trinket,' he growled.

'Archmage.' Nolyen appeared behind the Hearth Master. 'Jilseth.' He greeted her with muted relief.

'I take it we are scrying after this Mandarkin again?' Troanna barely acknowledged the younger mage's arrival as she contemplated the table where a shallow bowl stood beside vials of perfumery oils and a bowl of crumbled bitumen, now mostly dust.

'Once we have seen what Jilseth's prize can tell us.' Planir gestured towards a second tile-topped table bearing a tall-sided copper bowl.

'Necromancy?' Troanna shook her head, dismissive. 'If you really believe there is anything of value to be learned from a dead man's hand, you may proceed without me.'

'A moment—if you please, Flood Mistress.' Kalion's belated courtesy did little to blunt the sharpness of his rebuke. 'Archmage? Do you bring any worthwhile news from Suthyfer?'

'Any aetheric insights into how we might deal with this Mandarkin?' Troanna's sarcasm was withering.

'Unfortunately, no.'

Jilseth wondered if anyone else had noticed the Archmage's infinitesimal hesitation before he answered.

'Yet it took you four days to establish this?' queried Troanna.

'While Relshaz's wizards have been forced to bar their doors or bring their families to shelter in Hadrumal.' Kalion shook his head, jowls wobbling with disapproval. 'If wizardry had greater standing on the mainland, more influence with the Magistracy and other such rulers—'

'Who has been scrying after the Mandarkin while I have been away?' Planir asked sternly.

'Ely and Galen.' Kalion squared his plump shoulders.

'That's one question answered then.' Planir shared his displeasure between the Hearth Master and the Flood Mistress. 'I wondered why I returned to find the wine shops humming with rumour and speculation.'

'You think questions weren't already scurrying around the city?' Kalion was indignant. 'Your absence has added far more fuel to those fires.'

'I know,' Planir assured him. 'I have discreet ears listening for every whisper and ready to damp down any unruly blaze. At the moment I see no great cause for concern.'

'Pupils and prentices may swap gossip as they wish from sunrise to sunset but the Council must be kept fully informed and soon.' Troanna scowled.

'So tell me what Ely and Galen have learned,' Planir invited. 'Unadulterated by wild surmise.'

'Only that these mageborn have yielded to the Mandarkin's teaching. Not that they have much to show for it as yet,' Kalion admitted.

'It takes a full season for Hadrumal's mentors to channel a raw apprentice's affinity into the most paltry cantrips,' Troanna observed. 'I cannot imagine this Mandarkin will work wonders in a handful of days.'

Planir smiled. 'Then my absence in Suthyfer is neither here nor there.'

'We have no notion how the Mandarkin might train their mageborn,' Kalion retorted. 'Nor of these artefacts he has gathered up. And forgive me—' he spared Jilseth a brief nod '—I fail to see what we may learn from the death of some unfortunate corsair in Relshaz.'

'The more we know, the more complete narrative of recent events we will have to lay before the Council,' Planir countered. 'Hence the need for this necromancy.'

Kalion snorted with something perilously close to scorn. 'Then why was this spell not worked when these two arrived?' A gesture shared his ill-temper equally between Jilseth and Nolyen.

'Necromancy is a demanding magic,' Planir replied calmly. 'Any stone mage would be ill-advised to attempt it without being fully rested.'

Jilseth did her best to look both refreshed and confident in her abilities. She had assuredly slept better here in her own bed.

Troanna opened her mouth but before she could speak, booted steps echoed in the curve of the stairwell.

'Good day to you all.' Rafrid appeared at the door, prompting the rest to advance further into the study. 'Forgive me, Archmage. I had pressing business in Wellery's Hall.'

'We all have other pressing business as well as commitments to those mages who share our affinity and to all those pupils studying each element's magic and the quadrate spells that combine them,' Troanna snapped. 'You may bespeak me when you've worked this necromancy, Archmage, and I will return to go scrying after this Mandarkin.'

Jilseth honestly believed that the Flood Mistress would have left the room if Rafrid hadn't been blocking the doorway.

'Or you could scry with the Hearth Master's assistance,' Planir suggested, 'while Rafrid and I witness Jilseth's spell?'

'That seems eminently sensible,' Kalion said instantly. 'We must not let this Mandarkin go unobserved.'

'Very well.' Troanna shooed Nolyen out of her way and sat down at the scrying bowl.

Jilseth recalled Nolyen saying that Sannin had told him that Hearth Master Kalion was itching to try his hand at the bitumen-enhanced scrying.

The fat wizard quickly took a seat opposite Troanna, arranged the fullness of his mantle so the velvet wouldn't crease, and leaned forward to peer into the empty bowl.

Troanna swept her hand in a swift circle. Jilseth heard the muted ringing of the silver as water flowed around it. Nolyen stood ready to hand over the perfume oils which Troanna might ask for.

Jilseth frowned to see how little bitumen remained. There had assuredly been a good deal more when she had left that dish in Relshaz. Had Ely and Galen been so profligate? But Planir had mentioned scrying after Corrain when the Caladhrian had gone to Solura. Had he taken some of the bitumen to Suthyfer to enable his mageborn allies there to see what was afoot in the Archipelago?

'I'm glad to see you so fully restored,' Rafrid said quietly as he joined Jilseth and the Archmage beside the tiled table.

Jilseth gathered her wits. 'Thank you, Cloud Master.'

If she and Rafrid had been alone, or if only Planir had been with them, Jilseth would have admitted her qualms. She felt confident that she had recovered all her elemental strength but her control was wont to falter unexpectedly. Worse, she was forced to acknowledge that her affinity sorely lacked its former stamina. But she wouldn't admit any such thing with Troanna or Kalion in the room.

'So this is your prize from Relshaz.' Rafrid looked into the copper pot with an involuntary shudder, though the dead man's hand was barely visible through the viscous yellow rock oil.

'You can work necromancy with a single finger bone?' He looked at Planir, visibly steeling himself. 'Shouldn't we cut the thing up? To learn as much as we can from successive spells?'

'I think not.' Planir's tone suggested he'd already considered this. 'We already know how this unfortunate died. We want to look much further back, as far as we can beyond his few last days, if we're to learn all we can from that galley's progress through the Archipelago. The more substantial the remains used in the spell, the more chance Jilseth has of success.'

If the Archmage had no necromancy skills of his own, he was as well informed on the quirks of this magic as he was on every other.

Rafrid stood up straight, the rim of the bowl blocking his view of the grisly contents. 'Can I be of any assistance?'

'Look for any detail in the necromantic visions which you think I might miss?' Planir suggested with a wry smile.

'As you command, Archmage,' Rafrid answered with a grin.

'Whenever you are ready, Jilseth,' Planir invited.

She could already see the emerald glow of Troanna's scrying across the room. Nolyen's back was to her so she couldn't see his expression but Kalion's face was avid as he peered into the spell's broad reflection. The Flood Mistress's expression was coldly intent, revealing nothing of Troanna's inner thoughts.

Warding her affinity against any hint of that rival spell, Jilseth laid her hands on either side of the copper bowl. She focused all her wizardly instincts on the rock oil within it. In some remote corner of her mind, she observed that she was concentrating more thoroughly on working this necromancy than she had done since she had first perfected these spells, in that season after she had advanced from her apprenticeship to her first pupillage.

She promptly dismissed that thought lest it prove a distraction in itself. Within a breath, the oil began to stir. It came to a boil as though a fire had long since been lit beneath it. Ensorcelled smoke and steam rose from the seething surface though the copper bowl was merely warm against her palms.

The dead corsair's calloused hand in the depths of the oil was now completely obscured. No matter. Jilseth did not need to see it. Reaching through the copper and through the oil, her earth affinity found the infinitesimal traces of everywhere this dead man had been, of everything which he had encountered, all now part of his blood and bone and skin in a manner beyond mundane sight and sense.

Dull amber magelight began to shimmer through the mist rising from the bowl. Jilseth raised her hands to gather the swirling opacity between her clawed fingers. The threads of magelight brightened to vivid gold as she shaped and reshaped the unruly vapours into a churning globe.

Now her wizardry drew every key to the puzzle of the nameless oarsman's life out of his dead flesh. She lifted those intangible wisps up through the oil to be woven into the glowing haze. Though this was only the beginning and barely one in ten earth mages ever mastered even so rudimentary a skill.

Now Jilseth had to send true necromantic magic through the interstices of every trace drawn from the dead man's hand. She had to find those arcane resonances woven betwixt and between the physical memories embodied unseen in his remains. Only then could her spell extract some reflection of whatever had happened to this hapless Archipelagan.

The first such remembrance already lay within her reach. Jilseth ignored it, concentrating instead on the fainter reverberations behind it. She stretched her magecraft further. Now she was questing ever deeper into this unseen realm of infinite space bounded by the essences of elemental matter too seemingly insignificant for any but wizardly senses to comprehend.

There it was, she realised; the most remote recollection that she had any hope of grasping. Try to go any further and she risked losing control of this entire spell. Such a disaster didn't bear contemplating. Her hands shaped the swirling greyness with quick resolve and the magelight wove itself into a lattice of golden threads.

A vision appeared caged amid the haze above the bowl, as tiny and as perfect as the most skilled artist's miniature work. Except where a painter could only offer a vision as flat as a scrying, this image was as complete from all angles as the finest sculpture.

The dead corsair was standing on a crowded shore, the battered galley listing behind him. It was one of a host of ships anchored close together along the broad sweep of this bay. Archipelagan men and women thronged round the gaunt, hollow-eyed mariners. Their expressions were concerned and their outstretched hands welcoming.

Jilseth felt her affinity attuned to the necromancy as never before. The vision caught in the heart of the wizardry grew clearer, the distant voices louder. A necromantic spell needed no clairaudience to enhance it.

'This is their first landfall.' Fluent in the Archipelagan tongue, Planir picked the most vital information out of the riot of questions and pleading. 'On one of the Nahik domain's trading beaches.'

Despite her firm intentions, Jilseth yielded to a silent moment of pride in her own achievement. She had become accustomed to drawing out the last moments, the last day of some unfortunate's life and death. Going back this far, tracing the fleeing corsairs' fate almost all the way back to their galley's frantic departure from the prison which the Mandarkin's magic had wrought for them? This was an achievement worthy of Hadrumal's most celebrated necromancers.

Jilseth reminded herself of that other staple of chimney corner wisdom; as soon as pride lifts the chin, the feet are apt to trip. She turned her attention from the dead corsair back to her magecraft. The Archmage stood at her side with Cloud Master Rafrid opposite them both. The Element Masters could make note of whatever had befallen the oarsman. Jilseth's responsibility above all else was to sustain this spell.

She could already feel tremors of exertion in her thighs and across her shoulders. Gritting her teeth, she forced her hands to shape the swirling magic with steady care and tried to block her ears to the sounds forcing their way past her fingers.

Except in the corner of her eye, Jilseth could see that the Nahik islanders who had so solicitously crowded around the starveling corsairs were now all recoiling with cries of unmistakable horror.

'They are saying that all these ships must leave and at once.' Planir translated the Archipelagan shouts. 'They are refusing them food and water. They say they must not make landfall anywhere else within the domain.'

Jilseth could hear the hapless corsairs' protests being shouted down with fearful fury by the other islanders. With ominous speed, the cacophony turned savage; yells of hatred cutting across screams of pain and despair.

The crowd surged forward again, this time with raised fists. Jilseth wondered how the galley's exhausted crew would ever be able to fight their way free. But clearly they had done so. This poor wretch had survived to be hacked to death on Relshaz's dockside.

'Courier doves.' Rafrid jabbed a finger at the magecrafted vision.

'Have a care!' Jilseth said sharply as the Cloud Master's finger came perilously close to the flutter of white wings disappearing into the blurred haze edging her spell.

Speaking was a dreadful mistake. The words rasped in her throat as the reek of parboiled flesh and the acrid fumes of the rock oil instantly filled her nose and mouth. Her next breaths came fast and shallow but offered no relief from the sense of suffocation.

She had already been feeling light-headed. Now Jilseth fought an impulse to gasp desperately for air. In that remote corner of her mind, calm consideration told her that sucking these fumes so deep into her lungs would leave her coughing uncontrollably. Worse she would be wholly incapable of sustaining her spell.

Nostrils flaring, she succeeded in forcing her breathing into a slow and settled rhythm. The thumping pulse of blood in her temples eased to a dull drum beat and only the ache in the angle of her tightly clenched jaw remained as evidence of her silent struggle.

'More doves are being loosed over there,' Planir commented. 'That's how the word spread so quickly.'

'No great surprise.' Rafrid clasped his hands behind his back. 'He can have no understanding of the Archipelago at all if he truly believes they will pay him tribute.'

'How far has that word spread?' Planir mused. 'Has Velindre had any word from Kheda?'

The spell flickered in Jilseth's instant of surprise. She remembered the magewomen mentioning this Archipelagan but knew no more of him than that. In the next moment, she realised that Planir was asking Rafrid.

'There's no sight nor sound of him as yet.' The Cloud Master's reply betrayed his own exasperation.

'Troanna,' Kalion said sharply on the other side of the room. 'We have seen enough for the present. We cannot risk alerting this villain to our scrying. You know how close we came last time!'

'You need not tell me so,' the Flood Mistress snapped.

Planir took a step away from Jilseth's side. 'What have you seen?'

Jilseth spoke before either Kalion or Troanna could answer. 'What more do you need to see here, Archmage? Forgive me, I do not think that I can draw this vision back to its beginning,' she added with bitterest chagrin.

If necromancy could only be worked once with any

piece of dead flesh or bone, as long as the stone mage didn't let the spell unravel, the vision would play itself out time and again in a circle of memory as endless as a serpent devouring its own tail. A scene could be watched and rewatched until whatever secrets it held had been learned.

But though she had gone so far and so deep into this necromancy, Jilseth could feel the strength of her affinity beginning to fail her, faster and more brutally than ever before.

Planir stood motionless, his eyes distant with contemplation. An instant later, he turned quickly to Rafrid. 'Make a note of all the domain pennants represented on that beach. That will suffice.'

As Rafrid nodded and fetched paper and pen from the Archmage's writing desk, Planir took a few swift strides across the room to look at Troanna's scrying.

Jilseth looked after him. She couldn't help herself.

The Flood Mistress ripped her hands away from the bowl, the curt gesture embodying her frustration. The perfume essences gliding across the water evaporated to fill the air with a riot of discordant scents.

Jilseth glimpsed Kalion clenching his fists as though something had stung his palms.

She hastily returned her attention to her own spell as it dimmed. Rafrid deftly copied the Archipelagan symbols fluttering in the breeze. For a moment, the scrape of quill on paper was the only sound in the room.

As the emerald magelight of her scrying faded, Troanna glowered at Planir. 'We would learn a great deal more and a great deal more swiftly if we could work a clairaudience into this scrying.'

Her gaze shifted across the room. 'Cloud Master?'

The emphasis she laid on Rafrid's title turned her question into a barely veiled rebuke.

Jilseth tensed. Rafrid looked up from his sketching. His weathered face hardened but rather than turn to acknowledge Troanna, let alone reply, he flicked his upraised hand. A brief glimmer of sapphire magic sped across the room to open one of the narrow windows. Clean cold air obeyed the Cloud Master's summons, carrying the cloying perfumes away to be lost on the winds curling around this high tower.

Rafrid returned his attention to the necromantic vision, making a few last notes before smiling at Jilseth. 'We have all that we need. You may release your spell.'

Once again, Jilseth couldn't help stealing a quick look across to Planir. At the Archmage's barely perceptible nod, she spread her hands wide and let the glowing lattice unravel. Swirling threads of golden magecraft faded to amber and to dull ochre before vanishing entirely.

'My compliments, madam mage, on a notable achievement.' Rafrid's gesture swept the noisome smoke and steam away to follow the perfumes out of the window. 'I told you that your magic would return, didn't I? Better than ever, it seems,' he added with warm approbation.

Jilseth settled for a modest smile. If she tried to speak, she feared some quaver in her voice would betray her exhaustion to Kalion and Troanna. The Element Master and Mistress were looking across the room, no hint of sympathy and scant patience on their faces.

If only the Cloud Master had some spell to relieve the unpleasant atmosphere between these senior mages.

She swallowed her nausea at the sight of the pathetic

carrion in the bottom of the bowl. As the roiling oil slowed, the corsair's hand was revealed, as thoroughly cooked as some pig's trotter in a vat.

Rafrid peered at it, his wrinkles deepening as he grimaced with distaste. 'What shall we do with this, Archmage?'

'Burn it.' Kalion gestured and the dead hand rose from the oil's surface.

The wizened fingers were as clawed as Jilseth's own had been when she worked her spell. She found the sight oddly disquieting.

'No.' As Planir spoke, the hand sank back down out of sight. 'The Archipelagans abhor such rites for the dead.'

'They abhor all our magecraft,' Troanna said with icy contempt. 'In which case, wouldn't the Aldabreshi insist on fire's purification for any mortal remains which have been so thoroughly defiled by sorcery?'

'This man had no say in the use we've made of him.' Planir gestured and the hand vanished.

Jilseth saw Troanna and Kalion looking at each other. She needed no magic, elemental or aetheric, to foresee their criticism of his behaviour, when this morning's work was laid before the Council of Hadrumal.

'Hearth Master?' Planir smiled courteously as though nothing untoward had happened. 'Flood Mistress? What did you see the Mandarkin doing?'

Kalion answered curtly. 'He has gathered them all together, these slaves or apprentices or whatever he considers them.'

'We would know more on that score if we could hear what they were saying,' Troanna interjected.

'And if there is a single trinket there with clairaudience

bound within it,' Rafrid said instantly, 'our own spell would immediately resonate with it and let this wizard know that he has been found.'

'But not by whom,' Troanna retorted.

'You'll wager against him having some means of pursuing such a resonance?' demanded Rafrid.

'Don't you think we should learn all we can,' Troanna countered, 'before some ham-fisted Soluran scrying blunders against his affinity and ruins all our chances?'

'No Soluran can scry that far,' Rafrid scoffed. 'They have no quintessential wizardry.'

'You're certain that they have no artefact that might overcome such deficiencies in their magecraft?'

'The Mandarkin seems—' Kalion shot both the Flood Mistress and the Cloud Master a sour look as he raised his voice to speak over them '—to be challenging his slaves to use their own affinity to stimulate the magic instilled into the artefacts which he has given them.'

'We cannot be sure of that,' Troanna objected.

'What else could they be doing?' Kalion retorted. 'You saw—'

Planir interrupted. 'What exactly did you see? Nolyen? Tell me what you saw, not what you think it might mean.'

Jilseth was as startled as he was by the Archmage's command. She also saw that Nol would probably rather face the Mandarkin mage than Troanna and Kalion's indignation. But he was equal to this challenge.

'They were in the central garden of the mage's pavilion,' he said promptly, 'gathered in a circle. The Mandarkin had them each stand up in turn and we saw magelight rising from the artefact which each one held or was wearing.'

'Are they all there?' Rafrid asked. 'Including the women?'

'Yes, Cloud Master.' Nolyen nodded.

'As untutored as they are,' Kalion broke in, 'I believe we can determine their affinities by their innate magelight.'

'Though that's no guide to the strength of their aptitudes,' Troanna said acidly.

'Obviously,' Kalion glared at her.

'What's the tally?' Rafrid asked Nolyen.

The water mage cleared his throat. 'Four have an air affinity, five with the earth, six with fire and eight are born to water magic.' His gaze slid sideways to Troanna.

She glowered. 'Since we know this vagabond has a water affinity, we can assume he will find it easiest to teach them to master their talents.'

'A dual affinity,' Rafrid corrected her. 'We've seen him commanding lightning to deadly effect.'

'Indeed.' Troanna's gaze challenged Planir once again. 'How do you propose to contain this threat?'

He shrugged. 'The Aldabreshi warlords seem to be making their own preparations, given all we hear of them buying boatloads of slaves from Relshaz.'

'I have no interest in Aldabreshin warlords. What do you propose to do, Archmage?' she repeated. 'Where we faced a single renegade mage, soon we will face thirty!'

'They are not all mageborn,' Jilseth said suddenly. 'That lad with the injured face, the first one whom the Mandarkin bound with an artefact, he is a Caladhrian and doesn't have a scrap of magic within him.'

Troanna looked at her, incredulous. 'You think that makes a difference? One less mageborn? One more nameless slave?'

'His name is Hosh.' Planir said with quiet authority. 'He was enslaved alongside Captain Corrain and the others, when the former Baron Halferan and the rest of his men were murdered. His mother, Abiath—'

'Captain Corrain!' Kalion's fury turned the water in the scrying bowl to steam which heated further to vanish in the blink of an eye. 'The man responsible for all this, defying Hadrumal's edicts, summoning an unknown wizard from some nameless tradition—'

'That's hardly fair,' Rafrid objected. 'The man had no say in his own enslavement. What he's done since may have proved catastrophically ill-advised but he has been striving to defend his home, his kith and kin—'

'That means nothing,' Kalion snarled. 'He has easily as much to answer for as this Mandarkin.'

'To this point, perhaps,' Planir said drily. 'I suspect Anskal will prove the greater threat from now on.'

'And you believe that the Aldabreshi are fit to challenge him?' Troanna demanded.

'Perhaps they won't have to. Perhaps the Mandarkin and his apprentices will manage to kill themselves with arrogance and indiscipline,' Rafrid offered in a grim attempt at humour.

Distasteful though it was, Jilseth couldn't help hoping the Cloud Master was right.

— CHAPTER TWENTY-FIVE —

Black Turtle Isle
In the domain of Nahik Jarir

HOSH WAS ALREADY half-awake when Anskal opened the door to the pavilion's entrance hall. Sitting up on his stacked palliasses, he squinted in the grey half-light that presaged dawn.

The Mandarkin mage was silhouetted against a faint green glow.

Scrying magic. Hosh had seen enough of that worked by now to recognise the tell-tale radiance. What had the wizard found so fascinating in his silver bowl all night long? Hosh had first woken to the sound of the Mandarkin's stealthy footsteps crossing and recrossing the inner chamber shortly after midnight, as best he could reckon.

Anskal snapped his fingers. 'Get them all here, now. Run as silently as you can,' he warned, 'or you will surely die.'

Hosh's hand went to his arm ring.

'That will not help you,' the Mandarkin assured him, 'if you are caught before you return.'

Hosh had never heard Anskal so implacable. By all that was sacred and profane, what did he mean? He opened his mouth to ask but the wizard was already striding back towards his scrying spell.

Throwing off his quilts, Hosh grabbed his tunic and

ran for the door, lacing his trousers. He barely paused at the top of the terrace steps to pull the tunic over his head. Anskal's words chilled him more thoroughly than the night air.

One of the raiders was awake, sitting on their pavilion's terrace. Whatever Anskal might be teaching them of magic, these Aldabreshi swordsmen kept to their lifelong habits.

'He sends for all of you, now!' Hosh ran half way up the pavilion's stair as the swordsman came to meet him. That was close enough to pass on the message without having to raise his voice.

The swordsman nodded and turned back towards the pavilion's door. Hosh had noticed that these men and the mainlanders, both the mariners and the militiamen, now obeyed Anskal's orders without question. With no option but to yield their allegiance, they followed him as they had followed their former captains, afloat or ashore.

He jumped down to the bare earth and ran for the women's pavilion. The door and shutters had been repaired by one of the Ensaimin who proved to have been a merchant ship's carpenter. The man had done a good job with no call for wizardry; finding tools, fixings and other necessities in the ransacked cellars.

Hosh rapped hesitant knuckles on the freshly varnished wood. He wasn't about to enter without invitation and have them pin him to the floor, one ripping off his arm ring to allow another of her sisterhood to slash his throat.

'Who's there?' Someone within was already wakeful.

'He wants you, all of you, now.' Hosh's voice cracked with apprehension. 'Something is amiss.'

'What?' the unseen woman demanded. 'Why?'

'I don't know,' Hosh protested.

None of these women believed in blind obedience any longer, if they ever had before. The simplest instruction prompted a silent pause as each one thought through her choices.

To Hosh's surprise, Anskal would often explain his reasoning, and was usually more inclined to come to the women himself with requests than to send Hosh to relay his orders.

'He said to hurry.' Hosh shifted from foot to foot outside the immovable door.

'Very well.' The woman within was audibly suspicious. 'Tell him—'

Hosh wasn't waiting to carry any message. He was already half way down the steps.

The light was strengthening all around him. The air was still but Hosh could hear faint noises beyond the deserted hutments and the vile stone-ringed hollow.

It sounded as though a gentle wind was blowing through the fresh growth sprouting from the stumps of the trees. But Hosh knew it would be a good while yet before the strengthening sun warmed the island sufficiently to draw the day's breeze from the sea. Whatever that noise might be, it was something new.

The back of his neck crawled with unease as he ran for the *Reef Eagle* pavilion where the Aldabreshi slaves now lived. He threw open the unlocked door to the entrance hall. The slaves were all sleeping in huddles of quilts on the floor.

Hosh's foot found an empty bottle in the darkness. The brittle clatter of glass on tile startled the whole handful of them awake.

'Quiet!' Hosh risked a muted shout within the protection of these walls. 'He has sent for you all, at once!'

Lifelong submission beaten or bred into them meant that the slaves asked no questions. Hosh barely had time to recover his breath before he was alone in the deserted hallway as they all ran through the door.

He stooped to pick up the bottle, sniffing at the uncorked neck. Palm wine. So at least one of the slaves was rebelling against Anskal's ban on intoxicating liquors now that the Mandarkin had begun their wizardly training.

Hosh sniffed the air but he couldn't detect any hint of dream smoke beneath the rankness of sweaty quilts. Whoever was defying the wizard had the sense not to indulge themselves beyond a little liquor. It would be hard to hide such vice from Anskal, with the clinging aroma of dream smoke so persistent in cloth and hair.

Hosh hurried to the last dwelling where the mainlanders slept. Like the Aldabreshin raiders, the Ensaimin mariners and Lescari militiamen posted a nightly watch. The shorter of the two Lescari had already seen Hosh's frantic rush from building to building. All six stood ready on their terrace, waiting for confirmation of their summons.

'Does he want us all?' the Ensaimin man who'd tried to make a deal for Hosh's arm ring demanded.

Hosh didn't blame him for his caution. They had all seen Anskal lash one of the raiders with whips of scalding crimson for daring to follow when only two of his companions had been sent for.

He nodded. 'Everyone, at once, and as silent as you can.'

The men exchanged glances, reserving judgement though not about to refuse.

'Do you know what he has in mind?' The taller Lescari asked warily.

Hosh shook his head. 'But he told me to hurry, before I was caught.'

As he spoke, the faint sound from the distant trees was growing louder. Now they all heard it, though Hosh couldn't decide what it meant.

'Come on,' one of the Ensaimin said grimly.

Hosh ran with them. As they crossed the open expanse between Anskal's pavilion and the rest, the first hint of true dawn warmed the cold grey light.

Hosh fell a few paces behind the last seaman as they climbed the steps. His hand strayed to his gilt and crystal ring. His upper arm remained painfully bruised.

The Mandarkin was already surrounded by the other mageborn. As the mainlanders entered the audience chamber, Hosh hung back from the threshold. Anskal saw him and frowned.

Hosh raised submissive hands, ready to retreat and wait on the terrace. That was where he was always sent when they were working their magic.

Anskal surprised him. 'No, you will stay here.'

Hosh wasn't about to disobey. He slid along the wall, keeping as many of the mageborn between him and Anskal as he could. All their attention was on the wizard.

'What do you want with us?' one of the Ensaimin men asked, a tense edge to his dutiful tone.

Anskal gestured towards the scrying bowl and multi-hued magelight leaped upwards to dapple the walls with shifting images. Hosh had never seen the like and judging by their gasps, neither had the assembled mageborn. Everyone took a step to huddle in the middle of the room.

It took a moment for Hosh to make sense of what he was seeing on the walls all around them. Then he recognised one of the prowling shadows for an armed and armoured man. With that round helm and the veil of chainmail hanging from it, the swordsman was clearly an Archipelagan. One of the Aldabreshin raiders gasped and reached for a blade before checking himself.

Doubtless he'd realised he could do no harm to a mere shadow with that weapon. Since it was Anskal who had summoned these shifting images, Hosh fervently hoped the misty figures could do no damage either. Unless this was another of the Mandarkin's brutal lessons.

'Watch,' Anskal ordered, 'and your peril will become clearer.'

Your peril, Hosh noted, not the Mandarkin's.

The translucent visions showed an overwhelming Aldabreshin force advancing through the trees. There could be no doubt that they were on this very island. The first swordsmen scouting ahead had reached the hollow with the killing ground and its compass of stone markers.

'Galleys landed these men on this island's far beaches after dusk last night.' The Mandarkin smiled blithely as all the newly-discovered mageborn looked at him in horror.

'They have come here to kill you. If you wish to live, you will have to kill them,' he added unnecessarily. 'You may not be slaughtered as easily as they doubtless hope, thanks to the gifts which I have given you, but you have seen for yourselves how a wizard's defences can be overwhelmed by sufficient numbers.'

Anskal paused to bow with apparent thanks to the women who had killed the trio of mercenaries.

'There can be no doubt that they intend to kill you,' he continued, dispassionate, 'should that cost a thousand dead of their own. No wizard, however skilled, can sustain endless magic. Barely tutored as you are, you will soon be exhausted.'

He pursed his lips. 'Once you have been captured, from all that you have told me, you will be stripped naked to make certain that you cannot kill yourselves before you face unspeakable torment. My gifts will be no use to you then.'

A cacophony of Archipelagan speech filled the room but none of the Aldabreshi or any of the island-born slaves were paying any more heed to Anskal. They were all shouting at each other.

The Mandarkin slipped past a gesticulating slave to Hosh's side. 'What are they saying?'

Hosh did his best to make sense of the frantic babble. 'They are looking to the stars for guidance.'

The satisfaction that curved Anskal's smile filled Hosh with even deeper dread.

'What course does the heavenly compass advise?' the Mandarkin enquired.

Hosh struggled to pluck some meaning from the rival dialects echoing back from the walls.

'The Amethyst for clear thinking and for new ideas has moved in the arc of Honour. Not only of Honour. That part of the compass also sees omens for the outcome of ambition and that makes it doubly important that the Ruby is already there, standing for strength and courage.'

One of the raiders had shouted down the rest to

insist that since their magic couldn't be denied, these stars were saying that they must now have the courage to interpret the heavens in the light of their changed circumstances. The time had come for new ideas, the swordsman insisted, his face twisted with anguish. The stars of the Bowl in that same arc of the sky always advocated the benefits of sharing knowledge as well as anything else.

One of the women spoke into the momentary shock of silence at this radical notion. Hosh repeated her hesitant words for the wizard.

'The Diamond, talisman against corruption is now in the arc of Death, alongside the Canthira Tree's stars, talisman against decay. Perhaps that means if they can save themselves from being corrupted by their magic, they can save themselves from dying. If they stay true to themselves.'

One of her sisters nodded, her eyes still sorely troubled even as faint hope relieved her fearful scowl.

'She says that the Opal for truth is bright in the arc of Travel and Learning where the Mirror Bird urges wisdom through self-knowledge and reflection. The Mirror Bird itself is a talisman against magic's corrupting influence. Then the Pearl that's talisman against madness has shown its first new gleam in the arc for omens of children and the future, where the Walking Hawk urges vigilance at the same time as warning against unfounded suspicion while its stars are below the horizon.'

As the other raiders and the slaves exchanged guilty glances and guiltier nods of agreement, Hosh recalled that the two moons, Opal and Pearl, the lesser jewels as they were known among the Archipelagans, were considered powerful talismans against dragons. Those beasts were the most violent and mindless manifestations of magic's destructive might. But these people were not dragons.

'They all know that they are not evil folk. This magic discovered in their blood is wholly unsought.' Hosh swallowed hard before continuing. 'So they say that the heavens are telling them they may use their magic to save themselves.'

He supposed that he shouldn't be so surprised. Those Archipelagans unable to live with the knowledge that they were mageborn had already killed themselves.

'An excellent conclusion.' Anskal was very well satisfied.

Hosh stared at him. Didn't the Mandarkin see how distressed the assembled Archipelagans were? How fearful, lest they had made some fatal error in their reasoning?

Only the Ensaimin mariners and the two Lescari were looking discreetly relieved as they listened to Hosh.

'Then we're not fighting on our own,' one seaman muttered to his neighbour.

'Or with each other to save those incoming bastards the trouble,' the taller Lescar agreed with greater relief.

'So what do we do now?' the most weather-beaten of the mainlanders demanded of Anskal.

The Mandarkin shrugged and the shadowy visions vanished along with the emerald radiance casting them up from the scrying bowl.

The assembled mageborn gasped and protested, some angry and others more shocked. As Hosh blinked he realised how strong the daylight had now become. True dawn was not far off.

'If you wish to fight, you need to see your enemy.'

Anskal pointed towards the door. 'They hope to catch you sleeping,' he added with some amusement.

'Will you not fight?' the second Lescar demanded.

Anskal looked at him with that secretive smile. 'I have no need to fight. I can be a thousand leagues away from here in a single stride.' He looked around them all. 'Prove to me that you are worthy of learning such magic by driving off these invaders. Then I will teach you all that I know.'

The Ensaimin mariners and the two Lescari were first to the door. Hosh saw them skidding on the entrance hall's tiles in their urgency to reach the terrace. The raiders followed closest with the slaves barely three paces behind.

The women looked at each other, swapping their thoughts in such brief, swift sentences that Hosh couldn't catch their intent. Then they hurried out.

Anksal followed at a leisurely stroll and Hosh stayed close behind him. Standing in the entrance, they saw the raiders, the slaves and the mainlanders all crouched along the edge of the terrace.

Stealthy shadows were now creeping through the pathetic remnants of the abandoned huts. The multitude following stirred the trees further away like the rising wind of a winter storm.

Hosh pressed himself against the doorpost. Couldn't the invaders see the waiting mageborn? Then he realised that the pavilion's cringing defenders must be all but invisible with no need for magic; motionless in the dusky shadows beneath the wide eaves.

The advancing Aldabreshi had no reason to pay exclusive attention to this most distant building. They were dividing their attention and their forces between the other dwellings where they hoped to catch and kill the sleeping mageborn.

As they surely would have done, Hosh reflected, if Anskal hadn't been keeping watch for such an attack. The raiders' and the sailors' sentries could not have raised an alarm quickly enough for the rest to save themselves.

As the Mandarkin moved a few paces along the terrace, Hosh followed as closely as he could.

He was clinging to one hope. Anskal had come here with Corrain. The Mandarkin had said as much himself. Hosh knew that the captain didn't have a mageborn bone in his body. So that must mean that one wizard's magic could sweep two people across infinite distances.

If he stayed within arm's reach of Anskal, if the battle went against the mageborn, if he saw the Mandarkin about to depart, if he grabbed a handful of his tunic, perhaps the magic would carry him to safety?

As long as he didn't miss his moment. As long as Anskal didn't strike him down, thinking that Hosh was attacking him or merely to punish him for such temerity. As long as a wizard didn't have to deliberately choose to carry a passenger along with his magic. If so, there was every chance that Anskal would opt instead to abandon Hosh to his ghastly fate.

With all these frantic doubts and fears, the advancing Aldabreshin threat seemed almost trivial by comparison.

Anskal was oblivious. He was watching the women. Hosh realised the five of them intended to circle around the building to make sure there was no assault sneaking up from behind the pavilion, where the headland sloped down to a rocky shore.

'Girl children learn the value of attacking from an

unsuspected direction since they lack the strength to take down an assailant directly,' the Mandarkin observed.

Hosh's terror momentarily ebbed as he wondered yet again what manner of place the Mandarkin realm might be, where such violence was seemingly so commonplace.

Then the first wave of Aldabreshin attackers surged towards the shuttered dwellings where the slaves and the mainlanders had sheltered and all such thoughts fled.

Now that they had got so close, the Archipelagans abandoned all thought of stealth. Screaming incomprehensible abuse, tens and tens of men swarmed up onto the stone platforms that supported the pavilions. They came from all sides, not bothering with the narrow steps. The first men bent low, their linked hands offering a step for those that followed. Those first attackers were thrown bodily upwards to land balanced and alert, their swords ready to kill. As soon as they found themselves unopposed they began hacking the shutters to kindling.

'Why swords?' one of the Lescari demanded of the raider kneeling beside him. 'Why not burn us all with sticky fire hurled from triremes? Isn't that the island way to raze a settlement to the ground?'

'When wizards can turn fire to do their will?' The raider stared intent at the unfolding destruction. 'The only way to know your foe is truly dead is to hold his severed head in your hands.'

In the time it took the raider to share this wisdom, a second line of armoured men followed those pathfinders up onto the terraces. They advanced ready to slaughter anyone breaking out of those shattered windows.

The third wave dropped momentarily to one knee on

the terrace edges, empty hands extended downwards to haul more armoured assailants up to join them. Those in the vanguard were already inside the buildings, smashing their way through empty rooms, yelling their threats and hatred.

— CHAPTER TWENTY-SIX —

Black Turtle Isle
In the domain of Nahik Jarir

EVEN AT THIS distance, the noise of the onslaught on the pavilions was deafening. The Aldabreshin assault had reached the women's dwelling and the raiders' house. The attackers smashed their way inside with the same swift violence.

Hosh recalled Captain Corrain scaring callow recruits to Halferan's guard troop into stammering confusion. He would run at them yelling a torrent of obscenity in the midst of a peaceful sword drill.

Noise was as much a weapon as their blade, so Corrain had told them. Hadn't they just seen the proof of that? Couldn't he have stabbed each one of them a handful of times while they stood there gaping? If they found themselves in a battle, they should yell and curse with the language their grandmothers threatened would turn a bad lad's tongue black as the Eldritch Kin's.

Hosh remembered Corrain sticking out his own tongue to show the trembling recruits that hadn't yet happened to him, to ease their shock with relieved laughter.

There was nothing to laugh at here. Yet more Aldabreshi came, contingent after contingent clad in mail and brandishing swords. Some swarmed through the abandoned huts, ripping every last crude shelter apart to leave no hiding place for anything larger than a mouse. And still they came. There was no sign of a rearguard emerging from the line of ironwood trees between the settlement and the bloody hollow.

What would they do when they found no one inside those ransacked pavilions? When they realised that this lone building must surely house their prey?

Hosh looked at Anskal and wondered if the Mandarkin was somehow hiding this furthest dwelling with his own wizardry. He didn't imagine that Anskal would do so for those coerced mageborn's sake but the wizard had the highest regard for his own hide.

Were any of the mageborn going to act? Hosh was beginning to doubt it. He readied himself to grab Anskal's tunic at the slightest sign that the Mandarkin was about to flee.

The oldest of the Ensaimin swore under his breath in the dockside slang of Col. Standing upright, he flung out his calloused hands. A vast crack appeared in the stone foundation of the raiders' pavilion. Amber magelight shone in the depths of the cloven stone. The terrace split from the edge of the steps to the front door, leaving a void too wide for a man to step across.

The Aldabreshi recoiled, their shouts coloured with alarm. They could not move fast enough to keep their footing though. The dark gold radiance pulsed to match Hosh's heartbeat. That first gulf cut deeper into the house. The wall beside the door began to crack. From the depths of the widening crevice, magelight spread outwards, cutting angled lines between the closely laid stones. Tiles began to slide from the roof as the walls shivered with their footings crumbling away.

One of the Ensaimin's shipmates stood. He jabbed a

hand at the distant pavilion, ire twisting his face. Darts of golden magelight shot from his fingers.

Each dazzling flare was drawn to a falling tile, a lump of cracking plaster, as surely as pins to a lodestone. In the instant that magic touched the debris, each piece was transformed into a deadly missile. One of the slaves sprang up with an exclamation of belated understanding. His hands moved with swift certainty, his own magelight twice as bright.

Now the Aldabreshi weren't only fighting to keep their footing on the disintegrating terrace. Swords were little use against lumps of rubble smashing their hands and faces into bloody ruin. Armour was ineffective against crippling blows to the backs of their heads and the sides of their knees and elbow joints.

Anskal said something in his own tongue. Hosh didn't understand the words but he could hear the wizard's approval. Nevertheless, the Mandarkin watched the assault unfolding on the invaders with impatient expectation.

All the mageborn were on their feet now, savage intensity in their eyes. Hosh shivered in a chilling breeze as the two Lescari summoned jagged lumps of ice out of the humid air and sent them hurtling to knock Aldabreshin swordsmen senseless.

Two of the raiders came to stand beside them, joining in that bombardment. The same green radiance was now wrapping them all in a fine cold mist though none of them seemed to notice it. Hosh could feel the chill creeping through the very stones beneath his cringing unshod feet.

Swathes of Aldabreshi were collapsing; dead or stunned.

'Saedrin!' Hosh was startled into an exclamation as the raiders' pavilion convulsed.

Amber magelight flared from every door and window as though oil had been thrown onto a fire within. The tilting roof collapsed as the walls crumbled inwards. The screams of crushed Aldabreshi were lost in the roar of the building falling all the way down into the cellars within the foundation.

Anskal laughed. Hosh saw why. Before the clouds of dust had risen up beyond the falling beams and roof tiles of the raiders' erstwhile shelter, the same golden promise of mageborn destruction zig-zagged through the carefully laid black stones underpinning the women's dwelling. In the next breath, the foundation of the *Reef Eagle* pavilion cracked asunder with that same glow.

But Hosh saw no sense in Anskal's delight. However many Aldabreshi were dying, crushed in those ruins of the pavilion, however many lay knocked senseless or killed outright by the lumps of ice or rubble, countless more Archipelagans survived.

They were all turning towards this distant pavilion. The rainbow hues of magelight swirling around the terrace left no doubt where the wizards were gathered. Their fierce magic outshone the rising sun.

The Aldabreshi gathered together, heedless of their injured comrades. They stood shoulder to shoulder between the pavilions. Their ranks massed ten and twenty deep. The throng stretched back further than Hosh could count.

The foremost began to advance. If they were reluctant, they were given no chance to show it with so many more armoured men pressing so close behind them. As the front rank broke from a walk into a run, the rest followed hard on their heels. Upraised blades glinted in the fresh sunlight.

Hosh looked up as a shower of glittering metal showed that as yet unseen Aldabreshi had come armed with arrows and bows.

The first surge of attackers was barely two ploughs lengths away. The mageborn would all be hacked into oblivious pieces. Assuming they avoided being filled with so many arrows they looked like his mother's pincushion.

Hosh couldn't see anyone wielding any control over this howling mob. The mageborn wouldn't be captured alive and chained for later punishment. He wouldn't have the slightest chance to protest that he was no wizard. Not that anyone would believe him if he tried.

So finally, after all his trials, he would answer to Saedrin before this day had got half way towards noon. Hosh found himself surprisingly calm at this prospect of imminent death.

A soaring wave of scarlet light swept through the air. It traversed the advancing Aldabreshin force from the sands by the water of the anchorage to the trees beyond the raiders' devastated pavilion. The shafts of soaring arrows burned to ash drifting on the breeze as their steel heads plummeted towards the ground.

None of the arrowheads landed. Two slaves and two of the raiders watched the deadly hail intently, oblivious to the rosy flames licking up and down their forearms. Why should they fret, Hosh noted numbly. The magefire wasn't even singeing the fine down of black hairs on the closest slave's arm, let alone his skin.

The arrow heads melted. Searing gobbets of liquid metal flew though the air, tracing their path back towards the unseen archers. Tearing screams of fear and pain rose from the rearmost ranks, loud enough to be heard above the yells of hatred close at hand.

The first line of Aldabreshi stumbled. Not singly or in pairs. They fell headlong in tens and handfuls; their feet vanishing up to the knee in cracks cutting through the dusty earth. Those following so close behind couldn't help trampling their helpless comrades. As the ground continued to fracture, those second ranks fell to be crushed themselves by the inexorable cohorts behind them.

The Lescari and the two raiders who had been hurling ice at their attackers turned their attentions to the straggling undergrowth, lately flourishing in the island's moist warmth, only to be trampled beneath these invaders' nail-studded sandals.

The bruised tendrils writhed. They began to grow impossibly fast. Inside a few breaths, vicious green tangles snared the closest Aldabreshi. Within the next moments, red blood flowed where wiry stems cut deep into their flesh.

Hosh pressed a shocked hand to his mouth as he saw one unfortunate decapitated by a leafy noose. Gouts of the man's lifeblood spurted into the air as the headless corpse teetered; still standing upright, as though the dead man couldn't believe what had befallen him.

The closest Aldabreshi were swift to try cutting their comrades free. That was a fatal mistake. Any hand or blade touching the mage-inspired greenery was instantly captured by twining tendrils.

Those further behind, in the midst of the undergrowth and the ironwood trees between the anchorage and the bloody hollow found themselves in worse straits. Twigs curled around upraised hands. Branches flexed to pull men bodily off their feet. Where an Archipelagan was caught between two trees, he was ripped into bloody halves.

Hosh saw two of the raiders and one of the slaves conferring on the corner of the terrace. With a resolute nod, they clasped their hands together and reached up for the milk-pale sky.

A deadly shaft of lighting skewered a struggling group of Aldabreshi who had fallen victim to the twin hazards of the ground opening up beneath their feet and the malevolent coils of vegetation. Azure magelight stilled their thrashing. The only movement was the stinking smoke rising from the blackened corpses.

One of the slaves laughed out loud as the three of them summoned a second devastating lightning strike. A third followed and a fourth, as quick as a minstrel snapping his fingers.

Hosh saw the Aldabreshi wavering. Their advance slowed. But enough were driven onward by fear and hatred to kill everyone on this terrace fifty times over.

The raiders and the slaves who had melted the arrows linked their hands. A curtain of crimson fire surged up from the blood soaked ground to ring the pavilion. Hosh pressed harder against the wall at his back. The searing heat struck him like a blast from a blacksmith's furnace.

The four mageborn grimaced with effort. Slowly the flames began to shift outwards from the terrace. Abruptly, one of the slaves screamed. He leaped backwards away from the rest, looking at his outstretched hands with absolute horror.

His skin was blistering beneath the flames that

cloaked his forearms. The magewrought fire darkened to bloody maroon as his skin blackened and cracked to show vivid red flesh beneath. The slave threw back his head with a shriek of despair and the flames surged up to his shoulders. As the wizardry enveloped his skull, his hair blazed in a brief moment of agony. The blaze cascaded down his body, his clothing vanishing in a flare of commonplace flame oddly out of place amid the scarlet magefire. His flesh was utterly consumed within the next moment, leaving only his blackened skeleton to collapse and shatter on the the terrace's cold stones .

Even as Hosh recoiled from those splintered bones, he saw the remaining three fire mages intent on sustaining their spell. Though he hated himself for it, Hosh was relieved. He didn't want to see anyone else die like that. He didn't want to die himself.

He couldn't see what was happening through that curtain of opaque crimson brilliance. He didn't need to. They could all hear the screams of the Aldabreshi being burned alive. As the magical blaze advanced with paradoxical slowness compared with the untamed rush of a natural grass fire, their attackers' charred corpses were revealed. Tears filled Hosh's parched eyes as he saw those burned bodies now locked forever motionless in a futile struggle against their abhorrent fate.

The wreckage of the raiders' pavilion caught alight. The mageborn with the air affinity let their clasped hands fall and the lightning ceased. The slave collapsed to lie motionless on the terrace. The raiders clung to each other, each man's head on the other's shoulder. Their chests were heaving as though they had just run for their very lives. Untamed sapphire magelight crackled around them.

Hosh saw no such azure bathing the fallen slave. He realised with cold horror that the man's bony chest wasn't moving. He wasn't breathing.

Now emerald radiance showed Hosh exactly who shared the Lescari's arcane power over water up to and including the sap within those deadly plants. They seemed less fatigued, perhaps because there were six of them in all. Those four born to command the earth were sitting by the steps, their hanging heads all wreathed in darkening amber magelight.

The flames on the remaining mageborn to fire began to flicker. Their deadly wall of fire started to shrink. By the time it reached the ruins of the women's house, the crimson blaze was barely man-high. No matter. It had served its purpose. As the flames subsided to vanish into the scorched earth, Hosh could see the fleeing Aldabreshi vanishing out of sight. The plants and trees no longer stopped them.

'Do they—?' One of the Ensaimin mariners was so out of breath that he had to make a second attempt at his question. 'Do they have ships waiting?'

If they did, Hosh couldn't see any of these would-be wizards were in a fit state to do anything about it. But what of Anskal?

Before the Mandarkin could answer, a figure appeared at the corner of the building. It was one of the women who had taken themselves off to safeguard the far side of the pavilion overlooking the sea.

'Come!' She was hoarse with weariness, leaning on the building as though her legs might fail her at any moment. 'You must see this!'

The urgent exultation in her voice lifted even the two exhausted raiders' heads from each other's shoulders.

The woman said something more in the Aldabreshin tongue. Between her dialect and the breathlessness swallowing her words, Hosh barely caught half of it.

'What is she saying?' Anskal demanded all the same.

'She has seen an omen,' Hosh replied.

All the Archipelagan born were following the woman to the far side of the pavilion. The Lescari and the Ensaimin mariners were drawn along with them, albeit casting wary glances across the island to be certain that they had truly beaten off that Aldabreshin assault.

Since he had done nothing more arduous than stand and watch, Hosh easily outstripped the staggering mageborn.

He found the other women in a state of collapse much like their fellow mageborn. One pointed wordlessly as he appeared. Hosh looked first at the wrecked ships off shore; galleys and triremes alike sunk to their oar rails. Bodies bobbed in the water. For one horrified moment Hosh thought that he saw a desperately waving hand amid a slick of blood, only to see an angled fin betray the shark dragging the lifeless corpse beneath the soiled waves.

'Rek-a-nul,' gasped the woman who had suffered rape for the sake of killing the mercenary.

Now Hosh understood. He moved for a clearer view of the sea beyond the bloody catastrophe that had befallen this outflanking attack.

There it was. A sea serpent. It reminded Hosh of an eel; the ones the Halferan villagers caught in the stream that flowed past the manor. Not scaly like a snake or a fish but with a rough dark hide. Like those eels, this beast had a blunt head now questing above the waves. Its gaping mouth was filled with knifelike teeth, small black eyes barely visible. As it plunged back down beneath the waters, the long coil of its sinuous body broke the surface. Sunlight shone through the single translucent long fin running down to the tip of its equally blunt tail.

'What is that?' Arriving at Hosh's shoulder, Anskal was awe-struck.

Hosh could hardly blame him. Unlike those eels at home, this evil looking beast could comfortably have wrapped itself around the entire circumference of the manor wall.

'Rek-a-nul, a sea serpent.' Seeing neither explanation meant anything to the Mandarkin, he tried again. 'It looks like a snake but folk say that it's some kind of fish, though the beasts can move between the rivers and the sea.'

'Dastennin save us, where's the river where something like that could spawn?' One of the Lescari had come to join them, as astounded as Anskal.

Hosh had to agree. Only the god of storms and oceans could possibly understand such mysteries.

'What does it mean to them?' Anskal demanded.

Hosh saw all the Archipelagan-born huddled together, the last glimmers of their magelight fading away. For all their weariness, new animation brightened their eyes. Even the women seemed inclined to share their triumph with the men.

'The sea serpent is a powerful omen—' Hosh broke off as the great beast reappeared beside a wrecked trireme.

The waters foamed as the creature thrashed and the stricken ship rolled over to sink to the unseen seabed. The mageborn cheered, all of them including the mainlanders.

'The stars of the Sea Serpent speak of mysteries, of darkness, of unseen perils and hatreds.'

Those stars were currently on the westernmost horizon Hosh recalled, as he tried to understand what interpretation the Archipelagans were putting on the creature's appearance here and now. That most westerly arc of the sky was where one looked for omens and portents of foes.

'Though to see one in the flesh is always considered the greatest good fortune,' he added, 'as well as a warning to think deeply on any choices or future paths.'

Anskal waved all this away. He turned his back on the creature now investigating a galley charred to the waterline. The Mandarkin mage looked instead at the assembled mageborn.

'There can be no doubt as to their future path,' he said with profound satisfaction.

— CHAPTER TWENTY-SEVEN —

'WE MUST ASK Velindre what those islanders will make of that serpent's appearance,' Planir remarked, 'especially under these stars.'

'That attack didn't take him unawares. He must have been watching and waiting.' Bitter with chagrin, Jilseth removed one hand from the side of the scrying bowl set between them on the table in Planir's study.

She reached for her tisane glass and took a sip. The ginger and lemon infusion was cold but she didn't care. She didn't bother warming it with a touch of magic. After such exhausting wizardry, the last thing she needed was the glass shattering in her hand through some momentary lapse.

'So much for Ely and Galen assuring us that our friend was settling down for the night,' Planir said thoughtfully.

'They could only tell us what they saw.' Jilseth felt compelled to offer that in their defence.

As midnight had approached, Ely had come up the steps from the sitting room to detail the Mandarkin renegade's familiar routine of gorging and drinking. She and Galen had surveyed the other pavilions to see the coerced mageborn similarly making ready for bed. Planir had agreed that there was nothing to be gained by spending their dwindling stock of bitumen on watching people sleep. So had Nolyen and Cloud Master Rafrid who'd kept watch all through the previous day, discussing their observations and theories with Planir and Jilseth at the time.

Jilseth had wondered if it was really worth her rising a full chime before dawn to join the Archmage in resuming this vigil. So much for those doubts. Had Planir had some inkling of what was in the wind, when he had insisted on their early start? She searched his face for some clue but found nothing.

Planir looked up from the bowl. 'Should we suppose that he knew he was being observed? That he sought to trick us into looking elsewhere by lulling our suspicions?'

Jilseth frowned. 'None of us have felt any brush of his magic against our scrying.'

'Can we be certain we would know it if we had?' Planir countered. 'We are so unfamiliar with Mandarkin spells.'

Jilseth had no answer to that. She gazed down at the scrying bowl where the renegade and his apprentices were still watching the sea serpent. 'He's not watching the attackers now.'

'Why should he?' Planir gestured and the vision in the scrying bowl slid with dizzying speed across the distant island.

Jilseth watched the frantic men scrambling through the scrub beyond the bloodstained hollow with the ring of stones. Where thorns ripped their clothing, their skin showed deathly pale amid the shadows beneath the dark trees.

These were mainland slaves, such as the men whom

she and Nolyen had seen loaded aboard ship in Relshaz. Mellitha continued to report that men of fighting age, regardless of any lack of proven skills with bow or blade, were being purchased in unprecedented numbers from the city's slave traders.

Now the survivors of that magewrought massacre fled in terror. They were casting aside their unfamiliar armour, too frantic to cut their path clear with the swords they had surely never expected to be given by their new masters.

'What do you suppose they were promised for killing the mage?' She took another sip of cold tisane to quell her queasy apprehension. 'How is their failure likely to be punished?'

'I have no idea.' Planir slowly shook his head. 'But whatever they fear might happen, they're far more terrified of staying ashore.'

The first of the slaves, those who had been the last to disembark, were already stumbling back onto the beach strewn with the bones of the dead corsairs trapped by the Mandarkin mage's arrival. Those skeletons had been picked clean by the crabs and the seabirds.

'He's made no effort to sink these ships,' Jilseth contemplated the swift galleys with their sterns turned to face the beach.

None had thrown down an anchor, held in place instead by gently feathering oars. She could see their crews rushing back and forth, horrified by the bloodied slaves' return and still more terrified of what might be following the fugitives. One galley was already rowing away, abandoning the frantic men splashing into the shallows.

'He wants them carrying word of his power and those

mages now backing him to spread as far and wide as possible,' Planir observed.

'And they'll spread word of exactly how destructive unbridled wizardry can be.' Jilseth wondered how long it would take for such stories to get back to the mainland. How exaggerated would those tales become? Or would the simple truth suffice to poison the atmosphere in Relshaz against the mageborn further?

The first stirring breeze of the day plucked at the galley's masthead pennants, proclaiming this unlikely alliance of northern Archipelagan warlords: Khusro, Jagai, Esul and even Nahik whose spineless ruler Jarir had turned a blind eye to the corsairs for so long.

Jilseth cupped both of her own hands around the scrying bowl again, seeking to shift the spell back across the island to see what the Mandarkin mage was doing now. Emerald magelight flared as Planir's magic confounded her own. She looked up with a puzzled frown.

'I want to see where these galleys go,' the Archmage explained. 'To see if they scatter or if whatever treaty these warlords have made with each other holds in the face of this disaster.'

Jilseth nodded her understanding. She and Planir had watched the laden galleys trace their final path to this island far from the usual sea lanes. There could be no clearer evidence of the warlords' alliance. It was unheard of for an Aldabreshin ruler to allow a rival's ships and mariners to see the jealously guarded routes and vital shortcuts through backwaters so vital for a domain's defence.

The triremes had led the way from Jagai Kalu's home island, their stern lanterns showing the following vessels how to pick a route southward through the reefs hidden beneath the dark waters. More ships had joined the fleet as their path curved westward through Nahik waters and as they approached the corsairs' erstwhile anchorage, their numbers were swelled further by vessels flying Khusro Rina's standard.

Three vessels had strayed too far from the choppy wake of the ship ahead to founder on an unsuspected reef. There could be no greater proof of the warlords' desperate urgency to rid the Archipelago of the Mandarkin wizard. They had all commanded their ship masters to risk the hazards of night rowing through unknown waters in uncertain light. If the Greater Moon was only two days past its full, the Lesser was the merest fleeting suggestion of an iridescent arc.

'Do you suppose they will be allowed back on board, now that they have been attacked by magic?'

Watching the ship masters on the remaining galley's stern platforms, she stretched to ease the stiffness of long concentration in her back and shoulders. Slaves were standing in the shallows, their weaponless hands raised in appeal rather than reaching for the wooden ladders to scramble aboard. The reason for that was easily seen. The waiting ship masters were all flanked by archers.

Before Planir could reply a fiery circle appeared in the empty air above the scrying bowl.

'*Archmage?*'

'Flood Mistress,' Planir acknowledged the bespeaking spell courteously.

'*We must lay all this before the Council. They will agree that we must curb this menace at once.*'

'What menace?' Planir enquired mildly.

Jilseth could only see the reverse of the spell, a shimmering haze bounded by swirling crimson. She didn't need to see Troanna's face. She could hear the ragged weariness in the magewoman's words.

'*Do not play the fool, Archmage, nor play me for one.*'

Jilseth guessed that Troanna had been up before dawn, perhaps all night, scrying as Planir had done. Who had been supporting the Flood Mistress? Canfor? Jilseth wondered how many other mages across Hadrumal's halls were sitting over silver bowls of ensorcelled water, trying to fathom the mystery of the Archmage's latest interest in affairs beyond their island's shores.

Not that they could have succeeded, even if they had guessed at some upheaval involving the corsairs and the Archipelago. Not without some bitumen and the magecrafting vital for using it.

She stiffened. Where had the Flood Mistress obtained some of their limited supply?

'Troanna, I have the greatest respect—'

The bespeaking spell blinked and died. A bell's sonorous toll echoed across the city.

Planir looked at the morning still so pale though the windows. 'It seems that the Flood Mistress has as little respect for Council members' sleep as she does for her Archmage,' he said lightly.

The bell tolled again. Jilseth could only imagine the scene in tower bedchambers across the city. The ancient, quintessential enchantments which Trydek, first Archmage, had instilled in that bell meant that no Council member could ever sleep through its summons.

She tried to think who among the Council members was currently away from Hadrumal. Those same enchantments would be startling them, however far away they might be. Distance was no object to a mage after all and the honour of a seat on the Council was balanced by the obligations that such rank laid upon those wizards. The foremost was to assemble whenever they were summoned. To safeguard this island with their wisdom and vigilance.

Though the Council had agreed in recent generations that members were allowed to send proxies. Jilseth tried to think who else might arrive in the chamber on that basis and what influence their presence might have on the subsequent debate.

No, it was no good. She was too woolly headed with weariness to tally up Planir's likely supporters and detractors. Besides, she had no clear idea what the Archmage would say.

What course of action might Troanna propose, come to that, demanding the Council's endorsement? Jilseth had heard the implacable anger in the Flood Mistress's words.

She also wondered what Troanna had seen while she had been scrying. If the Flood Mistress had been keeping watch on the Mandarkin mage when Planir was not, perhaps she had seen something which the Archmage had missed. Something vital? Would Troanna share it, for the greater good of Hadrumal? Or seek some personal advantage at the Archmage's expense?

The Council bell repeated its insistent summons and startled her out of such thoughts. Jilseth headed for the study door.

'One moment.' Planir had crossed over to the fireplace. A snap of his long fingers kindled scarlet flames beneath the kettle. The water started seething barely a moment later. The Archmage assembled two fresh tisane glasses, filling their pierced silver balls with herbs for steeping from several jars along the mantel shelf.

'Here.' He raised the lid on a covered dish and tossed something to Jilseth.

She found herself catching a honey cake.

Planir smiled through the tiredness deepening the fine wrinkles around his eyes. 'There are plenty of mages who have much further to walk than we do. So we can take a few moments to restore ourselves.' His smile faded. 'I suspect that we'll need all our wits about us.'

'What do you think Troanna will say?'

Jilseth couldn't help asking, though she found she wasn't surprised to see Planir shake his head.

'We'll know soon enough and there's nothing to be gained by going looking for trouble.'

He poured boiling water and handed her the tisane glass. The steaming liquid was dark and oily with an unfamiliar scent. Jilseth couldn't help looking at the Archmage, a question in her eyes.

He grinned, sipped his own drink and grimaced before replying.

'It's said that the Mountain Men thrash themselves with holly leaves before going into battle, to make sure that they are alert. Aritane, the *sheltya* woman in Suthyfer, has told Usara in no uncertain terms that this is yet more lowlander nonsense. The truth is there are varieties of holly whose leaves and twigs make this particular tisane which is remarkably effective in repelling tiredness. But you will want to eat that honey cake,' he added.

Jilseth took a cautious sip and found out why. Bitterness puckered her lips before the hot liquid had reached her throat. She took a hasty bite of the sweet pastry and contemplated the glass with misgiving.

Planir had already drained more than half of his own drink. He crammed a second cake into his mouth, urging her on with an impatient hand.

Jilseth forced herself to drink the tisane. After the initial shock, the taste wasn't so revolting, if only something could be done about that jarring bitterness. She ate the rest of her cake, remembering her mother promising a spoonful of honey to follow childhood doses of physic.

Planir shucked off his shabby faded doublet and took an elegant sleeved jerkin from the hook on the back of the study door.

'Ready?' He shrugged himself into the black garment.

Jilseth nodded. 'Archmage.'

She smoothed her grey wool gown and reassured herself that the forgiving cloth would see the worst creases fall away as they walked to the Council chamber.

Whatever was in that tisane was already proving itself. She could feel the liquid's warmth washing away the tiredness weighing her down.

She followed Planir down the stairs. Even so early in the day, people were coming out of their lodgings to stand in the courtyard. Wizards with no warrant to join in the Council's deliberations huddled in twos and threes in their doorways.

Every low-voiced conversation stopped as the Archmage emerged from the door at the base of Trydek's Tower. Jilseth noted that few of the onlookers paid any heed to her, every gaze following Planir's long strides across the quadrangle.

The Archmage's pace quickened. Jilseth had to hurry

not to be left behind as he went out through the hall's main gate and took the flagstoned path around to the open square with the circular Council Chamber at its centre. Later, taller edifices overshadowed the ancient, modest building on all sides.

Not for the first time, Jilseth wondered what Hadrumal had been like when Trydek and his first followers had sought refuge on this island. When the single hall and this council chamber had satisfied all the first Archmage's needs as he instructed his pupils and debated the future of wizardry with his chosen companions.

The Council Chamber's door already stood open with mages heading up the short flight of stairs to the vaulted room within. Some wizards looked as though they had rolled straight out of their beds to rush here. Others had taken the time to wash the sleep from their eyes, their garments neatly ordered. Some wore colours denoting their affinity; others had long been heedless of such traditional practise.

The only sound was the slap and shuffle of footsteps on the cobbles and flagstones. Jilseth wondered at the absence of fervid speculation. In the usual course of affairs, for every Council member caught unawares by such a summons, there would be one or more already sounded out by whoever was using the privileged enchantments of their office to sound the ropeless, warded bell.

Jilseth found the eerie silence unnerving, all the more so when she saw Kalion appear with Canfor at his elbow. Both mages wore clothes sufficiently crumpled to convince her that they had been scrying all night as well. Would their conclusions tally with Troanna's or with Planir's?

She looked around for Rafrid and for Herion, for Sannin, for any of the Archmage's other allies. As she did so, she noted that none of the Council's current wizards had sent anyone else in their stead, not as far as she could see. However early the hour, every one of Hadrumal's most honoured mages wished to hear what might be said for themselves and doubtless to have their own say.

The last toll of the bell warned all the approaching mages to quicken their step before the chamber was sealed against the uninvited. Jilseth made haste up the stairs, ignoring the finely mage-carved stonework that normally so delighted her earthborn affinity.

Council members were taking their seats without the typical greetings or inconsequentialities between those mages whose paths rarely crossed in the normal pattern of Hadrumal's days.

Jilseth seized her chance to claim one of the six seats for guests and witnesses, set against the uncarved stonework flanking the wide door. She saw Troanna already sitting in the niche which accommodated the chair of her office.

The Archmage's chair stood opposite the entrance; flanked like the rest by pilasters reaching upwards to spread fingers of stone to interlace in the domed vault of the ceiling. Planir had already skirted the room's central circular platform to take his seat. He didn't even pause to greet Sannin whom Jilseth now saw smoothing her scarlet skirts before sitting down.

The elegant fire mage might have come straight from her seamstress and surely some maid's deft hand had just finished dressing her hair and applying her cosmetics. The gold and rubies of her rings and bracelets were burnished by the cool white light of the ball of magefire that hung in the highest point of the roof to illuminate the windowless chamber.

'Are we all assembled?' Planir barely waited for nods of assent to swirl around the gathering before he gestured at the heavy double doors. As the iron-banded oak swung together untouched by any hand, every mage in the room turned their attention to the entrance.

Magelight glistened along the edges of the hinges, studs and bindings, in every crevice of the wood. The iron shivered and spread across the oak like spilled quicksilver. As the solid sheet of metal closed off all those within from anyone outside, everyone knew that not even quintessential scrying could penetrate this Council's deliberations.

Planir stood and turned to Troanna. 'Flood Mistress?' He sat down with as little ceremony.

'Archmage.' Troanna rose to her feet but did not cross the flagstoned floor to address the gathering in customary fashion. Instead she extended her hands, calloused palms uppermost. A shimmering enchantment rose above the dais in the centre of the room.

From where Jilseth sat, it seemed as though a window hovered in the air. The reflection was even edged with the pale green of light bent and trapped within a sheet of glass. It appeared to be angled to face her directly but Jilseth would have wagered good gold that every wizard in this room saw the same flat pane before them.

Troanna's face hardened and images appeared on the magewrought window. The most reticent of wizards couldn't restrain muffled gasps as Troanna's magic showed them shocking glimpses of the previous night's events on that distant isle.

Jilseth wondered how much of that reaction was astonishment at the raw magecraft let loose in Nahik waters and how much was envious surprise that Troanna commanded the art of reflecting an earlier scrying in such impressive fashion.

Jilseth knew little of the detail, having scant interest in the blended magics of air and water, but she knew enough from her apprentice days spent reading endless annals in Hadrumal's libraries that few mages, even the most notable Element Masters or Mistresses, had ever succeeded in sustaining such a spell.

Troanna curled her fingers into fists and let her hands fall to her sides. The visions vanished. Jilseth blinked as the shimmering radiance seemed to linger before her eyes.

Now every Council member could see what the renegade Mandarkin and his coerced mageborn were capable of; Planir's allies, his rivals and those indifferent to such machinations as well as those wholly uninterested in what might be happening beyond Hadrumal's shores. Now they would debate what was to be done about this threat.

Jilseth wouldn't have wagered a copper cutpiece on the outcome. She had no idea what course of action this Council might decide on.

— CHAPTER TWENTY-EIGHT —

'THERE YOU HAVE it,' Troanna said curtly. 'Untamed magic loose in the Archipelago. An intolerable threat to us all. Archmage?'

Rafrid was already on his feet. 'This renegade may have taught his captives some of his own destructive magic but we all saw that they had to combine their efforts to use it. Doing so has left them all nigh on exhausted. I doubt that individually they have any magecraft worth the name.'

'That is worth noting of itself.' A balding mage combed his sparse beard with thoughtful fingers. An emerald shone on a tarnished silver ring as dirty as his fingernails. 'Mages working together to bolster each other's affinity in such a fashion surely warrants further study in our halls.'

Herion raised a hand 'These unfortunates may not even have sufficient affinity that would see them considered for training in Hadrumal.'

He rose to his feet at Rafrid's nod. 'It is the case, is it not, Archmage, that this renegade from Mandarkin has given them all some ensorcelled artefact? We know full well that such things can bolster an individual's magic, for a short while. Just as we know the price they will pay for such a boon.' The mild-faced mage shook his head, clearly troubled.

Nolyen surprised Jilseth by speaking up from a seat across from her, beyond the sealed door. 'If any had sufficient affinity for their magic to have manifested before now, surely that would have been the death of them anywhere in the Archipelago.'

A shiver ran around the room at the thought of the bloody Aldabreshin hatred of wizardry.

Kalion stood up, frowning more in thought than in rebuke. 'I don't think we can necessarily assume that, Nolyen. We have all seen evidence in recent years of how thoroughly the *sheltya*'s disapproval of elemental magic can stifle any expression of magebirth among the Mountain Men and Forest Folk.'

'Such instinctive suppression of wizardry will surely be doubled and redoubled among the Aldabreshi,' Canfor said in quick agreement.

'Quite so.' Rafrid nodded. 'Surely that makes it all the more unlikely that these unfortunates will be able to use their magic to any effect if they are left to their own devices.'

'If they are deprived of these artefacts perhaps.' A stubbled wizard, his scarlet doublet unbuttoned over yesterday's shirt contemplated the empty air above the dais. His face was nakedly acquisitive. 'And surely the best place for those trinkets is Hadrumal, so that we might learn their secrets.'

'Or we might use them to strengthen our own lesser mageborn's talents,' a young wizard in a plain grey doublet instantly suggested. 'Rather than dismissing such islanders as beneath our notice.'

Urlan. That was his name. Jilseth had heard something about him encouraging those Hadrumal-born with an affinity judged too weak for training in the wizard city to try their luck in Suthyfer. Though she hadn't heard of any successes among those fleeing such humiliation.

'Can any of us think of the least talented mageborn who has chosen to forgo even their paltry magic?' Troanna demanded from her intricately carved chair. 'No matter if they must work together or rely on looted trinkets to stir their aptitudes, this Mandarkin renegade's pupils have now all had a taste of elemental magic's true power.

'Can any of us doubt that they will do all they can to learn how to strengthen and sustain their magecraft?' she demanded, 'especially when that's all that saves them from an Archipelagan warlord's skinning knife?'

'True.' Sannin's crisp agreement merely reflected the consensus which Jilseth saw all around the chamber.

'And for myself,' the elegant red-gowned magewoman continued, clearly troubled, 'I have no doubt that this Mandarkin knows full well how an excess of fear, emotion or pain can provoke an outburst of magic from the most disciplined wizard, or in this case, from the most reluctant prentice mageborn.'

Kalion nodded sombrely. 'We should not doubt this swine will be happy to inflict such pain and fear on his captive pupils.'

'We saw no such untrained wizardry loosed,' Nolyen insisted doggedly, 'when some mercenaries originally among this contingent of mageborn attacked the women trapped on that island.'

'I have considered that, in the light of my recent researches into ensorcelled artefacts.' Though Troanna's reply was composed the look she gave Nolyen boded ill for the younger mage's prospects in the Seaward Hall.

'It seems that such instinctive, unguided magecraft can be immediately drawn into some ensorcelled ring or bracelet, some weapon that has already had spells instilled within it.'

'That is quite likely,' Rafrid allowed.

'Does that unguarded magic have to be of the same affinity?' the stubbled mage with the lust for such artefacts demanded, 'as the magecrafting bound within the thing?'

'Vedral, can we please address the matter at hand?' snapped Kalion. 'Archmage, we must act!'

Planir stirred in his seat and all faces turned towards him. Jilseth wondered what he might say to prompt those other Council members who were always so easily inclined to pursue debates along unexpected tangents. She had seen how skilfully and indeed how often the Archmage used the gathering's predilections for his own purposes. Instead, he surprised her.

'When considering such serious abuses of magic, I consider arguments based on 'might' and 'likely' as perilous a foundation for firm conclusions as shifting sand beneath a building.' The Archmage inclined his head in a polite half-bow to Rafrid, Herion and Nolyen before gesturing to the central dais.

The shining pane of reflected scrying reappeared to show the entire room the appalling death by untamed fire affinity that Jilseth had witnessed earlier. A murmur ran around the chamber, all the mages aghast.

Planir swept that horror aside only to show the assembled wizards the second mageborn to die on that island; the emaciated man with the air affinity who had so utterly exhausted himself that he could no longer breathe unaided.

Jilseth laced her hands tight together in her lap. It was all too stark a reminder of the fate which she had so nearly suffered when she had thrown all her magic into Halferan Manor's defence. It was little comfort to see ashen faces around the circle of the chamber walls betraying those wizards who recalled a similar experience.

Planir drew his hand back and the nightmare vision vanished.

'However this Mandarkin is drawing affinity out of these unfortunates,' he observed with distant compassion, 'he's not teaching them how to protect themselves from their own magic.'

Rafrid shook his grizzled head. 'How long do you suppose it will be before they are all dead?'

'Not soon enough to stop this Mandarkin using them for his own foul purposes,' Troanna insisted coldly. 'Archmage, you have a sworn duty to curb the abuse of magecraft!'

Her challenge echoed back from the highest recesses of the fan-vaulted roof.

Planir answered with a measured nod. 'It is indeed the obligation of my office to curb excesses perpetrated through wizardry here in Hadrumal and across those lands that once encompassed the Tormalin Empire.'

He looked at the emptiness above the dais and then at Troanna. 'I have no such authority to act anywhere in the Archipelago. No Aldabreshin warlord will ever acknowledge my writ.'

'But what of those warlords?' Kalion gestured aimlessly, frustrated. 'Do you think that they will stand idly by while this villain does whatever he pleases with his own wizardry and with that of these mageborn he has coerced?'

'Not at all,' Planir assured him. 'So why should Hadrumal risk incurring Aldabreshin enmity through some high-handed intervention when there's every chance that the neighbouring warlords will rethink their strategy, renew their attack with yet more men and ships and rid us all of this pestilential Mandarkin? He is only one mage and for all that he may have a boatload of artefacts to draw on or these underlings' own affinities to plunder, his strength is not inexhaustible. On the other side of those particular scales, Archipelagan willingness to send newly bought slaves to their death would seem to be limitless.'

The Archmage's calm words chilled Jilseth more thoroughly than anything Troanna had said.

'You speak of likelihood, Archmage, when you yourself have told us that is no foundation for action.' The Flood Mistress flung Planir's words back at him. 'We can make certain that this menace is dealt with before this day is out. There are fire islands sufficiently close at hand for a mastercrafted nexus to provoke an eruption or an earthquake. There would be no reason for any Aldabreshi to suspect that Hadrumal had a hand in contriving such a disaster. They will doubtless consider natural justice struck that island, according to their own philosophies, if they ever summon up the courage to return.'

The Flood Mistress didn't bother hiding her contempt for such cowardice.

'No,' Planir said flatly. 'Such a hasty strategy served neither our own ends in the longer term nor the innocents of the Ice Islands. We will not repeat that error.'

Troanna opened her mouth, about to refute this. Instead, she pressed her lips into a thin line, her eyes narrowing unpleasantly.

Jilseth could see the Council members were divided between those who knew exactly what the Element Mistress and the Archmage were referring to and those, like herself, who didn't. She made a mental note to ask Sannin for an explanation at the earliest opportunity. She also wondered why the elegant magewoman looked torn between supporting Planir and reluctantly agreeing with Troanna.

Kalion forced himself to his feet. Though his jowls were sagging with weariness, his eyes were bleakly unyielding. 'Then let us consider burning that single island back to the bedrock, Archmage. After all, that's doubtless what the Archipelagan warlords will do next, with their triremes bringing catapults and barrels of sticky fire to set a blaze ashore without anyone having to land.'

'You intend killing all these unfortunates who've been coerced by the Mandarkin?' Planir queried. 'You would have to, after all, to make certain that there are no witnesses. Will you do that directly or merely hope that they perish in the flames? I wouldn't be too sure of that. At very least, some mageborn instinct could safeguard those born to a fire affinity, though of course you would know better than me on that score.'

The Archmage's voice hardened. 'You argue that I should abandon my duty to nurture and defend the mageborn? When that's as much a sworn obligation of my office, laid down by Trydek himself?'

As the Archmage raised his hand, the great diamond of his ring glowed with rainbow magelight. The cold white light in the roof above struck still more vivid hues from the four gems set around it.

'If you insist that I have the authority to act to curb

renegade magic in the Archipelago, then the reverse of that rune means I have an equal duty to protect any mageborn found in those islands. Those mageborn in particular.' Planir's tone hardened. 'These unfortunates who if they can be freed from this Mandarkin's tyranny are surely no more of a menace than any other newly-apprenticed mageborn in Hadrumal.'

'Those mainland mageborn who are sent to us after setting a chimney alight in some fit of adolescent temper or because they have stirred lurking heat deep within a granary into deadly flames?' Troanna demanded. 'Who have shattered windows with a sudden frost in midsummer or with a dust storm on a calm day, or brought a millstream into unforeseen spate to shatter waterwheel, gearing and millstones, leaving an entire district to grind their daily corn in pauper's querns? Sent here precisely because they are such a menace to the mundane?'

'You cannot buy your bun and still pocket your penny, Archmage,' Kalion said crossly. 'You refuse to attack these mageborn directly yet you are content to see the warlords slaughter them. How are you defending the oaths of your office then?'

'I said I was content to see the Archipelagans rid us all of the Mandarkin,' Planir reminded the Hearth Master with cold precision.

'These mageborn can hardly be considered as guilty as the Mandarkin,' Rafrid interrupted. 'They have been coerced. Those of us already in the Archmage's confidence have all seen this for ourselves,' he assured the gathering.

Jilseth saw that revelation prompt an unwelcome variety of expressions. Rather too many of the Council members looked affronted that the number of those evidently already well aware of this crisis didn't include them.

'Then let us bring these unfortunates here.' Kalion threw up his hands, exasperated. 'I take it that's what you intend, Planir. By all means, let us train them properly.'

'How would you propose to keep that a secret?' Planir nodded towards the sealed door and to the high road beyond Trydek's Hall. 'From the wine shop gossips? From the wharf rats in Relshaz or Col when the ships which bring us mainland cargoes return to their home harbours? The Aldabreshi will learn of it, sooner or later,' he assured the assembled wizards. 'How do you think the warlords will react to news of us abducting their slaves and vassals?'

'These mageborn are all corsairs,' Kalion said hotly. 'As guilty of attacking the Archipelagans as they are of murdering the mainlanders.'

'Then Aldabreshin justice has a claim on them,' Planir replied, 'along with the Caladhrian parliament and the Magistracy of Relshaz and the Elected of Col. Do you imagine any of those will look kindly on Hadrumal usurping their authority?'

'The first pebble lobbed into these waters was Minelas's betrayal of Baron Halferan,' Troanna spat. 'All that has followed stemmed from that first treason against Hadrumal. That gives you all the authority you might require, Archmage!'

'Do you think that the Elders of the Order of Fornet will agree?' Planir wondered. 'Or those of any other Soluran Order of wizardry? Do we believe that we're the only ones scrying after this Mandarkin?

'I very much doubt that,' he continued thoughtfully, 'just as I have no doubt that the Mandarkin lord to whom this renegade was once sworn seeks to track him down by some magical means, if he hasn't already done so.'

'If Mandarkin wizardry was capable of dealing with him, we would already have seen it,' Troanna asserted.

'Unless whoever is scrying on him from afar has chosen to wait and see,' Rafrid said suddenly. 'To see what becomes of him. To see what becomes of this collection of artefacts which he has amassed,' he added with growing concern.

'The Soluran Orders will not stand for seeing those fall into Mandarkin hands. And whatever lore may be gleaned from the things will be lost to us if any other wizardly tradition seizes them.' It was hard to tell which prospect alarmed Kalion more. 'Archmage, we must act!'

'We will act when I decide the time is right,' Planir said sternly. 'In the meantime, let us see how the Mandarkin mage handles his surviving apprentices.'

The Archmage gestured towards the emptiness above the central dais with a wry smile. 'I'll wager good gold that we see he is as capable of quelling unruly magic as any of our pupil masters and mistresses.'

No one else in the circular chamber seemed remotely amused.

Planir shrugged. 'Then make your feelings known.'

A flick of his wrist sent a beam of amber magelight soaring up to the white sphere floating high in the vaulted roof. The Archmage's wizardry turned the light filling the chamber to soft gold. Rafrid, Sannin and a handful of other mages added their own colours to brighten the rippling brilliance.

Just as swiftly, Troanna flung a shaft of mossy darkness upwards, dimming the sphere with her disapproval. Canfor's indigo endorsement of her action was followed more slowly by Kalion's maroon rejection of Planir's proposal. Other mages proved similarly unconvinced by the Archmage's reasoning. Their verdicts dulled the magelit sphere with a tangle of rainbow shadows.

Jilseth added her own magelight to the next surge of wizardry, bright as brimstone. Cyan, rose and palest jade coloured declarations of support for Planir. The beams of radiance writhed and shifted amid the ochre and cobalt wizardry of those equally fervent in their opposition.

She set her jaw as she poured all her conviction that the Archmage's strategy was correct into the light soaring upwards from her outstretched palm. The mundane magistracies and assemblies of the mainlanders were welcome to make their decisions on a simple show of hands or some tally of tokens dropped into empty barrels. Trydek and the first Element Masters and Mistresses had ensured that the wizards of Hadrumal had the means to gauge the strength of feeling behind every vote.

Sweat beaded Jilseth's lip. Her magelight shivered as her affinity vacillated between ominous weakness and the terrifying possibility of wild magic escaping her control once again. She gritted her teeth as she bound her affinity with iron determination neither to abandon Planir's cause nor to disgrace him with some undisciplined outburst.

If such a thing was possible in this chamber warded with ancient spells to prevent any wizards' quarrel being settled by direct assault, magical or physical. All of

Hadrumal's current residents might agree that tales of battling mages belonged to those long-lost days before Trydek and his followers had settled this island but no Archmage had ever seen fit to unpick those particular sorceries.

Sorceries which would doubtless be as effective in quelling unbidden rampaging magic as they would be in stifling malicious intent. With that realisation soothing her fears, Jilseth found her affinity strengthening. Her magelight brightened.

Just as well, she realised, and just in time. The great chamber was dimming almost to twilight as the magelit sphere was veiled by the strength of the opposition to Planir's proposed plan of action, or rather, inaction.

Jilseth wished she could see who was supporting the Archmage and who did not but she dared not spare the merest flicker of concentration from the gleaming sphere up above. The silence in the council chamber was broken only by the rustling as wizards here and there shifted in their seats and by the increasingly harsh sound of breathing.

Someone on the far side of the circle let slip a wordless snarl compounded of disgust and exhaustion. A rising spiral the colour of clotted blood vanished to leave a shaft of magelight tinged with leaf-green soaring upwards unopposed.

A single slipping pebble can start a landslide. Every earth mage knew that. Jilseth was intensely relieved to see that first breach in Troanna's support was followed by other wizards abandoning their opposition to Planir's authority. Though she noted uneasily that the remaining magelight, from all those endorsing the Archmage's strategy, shone nowhere near as brightly as the floating sphere had done before the vote.

'Very well.' Planir rose to his feet, his face impassive. 'Now that is settled, let us see what the rest of this day has to show us of events in the Archipelago and elsewhere. There are any number of possible considerations that might better guide our actions along the most prudent course for Hadrumal.'

He snapped his fingers at the magical warding barring the entrance and the ensorcelled metal flowed aside to remake hinges, latch and burnished bindings. The Archmage gestured and the door swung open. He left the chamber before half of the Council members had even risen to their feet.

Jilseth hurried to catch up with him, pushing Canfor's arm aside when he would have blocked her path. The tall mage was so taken aback that she left him standing on the staircase, gaping after her lost for words.

She reached Planir's side as he turned into the narrow alley between the original outer wall of Trydek's Hall and the later range of accommodations built beside it. 'Do you want me to scry after the Mandarkin with you, Archmage?'

As they did so, perhaps she could find the right questions to draw out some hints as to what he really intended for those coerced mageborn. He must have a plan. Jilseth had no doubt of that. Where could he send them to avoid outraging the mainland's rulers? Suthyfer? Hadn't the Tormalin Emperor himself decreed those islands were beyond his own or any other jurisdiction?

Planir halted to look at her as he considered her offer of assistance. 'No, I will scry alone for the moment. Go and get some rest and a decent meal, then come to my study when you're fully refreshed.'

'Yes, Archmage.' Now Jilseth allowed herself to long for bread warm from the oven spread with soft cheese and quince preserves as well as a sweetly aromatic tisane to take away the lingering taste of Planir's holly draught.

She would have time to breakfast properly. The Mandarkin and his coerced mageborn would need far more than a meal and whatever it was the Archipelagans drank before they could make any more mischief.

— CHAPTER TWENTY-NINE —

Black Turtle Isle
In the domain of Nahik Jarir

HOSH CONTEMPLATED THE marks he'd scratched on the wall plaster, mostly hidden by his makeshift bed. He tucked the little folding knife back in his trews pocket.

Had he kept his count correct, when he'd begun this fresh tally? He hoped so. After all, he'd had plenty of leisure to check and recheck his count these past few days. Anskal had largely ignored him, beyond summoning him to bring food or drink each morning and evening.

It had proved simple enough to establish that the island was free of invaders. Scrying spells and a sweep across the island led by the raider-mages had confirmed that those fleeing the calamitous attack on the anchorage had either been carried off by the waiting galleys or had drowned in their desperate attempts to swim after the departing vessels.

Now the Mandarkin was intent on training his new apprentices.

So now Hosh reckoned, as best he could without an almanac, another sixteen days or so would see the equinox. Even if the Archipelagans paid it no particular heed, the three-quarter mark in the year would signify the end of the sailing season between the Archipelago and the mainland. Aft-Autumn's brutal storms would come wheeling in from the western sea. The most reckless sailors shunned the choice of being overwhelmed out on the trackless billows or driven onto rocks ready to smash bone and timber alike.

So that was all the equinox meant to the Aldabreshi and there was little more point in Hosh marking it. He had no more chance of ever enjoying a Caladhrian festival again than he had of catching a moon in a net.

'You.' One of the new-fledged wizards, one of the erstwhile raiders, appeared in the inner chamber's doorway.

Hosh scrambled to his feet, shoulders hunched and craven, to save himself from some casual beating. This was one corsair who'd regained all his former arrogance now that they had all proved themselves as mages.

'How may I serve you?'

'You are to keep watch.' The swordsman gestured through the outer door. 'For ships.'

'Of course.' Hosh ducked his head again though this instruction made no sense.

'Go now.' Without any further word, the raider-mage walked back into the inner chamber.

Hosh heard the man open the far door into the pavilion's central garden. He heard Anskal's voice.

'You must draw the fire from the air to make the water that remains visible. Send the fire deep into the earth. Picture your breath on a snowbound morning—'

The Archipelagans voiced their confusion at such a notion. There was no sign of their former reluctance to learn the secrets of magecraft now. The Ensaimin mariners spoke over each other in their attempts to explain what winter truly meant in more northerly climes.

Hosh lifted the corner of his stacked palliasses and retrieved a round of unleavened bread which he'd hidden there the night before.

Now that all the previously cooked and stored food had all either been eaten or spoiled, the women had deigned to show the Aldabreshi raiders and slaves how to cook, in return for a share of the loot which they were currently recovering from the ruined pavilions.

They weren't only recovering coin, gold and gems as they used their newly honed wizardry to toss aside cracked stone and charred timber. The buried cellars held stores that had escaped the general destruction but few of the foodstuffs would make a meal without someone making an effort.

Hosh preferred to join the Ensaimin mariners and the two Lescari, offering them his unskilled hand to chop and peel and stir when they claimed some time in this remaining pavilion's kitchen. All of the mainlanders proved to be competent if basic cooks, thanks to their time spent afloat or in a militia camp, far from helpful mothers, wives or sisters.

He walked to the corner of the pavilion's terrace, to secure the best view of the headlands framing the mouth of the anchorage. Why had Anskal sent him out here? It wasn't as if Hosh could understand any of those arcane conversations revolving around wizardry, still less make any use of such knowledge.

If he was concerned to keep watch, surely Anskal would do better to set one of his apprentices to gazing into a scrying bowl? Such a spell would warn of trouble well ahead of its arrival. What was the good in hoping for Hosh to glimpse some ship with his own unaided eyes? Assuming there was the faintest possibility that the Aldabreshi would launch a second attack after the magic-soaked slaughter of their first.

Hosh couldn't see anything in the stars to encourage such fresh folly among the Archipelagans. He couldn't begin to imagine what manner of omen might convince the neighbouring warlords to send more men to such certain, accursed deaths.

He looked across to the wrecked pavilions and to the vast black stain on the bare earth beyond. The prentice wizards had piled up all the corpses and carrion retrieved from the beaches for burning along with the wreckage of the old abandoned huts. The mainlanders had no quarrel with disposing of the dead in such a fashion while the Archipelagans wanted no lingering hatred interred in this island's soil along with the bones of those they had killed.

Anskal had fired the makeshift pyre with magic, stoking it into a blaze that had raised a column of smoke undoubtedly visible from leagues upon leagues away. As it burned, the Mandarkin had asked his Aldabreshin apprentices what they made of the way the winds tore the smoke into rags, what omens and portents they read into the flares of sparks or dancing flames.

Hosh sat, his feet dangling over the edge of the terrace. As movement caught his eye, he choked on his mouthful of flat bread. As he spat the pulpy mess he was vaguely surprised to find that he hadn't vomited up everything he'd ever eaten.

So Anskal had known to expect these newcomers. That's why he'd had Hosh sent out to keep watch while he discussed their imminent arrival with his apprentices.

One galley. One trireme. One of the prentice mages scrying out these ships must have recognised the standards flying from their mastheads. But by all that was sacred and profane, Hosh wondered with sick terror, what had the coerced mageborn told the Mandarkin of the men who captained these vessels now heading down the anchorage, confident in their knowledge of these waters.

Hosh ran back inside the entrance hall. He threw open the door to the inner chamber and then the double windowed doors opening onto the garden. Anskal and his apprentices sat on a circle of cushions surrounded by once carefully tended plants now variously charred or blighted by unnatural frosts.

'Grewa is here.' Hosh wanted to scream his accusation but horror strangled him to a whisper. 'You didn't kill him, you fool!'

He didn't care if Anskal punished him. It was reward enough to see the same thought reflected on most of the other faces turned towards him.

Anskal shrugged. 'I can kill him whenever I wish. I am interested to see what he might have to say.'

Leaving his circle of apprentices exchanging dubious glances, he strolled out of the garden, past Hosh and on through the pavilion, heading for the terrace.

Hosh wanted to block the Mandarkin's path, to seize him by the shoulders and shake some sense into the villain. Instead he stood with his hands hanging by his sides, his feet as heavy as lead. He would have liked to think that some hostile magic had him in thrall. But he knew his inaction for simple cowardice.

The prentice wizards were all now following Anskal. Hosh retreated to make certain he gave none of them an excuse to take their own fear out of his hide. When the last had passed through the entrance hall, he finally followed.

Anskal was already down the steps and heading for the beach. The galley was wheeling around to turn its stern ladders to the shore. The trireme held its position some distance off.

What did the blind corsair hope to gain by that? No one could doubt that the wizard who'd claimed this island could sink any ship he wished. The anchorage was still cluttered with the three wrecks, one of them Grewa's own burned trireme, while the waves continued to batter the shattered timbers of the vessels which the women had sunk on the far side of this southerly headland.

Hosh's last desperate hope, that this ship merely carried some of the blind corsair's former followers flying his standard died as he saw the weather-beaten old man aboard the galley. Then as the ship drove its stern firmly into the sand, Hosh realised this day was more cursed than he had feared.

That black-haired, black-hearted bastard, the corsair captain whose name Hosh didn't even know, he had paid that treacherous mage Minelas enough gold to betray Lord Halferan. Aye, and he had murdered the noble baron for good measure. Now he was making his way carefully down the broad rungs of the wooden ladder a few steps ahead of Grewa.

As the brutal killer and slaver dropped down into the thigh-high water, a passing shaft of sunlight struck gold from the chains woven into his beard. He paused, waiting to guide the blind corsair ashore.

They were the only two men descending from the ships. Whatever this might be, it didn't look like an attack to Hosh. For a start, neither Grewa nor the raider captain wore a sword, and Hosh couldn't recall when he'd ever seen an Aldabreshi corsair thus unarmed. Even blind Grewa had carried a blade for show.

Though of course that didn't preclude any number of treacherously concealed knives and there were plenty of crewmen and rowers visible aboard both ships. Hosh had no doubt that archers were readying the short bows of the Archipelago to retaliate for any treachery ashore.

Hosh hurried down the steps. Not that he wanted to get any closer to the murdering swine but he didn't want to stand exposed and alone on the remaining pavilion's terrace to draw that cold-blooded killer's eye.

The last time the corsair captain had come here, Hosh had been merely another cowed slave of no account, trailing after Nifai when the overseer and all his peers among the ship masters and their most trusted crewmen had been summoned to the stone circle to hear Grewa's predictions. The blind old man's guidance had made them all so rich, after all.

Now Hosh had no such crowd to lose himself in. The best he could hope for was to hide behind the apprentice wizards now assembling behind Anskal on the beach.

One of the slave mages plucked at the Mandarkin's sleeve. 'His name is Molcho. He is not to be trusted.'

One of the former raiders instantly objected. 'He led us on some of our most profitable raids.'

The erstwhile slave glared at him with unaccustomed boldness. 'And what misfortunes pursued those who chose not to follow him? How many men died at his hand when they refused to surrender twice the customary share in their loot as he demanded?'

Before the raider could answer, the black-bearded raider shouted out as he waded ashore.

'Good day to you. As you see, we offer friendship.'

442

With Grewa leaning heavily on his other arm, he held his sword hand out, empty palm uppermost.

The villain's Tormalin was as fluent as Hosh recalled it. As it had been when the beast had concluded his business with that swine Minelas. When he had murdered Baron Halferan in the barony's own marshes. And now Hosh didn't even have the consolation of believing that the vile killer was dead, struck down with blind Grewa in Anskal's first assault on this anchorage.

The Mandarkin laughed. 'You hold no grudges?'

Hosh saw his own astonishment reflected on every other face ashore.

'For you trying to kill me?' The black-haired man shook his head, prompting a faint rattle from the chains in his beard. 'We were not friends then.'

Hosh couldn't understand it. The corsair captain Molcho's inexplicably confident smile was now both warning and invitation.

Worse, Anskal acknowledged him with an answering grin, equally vicious.

The blind corsair said something in a low tone and the black-haired man Molcho nodded before addressing the Mandarkin in Tormalin speech once again. 'May we come ashore? My companion finds the water unseasonably cold.'

Hosh would have given good gold to be close enough to hear if that's truly what Grewa had said.

The Mandarkin mage raised a forbidding hand. 'Not if you seek to reclaim what you have lost.'

'No.' Molcho shook his head once again. 'But we would like to help you make the best use of what you have won here.'

'Would you, indeed?' Now Anskal's tone was both

intrigued and menacing. 'Then by all means come ashore.'

Hosh felt for the folding knife through the cotton of his trews. He slid his hand inside his pocket and stealthily unfolded the blade. Short though the blade was, he could rip it into the side of Molcho's neck before he was killed himself. Everyone would be taken entirely unawares.

He eased himself between one of the mageborn slaves and a woman looking at Molcho with utter revulsion. As the raider captain led blind Grewa ashore, Hosh measured the narrowing distance between them.

'My thanks.' Molcho reached the sand left firm by the wash of the tide.

'So,' Anskal invited, 'tell me how you could possibly strengthen my hand?' He gestured at the mageborn flanking him. 'I have all the allies I need to use the treasures which I have won here. Better yet, I know exactly what I have. You can only have discovered their secrets by chance and piecemeal.'

Before Hosh could guess at the Mandarkin's meaning, Anskal pointed at Grewa's face.

The thick scarf hiding the blind corsair's eyes tore in half, the cloth falling away. Hosh heard his own gasp of shock mingle with everyone else's.

There could be no doubt that the old corsair was truly blind. His eye sockets were twin scarred hollows sunk deep into his head.

So how could he be looking straight at Anskal, holding up his hand as though to ward off the Mandarkin mage?

Anskal snapped his fingers and his magic ripped open the neck of Molcho's tunic. The raider captain took a step forward, his face as ugly as Hosh recalled it in his nightmares.

Between that step and the next, everyone saw an ornate silver amulet studded with turquoise bright against Molcho's dark skin. The ornament sprang upwards and flew straight towards Anskal's waiting hand. Its incongruously sturdy chain hadn't even snapped.

Grewa snatched for the thing, taking a long, confident stride as though he would chase it, blind man or not.

In the instant that Anskal's fingers closed over the amulet, the blind corsair gasped. He stopped dead in the knee-deep water. Now he held his shaking hands out before him, palms beseeching like any other blind beggar.

Molcho advanced regardless with no sign of fear. 'Return that—'

Hosh seized his chance. No one was looking at him. He wrenched the little knife free of his pocket, not caring that he cut both cloth and his own flesh as he did so.

One step took him towards Molcho before anyone noticed. The second brought him within striking distance of the black-hearted murderer.

But Molcho had seen him. With a sneer that infuriated Hosh, the man raised one brawny arm to block the puny knife's stroke. His fist was already swinging around to finish the ruination of Hosh's nose and jaw, begun when one of Molcho's men's sword pommel had smashed into his face in the Halferan marshes.

Hosh ducked and thrust. Captain Corrain had told him and the other lads often enough that they should always guard their crotch. Not only in hopes of fathering sons if they could find a girl near-sighted or drunk enough to bed them.

The captain had said that more men fell victim to a blade cutting the great vessels carrying blood down the inside of their thigh than died from a cut throat.

The little knife only cut empty air. Hosh sprawled forward to land on his hands and knees. He looked wildly around but Molcho had vanished.

'What has happened?' Grewa waved fearful hands lest someone might be approaching. His blind face quested helplessly from side to side.

Anskal was laughing as though he hadn't seen such a jest in a year.

Hosh screamed insensate fury at the Mandarkin. He scrabbled in the sand for the feeble blade as dry sobs of rage choked him.

'No,' Anskal chided.

Hosh found himself flipped over to land flat on his back, the breath knocked out of him.

In the next instant, Molcho reappeared. He stooped over Hosh, massive hands reaching to seize him. Through his dizziness and the crushing pain in his chest, Hosh realised that the corsair had no need of a blade to murder him. He would snap his neck as easily as Hosh's old mother could kill a chicken for the pot.

'No,' Anskal said again with that same infuriating amusement.

Molcho vanished a second time.

The deadly sense of suffocation faded. Hosh rolled onto his side. At first all he could see were the feet and ankles of Anskal's contingent of mageborn. Then he saw they were all staring down the beach.

Forcing himself up onto his elbow, Hosh blinked through bleary eyes. Molcho was half way around the curve of the anchorage.

Anskal smiled at his apprentice cohort. 'Let us see if our new friends have learned their lessons.'

In the next breath, Molcho was staggering in the knee-deep water before them. Hosh saw the gold chains that had been woven into the corsair captain's beard were now looped around Anskal's fingers.

'So you have had the wit to use these trifles of magic which you have found among your plunder.' The Mandarkin examined his loot; the silver amulet in one hand, the gold chains in the other. He might have been conversing with the two men over a glass of wine.

'No,' he corrected himself. 'You not only made use of these little magics—and I will be interested to learn how you did that—' he remarked '—you also had the sense to gather together other such treasures, even if you could not awaken their enchantments.'

He nodded. 'All admirable, and most unexpected, given this curious realm's hatred and ignorance of magic. But once again, I must ask—' his voice hardened abruptly '— what can you possibly offer to persuade me not to add these trifles to my spoils and throw you and your crewmen into the sea, to await the mercy of the sharks and serpents?

'As you see,' he added with more menace. 'I can stifle such trivial magic or stir it to do my will as I choose and you can do nothing about it.'

For a moment, Hosh truly believed that the two corsairs would turn tail and run. Only for a moment.

Molcho waded through the shallows to stand beside Grewa, offering a reassuring slap on his shoulder. The blind man's flailing hands stilled.

No, Hosh concluded miserably, these men wouldn't run. Where would they run to? Besides, they had already been using the magic in these two artefacts somehow, in defiance of all Archipelagan law and custom. They might be overawed by Anskal's wizardry but they wouldn't flee from it in blind panic like the trapped corsairs had.

'We can offer you men,' Molcho said warily. 'Ships. Knowledge of these waters and these people. You have fended off one attack but if you have half the skills we can guess at, if you can summon the visions that mainland mages claim, you must know that can only be the first assault—'

'You have taken this island and our plunder.' Grewa turned his blind gaze towards the Mandarkin's voice. 'We yield to you as our conqueror. We ask what you would have us do next?'

'If you wished to go back to whence you came, why haven't you already done so?' Molcho challenged Anskal.

'But you are here and gathering allies,' Grewa continued more boldly. 'We can offer better men than these slaves and women. You have said that you wish to claim tribute in return for passage through these sea lanes?' He shook his blind head. 'The warlords will not offer that unless they have no choice.'

'While you can undoubtedly sink their defiant ships, each wreck is as much a loss to you as it is to them,' Molcho observed. 'And how many such losses will it take to convince them to yield? We can offer you the means to extend your reach beyond this island in a much more profitable fashion.'

'Can you indeed?' Anskal's tone gave no clue as to his thoughts as he contemplated his mageborn.

Motionless on the sand, Hosh could see the apprentice

cohort striving to hide their reactions. Those divided along predictable lines.

One of the corsair swordsmen couldn't conceal his vicious delight at the prospect of Grewa's return. Two of the former slaves were so unmanned by terror that Hosh expected them to collapse onto the sand beside him. The Ensaimin mariners and the two Lescari were united in barely veiled contempt for their erstwhile captors.

The only sound to break the tense silence was the lap of the sea around the galley's hull and the stir of the trireme's oars.

Anskal pursed his lips. 'Let us discuss this further, in more comfort.'

Molcho started forward though Anskal's invitation was far from warm.

'My amulet.' Grewa remained standing still. 'I must have use of that.'

Whatever else they might discuss, that was clearly not a subject for debate.

'To see through another's eyes.' Anskal nodded before turning to his apprentices with a sly smile. 'Then I choose—'

Hosh was startled out of his daze by Molcho's brutal attack. The bearded man stooped. He caught up Hosh's lost knife with one hand and seized his long tangled hair with the other. However slight the blade, the violence of his strike would have cut Hosh's throat from ear to ear.

The folding knife skidded down his neck leaving no more mark than the stroke of a feather. Molcho spat some Archipelagan obscenity and ripped the blade down Hosh's sleeve. The cloth yielded to reveal the silver-gilt and crystal arm ring.

Molcho drove the knife between the metal and Hosh's arm. Though his skin wasn't cut, the merciless pressure made Hosh squeal with pain.

His cry turned to a yell of panic as Molcho forced the blade downwards. The arm ring slid loose, down to Hosh's elbow. He pressed his arm tight to his side, wrapping his hand across his chest to dig his fingers into his far shoulder. His terror was only outstripped by his determination not to let the artefact be stolen.

A beam of amber magelight knocked Molcho's legs out from under him. Hosh fought frantically to free himself from the fallen man's grasp. Even with the corsair captain stunned by Anskal's attack, Hosh barely managed to escape and only by losing a skein of his matted hair to Molcho's clenched fist.

He scrabbled backwards on hands and heels, his backside scraping along the shore.

'Stop.' Anskal's hand fell heavy on his shoulder.

Hosh looked up, cringing.

The mage was staring unblinking at Molcho. Amber magelight wove painfully tight fetters around the raider's ankles.

'Power of life and death on this island is mine and mine alone.'

Before Hosh could breathe any sigh of relief, Anskal looked down at him with the same cold eyes. 'You would do well to remember that too.'

'What—?' Grewa's apprehension and frustration prompted him into an unwise step forward. A ruck in the sand nearly tripped the blind man. 'Molcho?' he bellowed.

'Here.' Anskal opened his hands and dropped the old corsair's amulet. Lithe as a live creature, the chain looped itself around Hosh's neck.

Grewa gasped, clasping at his empty eye sockets with clawed fingers.

'This boy's gaze will suffice for the moment,' Anskal said sternly. 'I may give you the services of one of your chosen once you have proved to be my friend. Until then I prefer to know that you are keeping no secrets from me.'

Hosh couldn't help seizing the amulet, ready to rip it upwards and over his head. Except that he couldn't. As his fingers closed around it, his entire hand and arm numbed. The chain slithered, tightening against the sides of his neck. Within half a breath he felt lightheaded and sick.

Anskal bent to tug the silver and turquoise trinket from Hosh's nerveless grasp. 'That is not your choice to make,' he reproved unnecessarily.

As Hosh swallowed his nauseating dizziness, he saw Grewa's blind gaze turned eerily towards him. Was he now truly bound to follow the old corsair everywhere and doubtless to report whatever he saw and heard to Anskal? The horror of that prospect nearly made him vomit.

Worse, what if Molcho or Grewa knew of some way to confound the wizardry keeping the cursed thing around his neck? Would killing him do it?

The corsair captain had managed to sit up. 'As you say,' he growled, 'all power of life and death on this island belongs to you.'

'Very well.' Anskal was pleased. 'Then let us find some refreshment and discuss how we might work together to our mutual advantage. How you might earn the return of these.' He tucked Molcho's tangled gold chains' links into his own pocket.

The amber magelight binding the raider's ankles vanished.

'Up,' Anskal chided Hosh.

Magic dragged him to his feet. 'Must I—?'

'You will stay with them.' Anskal's voice echoed oddly in Hosh's ears. Seeing bemused expression among the mageborn, he realised that no one else could hear the mage, though they could surely see Anskal's lips moving.

'You will tell me everything that they say when I am not present.'

'Of course.'

Amid his wretchedness, Hosh could only hope that Molcho and Grewa would easily see his role as Anskal's spy and take care not to betray themselves.

He looked up at the beached galley and beyond to the trireme. Just as long as someone else didn't come to the two corsair leaders with some news or a scheme that would mean they had to kill him, forcing them to accept the reversed rune of Grewa's blindness for the sake of keeping their true plans from Anskal.

— CHAPTER THIRTY —

The Terrene Hall, Hadrumal
35th of For-Autumn

'CAN YOU MAINTAIN the scrying?' Jilseth asked urgently.

Nolyen nodded. 'Go on.'

Jilseth withdrew her hands from the sides of the bowl and concentrated on clearing her wizardly senses of all engagement with water.

She hurried to her fireplace. As she took a wooden spill from the jar on the mantel, it bloomed with scarlet flame. As she took a polished metal mirror from her skirt pocket a crimson speck in the centre spread into a swirling spell. 'Archmage?'

'*A moment.*'

Jilseth had barely glimpsed Planir's study before the bespeaking vanished like a burst bubble.

'What have you seen?' The Archmage stepped out of the emptiness behind Nolyen's chair to peer over the mild-faced wizard's shoulder.

'Archmage?' Jilseth wanted to ask about the glimpse she had caught of Planir's sitting room. Troanna, Rafrid and Kalion had all been there and judging by their expressions, the conversation had been heated.

Planir looked up from the scrying bowl to offer her a brief smile before glancing at the window. Wet from an earlier rain shower, the ivy leaves stirred by the breeze were gilded by the setting sun. All too soon, Jilseth knew, it would sink behind the roofline and shadows would thicken around the courtyard.

The Council bell tolled.

'Archmage?' Emerald light flared to cast uncanny reflections under Nolyen's chin.

'You may release your spell.' As the magic evaporated leaving only the faintest perfume in the air, Planir looked from the younger mage to Jilseth and back again.

'I may need you to bear witness to the Council as to what you have seen. That is my summons,' he added.

Nolyen had no hesitation. 'What do you want us to say, Archmage?'

Planir spread his hands. 'The truth, no more, no less.'

He was striding for the door before Jilseth could frame a more meaningful question.

Nolyen was already rising to follow the Archmage. 'What are you waiting for?'

Since Jilseth had no answer to that, she let Nolyen go through the door and pulled it closed behind her.

Despite the dusk gathering in the courtyard, she could see the faces at surrounding windows. Planir's swift steps echoing across the flagstones had caught their curiosity. Now those onlookers were studying her and Nolyen.

She could imagine the questions running through the watchers' minds. The same questions that had been bandied about Hadrumal's wine shops for days now, running the length of the wizard city's high road.

When would the impasse between the Archmage and the Council be broken? Who would be the one to break the deadlock? What would the outcome be for Hadrumal?

They would know soon enough. Doubtless half the

council members would head straight to inform their favoured companions once this evening's meeting concluded.

She caught up with Nolyen as he passed beneath the outer courtyard's arch into the alleyway.

It came as no surprise to her that Planir took the swiftest route through the narrow ginnels running between and behind the high-walled halls to reach the irregular square in front of the Council chamber.

Jilseth was rather more interested to note how warmly the Archmage was greeted by two mundane born hall servants coming along the alley. Who, judging by their curious looks at her and Nolyen, were used to finding their humble paths customarily free of the mageborn.

Swift as they were, wizards were already assembling around the chamber door. Not only Council members. Jilseth could see a good number of mages who had no official reason to answer the bell's summons. Were they here with some argument or encouragement for those about to enter the debate, whatever that might prove to be? Or simply looking for more entertainment than sitting at a dinner table with their friends or on either side of a fireplace, swapping tales of a customarily arduous day.

She looked for the Element Mistress and Masters. If any of the three arrived with a coterie of Council members, that would surely be significant.

'There's Troanna.' Nolyen looked apprehensive.

'Ely is with her.' Jilseth wondered what that might signify.

'Galen is with Kalion,' Nolyen observed without surprise, 'and a good double handful of others,' he added, rather more concerned

Were there any Hall Masters or Mistresses among the Hearth Master's allies? Jilseth tried to see but she couldn't identify half the glimpsed shoulders and turning heads amid this throng. She had entirely lost sight of Planir.

'Let's go into the chamber.'

As the mages of Council rank climbed the short flight of stairs, the hum of speculation rose to a deafening pitch beneath the shallow drum of the roof vault. Jilseth's head was ringing by the time she arrived in the circular chamber.

Her relief was short-lived. Canfor's hand gripped her elbow.

'What are you doing here?' He looked down at her, his eyes intense.

So he wasn't challenging her right to be present. He was more interested in what he might learn before the debate started.

Jilseth took a little discreet pleasure in frustrating him. 'I am here at the Archmage's request.'

Canfor wasn't deterred. 'What have you seen?'

'Much the same as you, I would imagine.' Jilseth met his gaze boldly. 'Where have you been getting your bitumen from?'

He didn't answer, turning away to sit on the far side of the door.

'Here.' Nolyen had claimed two of the closest seats. 'No,' he said firmly to a rotund magewoman in puce velvet, 'this chair is required for the Archmage's witness.'

'Thank you.' Jilseth slid past the woman and sat down before anyone else could challenge Nolyen's claim.

She leaned close to him, keeping her voice low. 'Is there any limit on how many mages a council member can invite to observe a debate?'

'I don't recall.' Nolyen looked around. 'I don't recall ever seeing the chamber so crowded.'

The hum of speculation was only muted now because huddles of wizards were wary of being overheard, glancing over their shoulders to see who might be standing closest.

'There's Rafrid.' Jilseth was relieved to see the Cloud Master arrive with Sannin and Herion.

'There's Velindre,' Nolyen said, startled.

Jilseth followed his gaze to see the tall blonde magewoman standing beside Planir. Velindre was regarding the wizards bustling between their allies and their seats with a sardonic curl to her lip.

Jilseth found the expression reminiscent of Canfor's. Were all wizards born to the element of air naturally so aloof?

Planir took a lithe step onto the great chamber's central dais. The hovering sphere of magelight blazed with his urgency.

'Good evening, masters and mistresses.'

The Archmage didn't pause to allow those taken unawares to find their seats. A faint gloss of blue magic slid over the magelight above his head and his words rose more loudly above the hasty shuffle of feet and the rustle of clothing.

'Archmage? The door?' One of the oldest mages present, a snowy-haired, hatchet faced man indignantly waved his stick at the entrance standing wide open.

Planir acknowledged him with the briefest of nods. 'I see no reason to shut ourselves away, Master Massial, when the business that brings us here this evening concerns all of Hadrumal.'

That silenced the last whispers circling the room.

'It is my duty to see this Council is kept fully informed of recent developments in the Aldabreshin Archipelago, concerning the renegade Mandarkin mage. Jilseth, kindly tell us what your most recent scrying has shown.'

'Archmage.' She was on her feet at once. Then she realised Nolyen had stayed sitting down. 'Nol?'

'He doesn't need two of us repeating ourselves.' He pressed his shoulders back against the wall. 'I'll make note of who knows nothing of what we've seen, and who shows no surprise,' he muttered darkly.

Jilseth narrowed her eyes at him but she couldn't deny that such knowledge could well be useful. She could also feel the weight of every other gaze in the chamber upon her.

'You may speak from there,' Planir prompted.

Jilseth wondered who else realised the Archmage had no intention of yielding the central platform to any other speaker. She dared not look at Flood Mistress Troanna.

Lifting her chin, she looked straight at the Archmage.

'The Mandarkin wizard, Anskal, has made an alliance with two of the original leaders of the corsairs.' She strove to keep her subsequent explanation as succinct and unemotional as Planir's words.

'It seems that those men were already using some of the ensorcelled artefacts as best they might, for personal protection and assistance. These men do not show the same fear and hatred of wizardry as other Archipelagans. They appear to be persuading others to join them. They returned to the anchorage with two ships. This afternoon another three arrived, two galleys and a trireme.'

She broke off at Planir's nod.

The Archmage turned to Velindre who had moved to stand beside Cloud Master Rafrid. 'Are the Aldabreshin warlords aware of this?'

'They are,' she said crisply. 'Mellitha Esterlin and I have been scrying and gathering intelligence from a wide range of sources. The northern reaches' warlords have watched recent developments with great concern. Their patience with the corsairs had already worn thin but they were loath to intervene in Nahik Jarir's waters. Such an assault goes against all custom and law. The Mandarkin's arrival changed all that, as was clearly demonstrated when the neighbouring domains joined forces in that initial assault on this anchorage.'

Sinking back onto her seat, Jilseth saw that Troanna was ready to rise and to speak. Moreover the Flood Mistress wasn't the only mage intent on having a say.

Velindre ignored them all as she continued. 'The warlords have been considering what to do next ever since that first wave of slaves was slaughtered. We should not mistake their recent inaction for any lack of intent or courage. They will not tolerate the presence of a wizard in their waters.'

Her severe features hardened further. 'They will rid themselves of this wizard if it takes a year and a hundred lost lives for every day of that year to do it. But I can assure you that we will not need to wait a year to see the bloodshed start. As long as this Mandarkin stayed within the bounds of that single island, on land that was already deemed irretrievably cursed, the Archipelagans believed that they had time to regroup after those initial losses, to gather more men and ships while they consulted with each other in hopes of a strategy certain to kill him and all those mageborn—'

'And to consult their stars?'

It took Jilseth a moment to identify the source of that sarcastic interruption. Despin, the balding bearded mage who had been so interested in the notion of ensorcelled artefacts.

'To mock what you do not understand merely makes you look a fool.' Velindre shot him a fulminating glance before addressing the entire gathering once again.

'Now the warlords have learned that the Mandarkin Anskal has allies beyond those coerced mageborn. That those allies have galleys and triremes as well as detailed knowledge of their own sea lanes and islands. The warlords are preparing another attack even as we sit here and debate. They are most assuredly watching their skies for the most favourable stars. Because they know a conjunction is approaching which will offer their foes incomparable shelter and succour.'

The tall magewoman swept the chamber with a scathing glance.

'You may know nothing of and care less for the Aldabreshin heavenly compass but your ignorance has no bearing on this matter. The Archipelagans believe in their omens absolutely and will follow this most vital of portents' guidance to the uttermost end.

'The warlords have agreed that this wizard, his apprentices and all those corsairs who would sail under his banner must die,' she declared. 'Their attack will commence three days from now. It will continue until the Mandarkin and all those with him are dead. Then that island will be burned to black ash with no living thing allowed to escape it.'

'Then the matter will be closed.' An ancient magewoman hunched in her seat spoke up. 'There is nothing more to be said.' She planted her stick on the flagstones, ready to rise.

'Can we be sure of that, Shannet?'

In the centre of the chamber, Planir's question commanded everyone's attention.

'Aldabreshin swords are swift and so is their sticky fire but who here could not escape such threats, even taken unawares? This Mandarkin, this renegade mage Anskal, will have learned that this attack is coming, as readily as we have. This foolhardy Aldabreshin assault—' he broke off to acknowledge Velindre's unspoken protest '—though admirably courageous by its own lights, is doomed to fail in its ultimate aim.

'What of the consequences for Hadrumal?' he challenged the Council. 'Where will this wizard go next? A renegade mage whom we have already seen is as merciless as any tale of Mandarkin cruelty might suggest. Even if he chooses to throw his apprentices onto Aldabreshi blades to make his escape, at the very least we can assume he will make certain to save his trove of ensorcelled artefacts.'

Planir shot a look at Despin and some other mages whom Jilseth guessed had made representations to him about Hadrumal's supposed claim on such treasures.

'Many of you have reservations about our own new haven for wizardry in distant Suthyfer,' the Archmage observed. 'Do you want to see this Anskal establish himself in some remote place, to recruit a new cohort of mageborn to support those he has already coerced and to teach them his callousness and greed? Do we want to see those hoarded artefacts abused to further his purposes?

'What will the Soluran Orders do in such a case?'

Planir demanded. 'They tell us it is our duty to subdue this renegade, since it was a Caladhrian who lured him southwards. If we are seen to fail so signally in that duty, what of Hadrumal's reputation then? What is to stop the Solurans attacking this Mandarkin to defend their own interests if we have been found wanting? To secure those ensorcelled artefacts for themselves, giving us no opportunity to study them, now or in the future, to add to the sum of elemental knowledge.'

He raised a hand though Jilseth had seen no one open their mouth to speak, turning to address Shannet again.

'What will the Solurans do in years to come, if they have lost all respect for Hadrumal? Why should they abide by any ancient agreement signed between Trydek and those Soluran mages now as long dead as our first Archmage? Thankfully the Lescari strife seems to have ended, so we need not fear their wizards hiring out their skills in warfare to the highest bidder. But what is to stop the Soluran Orders offering their services to those Tormalin nobles and merchant adventurers so eager to explore those unknown lands far away across the Eastern Ocean?

'How long after that before King Solquen and his nobles consider they have an indisputable right to take an interest, if mages sworn to their service are engaged in such exploration? What will Emperor Tadriol and the princes of Tormalin's great houses make of such interference? How long before they look to Hadrumal to curb such insolence?

'What if the Soluran mageborn customarily obliged to swear oaths both to an Order and that Order's noble patron, decide to spurn such traditions? King Solquen will not take kindly to being deprived of his kingdom's defenders. Perhaps those defiant mageborn will seek to avert any retaliation by recruiting other mageborn to take their place. With Hadrumal proven so lacking, why shouldn't Caladhrian mageborn, or those from Ensaimin, Lescar or Tormalin look for wizardry whose strength is now plain for all to see? Whose mages are bold enough to explore those unknown lands and win a share in whatever riches might be found.

'What of Hadrumal's future then, if the brightest and the best of our mageborn turn their backs on our scholarship and libraries? Well, that is no great puzzle,' he concluded. 'At best the study of wizardry will become steadily more impoverished. At worst, the Soluran tolerance for magecraft in warfare will go unchallenged. How long before we see the lands of the Old Tormalin Empire laid waste by untamed magic as they were in the days of the Chaos?

'No,' Planir said briskly. 'I have a duty to protect Hadrumal's interests. Further, I have a duty to defend all mageborn and the time has assuredly come to offer these coerced unfortunates a future beyond a life of slavery or some agonising death as a sacrifice according to the Mandarkin's needs.

'So we will kill this renegade Anskal. That should remind the mundane powers from remotest Gidesta to the southernmost Archipelago and all the way across Solura to the Wildlands beyond that it is only wizards who have the right to discipline wizards. Because, as we will show them beyond any shadow of a doubt,' he assured the Council, 'it is only wizards who have the power to do such a thing.'

His words rang unchallenged to the ornate roof vault. There was a moment's utter silence. Then Jilseth saw mages all round the chamber exchange looks ranging from astonishment to satisfaction to frank apprehension.

Troanna was on her feet. 'Very well, Archmage.' She began walking towards the central dais. 'Let us debate how best to proceed and then we may vote accordingly.'

Planir made no move to yield the platform. 'You misunderstand me, Flood Mistress. There will be no debate. I have not brought the Council here to vote. I have simply fulfilled my duty to keep you all informed.' He looked around the room. 'I will call on each of you whose skills I require in the days to come.'

Now he did step down from the platform, taking all the wizards by surprise as he strode purposefully to the door.

As he did so, he looked straight at Jilseth and Nolyen. She didn't need to see his conspiratorial wink to prompt her to her feet. She followed the Archmage from the chamber, Nolyen barely a pace behind her.

Planir paused at the bottom of the steps, stopping barely half a pace beyond the threshold where Trydek's ancient spells nullified all but the magecraft permitted for Council purposes.

'Now,' he said urgently, 'we cannot do this alone.'

'Archmage?' Nolyen looked at him wide-eyed.

Planir grinned. 'Rather I should say, we should not do this alone. Not if we are to leave the Aldabreshi ignorant of our true involvement. I am content to have Hadrumal and the Soluran Orders, the Tormalin Emperor and every lesser mainland power suitably cowed by some flamboyant demonstration of Hadrumal's wizardly might but I would much rather offer the Archipelagans an alternative explanation.'

— CHAPTER THIRTY-ONE —

Halferan Manor, Caladhria
35th of For-Autumn

THIS MUCH HE could do. He could train Halferan's next troop of guardsmen. Whatever else he might merely be feigning, baron and husband in no more than name, Corrain was still a swordsman and the nearest to a captain hereabouts.

One of the first things he had done on his return from Solura was decree that half of the guard troop be released from labouring each morning to practise their sword drills. The rest were ordered to take their place on the makeshift practise ground after noon's five chimes.

Corrain watched intently as Linset and Reven sparred with blunted swords. The lads were the closest of the sweating pairs honing their martial skills on the cleared expanse of cobbles beside the shell of the manor's great hall.

'Use your left hand to cup that pommel,' he barked at Reven, seeing the lad's high thrust fade to futility. 'Drive that point through his nose and out through the back of his head!'

'And you!' He glared at Linset. 'You call that holding a squint guard? If you want to live through your first fight, you lift that hilt a handspan higher than your shoulder and keep that blade running crosswise down to your off-hand hip. Otherwise you're begging to be skewered through the belly.'

He paused as the two youths let their longswords hang slack by their sides, breathing hard and red-faced despite the cool, cloudy day.

'Again,' he ordered, relentless.

He would go to the Autumn Festival's forthcoming parliament in Ferl with as well-trained and disciplined a troop as had ever accompanied any former Baron Halferan. And he would arrive there in good time to secure accommodation befitting his rank, however much of the Archmage's coin that might cost. So these lads and greybeards only had a handful of days at best before they must all take the high road northwards.

The lads prepared to repeat their drill. The sour look they exchanged before they started didn't escape Corrain. He forbore to comment in favour of renewing his assault on their swordsmanship.

'Reven, get your whole body behind that second stroke, not just your shoulders. Linset, don't raise your guard and then hold it there until he moves on. Turn the blade straight into making your counterattack!'

That was sufficient, he judged, to spur them on to greater efforts in order to prove him wrong. Any more and their response to his criticism would be mutinous and unproductive resentment. He took a step towards assessing the next toiling partnership with a sternly disparaging eye.

'Eighth chime, near enough.' Fitrel appeared at his shoulder before he could move on. 'How long do you reckon to keep them at it?'

'As long as it takes,' Corrain said crisply. 'Half a season handling nothing but chisels and draw-knives has badly dulled their skills.'

'We all need a roof over our heads before winter,' Fitrel observed.

'So we will have.' Corrain wasn't going to be dissuaded from doing his duty, even if the pace of rebuilding had admittedly slowed somewhat this past handful of days.

He might have failed wretchedly in everything he'd attempted since his escape from the Aldabreshi but Corrain was now resolved to set all of that aside. Aye, up to and including the folly of playing the Archmage's envoy in Solura.

No more of such distractions. Home was where his duty lay and he was determined to see the Halferan Barony's reputation restored along with the manor's buildings and walls.

He remembered something he'd realised he needed to discuss with Fitrel. 'We need to send a troop out to ride the boundaries. We should decide who's doing that and who's coming to Ferl with me. The boundary troop will need to set out tomorrow or at latest the day after, if they're to be back in Ferl for the Autumn Festival.'

'Who will escort Lady Zurenne and Lady Ilysh back to Taw Ricks?' Fitrel queried.

'What?' Corrain looked at the old man, caught off-guard.

'Most of the demesne folk are still there,' Fitrel pointed out. 'Any celebration here or in the village can only be a makeshift effort at best.'

Corrain looked over towards the now roofed and weatherproofed gatehouse. Lady Zurenne, Lady Ilysh and little Esnina had taken possession of the upper floor, using the chambers that would become the manor's guest quarters once the baronial tower was renewed and they could reclaim their rightful accommodations.

'Lady Zurenne has said nothing of her festival plans.' Though Corrain realised he hadn't asked her. Their dealings were invariably of the past day's progress and the coming day's practicalities when they met to share a dinner in the gatehouse before he retired to sleep in his tent. Between such meals, they barely saw each other. They were all simply too busy.

'If Lady Zurenne wishes to go to Taw Ricks, she and I must discuss her journey,' he realised. 'We'll have to send some lad on ahead to warn Mistress Rauffe and Doratine to expect her. Where's Kusint?'

He was rapidly becoming Corrain's most valued sergeant. He hadn't said how long he intended to stay, when he'd agreed to return to visit Halferan but Corrain knew he'd miss the Forest lad sorely when he decided to return to Solura.

If he decided to go. Would he stay if he was offered the guard captaincy? Corrain was seriously considering it. Fitrel had declined the promotion and in his heart of hearts, Corrain was relieved. The old man had earned a second chance at retirement and captaining a troop was a younger man's task.

Granted, Corrain couldn't think of any baron's captain as young as Kusint. Perhaps he would find some opportunity to discuss the notion, in the most general of terms, with his former allies amongst the other lords' captains at the Ferl parliament.

Though it was a knife to Corrain's heart, whenever Kusint voiced his conviction that there must be some way to restore Hosh to Abiath's fireside, once the old woman's home was rebuilt. As long as he stayed, the Soluran wouldn't let that lie, would he?

Corrain did his best to hide his own despair over ever seeing Hosh again. He knew that he relieved such tension by subjecting the likes of Reven and Linset to occasionally undeserved rebukes but it would do them no harm to learn that life was seldom fair.

Of late Corrain had wondered how he had managed to forget that particular lesson from his own childhood.

'Have you seen Kusint?' he asked a second time.

Fitrel didn't answer. 'What does that lass want with the master mage?' the old sergeant mused instead.

'Who?' Corrain followed his gaze over to the rising walls of the kitchen and its associated range. Come the equinox, bakehouse, brewhouse and laundry should all be roofed and plastered and ready for refitting with all their necessities. Lady Zurenne had ordered a costly timepiece from some Relshazri artisan to be housed in the gable wall, to sound out the daily chimes for the benefit of all the household.

Corrain had expected to see one or other of the girls from the village. Those families who hadn't fled to Taw Ricks were now drifting back as the manor's renewal was proceeding. More than one of their intrigued daughters had flirted her petticoats at the Ensaimin wizard.

Instead he saw the lady mage Jilseth talking urgently to Tornauld.

'Keep them training,' he ordered Fitrel as he strode across the courtyard.

Corrain was still troubled by what Lord Licanin had told him on his return from Solura, of the growing misgivings about wizardry in Relshaz and the other port cities. Much as they needed magecraft's assistance to secure shelter for the demesne folk before the winter,

Corrain really didn't want to see their neighbours' attitudes to Halferan tainted by such reservations.

It wasn't that he wasn't grateful for all that the mages had done. He was also relieved beyond measure to know that he need no longer fear Soluran retaliation for his folly in enlisting Anskal. But now Corrain wished more than anything else to draw a final line across that ledger and look to Halferan's future. A future free from reliance on wizards.

Fitrel had already picked up something of such uncertainty among the barony's more distant folk finding some excuse to make the journey from their own villages to see the manor's renewal for themselves. Corrain knew better than to disregard such tavern talk. So that was something else he must tell the guard troopers sent out to make certain that the neighbouring barons' men were respecting Halferan's borders. To keep their ears open to learn what they might of opinions on the Ensaimin wizard's presence here.

To casually let slip in conversation that Tornauld was doing no more than any humble labourer's work, for all that his magic could shift more bricks, wood and mortar before noon than a double handful of men could hope to move in a long day. Corrain was making certain that everyone from the neighbouring villages knew full well that the wizard couldn't lay the bricks that were rebuilding the manor and its compound or cut the slots and tongues to joint the great hall's new roof timbers together.

'Good day—' His greeting was left hanging in the empty air as Tornauld vanished.

'Good day to you, Baron Halferan.'

Corrain immediately mistrusted the intensity in Jilseth's expression

'Where has he gone? What do you want?'

He could see heads turning all around the manor compound, as eager for answers as he was.

Corrain had one further question. Was Jilseth here to convey the Archmage's reproaches for his failure in Solura? The northern wizards might not have punished him. He'd had no such assurance of Hadrumal's forgiveness.

Every day, Corrain left his tent, waiting for Tornauld to pass on some caustic message from Planir. Every morning, as he woke and stared at the pale canvas overhead, he resolved when that reprimand came, that he would follow old Fitrel's advice, given over a bottle of white brandy in the old man's lost home when Corrain had first been raised to be a captain of Halferan's guard. Never apologise and never explain.

'What do you want, Corrain?'

He answered the magewoman's unexpected challenge with equal bluntness.

'To do my duty to my lost lord and his family.'

Jilseth's smile put him more on his guard as she looked past him to survey the men at their sword practise.

'Is Kusint still here with you?'

'He is.'

'We need you to fight the corsairs,' Jilseth said with no more preamble. 'The Mandarkin is drawing men and ships to join him. A handful of vessels have already gathered in that anchorage. The Archmage has no wish to see raiders return to the Caladhrian coast, to menace you all with magecraft as well as fire and swords.'

It was a cool day. Regardless, Corrain felt as though he had stumbled into the brook beyond the walls in midwinter.

'You cannot—' He was drowning in the horror of

that prospect. Of all the fears that burdened him, this was the heaviest. The fear that the Mandarkin wizard would make good on his threats to Zurenne. The fear that innocent Caladhrians would once again be subject to robbery and rape.

'I cannot fight Anskal!' He swept his hand around the manor compound with barely restrained fury. 'You recall his handiwork here? In that corsair anchorage? I dare say you have a far greater understanding of his strength than I do!'

'Indeed we do and the Archmage has decreed that Anskal must pay the highest penalty for his crimes against wizardry. We will ensure that he does.' The magewoman was adamant.

'Then you can sink those ships and drown those men when you're killing Anskal,' Corrain shouted, not caring whose attention his outburst drew.

Jilseth raised her chin and squared her shoulders. 'Magecraft has no place in warfare.'

Corrain had never hit a woman. He'd never been tempted to raise a hand to one. Now he forced his clenched fists inside his breeches pockets.

'Go and tell that to the Solurans. Go and tell that to Anskal. When Saedrin turns you back at the threshold to the Otherworld, tell that to all those who died along this coast because Hadrumal refused to help them.' He couldn't help taking a sudden pace forward. 'Tell my lord of Halferan.'

Though Jilseth paled she didn't step back. 'Wouldn't you like to hack off his killer's head and put it on the gibbet post's spike out by the highroad? Wouldn't you like to put the blind corsair's head beside it, the old man who first rallied that raiding fleet?'

Corrain shook his head as though to clear his wits after a stunning blow. 'They are still alive?'

How could that be? He had seen Grewa's trireme burn to the waterline. He had seen the blind corsair's pavilion reduced to dust and splinters. True enough, he realised in the next instant, but he hadn't known for certain that the old man was either aboard ship or in that dwelling. The old villain could have been anywhere else on the island.

Corrain looked around the compound, picturing the destruction which Anskal had wrought here, all in the name of driving out those thrice-cursed raiders. Corrain had dug into the rubble with his bare hands in search of a black-haired corpse with gold chains in his beard. He hadn't found the bastard before the Mandarkin's sorcery had swept them both away to that accursed island.

He shook his head all the same. 'You have no need of us. The Archmage can kill them all. As to your precious Edict, everyone from the lords in their parliament down believes that it has already been broken. They all believe they have Hadrumal to thank for the corsairs who died along this shore through Aft-Summer.'

'Just because they believe it, that doesn't make it true,' Jilseth retorted. 'We would much rather see Caladhrians reassured, to know that one of their own has finally secured revenge for Halferan's dead lord. That a strong sword arm and the courage to wield it remains their best defence. The Archmage would very much prefer that a wizard's talents are deemed best suited to hauling timber and serving stone masons.'

Her thin-lipped smile told Corrain that Tornauld had told her what he must have overheard. Corrain refused to feel ashamed for what he had done in Halferan's best interests.

He shook his head yet again. 'We cannot fight the corsairs.'

He gestured at the sweating guardsmen across the compound, their weapons slack by their sides as they wondered what was afoot, seeing their baron looming over the slender magewoman.

Mistaking his gesture, they hastily returned to their drills. Corrain was almost tempted into a smile. He shook his head, reclaiming his stern expression as he repeated himself.

'We cannot fight the corsairs. I have barely enough trained men to curb banditry on Halferan's roads.'

'Then find more men.' Jilseth was unmoved. 'You only need a sufficient force to tackle five galleys and three triremes and all those are undermanned as far as we can see.'

'As far as you can see,' Corrain echoed, sceptical.

'I can show you,' Jilseth offered. 'I can scry out the anchorage and you already know that land better than anyone else who we could ask to fight there.'

'You need ask no-one to fight there.' Corrain persisted in his refusal. 'I have seen what wizardry can do. Why so coy? If this mage and all who follow him are to die, what's to stay the Archmage's hand? There will be no witnesses left to tell the truth to anyone else.'

'Not everyone on that island deserves to die.' Jilseth bit her lip. 'What about your friend Hosh?'

Corrain stared at her. 'You cold-hearted bitch.'

Jilseth raised her eyebrows. 'Truly? When I offer you a chance to bring your lost friend home? To settle all accounts with the corsair captain who wears those gold chains in his beard?'

'How do you know about him?' Corrain was on the verge of seizing her shoulders and shaking the truth out of her.

'I am a necromancer,' she said unexpectedly testily. 'My magic showed me your lord's death when I found your murdered comrades in the marshes.'

Inexplicable as that sounded, her matter of fact tone offered Corrain a salutary reminder that he was dealing with a mage. Laying hands on her in anger would most likely be an appalling mistake.

Though hopefully not a fatal one since she was the one who had come to him with the Archmage's request.

Corrain stepped back and forced himself to think this through as rationally as he could. 'This will settle all accounts between this barony and Hadrumal?'

'It will,' Jilseth assured him.

Corrain allowed himself a wry grimace. He still wasn't sure he could trust any wizard, however much Halferan owed to Jilseth. He wouldn't accuse her of lying to him but no doubt there were facets to this tale which she was keeping hidden.

But how better to lay to rest any lingering rumour that Halferan was unduly indebted to the Archmage than to show that the barony was capable of pursuing its own vengeance and recovering the last of its lost men?

How better to show the parliament that Halferan was worthy of their full respect than by proving that the corsairs were defeated once and for all?

He rubbed a hand around the back of his neck, beneath his plaited hair. How better to fulfil his oath to his dead lord? To throw this weighty braid and the manacle encumbering his wrist into Talagrin's teeth. To be free of his burdens.

And if he died on this mad quest? Then he would have nothing to apologise for, if he truly found himself standing at Saedrin's door.

But no, he couldn't risk that and leave Lady Zurenne, Ilysh and Esnina all unprotected once again. A captain's life could be risked. A baron had a higher duty to his people.

For the first time, Corrain allowed himself to think the unthinkable. His dead master, the true Lord Halferan should never have taken command of that expedition into the marshes to drive out the corsairs. Captain Gefren had been perfectly capable of leading the guard troop. All the more so, surely, since they had all believed they had a wizard to call on. Until Minelas had shown his true treacherous colours.

Anger burned through his disloyalty. It was the renegade wizard who was to blame for his lord's death. He must never forget that.

He forced his thoughts back to the problem at hand. He had no captain to call on. No one competent to lead Halferan's troopers into a fight on some unknown Archipelagan isle.

'I will not send honest fighting men to their deaths,' he growled. 'Anskal could kill them all as soon as look at us.'

'We will not let that happen.' Jilseth wasn't offering reassurance so much as a plain statement of fact. 'Powerful as he is, the Mandarkin is only one mage. The Archmage will be bringing a nexus of Hadrumal's most powerful wizards to bear.'

'While we attack the galleys and triremes?' Corrain still couldn't bring himself to contemplate this. 'Where could we find ships ready to sail south with the equinox almost upon us? How could we possibly expect to reach that cursed anchorage with every warlord's sea lanes between Relshaz and the corsairs' island closed to us? A fleet of triremes would sink us before we were a day into the Archipelago.'

'You think we would give Anskal such advance warning? When we know he is scrying all the island's approaches for fear of an Archipelagan assault?' Jilseth looked at him, exasperated. 'Hadrumal's mages will carry you and your men to the anchorage as easily as Tornauld has been ferrying bricks for you.'

Corrain shook his head. 'I cannot abandon Halferan. I cannot risk leaving Lady Ilysh a widow.'

Jilseth narrowed her eyes. 'She will hardly find herself as friendless as her mother did. Besides, you will not be killed.'

'You can be certain of that?' Corrain demanded.

Jilseth pointed at Fitrel. 'Ask him if he would trust me to keep his hide whole. I saved his skin and countless others from those corsairs,' she said with unexpected bitterness.

Surprised to hear an echo in the magewoman's words of a swordsman's guilt after his first kill, Corrain was momentarily lost for words.

'No one will expect this attack,' Jilseth stressed. 'Neither Anskal nor the corsairs. They will be taken wholly unawares and the Mandarkin will have no chance to defend his new allies when he faces the Element Masters and Mistress of Hadrumal.'

'Five galleys and three triremes.' Despite his reluctance, Corrain found himself assessing the size of the troop he would need. He managed to turn his next ill-thought-out objection into a question. 'Will you see those ships driven ashore for us to attack?'

Now he was remembering the successful assault he'd led on the first corsair galley destroyed on Caladhria's coast. Halferan's men and the Tallat captain he'd duped into helping had killed those bastards without any need for magical aid.

Could he persuade Captain Mersed to lend his own men and expertise to this fight? Perhaps, if he made it clear to Lord Tallat himself that the slate between their two baronies would be wiped entirely clean by such assistance. That Lord Tallat would be able to claim a share in the credit for making certain that that Caladhria would never again see raiders' black ships on the dawn horizon.

Then there were Lord Licanin's men. They would be as eager as Halferan's own men to kill the last remnants of the force which had slaughtered their comrades here in this very manor and forced them into that humiliating retreat to Karpis's gloating shelter.

What of Lord Antathele? He had shown every sign of late that he was willing to be friends with Halferan, even if that was only thanks to his abiding dislike of Baron Karpis.

Fourteen days and Corrain would be seeing his fellow barons at the next quarterly parliament. Would it be better to try and convince them separately or to invite them all to dine and persuade them over some fine wine?

'I might be able to raise the requisite force,' Corrain said slowly. 'Sometime after the Equinox——'

'No.' Jilseth shook her head in absolute denial. 'We attack the day after tomorrow.'

Corrain threw up his hands. 'That is impossible.'

His heart twisted within him though. How could he throw away the slightest chance of rescuing Hosh?

He turned back to the magewoman.

— CHAPTER THIRTY-TWO —

Trydek's Hall, Hadrumal

37th of For-Autumn

JILSETH KNEW THAT other mages were watching her. Some would doubtless be scrying from their rooms in more remote towers and quadrangles; those who didn't have some excuse to visit a friend who could boast accommodation in Trydek's first sanctuary.

She could imagine what they were saying to each other. As fast as word of that astonishing Council meeting had spread through Hadrumal, it had been outstripped by fervid speculation as to what the Archmage planned to do.

But there hadn't been a whisper to indicate Planir's intentions. So all those wizards could be doing was wondering why she was pacing back and forth across this flagstoned courtyard below Trydek's tower.

The answer to that question was simple. Because she couldn't bear to sit down. Not until Tornauld brought them the final pieces for this game of white raven which the Archmage was planning. When the Mandarkin mage wouldn't merely be driven out of some painted forest to be dropped back in a box.

That was another reason why Jilseth didn't want leisure to sit and think. To contemplate the renegade Anskal's fate, however richly he might deserve it.

Wizards didn't take part in warfare. She had learned

that at her mageborn grandmother's knee. She had never imagined that she would see the day when wizards made war on each other. Still less that she would be part of it.

Jilseth turned on her heel to begin crossing the quadrangle again. All at once, Tornauld and Corrain appeared at the end of her path. Kusint, the Forest lad was standing behind them.

She quickened her pace. 'Well?'

Tornauld grinned. 'Lord Tallat will be honoured to lend his men's valour to such a noble enterprise.'

'I'm glad to hear it.' Jilseth would have liked to hear that news with her own ears, if only to save herself this past morning of frustration.

Until Planir had reminded her of the way in which she had both scared and humiliated Lord Tallat in front of all his peers when the parliament had last met in Kevil. When the hapless nobleman had been boasting how Corrain had secured Hadrumal's aid to drive off the vile corsairs. The nobleman had been wholly unaware of the captain's desperate lies, as indeed he still was.

Lord Antathele, only recently inheriting his father's honours, had clearly witnessed their encounter. Jilseth couldn't doubt that, after seeing his wide-eyed apprehension when she arrived on his threshold with Corrain. She certainly didn't think that Lord Antathele's haste to pledge his support was only rooted in his family's dislike of Baron Karpis.

'Where is the Archmage?' Corrain asked with strained courtesy. 'We should tell him our news.'

The Forest lad Kusint didn't say a word. He was looking around the quadrangle, overawed.

'This way.' Jilseth led them all up the stairs to the Archmage's broad sitting room.

The chairs had all been pushed right back against the windowed walls and the long table was piled high with books garnered from seemingly every shelf and dusty storage chest in Hadrumal's libraries. The closest texts that Jilseth could see left lying open were not merely printed in Tormalin letters. She could see angular Soluran writing and the arcane Mountain script.

The room was full of wizards. Corrain and Kusint advanced barely a handful of paces before halting in silent accord.

'I think that the Hearth Master will agree,' Canfor regarded Merenel with ill-concealed irritation, 'that I should go to this island.'

'Since we are embarking on such a vital endeavour,' Ely immediately concurred.

Planir broke off from his conversation with Troanna and Herion of Wellery's Hall.

'Much as I value your expertise, Canfor,' he said firmly, 'I also prefer to bet on certainties wherever I can. With so much nexus magic to be worked in such close proximity, I want established quartets addressing themselves to the complexities of quintessential wizardry. As you say, this is such a critical venture for Hadrumal.'

There could be no doubting his sincerity, his words coloured by no hint of rebuke.

'Archmage.' Canfor acknowledged Planir with a stiff nod.

Jilseth wondered that the tall wizard's neck didn't crack with the effort of it.

'Who is to square our circle without the Hearth Master?' Ely looked at Planir, doing her best to hide her anxiety.

'Sannin.' The Archmage smiled.

'Yes?' The elegant magewoman looked across the room. She and Rafrid were poring over a leather-bound tome so vast and weighty that the Cloud Master had brought it here in a lattice of magic complete with its own lectern.

'You will work with Ely, Galen and Canfor.' Courteous as Planir was, that was clearly an instruction, not a request.

'Naturally, Archmage.' Sannin smiled at Ely. 'I think we'll find our nexus all the better for a balance of two women and two men across the antagonistic elements.'

Troanna looked up from a faded scroll with a snort of derision. 'I have never found any truth in such assertions.'

'But you are exceptional, Flood Mistress, in this as in so much else,' Planir observed.

Once again, his demeanour was wholly sincere.

Troanna smiled without humour. 'Which is fortunate, given the circumstances.'

Kalion looked at Jilseth and Tornauld and at Corrain with Kusint standing uncertainly behind them. 'Well?'

'Lord Tallat begs for the honour of being of such service to Caladhria and to Hadrumal.' Tornauld grinned. 'And I think he'd welcome some help dredging the ditches in his low-lying pastures, if I have some time on my hands when we're done.'

'Congratulations, Archmage,' Troanna said drily. 'The mainlanders are indeed sufficiently reassured, if they're once again willing to ask us to save their menials from honest labouring.'

'I would like to think they'll have cause to show us rather more respect when this day's work is done.' Kalion shot her an exasperated glare before addressing Planir. 'So, we now have cohorts of guardsmen from Halferan, Tallat, Antathele and Licanin to carry to this island?'

Lord Licanin had shown no hesitation, when Corrain had explained how the wizards of Hadrumal were offering Caladhria the chance to put the last of the corsairs to the sword once and for all, to settle all accounts between them.

Jilseth had also been unexpectedly touched by the grey-haired nobleman's concern for her own well-being. Was she fully recovered, he had asked, from her indisposition?

She was, she had assured him. She was, she told herself resolutely, as she had done countless times already today. She could not allow herself the slightest doubt; either that her wizardry would desert her or that some wild magic would run riot beyond her control.

Besides, Planir had said he was only betting on certainties. He wouldn't be sending her to that island if he had any reservations about her abilities.

'Quite so, Hearth Master.' The Archmage smiled confidently at Kalion. 'A simple enough task for the elemental nexus composed of the strongest and most proficient mages in Hadrumal.'

'Where's that map of the island?' Rafrid looked at Corrain.

'I—' The Caladhrian looked at the table.

Jilseth couldn't see any sign of the chart which he had so painstakingly drawn, complete with every detail that his soldier's eye had noted during his enslavement. Planir had been more than ready to accept Corrain's suggestions for the disposition of their troops as they planned this attack.

'It's here.' Nolyen looked up from the far corner of the room where he sat at a small writing desk. An emerald glimmer challenged the clouded light coming through the window behind him. He had been scrying over the corsairs' anchorage almost without pause for these past three days.

Rafrid took a step towards him, stopped and swallowed an oath. 'Dastennin's —'

Velindre appeared in the perilously limited space within the crowded room.

Even the placid Herion was startled into a cross exclamation. 'What is so urgent—?'

'This.' Velindre gestured towards Nolyen. 'By your leave.'

She didn't wait for him to answer. Her swirl of azure magic carried the scrying bowl from his writing desk and set it on the carpeted floor in the centre of the room.

'Mellitha has seen this.' Velindre passed her hand over the bowl and jade magelight flickered wildly.

'If you don't mind,' Troanna said tartly as every wizard in the room crowded around trying to see.

The Flood Mistress snapped her fingers and emerald light blazed in the shallow bowl. A vision floated high above the rippling water. Not merely the usual reflection that a scrying spell carried from some distant place. This was a fully realised image, complete with depth and detail.

Far more akin to the images drawn forth by necromancy, Jilseth instantly realised. What spells had the Flood Mistress been working on with Ely and Galen?

'Aldabreshi ships?' Kalion was staring at the vision, puce with indignation. 'Why did Mellitha not see these earlier? I thought that she was scrying those neighbouring warlords.'

'She has been watching the domains who sent that first attack. These have come up from the south.' Velindre looked at Planir. 'We knew that the Aldabreshi would renew their attack. The southerly warlords have moved sooner than we expected.'

'Driven on by some omens or merely the stars?' Kalion seemed to be taking this as a personal affront.

Planir contemplated the ships. Was he trying to tally them up? As far as Jilseth could see, those galleys must surely carry a considerably larger force than the first Archipelagan assault.

'As you say,' he said after a long moment, 'while this is unwelcome news, it is hardly unexpected. However inconvenient its timing, we cannot let this deter us.'

'Archmage!'

Every wizard in the room turned, startled, to look at Corrain.

Nodding at Kusint's final whisper, the Caladhrian squared his shoulders. 'We can kill those corsairs, as long as you keep Anskal and his newfound wizards off us. But we cannot fight that number of Aldabreshi.'

'Then you had better defeat the corsairs,' Canfor told him curtly, 'before these Archipelagans arrive.'

'It would be better yet,' Planir rubbed a thoughtful hand across his bearded chin, 'if these Archipelagans don't arrive until we have all completed our business with these corsairs and their wizards.'

'Archmage?' Galen answered Planir's swift glance.

'I have a new task for your nexus.' The Archmage nodded at the vision of the scores of unexpected ships. 'You're to set the tide running against these vessels as soon as night falls. Moreover, I want them so thoroughly cloaked in mist that they have no chance to take their bearings from land or sky.

'This must be a subtle working,' he warned. 'Nothing to make them think that anything more than contrary winds and currents are holding them back. I don't want them suspecting that there's any more magic at work in these islands than whatever self-inflicted folly is going to rid them of this Mandarkin and all his followers, at least as far as they are concerned.'

'That won't win the Caladhrians much time,' Velindre observed, 'if the magic is to be so subtle.'

'Then we'll work fast,' Corrain growled from his corner by the door.

'Such a working will need to be led by water magic,' Canfor said sharply.

'Quite so.' Planir smiled at Ely.

'Archmage.' She couldn't help an apprehensive glance at Galen.

The stolid earth mage gave her hand an encouraging squeeze.

'You are more than capable, Ely,' Troanna said with asperity.

'But what of the Mandarkin's captive mageborn?' Merenel asked. 'If that second nexus is not here to receive them—?'

Planir looked around the assembled wizards, his face grave. 'That option is no longer open to us.'

'Archmage?' Herion voiced the gathering's growing concern.

'To confine each of those mageborn in turn, with the nexus on the island suppressing their affinity—' he nodded at Jilseth '—before translocating them here against their will to be held by more quintessential magic—' he gestured towards Sannin '—that will take time which we no longer have. Not if this business is to be concluded before those Archipelagan ships arrive.

'So we will offer them a more straight-forward, if more brutal choice,' he said coldly. 'We will confine their affinity and press them hard. If they yield, we will bring them here and we may hope to convince them of Hadrumal's benevolence and offer them sanctuary in Suthyfer. If they struggle against us, they will most likely destroy themselves.'

He looked at Corrain and Kusint. 'If any should survive, you may put them to the sword. That will be a mercy,' he assured the Caladhrian and the Soluran, 'rather than leaving them to the Aldabreshi's skinning knives. They will have lost all their wits along with their affinity.'

The two of them nodded with what seemed callous indifference to Jilseth. The prospect nauseated her.

'That is now our nexus's task, once we're on the island?' Merenel looked equally sick. 'Confining their magic?'

'No.' Planir shook his head. 'Disciplining the mageborn thus, any mageborn, is the burden of the Archmage and Hadrumal's Element Masters and Mistresses. The oaths of our offices forbid us to delegate such onerous duty to any wizard of lesser rank.'

'Then no wizard of lesser rank can ever have the temerity to attempt such fell magics.' There was no hint of mercy in Kalion's eyes. Then he grimaced with frank distaste. 'So we are to expand the working we're directing against the Mandarkin.'

'Expand it and refine it.' Rafrid looked inward, contemplative.

'Is this wise, Archmage?' Troanna asked with uncharacteristic hesitation.

'The alternative is to condemn all these mageborn to the same fate as Anskal.' Planir's expression was unreadable. 'Are we willing to do that? Masters? Mistress?'

For a long moment no one moved. Jilseth wasn't sure if anyone in the room was still breathing.

Troanna shook her head, in almost the same instant as Kalion and Rafrid.

'Then we are agreed,' Planir said grimly.

Canfor cleared his throat. 'Then, forgive me, but surely there is no need for the second nexus to go to the island at all?

Jilseth caught the veiled look of triumph that he directed at Merenel. 'By your leave, Archmage,' she interrupted.

'Yes?' he invited.

'I have been thinking,' she explained, 'about additional aid that magic might offer the Caladhrian troops.'

When she had visited Halferan Manor, and then Antathele and Licanin, she had been besieged by memories of the men she'd seen cut down when the corsairs had attacked Zurenne and her daughters. The bloody deaths on the road as she tried to shield their retreat with her magecraft. The final agonies of poor fat Captain Arigo, pulled from his horse and hacked to pieces.

Jilseth had asked herself time and again what more she could have done. What more she might try, if she ever found herself in such straits again and Archmage Trydek's Edict be damned.

Now the Archmage's plans had changed and

the Caladhrians would surely need every possible advantage, if they were to prevail before the Aldabreshi arrived to put every last one of them to the sword. Or a far worse fate, if they condemned any wizards' allies in the same fashion as wizards themselves.

Planir raised his brows. 'Black blade?'

'Indeed.' Jilseth ignored Nolyen's look of shock. 'And more besides.'

Tornauld had a very different glint in his eye. 'There's a good deal we could do. My magic could fracture doors and shutters before Jilseth could reduce that remaining pavilion's walls to dust. Nolyen can warp and split their ship's hulls as easily as Merenel can melt any blade that a corsair reaches for.'

'We need no such assistance.' Corrain stepped forward. 'Caladhrian valour will prevail against such foes. You take care of those mageborn and we will deal with the corsairs. Besides,' he added bitterly, 'I thought that wizardry has no place in warfare. I would prefer not to stand before the Caladhrian Parliament and tarnish our victory with lies.'

'That Edict has historically only applied across the lands of the Old Tormalin Empire,' Kalion said firmly.

'Then will you accept our assistance after your battle?' Jilseth challenged Corrain. 'Do you want your dead carried home to each barony for their funeral pyres to be lit in Caladhria? Will you allow Hadrumal's wizards to carry the wounded beyond Aldabreshin reach? We could save more of them if you accept the Hearth Master's wisdom and permit us to rescue the fallen from the midst of the fighting.'

She gave him a brief moment to contemplate the possible carnage.

'Or would you perhaps prefer to bring all your men safely home? We have the spells to help you do that.'

'You are entirely at liberty to decline such assistance, my lord baron,' Planir said mildly. 'But perhaps you might like to know what you are refusing, for yourself and your men. By way of magecrafted protection,' he added sternly, with a warning look for Tornauld in particular. 'That is as much as I will sanction.'

Jilseth met Corrain's hostile stare. She could see that he was torn between his desire to accept as little wizardly help as possible and his guilty wish to see all his men kept whole.

The Forest lad, Kusint, grabbed the Caladhrian's elbow. Turning his back on the whole gathering, he talked to Corrain, his voice low and urgent.

A moment later, Corrain raised his hands in brusque acquiescence.

'It can do no harm to discuss it,' he said warily.

— CHAPTER THIRTY-THREE —

Black Turtle Isle

In the domain of Nahik Jarir

'LOOK TO THE eastern horizon.'

Hosh was quick to follow Grewa's order. The blind bastard had found an overseer's whip from somewhere. If Hosh was too slow to turn his gaze where the old corsair directed him, he would feel the bite of that lash again.

He knew better than to appeal to Anskal. The Mandarkin had only smiled when he'd seen the weals through Hosh's torn tunic the previous day and asked instead what Molcho and Grewa had been discussing.

Hosh had told him. The corsairs were all studying the heavenly compass, watching for omens in every arc of the sky. Because something Hosh didn't understand was about to happen; he had gathered that much.

Now sunset marked the start of the new day by Archipelagan reckoning. Grewa had sent Molcho to summon the galley and trireme masters to this bloodstained hollow marked with the stones.

All the raiders were obediently turning their backs on the sun's last afterglow, to the infinity to the east shading between blue and black.

'Before dawn,' Grewa pronounced, 'the Emerald will pass into the arc of Death. The jewel is talisman for vision, for bravery and—' he smiled with satisfaction

'—talisman for clear sight. I have thought long and hard about what this might mean for us all. For those of us who have long had the courage and the insight to use the gifts which have fallen into our hands.

'These skies tell us to be bold,' he declared, 'as the Pearl for intuition joins the Diamond for strength in that self-same arc amid the stars of the Canthira Tree. The tree which defies death and fire, sprouting green even after it has been burned to a stump. Three jewels together while the Ruby and the Amethyst are both in the arc of Honour and Ambition. We see the Opal sinking in the arc of Foes amid the Sea Serpent's coils. We have seen those very serpents gather around this island's shores in unprecedented numbers. All this is token of mysteries to be uncovered. The mysteries that have so long been denied us by our overlords. The mysteries of magic.'

Hosh couldn't help looking to see how the assembled ship masters were taking that. When he realised what he had done, he cringed in expectation of the biting whip. No blow fell. He glanced at Grewa and saw the old corsair was more than satisfied with whatever he saw through Hosh's eyes.

'We did not seek out magic. These gifts found us. Who are we to question the turn of the earthly compass that put such wonder into our hands? But we can question all this talk of the evil and corruption of magic when these gifts have brought us the wealth and comforts that our overlords would deny us.'

Hosh watched the ship masters nodding. Grewa wasn't telling them anything they hadn't already heard. They wouldn't be here if they hadn't already been privy to the old corsair's secret. They wouldn't have escaped

Anskal's first attack. They would have been trapped here on the anchorage island along with Ducah, Nifai, Imais and all the rest.

So, Hosh realised, Grewa was telling him all this, knowing full well that he would repeat every word to Anskal.

He stiffened as the blind man turned his empty eye sockets towards him. Grewa hadn't replaced his blindfold. The scarred and empty pits beneath his grizzled brow were plain for all to see.

'Those warlords would claim absolute mastery over us all. They would deny me the means to see again through the sorcery in my amulet. Just as they stole my own eyes for the crime of not being my father's favourite son.'

Hosh didn't understand that, any more than he dared look away until Grewa turned his own blind gaze back towards the eastern sky. Hosh hastily followed suit.

'Let us look forward to the next shift in the stars,' the old corsair said with satisfaction. 'When the stars of the Sailfish swim above the horizon. That carries the Hoe for endeavour and virility into the arc of Death and now the Pearl sits in the arc of Travel to bridge the skies to the Amethyst and Ruby in the arc of Honour. The Opal sits directly opposite where the hidden Net may gather up wealth, if we have the wit so see where the omens lead us. To decide where we should attack first, to show these warlords of the northern reaches that we will not be denied.'

He turned his head as he heard the murmurs from the ship masters. They were all nodding thoughtfully.

Hosh wanted to see if Molcho's face gave any clue to his intentions. Except he knew, if he looked at the black-bearded raider, Grewa would see that he was taking an interest in the corsair captain. Then Grewa would surely tell Molcho and the last thing Hosh wanted was to draw that vicious bastard's suspicious eye.

The black-bearded raider would find some excuse, some justification for defying Anskal and then Hosh would pay with his own life for that failed attempt to kill Molcho. He needed no omens or portents to tell him that. He saw his death in the corsair captain's eyes whenever Molcho looked at him.

Hosh stared up at the sky instead, blinking away tears. What did it matter to him how the stars turned? He was back where he'd started, when he'd first been captured. At that murderer's mercy.

No, it was worse than that. When he'd first been captured, he'd had Corrain at his side and a double handful of other Halferans beside. Only they had been sold off elsewhere or had died, one by one. Then Corrain and that Forest lad Kusint had fled, leaving him utterly alone. Now he wasn't only at Molcho's mercy but Anskal's as well. How long before he was caught in the middle and torn to pieces like a rabbit between two hounds?

The whiplash bit into his forearm. Hosh recoiled, only to see that Grewa was no longer interested in him.

'We will all watch separately for omens from dawn until dusk tomorrow,' he proclaimed to the ship masters. 'We will gather here at sunset to discuss what the earthly compass has shown us.'

'We will decide which domain will be the first to feel our wrath,' Molcho added before looking at Hosh and jerking his head towards the path leading out of the hollow.

Hosh knew what he had to do. He hurried towards the anchorage, leaving the ship masters to their low-voiced speculation while Molcho offered Grewa his arm. The black-bearded raider wasn't trusting in Hosh's eyes alone to see the blind man safely through the rapidly darkening Archipelagan twilight.

Lamps were being lit in the distant pavilion ahead, aboard the ships anchored in the shallows and in the shelters of spars and sailcloth that the crews had erected ashore, beneath the fringe trees beyond the high water mark, well away from the cellar pits and rubble that was all that remained of the other dwellings and further still from the blackened burning ground.

Hosh was heading for the most distant pavilion. Anskal had decreed that Molcho and Grewa be given unoccupied rooms beneath his own roof.

Was that to honour them, Hosh wondered, or was it to remind them of their subordination as they ate and slept alongside their former underlings, now able to turn lethal magic on them whenever they might choose? The Mandarkin still hadn't given Molcho back his gold talismans.

Hosh picked his way carefully through the flourishing ironwood trees. How long would these survive, now that the crews of the returned galleys and triremes were hacking at them for firewood once again?

He stole a glance along the shore as he skirted the burning ground. There wasn't a shackle or a chain to be seen among the oarsmen and swordsmen from the ships. All of them, a motley rabble of Aldabreshi, mainlanders and mixed blood, they had chosen to be here. Just as they had chosen to defy every Archipelagan law and custom forbidding the slightest interaction with magic, for whatever reasons had driven them so relentlessly to revolt, just as Grewa's blinding had done.

So Hosh was the last real slave left on this island. He was the only one burdened with a chain, albeit only the one around his neck, holding that hateful amulet weighing so vilely on his chest.

Hearing the warning crack of that cursed whip behind him, Hosh returned his attention to the lamp-lit pavilion ahead. But if the blind corsair could direct his gaze, no one could dictate his thoughts.

Hosh had been interested to see that the slave mageborn had taken sides now that Grewa and Molcho had returned. Two had joined the Lescari and the Ensaimin mariners in the suite of rooms that they shared on the seaward face of the last pavilion. The third had sought refuge with the mageborn swordsmen who had claimed rooms on the opposite side of the hollow square, overlooking the headland. What did Anskal make of that?

What did the Mandarkin make of the women? Looking up, Hosh saw one; the hard-faced bitch who'd killed that mercenary with the melon knife was standing on the terrace. The open door behind her spilled a golden glow onto the dark stones while a savoury scent of dried meat stewing to succulence drifted through the dusk.

The lamp light was momentarily dimmed as a second woman appeared. Like the first, she ignored Hosh as he climbed up the steps and turned to look where Grewa was putting his feet.

Hosh recognised her all the same. She was the woman who'd endured rape to enable her sisters in captivity to kill those Lescari mercenaries.

As Grewa carefully made his way up to the terrace, the newcomer smiled down at Molcho as he followed. When the hard-faced bitch slid her arms around the old man, the slightly built woman twined her arm through the brutal raider's. Standing on her tiptoes, she whispered something into his ear.

Molcho laughed and gathered her into an embrace. As his mouth sought hers, his broad hand cupped her breast. A moment later, he tugged the wrapped silk from her shoulder to expose her, rolling her nipple between his finger and thumb.

Grewa chuckled and said something in an Archipelagan dialect. Molcho's head snapped around and he glared at Hosh. The woman looked at him levelly, unperturbed that he could see her nakedness.

The old corsair slid his hand down the woman's loosely draped gown to squeeze her buttock. He began hitching up the cloth to reach her bare skin beneath. She kissed him full on the mouth before turning her cold gaze on Hosh.

'Not with him watching,' she wheedled. 'Not tonight. You don't need to see me. Not when we're trading in touch and taste.' She angled her head to lick the skin at the base of Grewa's neck.

Her coquettish tone was in utter contrast to the warning her narrowed eyes directed at Hosh. He only wished he knew what he was being warned against.

Grewa turned his ruined face towards him. 'Find yourself a corner and don't distract me.'

'Of course,' Hosh nodded humbly.

Molcho broke off from pulling his woman's dress down to her waist the better to squeeze and suck at her breasts. Seizing her by the wrist, he dragged her inside the pavilion. Grewa's woman shepherded him through the door, kicking it shut behind her.

Hosh breathed a sigh of relief. How grateful he was that this cursed amulet didn't carry visions both ways. The last thing he wanted ever to see again was that woman sitting astride Grewa's sagging, wrinkled body, riding him and writhing, clasping his groping hands to her breasts, squealing with every appearance of ecstasy.

Though his stomach was growling with hunger made ten times worse by the enticing smell of that stewing meat, that was a trade he would gladly make. And he was unutterably relieved that the rooms Grewa and Molcho had been given were right on the far side of the pavilion beyond the central garden. Far too far away for any unwelcome noises to stir his unruly imagination.

Hosh walked to the edge of the terrace, to sit with his feet dangling over the edge. He gazed aimlessly out over the anchorage. The galleys and triremes floated placidly at anchor. Though it was a cloudless night, both moons were only at their quarters; Greater waning and Lesser waxing. Calm water reflecting the starlight lay like a slick of pewter between the velvet darkness of the headlands. That vision shouldn't distract Grewa from his pleasures.

'Do not look down.'

Hosh managed to avoid a startled glance into the shadows beneath the terrace.

'Have you learned what they want?' Anskal demanded.

'Not yet.' Hosh kept his eyes fixed on the closest trireme.

'Have the women said anything to hint that they have some scheme of their own?' the Mandarkin persisted.

'No,' Hosh said slowly.

Though he would wager that they had, when this particular rune bone rolled to reveal the truth. He didn't see these women whoring themselves in hopes that Grewa and Molcho could protect them from Anskal, any more than he believed they were spreading their legs in hope of learning secrets to offer up to the Mandarkin. Whatever these women sought, it would serve their own interests. They were mageborn, after all, even if they had only so recently learned it.

The grass beneath the terrace rustled irritably. 'Come to see me at dawn, before Grewa wakes.'

'I will,' Hosh said meekly.

Anskal climbed the steps, apparently paying no heed to Hosh at all. He went into the pavilion and closed the door behind him.

Some while later, the door opened again. One of the Aldabreshi raider-mages came to shove Hosh's shoulder.

'You're standing sentry?'

'If you like.' Hosh shrugged.

The man grunted but didn't say anything, going back inside and shutting the door.

No one else came out. Hosh guessed that the Archipelagan had told the Ensaimin mariners and the Lescari that there was no need for them to lose a night's rest.

The few night birds that had returned to the island of late began to call tentatively to each other. Faint noises from inside the pavilion gradually stilled and the lamps and cook fires of the encampment along the shoreline were doused one by one. The aroma of that succulent stew faded in the cool night air. Only the shuttered lanterns on the prows and sterns of the anchored ships glowed faintly in the subdued moonlight.

Hosh wondered what he was supposed to tell Anskal when he went to his room at dawn. Or was the Mandarkin going to tell him something he didn't want Grewa to suspect?

Hosh guessed that the wizard understood all the intricacies of this cursed amulet; in particular knowing that Hosh's eyes opening to a new day of misery and fear wouldn't wake Grewa too. If it did, even if the magic carried no words, only visions, surely Grewa would know for certain that Hosh was telling tales to his true master.

But the old corsair already expected that. He'd made that plain in the hollow clearing, when he'd been declaring the heavenly compass's omens to the rest. He'd be a fool not to know that Hosh was Anskal's spy. Whatever else Grewa and Molcho might be—murderers, thieves, despoilers of women, and that was only the start of it—neither of them was stupid.

Hosh heaved a sigh. Why try to puzzle it out? What did any of this matter? One way or another, he would surely soon be dead. Maybe Saedrin would offer some answers, before he ushered him through the door to blissfully ignorant rebirth in the Otherworld. If he didn't, that was no great concern since Hosh wouldn't remember any of this torment.

He blinked. He frowned and looked more closely. Was that a pale ripple of foam on the star-burnished water? Because that galley was certainly moving. Hosh could see the outline creeping along against the unchanging silhouette of the headland behind it, though the lanterns that might have betrayed it had been inexplicably doused.

But the vessel was moving so slowly. Far too slowly

to ruffle the placid waters. So what was that pale smudge? And there was another. And now that trireme was moving too, where it had been formerly settled at anchor.

Anchors. That was what those pale smudges on the water were; the stone slabs that the Aldabreshi used.

With metal so scarce in these islands, stone slabs were pierced to bristle with sharpened wooden stakes to catch on the reefs and the seabed like a real anchor's flukes. The stone was more than heavy enough to curb any tendency of the wood to float. Except those stones were now bobbing on the water's surface like some bladder full of air.

How could that happen? Magic. It had to be.

Hosh's breath caught in his throat. In the next instant, he looked up at the uncaring stars, drawing in a great gasp. His heart was hammering in his chest.

He so desperately wanted to look round. Were lamps being kindled behind the pavilion's shutters as someone inside had seen what he had seen? Anskal would be swift to draw the same conclusions. Hosh had no doubt of that.

Unless this was the Mandarkin's magic? But why would Anskal be sending those ships edging toward the shallows? Why would any of the other mageborn do such a thing, even assuming they had the skills? Even assuming they dared take such independent action.

With agonising slowness, Hosh looked casually across the anchorage to the encampment along the shore. There was no sign of a light anywhere, not a candle nor a lamp and assuredly no tell-tale glow of magelight. Nothing to offer him any answers or to raise Grewa's suspicions, supposing the old lecher was awake.

A soft bird call drifted through the trees. A brindle owl. Hosh stiffened and peered blindly into the darkness where the ironwood trees met the burning ground.

There were no brindle owls in the Archipelago. They hunted through Caladhria's thickets and woodlands far inland from the sea. No Aldabreshin, even one who had regularly prowled the coastal saltings would ever have heard one.

How could there possibly be Caladhrians here? Hosh's gut twisted between disbelief and frantic hope. Corrain had been here once before. Hosh knew that much. The Mandarkin had said so. The captain had brought Anskal to destroy the corsairs.

Not that the plan had worked out as Corrain had intended. Hosh knew that would infuriate the captain. Would he ever have let that go? No, Corrain would not rest until the Mandarkin had paid for his treachery. Hosh was ready to wager every last gold coin and jewel that Anskal had stolen on that.

No. Hosh was ready to bet still more on the roll of this rune. He was ready to risk his life. What was living worth to him anyway? To eke out his days as the blind corsair's eyes, to give Anskal the satisfaction of denying Molcho the murder which the black-bearded raider so plainly lusted for?

Hosh got slowly to his feet, careful not to glance towards the water. Feeling along the terrace's stone with his bare feet as much as seeing his way in the darkness, he made his way to the pavilion's wall and followed it to the pottery trough full of dead, dry herbs. His groping fingers found the scabbard of the sword which he had hidden there more in desperate defiance than in any real hope of ever using it.

So no one had discovered it. He could take that for a portent if he liked. Slowly, carefully, he edged the weapon out of the gap.

But he mustn't be too slow. He must act and quickly if that owl's cry had truly been a signal of some approaching Caladhrian attack. If he hadn't been mistaken, half drowsing and longing for home.

Hosh found he didn't care if he had been dreaming. He took the sword by its hilt and kept the weapon pressed to his thigh, the blade running down his leg to make certain that no jutting outline could possibly betray him.

He eased the pavilion's main door open, his body shielding the blade. His leathery soles scuffed on the tiles. As dim as the starlight was outside, the darkness within the building was absolute. He strained his ears for any hint of movement at either end of the hallway, where doors opened onto corridors linking the four sides of this hollow building.

He crossed to the inner door and went through the chamber to open the windowed doors overlooking the garden. Hosh had made up his mind. He would see this through to the end. Whatever that end might be.

He walked carefully through the garden, as silently as he could along the paths of crushed seashells. Reaching the far side, he could hear snoring. Hosh took a moment to remind himself where the raiders were sleeping. Grewa had taken the room in the off-hand corner for his own. Molcho had claimed the chamber beside it. The women had taken the central suite and Anskal slept at the other end.

Hosh didn't know what had governed their choices. He didn't care. But he had to get into Molcho's room without making any noise to raise an alarm. Gripping the sword, he stooped low and felt ahead with his off-hand. His questing fingers found the edge of the window.

On the other side of these perilous scales, he had to move fast enough to strike before the Caladhrians attacked. With their leaders to rally them, those galley and trireme crews would put up a ferocious defence. Hosh had no doubt of that after these past few days sitting in that audience chamber listening to the newly-returned corsairs discuss the Archipelagan assault with the mageborn raiders.

Without their leaders the returned corsairs would be thrown into disarray. Beyond that Hosh could only hope that the Caladhrians were backed by some wizardry fit to frustrate Anskal and his prentice mages.

His fingertips traced the join of the window's louvered shutters. One side jutted slightly proud of the other. The shutters weren't latched from the inside. Hosh dug his chipped fingernails into the oiled wood. He managed to ease the shutter open a hand's width.

The hinges squeaked, no louder than the most timid mouse. Hosh froze all the same before rebuking himself. What would serve him best now; stealth or boldness?

He hauled open the shutter and sprang over the low sill. With a little light now filtering through the room, he saw two figures sprawled satiated amid rumpled quilts. Three quick steps took him to the bedside. One figure stirred.

Hosh ripped the blade free from its scabbard. He drew the sword back as far as he could before slashing it down across Molcho's throat. He felt the blade bite deep into flesh and bone. No enchantments protected the black-haired raider now that Anskal had stripped those chains from his beard.

Warmth sprayed across Hosh's arm. The metallic scent of blood overrode the rankness of sex in the room's fetid air. As he tore the sword free, drawing it back for a second strike, he heard a moist gurgle and the dark shape on the bed lurched upwards.

Hosh staggered backwards, dazzled. The woman sat up, a mage flame dancing on her outstretched palm. Her naked skin glistened with sweat and blood as she took in the charnel scene.

Molcho was pressing one hand to the gaping wound in his throat, gasping in mute astonishment. His other hand grabbed for Hosh.

He smacked the empty scabbard down as hard as he could on Molcho's wrist. Something cracked; bone or the leather-bound wood.

The magewoman looked up at Hosh. He must decide whether or not he was going to kill her. Before he could, she vanished, leaving only the pale outline of her sleeping form amid the gore staining the mattress. Though for some reason, she had left him the mage flame hovering in the air.

Fresh blood splashed across the white cotton where she had lain. Molcho collapsed backwards onto the pillows, his hand falling away from his throat. The last spark of life in his dark eyes dulled, a final mist of blood spitting from his slack mouth.

Hosh stood there, trembling. He had really done it. If the Caladhrians were truly attacking, then he had deprived their enemy of their doughtiest captain.

If they weren't, he had finally avenged Lord Halferan.

That would be enough for him to lay before Saedrin, to win him passage to the Otherworld without delay.

Then he heard a shout of alarm from the room next door. Grewa was awake. Hosh kicked open through the inner door and strode down the corridor.

The mage flame followed him. Hosh didn't care. If the blind corsair saw his own death approaching, it was no more than he deserved.

— CHAPTER THIRTY-FOUR —

'*ARE WE ALL ready?*' Sannin's calm whisper floated through the burning circle hanging in the air.

Crouched beside Jilseth in the Archipelagan darkness, Tornauld turned towards the bespeaking. 'Are you?' His voice was uncharacteristically sharp.

'Is the Archmage?' That was all Jilseth wanted to know.

She heard a distant voice through the spell. Canfor. Then she heard the elegant magewoman reject whatever last minute argument the tall wizard had concocted.

Jilseth was relieved that the night hid her inadvertent smile. It wouldn't do to antagonise Canfor if he saw her satisfaction through Master Herion's scrying.

'*Planir says that everyone here is prepared*,' Sannin assured Jilseth and all those crouched beside her. '*Corrain and his men can make their way to their places, as soon as you are ready.*'

Jilseth looked at the Caladhrian. 'As soon as we make you ready.'

'Very well.'

In those two words, Jilseth could hear Corrain's voice shaking. Though the Forest-born lad, Kusint, looked more relaxed. Had he experienced wizardry's touch before, thanks to some Soluran mage? Jilseth realised she had neglected to ask.

'Relax and trust us.' Merenel laced her slim fingers together. Turning her palms outward, the Tormalin born magewoman flexed her hands back until her knuckles cracked. A shimmer of faintest ruby magelight came and went in the blink of an eye.

'Are you alright?' Jilseth heard her own whisper harsh with tension.

At least no one else could hear beyond the six of them, assuming that Tornauld's silence spell was wrapped as tight as he had promised.

One look at the Ensaimin wizard reassured Jilseth as to that but other doubts tormented her.

All the debate and argument and beseeching and planning for this night's work would come to nothing if these Caladhrian guardsmen couldn't set aside their own fears and uncertainty. If they couldn't make use of the spell which Merenel had now loosed to spread among them as one lurking man touched hands with the warrior beside him.

'I am ready. We all are.'

Corrain's resolute answer helped soothe Jilseth's uncertainty, though nothing could quiet the quivering deep beneath her breastbone.

'Give me your hand.' As she reached for him, his touch drew her into Merenel's spell. Now she could see the kneeling men outlined with faint red radiance, its elemental glow illuminating the trees and shrubs and the narrow goat tracks between them.

With the Caladhrians now able to see in the dark, no glimmer of the dimmest dark-lantern need betray their presence before battle was joined.

Jilseth concentrated on her own magic. She sent her affinity deep into Corrain's skin. Her magic sought out the roots of every fine hair on his forearm. She could feel each one bristling like a startled cat. Despite all his earlier promises, he recoiled.

'Stay still!' she hissed.

He grunted uncomfortably but he stopped moving. Jilseth gathered up the threads of her magic again. Now she was concentrating on that within his skin which was bound on a level beneath seeing to the hair and scale and horn which protected so many living creatures. Within a few breaths, Corrain's entire skin was imbued with all the toughness of the hardest turtle shell.

'Pass that on,' she muttered.

'Reven.' Corrain reached for the lad beside him. 'You won't like it,' he warned, 'but you'll like a corsair's sword through the guts less.'

Although Tornauld now relaxed his silence spell enough for the other men to hear their baron's encouraging words, the haze of amber magelight tracing this spell's progress was only visible to the four wizards. As Jilseth watched her magecraft spread through the Caladhrian cohort, she stole a glimpse at Merenel. Even through the eerily shifted vision granted by the fire mage's spell, Jilseth could see that particular wizardry had taken as much out of the Tormalin magewoman as magically armouring the men had drained herself.

And they both had to sustain these intense and subtle workings for as long as they were called on. Jilseth could only hope that Corrain was right, when he swore that this battle would quickly be concluded.

That was all the more likely, given Jilseth had spent

the past day and a half darkening the entire cohort's blades with the black wizardry which Planir had shown her before these same cursed corsairs had attacked Halferan Manor.

After all, as she had told Corrain, there was no telling if Anskal had gifted the corsairs with this same magic which turned the merest scratch from a blade into an ever-deepening gash.

Kusint had recalled how they had seen that very spell for themselves, when Anskal and his fellow Mandarkin spies had been fighting the Soluran mages in the far reaches of the Great Forest.

Planir hadn't forbidden them this wizardry, Jilseth told herself firmly, when the four of them in this nexus had laid their plans for defending the Caladhrians before the Archmage. Though to be strictly accurate, no one had mentioned the spell at all. Well, if necessary she would face his displeasure when this night's work was done.

'We can all see where we're going now, can't we, lads?' Corrain's whisper strengthened. 'And I want to see a corsair's face when he tries sticking a blade into me, eh? So let's show them what we can do!'

Jilseth heard murmurs answering with growing confidence. With a soft rustle of undergrowth, the guardsmen moved towards the shore and their unsuspecting victims.

'Don't touch the mageborn!' Tornauld sent that last reminder to every ear on an urgent breath of ensorcelled air.

Jilseth could only hope the Caladhrians remembered in the heat of battle. They had been told time and again. They were to kill the corsairs. The wizards of Hadrumal would put paid to the Mandarkin and his minions.

More than anything else they'd been warned, if any Caladhrian got in the way of Element Masters and Mistress's lethal magic directed at the mageborn, the Archmage would not be answerable for the consequences.

Sooner than she might have imagined, the four mages were left alone amid the humid, strangely scented undergrowth.

'They are still coming,' Nolyen said in strangled tones. 'Scores of galleys and triremes.'

He knelt, hunched over the smallest, most shallow scrying that Jilseth had ever seen. A glow worm would cast more light.

'They will not prevail against an ensorcelled tide,' Jilseth assured him.

Whatever she might think of Canfor personally, she would never deny his talents either as a mage or within a nexus. The same was true of Ely and while she had never warmed to Galen, Jilseth was ready to acknowledge his talents with the elemental earth. With Sannin to further strengthen them, Jilseth truly had no doubts that their distant nexus could hold off the approaching Aldabreshin fleets.

Nolyen wasn't mollified. 'Why do the Archipelagans have to attack tonight?'

'Velindre explained. It's all to do with their heavenly compass.' Tornauld answered with more tolerance than Jilseth could have managed.

'Why isn't Anskal preparing to meet their attack?' Nolyen persisted.

Why couldn't he be content that his last scrying into the remaining pavilions had shown them the Mandarkin wizard preparing for bed?

Jilseth's patience snapped. 'We don't know and it doesn't matter.'

Once again, Tornauld offered an answer. 'Velindre suspects he wants these southern warlords to attack, so he can drive them off as he did the first fleet. Then word of his power will spread further through the Archipelago. And he'll show these recently returned corsairs exactly how mighty his magic really is.'

Merenel agreed. 'So he's getting his head down before they arrive at dawn. He's in for a rude awakening.'

Jilseth fervently hoped so, before reproaching herself for this suggestion of doubt. The Element Masters and Mistress's nexus could surely hide the assembled legions of Toremal, never mind three contingents of Caladhrian guardsmen, from one Mandarkin mage's scrying or some sentry's unaided eye.

She looked across the anchorage, beyond the scatter of tents where the line of trees marked the edge of the beach. Was that wretched lad Hosh still sitting on that last pavilion's terrace while the corsair leader and the captain of his raiders rutted with those mageborn women who knew no better than to debase themselves so?

Jilseth was sorely tempted to ask Nolyen to scry the wretched boy out again. But they had no time for such indulgences. Either Corrain would find Hosh where he had seen him sitting or they would have to wait and hope that the pitiful lad managed to stay alive until the dust of this battle settled.

'Nol,' Jilseth prompted. 'The anchors?'

The Caladhrian mage nodded and closed his hand to extinguish the last glint of his scrying. 'The water is already moving towards the beach.'

That was good news; that the nexus led by Sannin was indeed managing both to repel the Archipelagans and to send a countercurrent to wash these corsair ships ashore so their crews might meet waiting Caladhrian swords.

Jilseth watched the water between the ships. Amid the woven threads of her own magecraft, she could feel the stone anchors' indignation as Nolyen's water wizardry ejected them from the depths, in defiance of all natural order.

'Tornauld?'

'Oh, hush.' He sounded amused.

Jilseth strained her mageborn senses but could hear nothing beyond the Ensaimin mage's spell. As well as drawing a wall of silence around the Caladhrians so that no one outside might hear them moving through the undergrowth on this slope, Tornauld was throwing a muffling shroud right across the anchorage and far inland.

No startled sentry aboard ship or down on the beach would be able to raise a hue and cry. No one in that last distant pavilion could be roused by some shout of alarm at the sight of those galleys and triremes drifting to shore.

Though that wouldn't stop some bright spark signalling with a lamp once they realised they couldn't make themselves heard.

Jilseth glanced at Merenel. The Tormalin magewoman's face was reassuringly intent. Jilseth looked back at the ships and saw that their night lanterns had already been snuffed.

'*Make ready.*'

Though she knew to expect it, Jilseth was startled

by Master Herion's voice murmuring through a new bespeaking spell. It was some small consolation to see the other three equally shaken.

'*The Archmage is readying his nexus once again.*'

Even through the spell, even over such a distance, Wellery's Hall Master sounded uncharacteristically tense and he wasn't even involved in the quintessential magic being worked so far away in Hadrumal. Like Velindre, Jilseth knew he had been ordered by the Archmage to stay well apart from such intricate magecraft, keeping watch for those who couldn't spare any such attention.

Sitting cross-legged, Jilseth reached out to Merenel and Nolyen. As they took her hands, Tornauld settled himself and spread his own arms wide. His grasp secured their circle.

He looked at Jilseth. 'No doubts.'

'None,' she confirmed.

Nolyen's firm squeeze of her fingers reassured her as did Merenel's resolute nod.

They could not afford the slightest uncertainty. Their nexus must summon and sustain the quintessential magic which Planir had shown them. That would be their only defence against the attack that the Archmage was preparing. If the four of them could not hold firm, then they would all suffer the fate which Planir had decreed for Anskal and his apprentices.

Jilseth reached deep with her wizardly senses; through the rich earth of this strange little island and into the curious rocks beneath. Jilseth was used to the grainy touch of granite and the solidity of marble. This was something else entirely; raw rock in the aeons-length terms of earth magic, so recently spewed out of some cleft deep beneath the seas.

She reached deeper and deeper still. Now Jilseth could see the boundary between solid and fluid rock. She felt Merenel's elemental understanding of fire blending with her own affinity. Their doubled magic anchored their nexus's working all the way down to the molten ores countless leagues beneath their feet.

Jilseth returned her attention to the substances making up this island. The ground beneath the island's greenery was seamed with finer, lighter rock than she had ever encountered. Layers of the strange stuff had settled, carried by the wind from some distant mountain destroying itself and all the land around it in a fiery cataclysm untold years ago.

The blend of her magic with Merenel's own was joined and redoubled as Tornauld's air affinity slid through those unseen layers of powdery grey. This strange rock was as riddled with holes as one of the sea sponges which Aldabreshi traders brought to Relshaz. Velindre had told them she had never encountered a stone so far removed from the elemental antipathy of air and earth. Then the austere magewoman had explained to Tornauld how he could take advantage of that.

Intertwined, their triune magic reached for the breezes drifting through the Archipelago. Now Tornauld bound their wizardry to the invisible tapestry of ever-changing, ever-moving air constantly rewoven across the countless Aldabreshin islands and extending over the vast uncharted seas beyond.

Those seas were Nolyen's province. Jilseth felt the cool shiver of his water affinity so far below, circling the boundary where the saturated rocks of the seabed yielded to the dry heat of molten fire below.

After all their experience working as a nexus, Nolyen

knew better than to try forcing any kind of union there. His water magic rose from the depths and mingled with the moisture drifting through the night air, drawn from the sea by the warmth of the now vanished sun and destined to fall as dew on the island. Nolyen's subtle magecraft bound this elemental water to Jilseth and Merenel and Tornauld's magic.

The circle was complete. The blending of three elements became four and their strength was doubled again. Jilseth could feel Nolyen's water magic drawing on her own affinity as he lifted the corsair vessels' anchors and parted the water before their prows. She was part of Merenel's wizardry laying the whole island open to the Caladhrians' mage-touched sight. Now she lent her strength to Tornauld's spell wrapping ships, tents and houses in invisible silence, and Jilseth felt his affinity in turn coursing through her own magecraft armouring Corrain and his men.

Now quintessential magic was within their reach and as they grasped it, the four wizards had the strength of four times their number. Immediately Jilseth could feel the other nexus's wizardry coursing through the seas. The spells woven by Sannin, Canfor, Galen and Ely were running along the seabed in the anchorage. Their subtle, inexorable magecraft pushed the corsairs' galleys and triremes onto the beach. A hundred oarsmen, a thousand, could not have resisted that gentle pressure.

Far out to sea, Jilseth's wizard senses saw the elemental water of the seas being turned against the advancing Aldabreshi. The nexus went further, repelling the metal and wood of the Archipelagan ships. Artfully woven mists all around the fleet obscured both their chosen paths through the sea lanes and their lack of progress.

Even if the Archipelagans had understood what they were facing, they would have needed a nexus of their own and one to equal Planir's own, to make any headway against the ensorcelled tide now denying them any route to this island.

How was it possible that Anskal had not yet sensed such phenomenal wizardry surrounding him?

Jilseth didn't know if that was her own incredulity or some thought shared by Nolyen, Merenel or Tornauld.

Hard on its heels came vengeful satisfaction.

However much the Mandarkin might be startled by that magic, he could have no conception of the wizardry now to be directed against him.

Here it came. The quintessential magic worked by the Archmage's nexus.

Remote as she felt from her own body, Jilseth could sense her own head instinctively ducking, her shoulders cringing. Through the nexus she knew that the other three were all doing the same, sat in this little circle amid the corsair island's darkened undergrowth.

Brilliance cracked across the sky. Not that anyone not mageborn could have sensed it. To any mageborn though, it looked like lightning carried from horizon to horizon in the blink of an eye. A rainbow shimmer lingered to stain Jilseth's magesight. The Element Masters and Mistress of Hadrumal had combined and magnified their already formidable powers with terrifying results.

The diamond brightness sheeted across the sky again. This time it did not fade. Now forked magelight struck downwards, branching and branching again, seeking out any hint of wizardry.

Distantly Jilseth could feel her fingers numbed by

Merenel's crushing grip. She knew she was punishing Nolyen just as painfully and could only be grateful that her helpless hand wasn't subject to Tornauld's strength. They could all feel their interwoven magic being lashed by those quintessential tendrils. Sustaining their protective magic, rooted in the elemental endurance of this island, took all the strength of affinity and of will that they could summon up between them.

The touch of the Archmage's nexus was as painful as a scald, as terrifying as a choking cloud of dust. The urge to recoil, to fight her way free of this endless anguish, was almost too much for Jilseth to bear. That impulse was only countered by the certain knowledge that any unguarded retreat would leave all four of them defenceless, senseless and dead.

In the next instant, the agony flowed through them to be carried away on the breezes, to dissipate in the boundless seas, to be consumed by the fires far beneath the island, unable to shake the foundations of their magic so deep in the bedrock. The Archmage's quintessential wizardry passed on.

Jilseth felt her own shiver of relief travel around their circle, only to rebound and return as that shudder struck equal shocks born of Merenel and Nolyen's exultation. A final tremor declared Tornauld's fears eased.

For a moment their combined magecraft was thrown into utter confusion. Only for a moment. Instinct combined with their shared years under Hadrumal's discipline and they reasserted their control of those spells so essential for the Caladhrians' success in battle.

Elsewhere, the quintessential magelight was searching out the chaotic wizardry now afflicting those mageborn unable to rally their affinity so readily. With her wizard senses, Jilseth could see those lightning strikes pinioning the Mandarkin's barely trained apprentices one by one. Trees and buildings, the mundane born Caladhrians advancing onto the beach; they all were no more than shadows, no obstacle to her quintessential vision as she picked out each one of the coerced mageborn within the faint outline of the distant pavilion. One here, two there, another couple, a cluster sharing some large room, each successively skewered.

As the Archmage's nexus struck, each hapless victim's affinity was woken. The mageborn were swathed in coils of magelight; sapphire, amber, ruby and emerald. Here and there Jilseth saw a more vivid spark kindle amid the blinding light; a necklace, a belt buckle, the hilt of a hidden dagger. The ensorcelled artefacts.

The first tangle of coloured magelight had already begun to pulse. The rhythm mimicked the beat of a panicked heart. Now that light became sharp-edged. Each swirl of pounding radiance was confined within a sphere of diamond luminosity faceted like a gemstone.

The next mageborn was similarly imprisoned, then the next and the rest. Each glittering sphere grew brighter and brighter. Now the colours of the imprisoned affinity began to bleed into the rainbow glimmer of Hadrumal's all-consuming magic.

Jilseth heard a despairing groan and realised that she had uttered it. None of these coerced mageborn was yielding to the Archmage's nexus. Whether they lacked the will or the skill was irrelevant. If they could neither surrender their affinity nor master it sufficiently to save themselves within the confines of the quintessential warding, then their magic would be the death of them. So the Archmage had decreed.

The closest sphere of magelight swelled alarmingly, collapsed in on itself and vanished in a coruscation of blue-green light. The Masters and Mistress of Hadrumal could at least ensure that each hapless wizard's death destroyed nothing else.

'No!'

Tornauld's protest cut across Merenel's confusion.

'He had a fire affinity!'

Jilseth didn't know if she was truly hearing them or they were sharing such insights through the nexus bonds.

Regardless, they were both right. That unknown mage should have died a fiery death, not stricken by ensorcelled air and water.

'Look!' Nolyen's alarm directed them all towards the next faceted sphere enveloped in diamond magelight.

This time they all saw the turquoise thread snaking towards the relentless magic imprisoning the hapless mageborn.

They saw the infinitesimal instant between the untrammelled wizardry within killing the man born cursed with its gift and the crushing magic of Hadrumal that would force catastrophe to consume itself rather than level the building.

In that immeasurable moment, the turquoise thread fastened leechlike on the dying wizard. Writhing magelight stripped every last vestige of power from flesh and bone. The Archmage's merciless warding closed on no more than an empty husk.

'The renegade!'

'How?'

'Where—?'

A turquoise dart answered Tornauld's question.

It wasn't heading for any of those mageborn already subjected to Hadrumal's trial. Jilseth saw a woman skewered, the magic ripping her chest open as surely as it tore into her affinity. The turquoise radiance swelled obscenely.

A diamond lance shot down from the magelit sky. The turquoise magic recoiled. The lance stabbed at it, twice, a third time. The leech spell twisted and looped back on itself, always evading the Archmage's strike. Another dart from Hadrumal had already found its vile prey. That didn't stop a third sucking thread from stealing the release of unfettered wizardry from the next victim of Hadrumal's nexus.

'What—?'

As Nolyen spoke, Merenel shrieked.

'The magesight!'

Jilseth had wondered how the Mandarkin could hope to hold such power within him. As it turned out, Anskal was no such fool. Instead he hurled a brutal blast of magefire towards a small troop of Caladhrians who had made a break from the tree line beyond the tents. They were racing across the beach towards the remaining pavilion.

Jilseth knew who they were. That troop was Corrain and his men, setting out to avenge their dead lord by killing the corsair captain who had murdered him. That was the signal for their allies to slaughter the rest in the tents ashore and aboard the corsair ships now beached below the high water mark.

But Anskal's magefire wasn't only seeking to burn those Caladhrians. Jilseth, Nolyen and Tornauld all shared Merenel's horrified insight. The Mandarkin sought to use their very own spell as a conduit. Wizard fire would burn the eyes out of each man's head. It wouldn't blind only this handful. The Mandarkin's lethal blaze would trace every path which their spell had taken, as it had been passed from hand to hand.

Quick as thought, Merenel gathered all their strength. In the next heartbeat, she was ready to throw a diamond barrier of quintessential magic between the Mandarkin's evil wizardry and the defenceless Caladhrians.

'No!'

Jilseth barely managed to show the fireborn magewoman the Mandarkin's next attack. More stealthy yet no less murderous. Hateful wizardry summoned from the earth crawled golden across the sand. It sought her own spell armouring the Caladhrians. Their bones would be turned to stone, their skin to hardened clay.

Life without eyes was surely preferable to whatever miserable, brief existence they might eke out in such torment?

Neither spell reached the Caladhrians. A shaft of sapphire-edged magelight tore down from the sky to intercept the ruby fire. The Archmage's nexus drove the Mandarkin's magic deep into the earth to be consumed by the banked fires beneath the deepest rocks.

A white wave foaming with emerald wizardry surged up the beach. Retreating, it carried away the dulled ochre splinters of his malice to scatter them across the seabed.

Relieved as she was, Jilseth could not exult at Hadrumal's momentary victory. While Hadrumal's Element Masters and Mistress had been forced to focus on saving the Caladhrians, the Mandarkin's loathsome magic had drained life and wizardry from another two of his captive mageborn.

Nolyen gasped. 'The sea!'

They all felt the waves of magic ripping through the depths as the spells ensorcelling the tide against the Aldabreshi vanished.

How was that possible? The Mandarkin knew nothing of quintessential magic. Before Jilseth could complete that panicked thought, new terror assailed her.

Some new magic had fastened on her own affinity. No, it wasn't only seizing on her wizardry. Her elemental link to the earth had given this unknown spell an entry to their entire nexus. They were all helpless to resist.

Jilseth fought it anyway. She could feel the others doing the same. She reached deep within herself and deeper still, searching for the elemental foundation of her power.

Too late she realised that was precisely what this unknown wizardry sought. Wild magic roared through her. Power that Jilseth could never have imagined. She had no hope of holding it back.

The shock of the untamed wizardry which she had felt before was as a candle set beside a blazing building compared to this.

Somewhere far away, she heard someone screaming.

It was her.

— CHAPTER THIRTY-FIVE —

Black Turtle Isle
In the domain of Nahik Jarir
38th of For-Autumn

WIZARDRY HAS NO place in warfare. Now Corrain was inclined to agree. The eerie crawling sensation of whatever spell had armoured his skin was something which he would gladly never feel again.

Seeing the world outlined in the dim red light of magesight, as the Tormalin lady wizard had called it, was already giving him a headache. Granted he could see what lay ahead but he was finding it horribly difficult to judge distance. Time and again as he looked down, he felt his foot touch the ground before his eyes told him that the step should land.

How were his men and the Tallats and the Licanin guardsmen going to fight, if they couldn't judge the heft and depth of a swing? On the other hand, yes, Corrain knew that they wouldn't get close enough to fight, certainly not with any hope of taking their enemies by surprise, if they came crashing through this undergrowth with blazing torches in hand.

Just as he knew full well that some arcane magic was silencing their approach from their enemies while ensuring they could all hear each other. So every captain and sergeant had told their men that speed was of the essence, not stealth.

Regardless, Corrain winced at every snapping twig. Every boot nail squealing as it found a stone beneath the leaf mould set his teeth on edge. Such heedless haste went against every instinct which Fitrel had trained into him.

The beat of his own blood hammered loudly in his ears. It pounded all the faster as they reached the margin of the undergrowth above the anchorage. Corrain glanced from one hand to the other, to satisfy himself that every contingent was where it should be. Crouched at his side, young Reven sounded the brindle owl's cry to warn all their allies against moving before they were bidden.

Now Corrain and his chosen double handful of Halferans had to cross this open expanse as Captain Mersed led the Tallats to seize and burn those galleys now drifting slowly into the beach.

With the Licanins to back him up, Mersed was confident he could take the triremes as well. Corrain was inclined to think he was right. The Tallat captain and his men had proved themselves most effectively along Caladhria's shore throughout both halves of summer.

He had also seen the Licanin troopers' eyes light up at the prospect of getting their revenge. They had all seen that black-haired bastard reflected in the meek Caladhrian wizard's scrying spells. There was no doubt that these were the very same corsairs who had ransacked Halferan Manor and cut down the Licanins' sword-mates and friends.

Meantime Kusint would lead the rest of the Halferans in wreaking their own bloody retaliation through the tents crews ashore. They would be ably assisted by the Antathele guardsmen, eager to bring some battle honour home for their new lord.

Corrain nodded at Reven and the other men pressing close behind him. Each one had lost some father, son or brother to these cold-hearted swine; their blood kin either cut down in the marshes with the true Lord Halferan or dying a wretched death in slave chains. Corrain had no doubt of their determination to see justice done.

He led them quickly towards the curved arc of the beach. The contorted fringe trees grew more widely spaced, finally straggling out into a line marking the high water mark.

Corrain barely needed the Tormalin girl's gift of magesight to show him the lie of the land. He could even pick out the ugly tree where he had been used to sit, gazing out to sea and wondering if he would ever see Caladhria again.

Now he could go home with his head held high. Once he had killed that black-hearted bastard with the gold chains in his beard. Once he had found poor Hosh. Then the lady wizard Jilseth's magic could carry them all safely back home.

He glanced towards the water. Yes, the ships were grounded in the shallows, still, incredibly, apparently unbeknownst to the corsairs.

So he and the Halferans must take the shortest route towards the furthest pavilion. Nolyen's scrying had shown them the corsair leaders rutting with their whores. Corrain had seen Hosh kicking his heels as he sat on the edge of the terrace.

Corrain broke through the trees at a run. His men followed, running across the firm sand left by the retreating tide, cutting right across the curve of the beach.

It didn't matter now if some wakeful sentry saw them, either aboard ship, in the camp ashore or over by the distant pavilion. The rest of the Caladhrians were only watching for Corrain and his Halferans to show themselves. That was their signal to attack.

Attack always provokes defence. Fitrel had taught him that too. Half way and Corrain halted, his boots digging deep into the damp sand. A furnace blast of wizard's fire was coming straight towards them. He should have remembered that the Mandarkin had no scruples about using magic in battle.

'Scatter!' Corrain bellowed.

Then before he could so much as decide which way to throw himself, a blinding shaft of white light snuffed out the fiery death hurtling towards them.

Before he could breathe a sigh of astonished relief, seawater swept across his boots, cold trickles through the lace holes tickling his feet.

Corrain looked down to see the retreating foam glittering like fool's gold. Whatever the Mandarkin was trying to do, the Hadrumal wizards were proof against it. Jilseth had assured him of that.

His heart was pounding fit to crack his ribs.

A clash of swords erupted away to his rear and off towards the water. The attacks on the ships and the tents had begun. Now he must reach that distant pavilion before the uproar roused the black-bearded leader and the old corsair.

Anskal, evidently, was already awake. He could only trust in the Archmage's promises to defend them all from the Mandarkin's killing magic. That was easier to believe in now with one success already tallied up for Planir.

Corrain began running again. They reached the foot of the pavilion's steps.

'Remember,' he bellowed at his following men. 'We do not touch the mageborn! Hosh!' he yelled as he drew his sword.

There was no reply. Corrain's heart sank. He scrambled up the stone stair, looking this way and that. Now he was ready to curse this blasted magesight. Where was Hosh in all this red-limned darkness? Why couldn't a man have an honest torch?

A woman screamed somewhere within the dwelling. Corrain saw that the entrance straight ahead was ajar. He led the Halferan contingent inside.

Three doors. The one straight ahead stood open. The woman screamed again. She was somewhere deeper in this building. Corrain pictured the hollow square as the Caladhrian mage Nolyen had shown it to him. The best place to get their bearings would be the garden.

'Come on!' He charged through the hallway and on through the inner chamber, passing through the glass-windowed doors to reach the dishevelled garden.

Now he heard sounds of a struggle and saw an eerie light cutting golden lines across a window's louvered shutters on the far side of the garden. The shutters of the room beside it swung open, only darkness within.

'Reven, secure our flank,' Corrain jabbed his sword towards the silent rooms on that hand. 'Linset, the off side. Weltray, watch our back! Follow me!'

Vigilant in all directions, the Halferans charged across the garden. Corrain planted one boot solidly in the crushed shells underfoot and swung his other leg to kick in the glowing shutters. If that was the only sign of life, that was where he would look for Hosh or for answers, whichever might come first.

Before the splintered wood had fallen to the ground, Corrain stood balanced and ready to take on whatever they might find within.

Madam Merenel's magesight was no match for the golden light filling the room. As the redness burned away, they all took in the scene. Corrain stood like all the other Halferans, stunned with disbelief.

A woman dressed in a plain white shift stood motionless in the middle of the room. She didn't seem to have noticed the armoured men kicking in her window. Then again, she was encased in brilliant magelight. Her head was thrown back, her eyes wide with terror and her mouth gaping. Corrain saw her jaw flexing as though screams were scraping her throat raw. If they were, no one could hear them.

Did that mean she was no threat? Corrain could only trust in the Archmage's promises. The woman didn't look as though she could move. He also remembered Jilseth's repeated warnings that they must not touch these mageborn.

Besides, far closer to hand, Hosh was grappling with the old corsair leader. A bloodied sword lay caught up in a tangle of quilts on the floor. Though from what Corrain could see, despite the gore spattering his tattered tunic, neither Hosh nor the old blind bastard had suffered any wound.

Not beyond scratches anyway. The blind corsair was as naked as the day he was born, no clothing to offer Hosh a handhold. That hadn't deterred the boy. Bloody gouges in the old man's shoulders showed where he had dug in his nails in hopes of a grip.

The old man had a firm handful of Hosh's stained tunic in each of his fists. He lunged forward, intent on smashing his eyeless brow into Hosh's broken nose.

As the boy recoiled, the corsair let go with one hand, twisting to reach right over Hosh's opposite arm. Keeping that forearm pinned against his chest, the old man dropped down, reaching to hook a hand under Hosh's knee and throw him off his feet.

Corrain had his dagger drawn now as well as his sword but he dared not try climbing into the room for fear of fatally distracting Hosh. Even if they reeled close enough, Corrain couldn't risk a thrust with either blade for fear of stabbing the boy.

Hosh stepped backwards to deny the old corsair the throw which he sought. Now his arm pinned to the old man's chest offered him an advantage. Wrenching his other hand free, he wrapped both arms around the blind man's bony ribs. Thrusting a foot between the corsair's knees, Hosh swept the leg bearing his weight out from under him.

The old man fell heavily onto his back. The quilts saved him from being winded. As Hosh bent to reach across him for the bloody sword, the sly corsair kicked hard and true for the boy's stones. Hosh saw his peril in time and a twist took the kick on his inner thigh.

With a brutality that Corrain would not have believed, Hosh dropped to his hands and knees on top of the old man. His hands pinned the corsair's shoulders to the tiles. One of his knees spread the old man's thigh. The other drove deep into his wrinkled groin.

As the corsair doubled up around his agony, Hosh reached for the sword a second time. As his hand closed around the hilt, he staggered to his feet.

The death blow to the old man's neck was no elegant stroke of swordsmanship. Truth be told, it would have disgraced an apprentice butcher. Hosh hastily stooped and threw a fold of quilted cotton over the spurting corpse.

Every Halferan man watching cheered fit to shake tiles from the roof.

'What—?' Breathless, his face blank in utter disbelief, Hosh stared at Corrain as he stood framed in the window.

'Captain?' Over by the open shutters, Reven's voice was shaking. 'Him with the beard, he's dead. My lord,' he added hurriedly.

'What—?' Hosh's white-rimmed eyes widened. He raised the bloodied sword.

'Never mind.' Corrain vaulted the window sill and seized the boy by the shoulders. 'Did you kill him too?' He didn't mean to shake Hosh but he could scarcely believe it. Hosh had killed the corsair captain?

The lad nodded dumbly.

For an instant Corrain was furious. In the next breath he recovered himself. What mattered above all else was that Lord Halferan's murderer was dead.

And that everyone would know he was dead. Corrain jabbed his sword point into the blind corsair's thigh and nodded at the trio who had followed him into the room before they had taken a moment to think.

'Somer, cut off this bastard's head. Reven, go and get the other one.'

'What's happening to her?' Linset quavered.

Corrain turned his attention to the imprisoned woman.

Her skin was splitting. Her gaping mouth had widened

into a gash showing the entire curve of the teeth in her jaw. The holes that had been her ears extended right down her neck, laying bare the vertebrae beneath. Her eyes rolled in the middle of a slash running from temple to temple now that the corners of her eyelids had parted.

There was no blood. Turquoise magelight suffused the quivering flesh laid bare by her torment. More gashes were opening up her body beneath her cotton shift. That same magelight shone through the flimsy cloth; the tarnished green of weathered bronze.

Corrain had seen men die the ugliest of deaths. This was worse than anything he had ever witnessed. He could still see a spark of awareness in the woman's frantic eyes.

She managed to raise one hand. As her fingers parted in desperate appeal, wounds opened between her knuckles, slicing down through her palm towards her wrist.

Corrain couldn't bear to look but dropping his gaze only showed him her feet being flayed to bony claws.

Never mind not touching these mageborn. Corrain didn't want to be within a plough length of whatever was happening to her.

'Out!' He drove everyone from the room, out of the window and back through the garden. Corrain had the edge of his blade ready if that's what it took but no one halted until they had barrelled through the windowed chamber on the far side, through the hallway and reached the terrace outside.

'Captain?' Reven turned to face the pavilion.

Corrain could see the sick terror in the boy's eyes as more golden magelight spilled out through the doorway. Then, with a searing shock, the radiance died.

No matter. A more punishing brightness was illuminating the entire anchorage. White and yet not white, it shimmered with all the colours of the rainbow on the very edge of seeing.

'Run!' Corrain barely took half the steps to the ground before trusting to luck and jumping the rest. Halferans landed all around him. If any of them had broken or sprained an ankle, that didn't slow them.

Corrain fled, half turning with every second stride, back and forth. He was desperately trying to see what unknown menaces might pursue them as well as what enemies might lie ahead.

He could barely make out the pavilion now veiled by that eerie radiance. Sharp-edged magelight burst out through the shattered windows and doors in successive waves; sapphire, emerald, amber and ruby. The rainbow colours in the white wall enclosing the pavilion grew brighter. The shifting patterns stilled. The colours trying to force their way through darkened against the brilliance.

A blade of azure magelight scythed through the wall and shot towards them. The white magic blazed and the cobalt crack was sealed. The azure magic vanished.

The Halferans had all dropped to the damp ground regardless. As he threw himself down, Corrain wondered what good such instinctive action could have done them. If it hadn't been cut short, that killing magic would have cut them all in half before their knees had reached the ground.

'What's happening?'

Corrain didn't know who was begging for an answer. It hardly mattered. He had none to give.

'Anskal's mageborn were in there.' Hosh alone was

still standing, using his sword to point at the mesmerising lights. He spoke as casually as a man idling by a tavern.

'Good to know.' Rising to his feet, Corrain gently took the bloodstained weapon's hilt from Hosh's slack grasp.

'I think,' he said carefully, 'we should make our way back to the wizards.'

Dragging his gaze from the eerie mage battle enveloping the pavilion, he looked towards the beach. If the ships and their crews were destroyed, then their work here was done.

Then Jilseth and the other wizards could send them home and they were welcome to kill Anskal in whatever fashion they chose. Corrain hardened his heart. They could inflict as vile a death as the Mandarkin had wished on that unfortunate woman and do so with his blessing.

He flinched as another spear of magelight tore across the night. This time the tip glowed white as a branding iron, dulling through venomous orange along its length to a sullen red. Corrain glimpsed the outline of a trireme before the menacing light winked out.

He squinted into the darkness but found it was impossible to make out any more detail along the shore. His magesight was long gone and looking at the brilliance shrouding Anskal's pavilion had left him completely night-blind. The rawest recruit lighting a candle for company on the midnight watch had a better chance of seeing something than he did.

He could hear shouts and cries from the beach but none told him what he so urgently needed to know.

'Come on.' Corrain headed for the beach where the ships had grounded regardless. His sense of direction hadn't deserted him and if they encountered some fleeing corsairs, they had the sorcery in their skin and blades to call on.

'Halferan! Halferan!' he yelled. He didn't want to run into a careless Tallat sword imbued with that deadly black sorcery.

The men following him did the same.

Corrain had barely taken five paces before he was blown off his feet. Helpless as a rag doll, he tumbled across the sand, the plaything of a wind such as he'd never encountered before.

The sky was suffused with a pale blue light as bright as a double full of the moons and the air was ringing with the cacophony of trees falling all across the island.

'Captain!' someone screamed.

Someone else grabbed his arm. Boots and elbows struck his back and his thighs as all his men were swept helpless back towards the pavilion which they had just fled.

Corrain struggled to breathe, not because he'd had the wind knocked out of him but because the roaring air pressed so hard on his chest. He felt as though his ribs were bound tight. His lungs were burning. All he could hear was the thunderous wind.

He struck the front face of the terrace with a bruising thump. The rest of the Halferans were blown against the masonry with the same merciless force.

At least Corrain was able to struggle to his feet, clawing at the black stones, bracing himself against the wind pummelling his back.

The sharp snap of beams overhead made him look up. He saw the heavy tiles ripped from the roof and floating away like autumn leaves. The sight defied all common sense with the brutal wind pressing him so hard. Trusses and rafters followed, plucked like straws from a harvest stook to drift away in lazy spirals.

Corrain shifted to brace one shoulder against the stones, trying to see who among his men were on this side of the steps. Were the rest safe on the far side of the stone stair?

Movement towards the shore caught his eye. He saw the triremes and galleys tumbling over and over in the shallow water. The ships were smashed to heaps of kindling. How many Caladhrians lay dead amidst the broken lumber?

How soon would he and these other Halferans join them at Saedrin's door? The masonry beside Corrain cracked from top to bottom. He could only hope this incessant wind would stop the stones from collapsing on top of them all. Only then, of course, there would be nothing to stop them being swept to their deaths. Blown across the headland, they would either perish with every bone smashed on the rocks of the shore or be drowned in the surging waters beyond.

The terrace shuddered. Corrain could see ochre light in every joint between the stones. As the magelight brightened, the gaps widened. The pavilion's very foundations were crumbling away. He could hear the walls cracking overhead.

He staggered and fell amid roiling stones. He could see his guards struggling like drowning men. Their arms flailed desperately to save themselves from being overwhelmed by the collapsing rubble.

It took a few moments before Corrain realised that however violently he was being jostled, he wasn't being hurt by the sharp-cornered stones. One block rolled across another in front of his face, trapping his hand before it went on its way. He saw the flash of golden magelight beneath his skin. So Jilseth's armouring spell was proving its worth.

That was meagre consolation. He had no hope of fighting his way free. Now great lumps of plastered wall and splintered doors and shutters were smashing down on top of them all. Corrain lost sight of his men entirely. All he could see was the wreckage trapping him.

What about Hosh? The poor, fool, valiant boy didn't have Hadrumal's magecraft to protect him. Corrain fought ferociously to free himself. In vain. His legs were trapped. One arm was pinned. He couldn't reach anything that might give some purchase to haul himself free.

Scarlet light crackled along some splintered laths sticking through a slab of plastered wall jammed hard up against his cheek. They looked like broken bones piercing skin.

Corrain smelled smoke. He watched the dusty wood darken. Faint yellow crept along the charred lath's edge towards his eye. The colour deepened and a little flame blossomed. It grew. The next lath kindled. Sparks flew through the air to fasten on the frayed end of a snapped beam jutting up beside his shoulder.

He twisted, trying to see where the flame was heading, but in vain. He was irretrievably stuck. Now the wind roaring in his ears deepened to the ferocious rage of a fire tearing through the Caladhrian marshes at the end of a long dry summer.

Corrain remembered riding the Halferan coast highway one year not so long after he'd formally joined the guard. The saltings were left to burn; there was no hope of fighting the blaze skimming the marsh's surface and the plants rooted beneath the water would recover.

His troop was keeping watch for any new blaze started by wind-borne embers falling in the drained and valuable pastures on the inland side of the road. Corrain recalled seeing a marsh deer dashing out in front of his horse, too maddened by the pain from its burning hide to fear the bigger animal.

When the flames in the saltings had finally died, they had found countless smaller beasts burned to blackened skeletons amid the ashes and stumps of the twisted thorns. He had wondered how they could be so foolish. Even an animal should know to run away from an approaching fire.

Perhaps the lizards and weasels had been surrounded as he was now. Perhaps the same deadly despair had consumed them just as surely as these flames were about to be his death.

Corrain closed his ears and clamped his jaw shut. Whatever was going to happen, the last thing that his men heard would not be him screaming.

He could hear the timbers and laths amid the tumbled masonry burning, crackling and spitting. He could feel the warmth on his face growing ever hotter. He braced himself for the first agony.

Would his hair catch alight? He recalled a careless village woman who'd set her own skirts on fire when he was a boy. As she fell into the hearth in her panic, so village gossip around the well had said, her braids had blazed like rush lights.

Corrain screwed his eyes tight, trying to drive such ghastly images out of his imagination. All around him, the heat grew. Fiery brightness penetrated his closed eyelids as the sounds of burning buffeted his ears.

But the pain didn't come. Was this what the wizards' magic had saved him for? Enduring an eternity of such assaults on his senses, helpless to escape?

Something surged up beneath him. His legs felt cold and wet, all the more shocking with the scorching heat threatening his face.

Then the vividness searing his closed eyes dulled. The fiery threat receded. Where the masonry and timbers trapping him had been grinding together like stones in a mill, now they were rolling away. Giving him room to move.

Corrain forced his eyes open as he ripped his sword hand free. Now he had both arms above the shifting surface of the wreckage. But the rising water was up to his chest now. He kicked frantically for some foothold but every time his boot struck something solid, it floated away.

Green-laced foam was washing through the ruins of the pavilion. Except the wood was still burning, even when the waters sloshed right over the flames. That wind was blowing ever stronger, rucking up the rising waters into swelling breakers.

One such wave swamped him entirely. Corrain broke free of its trailing side, spitting and cursing as he looked wildly around for any sign of his men.

All he could see was a featureless sea dotted with burned flotsam. Here and there a gout of foam burst boiling from the depths to scatter the debris more widely or to suck it down in a murderous whirlpool.

Corrain looked up. All he could see overhead was starlight. Then something dragged him beneath the waters.

— CHAPTER THIRTY-SIX —

'WHAT HAPPENED, EXACTLY?'

Zurenne had been steeling herself to ask this question all morning. Ever since Jilseth and that other, unfamiliar magewoman had appeared outside the manor's gates, asking courteously for admission.

Jilseth had introduced the tall blonde wizard woman as Velindre. Now she was talking to Hosh, sitting with him outside the shrine. Abiath perched on a third stool, leaning close to hear whatever her son had to say about all he had endured in his long absence.

That left Jilseth sitting on a bench beside the gatehouse, watching with interest as the master carpenter and his workmen tiled the great hall's new roof.

Zurenne really hadn't needed Lysha's urgent prompting, when the girl had seen the approaching magewomen from her bedroom window up above in the gatehouse. She was as curious as her daughter to find out what had befallen the Halferan guardsmen and their allies. Or rather, what their wide-eyed tales of wizardry and confusion might truly signify.

Jilseth looked up with a polite smile. 'Fair festival, my lady.'

'Fair festival to you.' Zurenne took a seat on the bench.

Before she could repeat her question, Jilseth asked one of her own.

'When do you expect Baron Halferan to return from Ferl?'

Zurenne pretended to consider this. 'It's wise to allow six days for that road in all but the finest weather.'

Though given Corrain's determination to reach the Parliament before its first sitting, she wouldn't have wagered against him making that journey in the three days he'd had left to him. Even after spending three days and nights senseless and two more rounds of the manor's new timepiece's chimes so weak that he could barely get out of bed.

But he had been determined to go. Even more so after courier doves had brought him messages from Licanin, Tallat and Antathele. Kusint had gone with him, ready to tie him to his saddle if that's what it took to keep Corrain on his horse and on the road.

Zurenne had read the messages brought by the doves after Corrain and the guard contingent had left. It seemed that the noble lords all agreed that the parliament must be told in no uncertain terms that there truly was no place for wizardry in warfare.

Not now those who'd gone to fight the corsairs had seen magecraft wreak such terrifying, unstoppable destruction. Not now that the corsairs' island had been utterly sunk beneath the Archipelago's seas. None among them, the barons were agreed, must ever consider enlisting such an ally for fear of facing such implacable annihilation by way of retaliation.

Never mind any of Hadrumal's edicts. This must be enshrined in Caladhrian law, subject to the gravest penalties. Every power and fiefdom on the mainland must also learn this truth, from the trading cities of Ensaimin, through the newly fashioned Conclave of Provinces in Lescar to the generations-old Imperial throne of Tormalin. Though hopefully the Tormalins would remember that magic had been the cause of the chaos which had engulfed their ancient Empire.

Jilseth looked across the manor compound. 'Hosh didn't go with him to the parliament?'

Clearly the boy hadn't, Zurenne was tempted to reply. But she understood what the magewoman was asking.

'He wouldn't leave his mother.' She watched Abiath rest a wrinkled hand on the lad's knee. His own fingers closed on top of his mother's as he spoke to Velindre.

Jilseth's gaze slid sideways to Zurenne. 'Not to be honoured by the parliament for killing your lamented husband's murderer? Or does Corrain take credit for that?'

'No, he does not,' Zurenne said indignantly.

It had been the first thing Corrain had said, that Hosh had avenged their lost lord, when he had finally opened his eyes to look with wonder at the gatehouse bedchamber ceiling.

Even before he knew that three of the other men who'd gone with him had already woken down in the roughly furnished barrack hall, to gasp out their terrified tale. Whatever else had been incomprehensible, the news of the black-bearded corsair's death had raced around the manor before leaping the brook to the half-built village beyond.

Jilseth looked towards the kitchen buildings and the storehouses and servants' dwellings rising anew. 'The rebuilding proceeds apace.'

'Even without Tornauld's assistance,' Zurenne agreed. 'Where is he?'

She wasn't going to sit here exchanging idle pleasantries with Jilseth. She wanted to know what had happened on that corsair island.

'In Hadrumal.' Jilseth hesitated. 'Our victory took a great deal out of him.'

'Your victory over the Mandarkin wizard?' Zurenne demanded.

Jilseth looked startled. 'He told you about Anskal? Corrain did?'

'Of course.' Zurenne wondered why the magewoman should be so surprised. 'But is the villain dead or merely defeated?'

Corrain had been unable to tell her. His distant gaze had fixed on some awful memory. All that he could say was he couldn't imagine how anyone, man or mage, could have survived such an overwhelming magical onslaught.

But that was nonsensical as far as Zurenne was concerned. Corrain had survived, and so had every man gone with him. Even Hosh had been brought back from the distant Archipelago.

'What happened?' Zurenne repeated her question.

What had happened before the Tormalin magewoman Merenel had appeared in the manor compound? Hollow-eyed and tear-stained, she had shouted at them all to make ready to receive their injured men before vanishing just as abruptly.

Since Merenel had spoken of injuries, Fitrel had immediately begun shouting for linen and hot water, for whatever salves and stitching needles the carpenters and bricklayers might have in case of accidents and injuries.

Then the unconscious men had appeared, swathed in white mist and laid as gently on the cobbles as any mother might lay down her child. There had been no blood. Their sufferings looked more akin to someone who had been lost for days in the salt marshes through the height of summer.

Their faces had been reddened and peeling while their feet had been sodden and foul. Stripped and washed they had all been so bruised that they might have been beaten from head to toe with fence posts.

All except Hosh. He had looked like a drowned rat but once he'd spewed up a bucket of seawater, there hadn't been a mark on him. Not beyond that shocking, ill-mended old injury to his poor thin face. Though he had been mute for two days before suddenly bursting into tears and begging pitiously for his mother.

Zurenne looked towards the shrine. She saw the lad reach into a pocket of his smart new tunic and take out something that shone bright in the autumn sun.

Velindre reached for it before suddenly withdrawing, her fingers knotting into a fist. A moment later, she held out her palm. Zurenne could see the tension in the tall woman's shoulders as Hosh laid the thing on her hand.

'He says there is magic in that arm ring.' She twisted on the bench to look straight at Jilseth. 'He says that it saved him. He says the wizard had a trove of such treasures. How do you know that some such thing didn't save this Mandarkin?'

Her voice rose with her anger. She was angry because she was frightened. If half the mumbled tales from the barrack hall were true, the notion of that wizard surviving was truly terrifying. Now he would surely be Halferan's sworn foe until his dying day. Zurenne had seen that very fear in Corrain's bruised eyes, however much he insisted that the Mandarkin had perished.

'Anskal is dead.' Jilseth paused to choose her words. 'The Archmage turned his magic upon him, and not only his own wizardry. When four mages join their affinities together into what is called a nexus, their strength is not merely the sum of their individual power. The first mage's might is doubled, then their joint strength is redoubled by the third and that magecraft is doubled again by the fourth.'

'I see.' If Zurenne understood little about wizardry, this past season of tallying Hadrumal's ledgers and accounts had taught her more than she ever expected to know of arithmetic. 'And so they were stronger than Anskal? They were able to kill him?'

Jilseth hesitated again. 'Anskal had secrets of his own. He had some means to steal another wizard's strength, whether or not they were willing. He had gathered a number of mageborn to follow him and he didn't hesitate to kill them in order to add their strength to his own. Then there were these artefacts and other, unexpected influences on our magic...'

She broke off with that same distant look which Zurenne had seen on Corrain's face. Which she could see across the compound when Hosh's eyes drifted away from Velindre as he answered whatever questions she had.

Abiath took his hand again and Hosh recovered his crooked smile. Zurenne wondered how long it would be before the poor boy truly recovered from all that he had endured. His neat, clean clothes, a shave and a close-cropped haircut could only be the first and most trivial of steps along that road.

'We hope that aetheric magic might offer some hope of relieving Hosh's disfigurement,' Jilseth said with discreet pity. 'We have an ally, a healer called Aritane, in the Suthyfer islands—'

'What happened to him? To Anskal?' Zurenne realised she had very nearly been lured into changing the subject. No, she would not stand for that. 'Did the Archmage's magic prove stronger or not?'

Once again, Jilseth chose her words carefully. 'The union of four affinities helps the wizards in a nexus reach for higher magecraft. Quintessential magic. Anskal had no such spells and so his answer was merely more violent and brutal attacks as he murdered his followers for the sake of plundering their magic. As he killed so many of them so swiftly, the Archmage saw the very real danger that he could outstrip Hadrumal's master nexus.'

The magewoman shuddered so suddenly that Zurenne was startled into a shiver of her own.

'So the Archmage wrought a still greater nexus.' Now wonder coloured Jilseth's words. 'There were already two more such quartets working higher magic as part of our plan to defeat the corsairs.' She nodded towards Velindre. 'She was there with another mage and they called on two more to square a fourth circle. Planir drew them all into his magecraft.'

Zurenne did her best to understand this. 'And so that first higher magic already summoned by the Archmage, it was doubled and redoubled and doubled again?'

She couldn't do that sum without pen and ink but surely that must mean Planir had amassed magic to equal every wizard in Hadrumal.

'Anskal didn't expect this? He had no answer?'

'He was so utterly crushed beneath the Archmage's wizardry that the very elements making up his flesh and bones, his blood and brain were scattered asunder. There was nothing left of him larger than the smallest grain of dust.'

There was no triumph in Jilseth's voice, only awe and more than a little shock.

'None of us expected the Archmage to do such a thing,' she added grimly. 'We didn't know that he could do such a thing. It was—a draining experience. More so for some than for others.'

She forced an unconvincing smile. 'But it lent us the strength to save your men and their allies.'

Zurenne thought of those cryptic messages carried by the courier doves. 'Is the corsairs' whole island truly destroyed?'

Was that really possible, even with wizardry as potent as Jilseth had described?

'It is.' The magewoman shivered again. 'Caladhria need never fear such raids again.'

Zurenne suddenly remembered the noble-born Caladhrian wizard who had so reassured her in the past. 'What of Master Nolyen? How is he faring?'

'He's well enough and recovering his strength in Hadrumal.' Jilseth's mood visibly lifted at that thought.

Zurenne caught sight of Lysha and Neeny walking back towards the gatehouse. They had been to collect the eggs from the hen houses currently standing on the plot that would be a new herb garden.

She was so relieved that the guardsmen had not returned with gaping wounds and gashes and not only for their own sakes. Zurenne knew that it was selfish and she had sought Drianon's forgiveness but she was thankful that her children, especially Neeny, hadn't had to endure the sight of more bloodshed.

'It really is all over?' She hesitated between a question and hopeful wonder.

'For Halferan? Let's hope so. For Hadrumal?' Jilseth shook her head. 'We cannot say. There were Archipelagan ships on the horizon. They will have been close enough to see unbridled wizardry destroying that island. The warlords will take that very ill.'

'The Archmage has retrieved Anskal's trove of artefacts.' She looked over at Velindre with a wry twist to her mouth. 'There are a great many wizards who will claim an interest in such treasures and a good number of those live beyond Hadrumal's shores and do not bow their head to the Archmage's authority.'

'But none of that is Halferan's concern,' Zurenne persisted.

'I have no reason to think so,' Jilseth allowed.

No reason to think so. Zurenne hugged that reassurance close. 'Then we can put all this behind us and look to the future.'

Once he returned from the Autumn Parliament in Ferl, Corrain could cut his own hair and lay aside that broken shackle that he still wore. Whatever oath he had made on those tokens must surely be fulfilled by now.

Though, for some reason, Zurenne thought of Kusint. The first thing that the Forest lad had done, as soon as he recovered his senses, was beg for a bag of runes.

Lysha had found him sitting by Corrain's bedside, casting trio after trio. He wasn't gambling, he had said tersely. He was seeking guidance.

But he had refused to share whatever he read in those runes.

ACKNOWLEDGEMENTS

I am indebted as always to the family members and friends who've helped this book on its way with support, encouragement and interesting comments, ideas and information.

Special mention goes to Sue Rumfitt, for referring me to Bran Symondson's 'mouse and scorpion' photograph, and to David LeTocq, our excellent family dentist, for advice on the longer term consequences of maxillofacial injuries. I am also most grateful to Karen Williams for her wonderful hospitality in California, and to everyone who made me so welcome on my trip to Sunnyvale and at the World Fantasy Convention in San Diego.

My thanks to Jon, David, Jenni, Ben and Mike at Solaris and Rebellion for their professional contributions to my work and for their excellent and amusing company at science-fiction conventions and other events.

I remain continually thankful for the good fellowship of other writers, for my own keen readers and for all the SF&Fantasy enthusiasts who read, review, blog and keep our wonderful genre thriving.

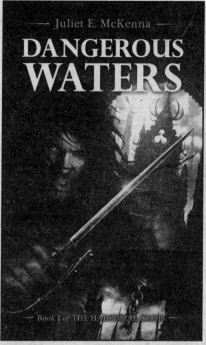

Juliet E. McKenna

DANGEROUS WATERS

Book 1 of THE HADRUMAL CRISIS

UK ISBN: 978 1 907519 97 0 • US ISBN: 978 1 907519 96 3 • £7.99/$7.99

The Archmage rules the island of wizards and has banned the use of magecraft in warfare, but there are corsairs raiding the Caladhrian Coast, enslaving villagers and devastating trade. Barons and merchants beg for magical aid, but all help has been refused so far.

Lady Zurenne's husband has been murdered by the corsairs. Now a man she doesn't even know stands as guardian over her and her daughters. Corrain, former captain and now slave, knows that the man is a rogue wizard, illegally selling his skills to the corsairs. If Corrain can escape, he'll see justice done. Unless the Archmage's magewoman, Jilseth, can catch the renegade first, before his disobedience is revealed and the scandal shatters the ruler's hold on power...

The first book in a thrilling new series.

"Fantasy in the epic tradition, with compelling narratives, authentic combat and characters you care about."

— Stan Nicholls, author of *Orcs*

WWW.SOLARISBOOKS.COM

Follow us on Twitter! www.twitter.com/solarisbooks